CHANGES

THE BELLE MORTE SERIES

BELLE MORTE

REVELATIONS

HUNTED

CHANGES

CHANGES

BELLE MORTE BOOK FOUR

BELLA HIGGIN

wattpad books **W**

wattpad books **W**

An imprint of Wattpad WEBTOON Book Group

Content warning: mentions of blood, death, violence; language

Published in Canada by Wattpad WEBTOON Book Group, a division of Wattpad WEBTOON Studios, Inc.

36 Wellington Street E., Suite 200, Toronto, ON M5E 1C7 Canada

www.wattpad.com

First Wattpad Books edition: December 2025

ISBN 978-1-99834-100-9 (Trade Paper original)
ISBN 978-1-99834-101-6 (eBook edition)

Library and Archives Canada Cataloguing in Publication information is available upon request.

Printed and bound in Canada

1 3 5 7 9 10 8 6 4 2

Cover design by Ysabel Enverga
Images © Sanit Fuangnakhon, © Yoko Design via Shutterstock;
© Naborahfatima via iStock
Typesetting by Delaney Anderson

For my readers.

You made this journey possible.

CHAPTER ONE

Jason

When Jason woke up, he knew the other side of the bed was empty, but he still rolled over to check.

No Roux.

They'd only shared her bed for a few days, first when Renie had struggled through the turn, and then again when they'd fled to Fiaigh, but he'd grown used to the sight of Roux's head on the pillow next to his, and he missed the comfort of snuggling up with his best friend.

Now both Renie and Roux had hot vampires to snuggle with instead.

Jason got up, running his hands through his hair.

Roux and Renie's old bedroom stared back at him: the flocked gold wallpaper, soft cream carpet, and lavish curtains more familiar to him than the room he'd been allocated when he'd first arrived at Belle Morte.

That had only been a few weeks ago, but it felt like forever.

On the nightstand, his phone buzzed, but Jason, recognizing his mum's number, didn't answer it. He already knew what she'd say, and he wasn't in the mood for that argument again.

A flurry of knocks sounded on his door.

"Jason, honey, are you decent?" Roux called.

Jason glanced down at his boxers. They were a little tight . . . eh, it was nothing his friends hadn't seen before. "Decent enough," he replied.

The door opened and his girls came in. Renie raised her eyebrows. "You call that decent? Those boxers don't leave much to the imagination."

Jason struck a Mr. Universe pose and blew her a kiss. "I didn't want to deprive you of a little morning eye candy."

She grinned wide enough to show off her fangs. "I'm sleeping with Edmond Dantès. That's all the eye candy I need."

"But he doesn't tease you with sexy poses, does he?" Jason said.

Renie's grin widened. "How would you know?"

Jason had no comeback for that.

"Just because we're both spoken for doesn't mean we can't enjoy the view," Roux commented, eyeing Jason's bare chest.

He promptly put both hands over his nipples. "Greedy wench! You have your own delicious vampire to ogle."

Roux smiled.

Barely a week had passed since she'd moved into the north wing with Ludovic de Vauban, and already it seemed strangely normal, as if they'd always been together.

"What can I do for you, ladies?" Jason asked, throwing on the nearest thing to hand—a floral silk dressing gown that was far too small for him.

"Isn't that mine?" Roux asked.

"Probably."

Little pieces of Renie and Roux were still scattered around the room—some clothes left in the wardrobe, a couple of lipsticks on the dressing table, a stray shoe in the corner.

His mum called again, Jason's phone vibrating against the wooden surface of the nightstand.

"Do you need to get that?" Renie asked.

Jason shook his head. "It's my mum."

"Isn't that more reason to answer?"

Jason sighed and crossed his arms. "I'm tired of explaining to her that I'm not coming home yet. I can't."

Unlike a lot of other people, Jason's mum didn't blame the Belle Morte vampires for everything that had happened recently, but so much had gone wrong here, so much blood and violence and death that Jason understood why she wasn't thrilled about him staying. But she didn't understand how important everyone in this house was to him, how completely they'd become intertwined with his life.

As the only donor left in Belle Morte—in the whole of the UK— Jason was no longer sure where he fit in, but he couldn't just walk away.

And, if he was honest with himself, there was another reason he didn't want to leave.

A beautiful, blond reason.

Gideon Hartwright.

From the moment Jason had laid eyes on the vampire, Gideon had been on his mind. It was pathetic, really, to feel so much for a man he barely knew, but the heart wanted what the heart wanted.

Roux made a sympathetic noise and touched Jason's shoulder.

"You still haven't told me why you're here," he said.

Clouds gathered on Renie's face, and she tucked a strand of auburn hair behind her ear. "Ysanne wants us all in the dining hall for a meeting," she said.

"That doesn't sound good," Jason noted, his stomach dropping.

Renie shrugged, but it was a tense, jerky movement.

"Give me a few minutes to get ready," Jason said.

He showered and dressed as quickly as he could, then followed Renie and Roux out of the donors' wing and down the main staircase to the vestibule. Seamus was just coming through the front door.

"How is it out there?" Jason asked.

Seamus pulled a face. "Honestly? I think it's getting worse."

Cold crept along Jason's skin.

Things had been bad enough for vampires after Etienne and Jemima's bloody coup, but the shit had hit the fan even more when Roger Schofield, a vampire Etienne had turned, had abducted and turned nine kids.

Public backlash had been grim, and while Jason had avoided a lot of the nastier stuff on social media, no one could ignore the protestors gathered outside the mansion's gates. Even with all the windows and doors closed, the faint roar of angry voices was audible.

Jason doubted any of the protestors would do anything other than yell from the other side of the gates, but the fact that Belle Morte was operating with a skeleton security detail made him nervous.

They all walked through a parlor to the dining hall, Renie and Roux flanking Jason, Seamus following.

Gideon and Isabeau were already there, and Jason's heart skipped a beat as he looked at the object of his affections. Gideon was tall and broad-shouldered, his skin smooth and pale, honey-blond hair curling around his ears, his eyes as gray as a winter sky. His white shirt clung to the muscles of his body in a way that made Jason's mouth go dry.

Every time he saw the man it was like the first time all over again—a bolt of electricity straight to the heart.

And straight to the pants.

Gideon glanced at him but his face betrayed nothing, and Jason's heart sank. If Gideon had been consistently neutral toward him then Jason might have got over him by now, but every once in a while Gideon did something to rekindle Jason's hope.

Like gently lick Jason's throat to seal the bite marks left by another vampire.

Or throw himself in front of Jason to protect him from an attacker.

Little things like that.

Jason's eyes moved past Gideon to where Ysanne stood at the head of the table, and the chill sweeping over his skin got worse. DCI Walsh stood with the Lady of Belle Morte, his face somber, dark eyebrows pulled down.

Jason had already guessed that Ysanne wasn't gathering them here for good news, but Walsh's presence suggested that whatever was going on was worse than he'd imagined.

He pulled out a chair halfway down the table and sat, Renie and Roux still on either side of him. Edmond and Ludovic joined them, but Jason spared them only a glance.

The atmosphere was heavy.

He focused on Ysanne.

The Lady of Belle Morte looked as polished as ever in towering heels and a sheath dress of palest green, her diamond pendant nestled in the hollow of her throat, her hair a sleek sheet down her back. Her face was an impassive marble mask, but there was something strained in the way that she placed her palms on the table, like she needed to physically ground herself.

"I'll cut to the chase," she said, her voice crisp and clear. "We have fought and bled and suffered for this House, and now it is under threat again, only this threat is not one we can fight with brute force."

She gestured with one hand and Walsh took a step forward.

"You may have noticed that your scheduled delivery of bagged blood hasn't arrived yet," he said.

Jason glanced around the table, trying to gauge the reactions of the assembled vampires. No one looked surprised.

Since every donor in the UK had been sent home, along with most of the human staff, the vampires had been relying on bagged blood rather than drinking straight from their live-in donors.

"What's happened?" Edmond asked.

"I don't know how aware you are of what's going on outside, but there's something you should see," Walsh said.

He took out his phone and turned it so those nearest him could see it. Jason leaned forward as Walsh pressed the Play button in the middle of the screen.

The video flickered to life.

Jason saw a street, one he didn't recognize, but which judging by the architecture could have been somewhere in Winchester. It was filled with people, shouting, chanting, waving placards, and at first Jason couldn't hear what they were saying; then individual chants coalesced, and a knot formed in his throat.

They were protesting against vampires.

"Protests like these are springing up all over the country. While some are small, localized, others are growing much larger, and potentially more dangerous," Walsh explained, pausing the video. "There are currently two online petitions calling for justice in the wake of Roger Schofield's death, claiming that no matter what his crimes were, he had the right to a fair trial."

"He deserved exactly what he got," Roux said hotly.

Walsh shrugged. "I'm more worried about the group calling themselves People Before Vampires. It started as graffiti—that phrase appearing all over the city—then several ex-donors filed reports about people harassing them on the street, frequently shouting the same phrase. There's also been an uptick in online abuse aimed at ex-donors and anyone else speaking in defense of vampires, with many of the accounts perpetrating the abuse being linked to the PBV group."

"Sounds like an STD," Renie muttered.

Jason swallowed. As bad as the protestors at the gates were, it hadn't occurred to him that they were a symptom of something much bigger.

Walsh pressed Play on the paused video.

A woman appeared on the screen, holding a microphone in one hand, though there was nothing to suggest she was from an official news channel. She tapped the shoulder of the nearest man, and he turned to the camera.

"Can you tell us why you're here today?" she asked.

The man rubbed the back of his neck. "I just wanted to see what it was all about."

"Do you think people are achieving anything by protesting today?" the woman asked.

"If nothing else, I think it's opening people's eyes."

"Opening them to what?"

Something cold slid through the man's eyes, so quick Jason almost thought he'd imagined it. "To what vampires are really capable of."

"You think they're dangerous then?" the woman said.

The man uttered a short laugh. "Don't you?"

She didn't answer, and the video clip ended there.

"This morning, a similar protest, believed to be linked to PBV, targeted the van that should have been delivering your supply of blood," Walsh said. "It wasn't captured on film, although witnesses claim that participants stated they were stopping the supply because that blood was needed more by hospitals than Vampire Houses."

"And what did the protestors do with the bagged blood?" Roux asked, though her heavy tone suggested she already knew.

Walsh sighed. "It was mostly destroyed in the scuffle."

"How the fuck does that help hospitals?"

Walsh lifted his shoulders in a short shrug.

"Blood banks across the country have been receiving threats, and two have already issued public statements saying they'll no longer donate blood to Vampire Houses," Walsh said.

"So where does that leave us?" Gideon asked.

"I don't know," Walsh admitted.

"The reality is that both the human and the vampire worlds are facing a situation unlike anything we've ever experienced. As vampires, we've become accustomed to being near worshipped, myths and legends come to life. Now the curtain has been ripped away and humans have realized how flawed we can really be. Suddenly, we're not so different from them, but we're still not human, and many people don't know how to reconcile those two things," Ysanne said. Her cool gaze traveled around the table. "We were prepared for the novelty of our existence to one day wear off, prepared to have to work harder to maintain public interest, but we weren't prepared for this."

Ysanne and Walsh exchanged a dark look, and Jason braced

himself, because what they'd seen so far wasn't the only reason Ysanne had gathered them here.

Walsh tapped at his phone then turned it again, showing another paused video.

Jason recognized the man on screen: Karl Kendrick, a politician he'd never heard of until Kendrick started speaking out against vampires.

Walsh pressed Play.

"—donor system is unsalvageable," Kendrick said, speaking to someone off camera. A small group of people were gathered behind him, listening.

"What makes you say that?" a male voice asked.

"The donor system was established on the basis that the donors in question would always be safe inside their respective Vampire Houses. But they weren't, nor do I believe that their safety could ever again be guaranteed," Kendrick said.

"You've spoken about the possibility of evicting vampires from their houses," the unseen interviewer asked.

"*What?*" Renie exclaimed.

Edmond squeezed her hand.

"That's right. After everything that's happened, I fail to understand why vampires should be permitted to continue enjoying the luxuries they have for the last decade, and their mansions could be put to far better use," Kendrick said.

"Such as?"

"Providing shelter for the homeless, for one," Kendrick said. "Imagine how many underprivileged people we could get off the streets if they were allowed to live in those houses?"

"But where would the vampires go? Wouldn't your suggestion be exchanging one group of displaced people for another?" the interviewer asked.

"Is it necessary for vampires to live in mansions? They have enough wealth to arrange normal homes for themselves, the same as everyone else," Kendrick said.

"What would you suggest they do for food with no mansions and no donors?"

"I'll admit I don't have an answer for that yet, but I believe there are options."

"Many MPs have been vocal about not punishing all vampires for the crimes of a few. What's your view on that?"

Kendrick made a rueful shape with his mouth. "My stance isn't about *punishing* vampires, it's about protecting humans."

"But vampires have rights too."

Kendrick tilted his head. "In what sense?"

The interviewer faltered.

"Vampires are still entitled to basic human rights," supplied a woman from the group behind him.

"Basic *human* rights," Kendrick repeated. "Only they're not human, are they? The Human Rights Act is for *humans*, not vampires."

The video abruptly ended.

"What the fuck?" Jason breathed.

"They can't do that, can they?" Renie asked.

Ysanne paused, seeming to weigh her words before speaking. "I don't wish to alarm anyone by looking at the worst-case scenarios. Equally, I don't wish to lie to you about how serious this could be. Kendrick may be legally correct. When the Humans Right Act was established in 1998, humans didn't know that we existed. Kendrick may have some footing here," she said.

"But we're still *people*," Renie said, her voice trembling with anger and emotion.

Ysanne raised one hand. "Let's not get carried away yet. Tomorrow, the prime minister will come to Belle Morte to discuss our future, and I honestly don't know what she's going to say. There's also the matter of the vampire children to consider, something that Kendrick appears to have forgotten about."

Since new vampires were so susceptible to the sun, the kids Schofield had turned couldn't go home, and were instead living in Belle Morte's west wing.

"The prime minister will be accompanied by people from Social Services to check on the children. This is an entirely new and unforeseen situation for so many people, in so many ways," Ysanne said.

"There's something else, though, isn't there?" said Edmond, looking intently at Ysanne.

Again, she hesitated before speaking, which wasn't at all like her.

"We've received reports of attacks," she said carefully.

"What kind of attacks?"

"Over the last few days, four people have publicly alleged that they were bitten by a vampire. So far no one has been seriously injured, but medical examinations appear to corroborate these claims," Ysanne replied.

"In what way?" Ludovic asked.

"Bite marks and blood loss," Walsh said.

"Of course, this isn't definitive evidence, which is why I'll be visiting these alleged victims myself today. If they're lying, I'm confident that I'll be able to tell," Ysanne said.

"But if they are telling the truth, then there's still a rogue vampire running around out there," Gideon said.

Ysanne inclined her head in a small nod.

"Etienne or Jemima must have turned more people than we realized," Gideon said.

"No," Ysanne said. "With Susan Harcourt's assistance, every person who was turned during that coup has been accounted for. No one is missing."

"Schofield must have turned someone, then," Renie said.

It wasn't like they could question him—not after Roux had driven a sharp piece of wood through his heart.

"I'm afraid that's impossible. Three of the four victims allege that they were attacked in broad daylight. Two of them were dog walkers, one a jogger, and all of them were in the countryside when it happened, making it extremely unlikely that a newly turned vampire could access the shelter they need from the sun."

"Unlikely, but not impossible," Renie countered.

Ysanne acknowledged that with another small nod.

"But that's not what you think, is it?" Jason said, feeling like he'd swallowed a bag of rocks.

Ysanne's eyes flicked to him, giving nothing away.

"I don't get it. What's the alternative?" Renie said.

"That there's another vampire out there somewhere, but a much older one," Jason said, the words tasting bitter. "A vampire who's been out there since long before vampires revealed themselves to the world."

CHAPTER TWO

Gideon

He felt like he'd been plunged into ice. Surely this couldn't be possible.

"I thought that all vampires came forward once Ysanne revealed their existence," Seamus said, scratching his head.

"We thought so too." Ysanne lowered her eyes. "But perhaps we were wrong."

"Did these victims say anything about who attacked them? Was it a man, a woman? Do we know *anything*?" Gideon asked.

"At present, I know nothing more than I've already told you. Perhaps my upcoming visit with these people will provide more details," Ysanne said.

"Why would a vampire want to hide away all this time?" Jason asked, frowning.

"I suppose that depends on the vampire."

"But it doesn't make sense. Even if this person didn't care about the fame and fortune side of modern vampire life, surely he or she would want to live in a world where they were accepted rather than having to skulk in the shadows?" Jason said.

"Jason, I don't have these answers," Ysanne said, and for the first time since she'd called this meeting, there was a note of real weariness in her voice.

"But we can't let another rogue vampire run around unaccounted for," Roux said. "Especially if they're attacking people."

"First, we need to ascertain whether these allegations are true or if it's some elaborate hoax to further blacken our reputation," Ysanne said.

She believed it was true, though; Gideon was sure of it.

Seamus said something else but Gideon didn't hear what it was. There was a strange buzzing noise in his ears, a growing sense of panic that threatened to drag him under.

The discussion continued around him but Gideon still didn't hear a word of it. He felt like he was caught in a riptide dragging him farther and farther out to sea, and there was nothing to grab onto.

Then Jason's voice rang out, brighter and clearer than the rest, and Gideon had an anchor.

"No matter what happens, the Vampire Houses need to modernize," Jason said.

Ysanne recoiled a little.

"I know you don't want to hear it, but even in the best-case scenario the Houses can't go back to how they were before. Not completely, anyway. Changes have to be made," Jason said.

"That may be a discussion for another day," Ysanne said.

"Okay, but you can't ignore it forever."

Ysanne's expression hardened, but Jason stared back at her, uncowed.

Gideon felt a spark of something that might have been pride.

For ten years Belle Morte had been almost entirely technology-free, which was how most of them liked it. Asking them to modernize their private space was a big step. Although hadn't they already made steps? The younger vampires had phones, and so did

Jason. In the week that had passed since Roux had killed Schofield, Gideon had spotted Seamus quietly bringing two boxed laptops into the house, although Gideon wasn't sure where they were now. Even Ludovic, who'd been one of the most averse to technology, now had a rudimentary understanding of mobile devices.

"Jason's right," said Renie quietly.

Ysanne stiffened.

"Even little things like CCTV would make a difference. If we'd had cameras in this place, Etienne couldn't have covered up June's murder," Renie went on, her voice hitching on her sister's name.

Ysanne said nothing.

"And you already *have* tech here. The passageways?" Roux added.

Gideon sat up straighter, feeling foolish. That hadn't even occurred to him. For years whispered rumors had claimed there were secret passageways behind the walls of Belle Morte, but it wasn't until Etienne's scheming that the rumors were proven true. Each passageway was accessed via a code entered on a small keypad.

"The technology we have in place was for emergencies only," Ysanne said.

Renie spread her palms. "I'm pretty sure that what's happening now counts as an emergency."

Tension thickened in the room.

Ysanne lowered her eyes. "My arrogance has been assuming that I always knew what went on in my house, but recent events have proved how very wrong I am in that regard. Difficult though it is to accept, I suppose we cannot continue to let progress pass us by."

"But isn't that one of the things that's made us popular?" Isabeau spoke for the first time. Her hands were clasped on the tabletop, her shoulders slumped. "We're not just myths come to life, we're pieces of the past. We've carved out our little empires separate from the modern world, and it seems foolish to pretend that humans aren't fascinated by that."

Ludovic shook his head, a strand of blond hair slipping free from his ponytail. "I'd argue that recent events have changed the public's perception of us. What they once found quaint will now seem short-sighted. A refusal to implement better security measures in the wake of so much death and tragedy will hardly endear us to anyone."

"It would help if donors were allowed to communicate with friends and family on the outside too," Renie said.

"They *are* allowed," Ysanne said.

Renie rolled her eyes. "I mean in a twenty-first century way. Phones, not writing letters."

"What difference would that make?"

"It would make the houses seem less isolated. That's one of the problems we're having now. Vampires are so separate from the rest of the world that it's become easy to dehumanize us, to stop seeing us as people. Letting donors keep their phones is one more step toward removing some of those barriers between us and them."

"Those rules are in place for a reason, to prevent donors from sharing unauthorized material," Isabeau cautioned.

"Oh come on, that's not the only reason. Vampires don't like cell phones because they don't understand them, and *that's* why you don't want them in the houses."

"If privacy breaches are the only problem, then add new stipulations to the donor contracts," Roux chimed in. "Make it so you can sue the pants off anyone who releases anything unauthorized."

Isabeau pursed her lips. "We're talking about donor contracts as if they still exist."

"For now, they do," Jason said.

"Contracts without donors are meaningless. Besides, you heard Kendrick. The donor system might be beyond saving," Isabeau said.

"And it might not be. Things are bad, but they could be worse."

Gideon rubbed his thumb along the tabletop, tracing the whorls of wood. "Maybe we need to face the possibility that this is one battle we can't win," he said.

Jason's face softened. "Don't say that."

"Why not? With everything that's happened, I don't see how we'll ever fit in with the human world again, so maybe it would be easier on everyone if we simply faded back into the shadows."

"Bullshit," said Jason at once. "You all have as much right to be here as anyone else."

Renie nodded in fierce assent.

Jason's eyes met Gideon's, and he smiled.

Gideon looked down at the table.

Shortly after, Ysanne called an end to the meeting so she and Walsh could go and visit the alleged victims of the rogue vampire.

Renie and Roux disappeared with Edmond and Ludovic, Seamus returned to his duties, and Jason hovered a few moments longer, looking somewhat lost, before he finally left too. Then it was just Isabeau and Gideon.

Isabeau's eyes had lingered on Ysanne as she left the dining hall, her expression caught between longing and anger, and now she stared blankly at the seat opposite.

Gideon pulled his own seat closer to her. There were few people in this world he truly trusted, but Isabeau had been his friend for many years before vampires revealed themselves, and she was the reason he'd chosen Belle Morte as his home. She'd been the brightest spark in his life for so long, but she hadn't been the same since the Council had imprisoned her for crimes she hadn't committed. Now she was a shadow of who she'd been, except when she was in a room with Ysanne, and then the air turned frosty.

Gideon wondered if Ysanne had tried to fix things. She was nothing if not proud, but would she throw away her happiness for the sake of her pride? He'd tried to broach it with Isabeau, but this was one subject she refused to discuss, even with him.

"What will we do if they take our houses?" Gideon asked.

"We survived without donors and bagged blood before. We can do it again," Isabeau said. Her voice was as flat as her expression.

"But then no one knew we existed. Now the whole world knows we're real, and knows our faces. How could we hunt on the streets without anyone knowing?" Gideon said.

Isabeau was silent.

"And what do we do if these attacks are real and there *is* another vampire out there somewhere?" Gideon went on.

No response.

Gideon gazed around the dining hall. Despite being one of the mansion's largest rooms, vampires typically spent less time in it than donors, who had eaten three meals a day here. Gideon had always considered it *their* room.

Now he wondered if donors would ever eat here again.

What would happen if vampires really were evicted from their homes? Would Kendrick follow through with his proposal to turn the mansions into shelters? Or was that just an excuse to turf vampires out?

It had only been ten years since Gideon had come to live at Belle Morte—the blink of an eye to many vampires—and already it seemed impossible to him that Vampire Houses could one day be *without* vampires.

Yet it wasn't.

He glanced back at Isabeau but she was still staring at the opposite chair, her expression downcast. Clearly she didn't want to talk about this now.

Quietly, Gideon got to his feet. He rested his palm on Isabeau's shoulder, and she patted the back of his hand, but she still didn't look at him, and after a moment he left.

There was something he needed to do.

Jason

Once the dining hall had emptied, Jason had realized he didn't know what to do with himself.

Now, as he lay on his bed staring up at the ceiling, a small knot of loneliness formed behind his ribs.

Ysanne had included him in that meeting because she considered him as involved as anyone else, and Jason was happy about that, but at the same time he was still the odd one out, the puzzle piece that didn't quite fit.

Someone knocked on the door and he perked up. Maybe the girls had realized he was lonely.

He climbed off the bed, opened the door, and froze.

Gideon stood on the other side.

Jason almost forgot how to breathe. How many fantasies had started with Gideon knocking on his door? He fought the urge to pinch himself in case he'd fallen asleep and this was some beautiful dream.

"Hello," Gideon said, shifting his weight.

He couldn't quite meet Jason's eyes, and that more than anything told Jason this was reality. In his dreams, Gideon never hesitated to look him in the eye.

"Hi," Jason said.

An awkward moment passed.

"Can I help you?" Jason asked.

Gideon squared his shoulders, as if gearing up for something. "I hope so."

Another awkward moment passed.

"Okay, if you need my help, you need to tell me what with. I can't read your mind," Jason said.

He wished he could. Gideon was an enigma, a code he'd love to crack.

"I'd like you to teach me about the modern world," Gideon said.

Jason blinked at him. Obviously, Gideon hadn't come here for the sexy fun times of Jason's dreams, but he hadn't expected this.

"Why?" he asked.

"Because if we lose the protection of this house, I want to understand the world I'll be going back into."

Jason had the urge to hug him, and not just because he fancied the pants off him. Gideon had been around for longer than Jason knew, but, in that moment, he looked . . . lost.

"First things first," he said, beckoning Gideon into the room. "You are not going to lose Belle Morte."

Gideon turned bleak eyes on him. "You don't know that."

"Okay, no, I don't, but—"

"Please don't," Gideon interjected. "I know you're trying to be comforting, but I need to be prepared."

Jason shut his mouth. It was his turn to feel awkward.

Gideon Hartwright was in his room, and Jason didn't know what to say to him.

"Why me? You know that Renie and Roux are teaching the others about the modern world, right?" he said.

Gideon finally looked at Jason properly, and there was the faintest hint of amusement in his eyes.

"Renie and Roux have both been a little preoccupied lately," he said.

Jason laughed. "Yeah, I noticed."

"Besides," Gideon said, "I need to understand more of this, but I'm afraid of how negative it will be. Renie and Roux have been through more than enough lately, and I don't want to expose them to any more ugliness. They deserve some time to be happy."

Jason's heart thumped.

Once, at a Belle Morte ball—it seemed like years ago—he'd warned Renie not to fall for Edmond. Even if human/vampire relationships weren't forbidden, they would only end badly. Vampires lived forever. Humans didn't.

But Gideon was like the sun coming out on a cloudy day, bright and beautiful, and Jason couldn't ignore the way he felt when he looked at the vampire. And he couldn't ignore the spark of hope in his chest that Gideon had chosen to come here, to *him*.

"Will you teach me?" Gideon asked.

"Of course," Jason said.

He started with something obvious, talking Gideon through the basics of a cell phone while trying not to freak out over the fact that Gideon was *sitting on his bed*.

"So I can contact anyone, anywhere in the world?" Gideon said.

"As long as you've got their number. And reception."

"Fascinating." Gideon turned the phone over in his hand, marveling at it. "They're so small."

"They used to be smaller. Originally they were great big bricks, and then the fashion was for teeny tiny flip phones, and now we've got these."

"And everyone has one?"

"Most people, yeah."

Gideon bent over the phone and practiced unlocking it, like Jason had taught him.

Jason admired his profile. Gideon's hair was a darker blond than Ludovic's or Ysanne's, like honey under sunlight, and Jason ached to run his hands through it. Preferably while kissing. The way that honey-colored hair curled into the nape of Gideon's neck, the shape of his Adam's apple interrupting the smooth line of his throat, the golden brushstrokes of his eyebrows, it all made Jason feel warm inside.

"What's this?" Gideon asked in a strange voice.

Jason looked over and his heart jumped into his throat. He tried to take the phone, but Gideon pushed his hands away. His eyes narrowed as he continued reading what was on the screen.

"Is this what people really think of us?" he asked.

He lowered the phone and Jason snatched it back. "Social media doesn't mean anything," he said.

"There are people calling for us to be burned alive. They're calling for us to be chained out in the sun or staked through the heart," said Gideon flatly.

Jason tossed the phone onto the bed behind him. "Listen," he said. "People say a lot of disgusting shit online. They get to be anonymous and that brings out their worst side. This isn't only about vampires. There are always people being vile on platforms like this because they know they can get away with it. That doesn't mean anyone agrees with them."

"I think the protests have shown that people *do* agree with them."

"That doesn't make them right," Jason countered.

"They said we were as bad as Schofield," Gideon said, still in that flat voice.

"Wait, what?" Jason hadn't seen that, and it sparked a wave of anger.

Gideon looked at him, his gray eyes unbearably sad. "Schofield kidnapped and turned those children, but some people think we're just as bad for keeping them here at Belle Morte."

"Where the hell else are they supposed to go?"

"Even if they *could* leave, this is the world they have to face now," Gideon said, indicating the phone.

"Then it's a good thing they're not alone," Jason said.

"Do you think that makes it any better?"

"Better? No. Easier? Maybe. When it feels like the whole world's against you, having friends who'll stand with you is incredibly important. Don't ever underestimate that."

Gideon didn't respond.

Jason wanted to push his point a little further, but sometimes Gideon was like a skittish animal. He didn't want to scare the vampire away.

"I should go," Gideon said, abruptly standing up.

Disappointment coursed through Jason's chest. Gideon had been here barely half an hour, but those minutes felt precious. Jason wasn't ready for them to end. But he couldn't make him stay.

"Okay," he mumbled, getting up too.

It felt faintly ridiculous to walk Gideon to the door when they both lived in the same house, but Jason did it anyway.

At the door, Gideon paused. "Thank you," he said.

"You're welcome."

"Can we do this again?" Gideon asked.

Jason's brain almost short-circuited before he realized what Gideon was actually asking—whether or not Jason would continue helping him adapt to the modern world.

"It's not like I've got much else to do," he said, smiling.

Gideon's gaze drifted to his lips, and Jason was sure the world stopped turning, just for a moment.

Nobody moved, and then, just when Jason was sure Gideon would lean forward, the vampire broke eye contact and reached for the door handle.

"I'll see you next time," he said, and walked out.

Jason shut the door and leaned his head on it, breathing deeply. He couldn't have imagined that. Gideon had looked like he wanted to kiss him, and that had been real.

Something had happened in this room. Jason wasn't quite sure what it was, but it felt like a beginning.

CHAPTER THREE

Jason

As evening drew in and Ysanne still hadn't returned, Jason hung around the vestibule, going in and out of the rooms on either side, up and down the hallways that branched off it, hoping to catch her without making it too obvious that he was waiting for her.

When she did return, without Walsh, Jason knew immediately she wasn't bringing good news. Her face was composed, her posture as straight as ever, but her eyes were heavy, like she was carrying a greater weight than before she left the mansion.

"What happened?" Jason asked, leaning one shoulder against the banister of the main staircase.

"I detected no lies from the people Walsh and I visited," Ysanne said.

Jason took a moment to appreciate how Ysanne spoke to him like an equal now. A couple of weeks ago she'd *never* have done that.

"So either they really were attacked by a vampire, or they sincerely *believe* they were," Jason said.

Ysanne nodded.

"Okay, let's look at this logically. A lot of people are mad at vampires right now, mad enough to protest, mad enough to destroy your blood supplies. Is it so farfetched to think that someone, maybe People Before Vampires, is faking vampire attacks to smear you all further? The victims wouldn't necessarily know the attacks were hoaxes," Jason said.

"The attacks aren't hoaxes. These people really have been bitten, or at least have puncture marks on their necks consistent with vampire bites, and they really have lost blood," Ysanne said.

"Right, but that doesn't mean a vampire did it. A human could still have attacked them and made it *look* like a vampire bite."

Ysanne smiled sadly. "While I believe there are people who hate us enough to do something like that, each victim described being immobilized by an assailant of incredible strength. They described the sensation of being bitten, the feel of a mouth on their necks, along with the fangs."

"And there's no way that any of them could be in on a hoax?" Jason clutched at straws.

Ysanne held up one pale palm. "I admire and appreciate your optimism, but we must face reality. A vampire did this."

The hope drained out of him. "How could another vampire have been out there all this time without anyone knowing?"

"Vampires existed for thousands of years without anyone knowing," Ysanne pointed out.

"But why now? Every other vampire came out of the shadows when you went public with their existence, so why not this one?"

Tension flickered across Ysanne's face. "What if it isn't just this one?"

"You think there's more?" Dread washed over Jason.

"At the moment I cannot possibly say if this is the work of a single vampire or a group of them. But even if it is just one, there's nothing to say that there aren't more out there."

"But why choose now to reveal themselves?" Jason asked. "And more importantly, what do they want?"

Ysanne tilted her head. Light gleamed off her sheet of blond hair. "Why do you assume they want something?"

"Why else would they be so careless? This vampire has hidden all this time, potentially hundreds of years, and it's only now that they've started biting people like this? That's not an accident. Whoever they are, they want us to know they're here," Jason said.

"I agree." Ysanne gave Jason an appraising look.

"And if they want us to know they're here, it's because they want something else. They've come out of hiding for a reason," Jason went on. "How the hell do we find out what it is when we don't know who or where they are?"

"*We* don't. This isn't your problem to solve," Ysanne said.

"Hey, we're all in this together," Jason told her.

"In many things, yes, but you can't help with this, Jason. Walsh and I will handle it."

Jason thought Ysanne was going to say something else, but then she stiffened, her eyes moving to someone behind him. Jason looked over his shoulder.

Isabeau and Gideon had appeared from the hallway to the left of the staircase. The temperature in the vestibule seemed to plummet; Jason half expected frost to creep up the walls.

"You should get some sleep," Ysanne said, and Jason wasn't sure if she was still talking to him. "The prime minister will be here in the morning, and we have a lot to discuss with her."

She swept into the parlor on the other side of the vestibule, her high heels clicking on the floor. Isabeau turned and went back the way she'd come, and Jason held his breath, wondering if Gideon would stay. But after a brief look at Jason, Gideon followed Isabeau.

Jason let out a long sigh.

Things were bad right now, in so many ways, but surely they couldn't get much worse.

At least, he hoped they couldn't.

Despite an uneasy night's sleep, Jason woke the next morning with hope in his heart. A dark storm still hung over their heads, but Belle Morte had weathered storms before.

He headed downstairs to the small kitchen beyond the ballroom, once off-limits to donors. With the mansion's staff now gone, Jason and the remaining security guards had free rein of the kitchen, and the set mealtimes had been abandoned, leaving people to grab food whenever they wanted or needed to. Belle Morte's rule about healthy eating seemed to have gone out of the window too—someone had stocked the fridge with bacon.

Jason promptly made himself a bacon sandwich, humming quietly as he flipped the rashers, getting them good and crispy before laying them on the bread.

He ate his sandwich in the kitchen, leaning against the nearest counter. It didn't feel right eating in the dining hall, not when he was the only one who did so.

Besides, nothing good ever seemed to happen in the dining hall anymore.

The door opened and Gideon walked in. Jason's heart did a little flip.

"Hi," he said, hoping he didn't have bits of sandwich stuck in his teeth.

The bagged blood that the vampires currently lived on was stored in the kitchen, meaning that vampires also visited this room a lot more than they used to.

Gideon approached him, his expression cautious. "Good morning." He opened the fridge and took out a bag of blood, staring down at it for a long moment.

"You okay?" Jason said.

Gideon lifted his eyes.

"This supply won't last forever. If we're not getting more, what will we do when it runs out?" he said.

Jason bit his lip. He hadn't really considered that. "You can drink animal blood, can't you?" he said, recalling how Ysanne and Isabeau had fed June Mayfield when she was chained in the west wing.

"We could survive on it for a while, but it can't permanently replace human blood," Gideon explained. "And newer vampires like Renie, Roux, and the children *need* human blood. They're not strong enough to survive on animals."

Jason rubbed his hand over his neck. "There's always me," he suggested.

Gideon stared at him, his face unreadable, then his gaze dropped to Jason's throat, and for a breathless moment, Jason thought Gideon was considering it.

Then Gideon looked away. "You can't feed all of us."

Seamus came into the kitchen.

"Hey. You want some breakfast?" Jason said, already turning to the frying pan he hadn't washed up yet.

"Actually, I was looking for you," Seamus said. "Ysanne wants to see you."

His tone of voice was casual, normal, but Jason's heart still sank. What could Ysanne possibly want him for?

"In her office?" Jason asked.

He hoped that Seamus would say no, that this wasn't that formal, but Seamus nodded, and Jason's heart dropped a little more. He cast a vaguely panicked look at Gideon.

Gideon looked at the floor.

"Okay," Jason mumbled.

His chest felt tight as Seamus led him to Ysanne's office. Besides the security guards, who had a job to do, Jason was the last human left in a Vampire House in the UK and Ireland. Since he no longer fed the vampires, he wasn't even sure he could be called a donor anymore. He'd been allowed to stay because he'd helped the vampires of Belle Morte face every threat that had come their way, but maybe that only gave him so much leeway.

What if Ysanne was bringing him to her office to tell him it was time to leave?

They reached the office, and Seamus knocked on the smoked glass door.

"*Entrez.*" Ysanne's crisp voice rang out.

Seamus pushed open the door and ushered Jason inside. For some reason, Jason had thought Seamus would come in with him, but as soon as he was across the threshold, Seamus closed the door, leaving him alone in the office.

Alone except for Ysanne.

She sat behind her desk, her pale hands clasped on the polished black surface, her eyes sharp and penetrating.

Jason swallowed.

"Sit," she said, indicating the chair in front of her desk.

Jason slid into the chair.

"I was contacted today by representatives from the *Daily Topic*. Do you know what that is?"

"Um . . . it's a talk show," he said.

Specifically, one of the longest-running, popular morning talk shows in British history, airing five mornings a week and dealing with everything from celebrity interviews to serious political discussions.

"They'd like you to appear," Ysanne said.

Jason frowned. This was the last thing he'd expected. "Why?"

"They're planning a special feature about vampires, and you hold the unique position of being the last donor in the UK. I believe the show is interested in why you've chosen to stay here, what your views are on everything that's happened, and what you'll do when this is all over," Ysanne explained.

If it was ever all over.

"How do you feel about this?" Ysanne asked.

"I don't know," he admitted.

"Perhaps you need some time to think about it. I should warn you, though, the show is hoping to air this feature in just a few days, so you'll need to make a decision soon."

"Right," Jason said, his mind churning.

"I will support whatever decision you make, but I do ask that you consider this," Ysanne said.

"Would it just be me?" Jason asked.

"No other guests have been confirmed yet, but I believe they are in the process of approaching former donors too."

"What about vampires? Shouldn't they be invited?" Jason said.

Ysanne pursed her lips, just a little. "I have discussed that point with the show and I volunteered to appear myself, but they diplomatically expressed their feelings that a less controversial vampire might be a better choice."

Jason frowned again. "Since when are you controversial?"

"Since some of these movements against vampires decided that, since I'm the one who brought vampires out of the shadows, I'm now to blame for everything that's happened."

Ysanne's voice was inflectionless; Jason couldn't gauge how she felt about that.

"What about Renie or Roux? I bet they'd do it," he said.

"I'm sure they would, too, but they've only been vampires for the blink of an eye. I believe the perspective of an older, more publicly familiar vampire would be more valuable," Ysanne explained.

Renie and Roux were pretty publicly familiar themselves these days, but Jason got what Ysanne meant. His girls hadn't been famous for long, whereas the other vampires of Belle Morte had a decade of celebrity under their belts.

"I'll do it," he said.

"Are you sure? You don't wish to discuss it with your friends, your family?" Ysanne asked.

"I'm sure."

Ysanne's shoulders slumped the barest amount, the only sign of relief she'd shown.

"Thank you," she said.

Jason had the sudden urge to reach across the desk and take her hand. Ysanne wasn't the unfeeling, ice-cold bitch that many people thought her to be, but her position could be a lonely one, forcing her to keep everyone at arm's length, and she was under more pressure now than ever. But something told him that she wouldn't appreciate it, so he kept his hands in his lap.

"I'm still waiting on some of the details, but I'll provide you with them as soon as I can," Ysanne said.

"Is there anything else you need me for?" Jason asked.

Ysanne gave him something that wasn't quite a smile, but it was close. "Not just now."

There wasn't much else to say, so Jason quietly slipped from the office. Farther down the hallway he spotted Gideon, leaning against the wall as if he was waiting, and his heart gave that flutter again.

"What did Ysanne want?" Gideon asked.

Jason told him.

Was it his imagination, or did a flash of relief cross Gideon's face?

"Are you sure you want to do this?" he asked.

Jason leaned against the wall next to him, hands behind his back. "It's important."

"That's not what I asked."

Jason shuffled his feet, trying to find the right answer. "I don't know," he admitted. "All these protests and attacks are pretty scary, and I get that I could be putting myself in the firing line, but I won't skulk around the mansion when I can do something to help."

"Do you ever think that this isn't your fight?" Gideon asked.

Jason gave him a friendly nudge. "Hell, no. I'll always fight for the people I care about."

Gideon fell silent, staring at the opposite wall. Jason peeked at him from the corner of his eye, admiring the strong line of Gideon's jaw, the way his hair curled around the curve of his ears, the straight slope of his nose.

"You mentioned the possibility of a vampire appearing on this program," Gideon said at last. "What if that vampire was me?"

Jason did a double take.

"Uh . . ." was the most eloquent response he could muster. This hadn't even occurred to him.

Gideon met his gaze, and Jason swallowed. Gideon's eyes were dark, churning, like a winter sea. A guy could drown in those eyes.

"You don't want me to?" he asked.

"It's not what *I* want. I'm not in charge of the show," Jason pointed out.

"But what do *you* think?"

A memory flashed in Jason's head. On the night that Roger Schofield had finally been brought to justice one of his accomplices had attacked Roux with a pitchfork, and Gideon had pushed her out of the way to take the injury himself. Jason hadn't been there at the time, but he couldn't forget Gideon returning to the mansion, covered in his own blood, and the gut punch of terror Jason had felt, not immediately knowing how serious the injury was.

Gideon never hesitated to protect the people he was loyal to.

"I honestly can't think of anyone better," Jason said.

That earned him a quick smile.

"Perhaps I should go and talk to Ysanne, then," Gideon said.

"Do you want me to come with you?" Jason offered.

Gideon shook his head.

Jason tried again. "Do you want me to wait for you?"

Another head shake.

Jason deflated. "I guess I'll . . . see you around then," he mumbled.

Gideon didn't respond, just walked away.

Jason slumped against the wall again and scrubbed his hands over his face. "You have *got* to stop mooning over him," he sternly told himself.

But he knew it would make no difference.

Somehow, Gideon Hartwright was under his skin, and he had no idea what to do about that.

CHAPTER FOUR

Jason

The next few days passed quietly. The *Daily Topic* accepted Gideon as an additional guest, and despite how hot and cold Gideon sometimes blew with him, Jason was glad there'd be a familiar face sitting beside him on national TV.

Especially when that face was so damned delicious.

There was no further news of attacks from the mysterious vampire—at least none that Ysanne had shared, though Jason wasn't naive enough to think that was the last Belle Morte would hear of it.

And then suddenly the day arrived, and Jason was lying awake in bed hours before he needed to be up, his stomach a writhing nest of nerves.

When he'd first arrived at Belle Morte, he'd relished the idea of achieving some level of celebrity, though it would pale in comparison to the vampires themselves. The thought of cameras flashing in his face, strangers on the street knowing his name, had thrilled him. Now it made him feel slightly sick.

He pushed back the covers and climbed out of bed.

As big as the bedroom was, it suddenly felt too small, like there wasn't enough air in it. Slipping on a pair of socks, Jason crept out of his room and down the darkened hallway to the main staircase. Even though donors hadn't used to creep around at night—except for Renie—Jason could somehow feel that they weren't here anymore. The house felt so much quieter, emptier, like once it had been singing but now could only whisper.

He'd almost reached the vestibule when a prickle of awareness ran up the back of his neck, and he turned. Gideon stood at the top of the stairs, his skin looking like ivory in the dark, and something warm spread through Jason's chest, easing his nerves.

No matter how difficult today was, at least he wouldn't be alone.

"What are you doing up?" Gideon asked.

Jason leaned on the banister, looking at the darkened lobby below. "What are *you* doing up?"

"I couldn't sleep."

Jason rubbed his chin. "Same. I hope the *Daily Topic* has good lighting to hide the bags under my eyes."

"You don't have any," Gideon said.

"Flatterer."

No response.

Jason swallowed a knot of frustration.

"Are you worried about today?" Gideon asked, moving closer.

Jason gave a little nod. "I know how much is riding on this—on *us*. It's a lot of pressure."

Gideon rested one pale hand on the banister. "It's not too late to cancel."

"To hell with that. I'm doing this," Jason said.

Gideon gave him a small smile. "Good."

They were quiet for a few moments, standing side by side in the shadows.

"Have you thought about what you'll say?" Gideon asked.

"I've rehearsed some stuff, but it depends on the questions, and what the other guests say. Ysanne's given me permission to bring up some of the changes to the donor system that we discussed, but other than that I really don't know," Jason said. "You?"

Gideon uttered a short laugh. "I have no idea."

"I guess being in the public eye in this way is different than what you're used to," said Jason softly.

Gideon lowered his head. Jason took that as agreement.

"A lot of people will watch this program, won't they?" Gideon asked.

Jason rubbed his hand along the wood grain of the banister. "Yeah."

"Including the people protesting against us."

Jason sighed. He'd been trying not to think too much about that. "Yeah."

"This could be dangerous."

Jason gave a half smile. "Hey, I work out." He flexed his bicep. "I'm not completely helpless."

Gideon's eyes flicked to Jason's arm, and Jason thought he saw *something* flash across Gideon's face.

"It's dangerous for you too," Jason said.

Gideon arched an eyebrow. "I'm a vampire."

"But you're not invulnerable."

A pause.

"Are you worried about me?" Gideon asked, his voice lower than before.

"Yes. Vampires can still be killed, and too many people hate vampires right now."

Gideon tilted his head. Shadows slid across his face. "You need to look out for yourself, not for me."

"I'm a multitasker. I can worry about two people at once," Jason said.

But his stomach felt like one huge knot.

What if he screwed this up?

What if he made things worse?

Dawn came and went, and all too soon it was time to leave for the studio.

Jason's friends were waiting for him in the vestibule, and he paused at the top of the staircase, gazing down at them, his heart stuttering in his chest.

Renie let out a loud *whoop*, breaking the silence, and clapped. "That's our boy," she called.

Jason managed a wobbly smile as he walked down the steps.

Renie threw her arms around him. It was a good thing she'd gained better control of her vampire strength. "You've got this," she whispered in his ear.

"I'm terrified," Jason admitted, hugging her back.

Roux took Renie's place. "We have complete faith in you," she said.

Jason swallowed hard. "I'm so scared that I'm going to fuck it all up."

"Why would you think that?"

"Because this is important, but I don't really know what I'm doing."

Roux held him at arm's length, regarding him intently. "Everyone in this house trusts you. You won't fuck anything up."

"I might," Jason said stubbornly.

Roux kissed his cheek. "You won't. I know you won't."

Everyone parted to let Ysanne through. The Lady of Belle Morte looked as cool and collected as ever, not a strand of blond hair out of place—but Jason knew she'd be feeling the pressure as much as anyone.

"The laws of this house were put in place to keep us all safe," Ysanne said. "But things have changed. We must change with them, or we will be left behind." She fixed her shrewd gaze on Jason. "Your ideas for modernizing the Houses and the donor system will likely be a point of debate today. I can only trust that you will present your suggestions logically and thoughtfully."

Jason had to swallow a couple of times before he could get the words out. "Thank you for trusting me," he croaked.

Ysanne offered a rare, brief smile. "You've more than earned it."

Gideon stepped forward, and Jason startled a little. It was the first time he hadn't noticed the blond vampire whenever he was in a room, which spoke volumes about how nervous he was.

Renie started forward as if she was going to hug Gideon, too, but stopped herself. Despite everything they'd all been through together, Jason and his girls still didn't *know* Gideon very well.

"Are you ready to go?" Gideon asked Jason.

No.

"Yes," Jason whispered, his throat still dry. The *Daily Topic* had better provide their guests with water; otherwise he wouldn't be able to get out a single word.

He'd been so worried about screwing up the interview that he'd almost forgotten about the protestors, but they'd obviously heard about his and Gideon's TV appearance that day—there were more of them than ever gathered at the gates, angrily shouting.

His heart plummeted and he ran a hand along his jaw, feeling the faint prick of stubble. He'd been too nervous to shave.

"You okay?" Seamus asked, stepping up beside him, and Jason jumped.

"Yeah," he said.

Seamus scrutinized him, not looking convinced. "It's not too late to change your mind. No one will think less of you."

Jason shook his head. "No way am I backing out now."

Seamus clapped him on the shoulder. "That's what I like to hear. Gideon, you still with us?"

Gideon was staring blankly at the gate; at Seamus's words, he blinked and focused on them. "Of course," he said.

"Great. Come on."

Seamus walked toward the black Belle Morte car parked nearby.

"Wait, you're coming with me?" Jason hurried after him.

Seamus grinned. "Someone's got to keep an eye on you."

Jason and Gideon climbed into the back seat. As the gates slowly opened, Jason fought the urge to duck down. The windows were tinted, so it was unlikely anyone could get a photo of him, but in case they did, he wanted to be sitting tall and holding his head high.

"Are you coming into the studio with us?" Jason asked.

"Yeah, but I won't be on the show itself. I'll hang around behind the scenes until you're done," Seamus replied.

The journey from Winchester to London took the better part of two hours, but all too soon they were arriving at the studio. Jason's heart climbed into his throat and lodged there, making it hard to swallow. People thronged the street outside, shouting and waving more placards.

"Oh my god," he whispered, closing his eyes and digging his fingers into his seat.

There were so many of them.

"They're not all protesting vampires," Gideon said in a strange voice. His fingers brushed Jason's arm. "Look."

Jason looked. Farther down the street, three people held up a massive banner with VLADDICTS FOR LIFE written on it in blood-red lettering. They cheered when they saw the black car, and hope swelled in Jason's chest. He'd grown so used to people booing vampires outside the gates of Belle Morte that it almost felt strange to hear people cheer for them again.

But there were protestors, too, clamoring against the metal barriers that had been placed on either side of the studio entrance, and the sound of their anger grew louder as the car got nearer.

"People Before Vampires," someone shouted, and more voices took up the chant.

"People Before Vampires."

"People Before Vampires."

"People Before Vampires."

Jason's mouth went dry again, and he glanced at Gideon, whose face was unreadable.

"There are more supporters than protestors," Jason said.

"You ready?" Seamus said, twisting in his seat to look back at them.

Jason gave a decisive nod, even though his stomach was starting to clench. "Let's do this."

There was a surge of noise when he climbed out of the car, and for a moment he paused, disoriented by it. It had been like this when he'd first arrived at the mansion, though nobody had booed then.

He turned to Gideon, who still stood by the car, one hand on the open door, his expression rigid, looking like he wanted to dive back inside and get the hell away from here.

"Hey." Jason pitched his voice so no one else could hear them. "I'm right here, okay?"

Gideon gave a short nod.

As they approached the studio, people reached over the barriers, phones in outstretched hands, shrieking for photos, and Jason was surprised that his name was shouted as much as Gideon's. He'd assumed the Vladdicts had turned out for the beautiful vampire, not him.

Seamus shook his head, and Jason took his advice, hurrying past them with an apologetic smile.

Something sailed through the air toward him, thrown by someone in the crowd. Gideon flung an arm around Jason's head, pulling him down and shielding him.

Time seemed to stand still; all Jason could think about were the Molotov cocktails that Iain Johnson and his friends had used to burn down Roux and Ludovic's hotel. If one of those hit Gideon—

A plastic bottle thudded on the ground in front of Jason.

No bombs.

Just a poorly thrown bottle.

Seamus pulled them upright. "You're okay," he murmured.

Jason nodded, not trusting himself to speak.

Yellow liquid had spilled out of the bottle and was forming a puddle on the ground.

It looked like piss.

Jason hoped it wasn't.

Then again, a bottle of piss was a lot better than a Molotov cocktail.

"Thanks," he said to Gideon.

Gideon scanned the crowd, a dark look on his face.

"You won't find out who threw it. Let's just get inside," Jason said.

Seamus hustled them into the studio, an arm around each of their shoulders. As the doors closed behind him, muting the cries of the crowd, Jason realized his heart was slamming against his chest.

It had just been a stupid bottle, but it could have been something more.

And once again, Gideon had acted instinctively to protect him.

Jason didn't want to read too much into that, but for a vampire who sometimes seemed so aloof, Gideon always seemed to have one eye out for Jason's well-being.

From there, everything passed in a blur, seeming to take no time at all, and before Jason knew it, the audience had arrived and he and Gideon were sitting with the show's hosts, Hari Morrison and Stuart Hall, on the famous blue sofa. On Jason's other side was a woman he guessed to be somewhere in her forties, her makeup a little too heavy, her hair teased a little too high.

Jason fought the urge to giggle. Being here felt too surreal.

That urge quickly died away as Hari, tall and lean with hair cut in a soft black bob, recounted everything that had happened to upend the vampire world. She didn't reel off the names of the victims—every news channel across the country, or even the world, had done that enough.

Stuart, handsome in a bland, forgettable sort of way, formally introduced Jason first, and applause greeted him, mixed with a few boos, and he smiled, trying to look more relaxed than he felt.

"So, Jason," said Hari. "You're currently the only donor left in a Vampire House in the UK or the Republic of Ireland."

"Not exactly. I'm not really a donor anymore. I don't feed anyone," Jason said.

Despite himself, his eyes slid to Gideon. Ever since he'd arrived at Belle Morte, he'd hoped that Gideon would pick him as a donor. But Gideon never had. The closest he'd ever come was licking Jason's throat to seal the punctures left by another vampire, and even now the memory of that made Jason squirm in the most delicious way.

"I see. But you're still choosing to live at Belle Morte," Hari said.

Jason nodded. "The people I've met there, both human and vampire, have become the best friends I've ever had."

Hari nodded. "How are things inside Belle Morte right now?"

"Everyone is a bit . . . tense," Jason said. "They've gone from being worldwide celebrities to complete pariahs, and they haven't done anything wrong."

"A lot of people died," Hari reminded him, but it didn't sound accusatory.

"Thanks to Jemima, Etienne, and Roger Schofield. Nothing to do with the vampires left in Belle Morte, or any other House," Jason said.

"Karl Kendrick recently made comments suggesting that vampires should be evicted from their houses, that the resources could be put to better use. What do you think about that?" Stuart said.

"That's—" Jason stopped himself from saying *bullshit*. "My friends fought to stop the vampires responsible for all this, and Kendrick's suggesting punishing them for it."

"You don't think there are two sides to this?" Stuart asked, crossing one leg over the other. His shoes were very shiny, and Jason focused on those as he assembled his thoughts.

"Those houses are the vampires' *homes*. The only reason he's suggesting this is because he doesn't really see vampires as people," Jason said.

"They're *not* people," called a voice from the crowd.

"Yes, they are. They have feelings the same as any of us, and the moment they found out what Etienne and Jemima were doing, they put their own lives on the line to stop them."

"That's not much comfort to the families of the donors who didn't come home," called another man, higher up in the tiered seating.

"No, it isn't, but what do you want anyone to do about that? The Belle Morte vampires didn't kill those donors, and they can't raise them from the dead. All they could do was get the remaining donors to safety, which they did."

"They don't live by the same rules as other people, though, do they?" said a woman in the front row, her voice quiet and serious. "I've been following all this since it started, and it's pretty clear that vampires have their own rules inside their houses, which they've kept hidden from everyone."

"On that note, let's go to Gideon Hartwright, one of the vampires of Belle Morte," Hari said, turning to the vampire at Jason's side.

Gideon sat too rigidly, like he wanted to be anywhere but here.

"The Vampire Council put their own laws in place because they thought it was best for everyone, both human and vampire. They didn't broadcast those rules to the human world for the same reason," he said.

"That seems like a poor excuse, if you ask me." The woman's voice was challenging, though not hostile.

"All the majority of vampires have ever wanted is to peacefully coexist with the human world. For most of our lives we've had to hide in the shadows, never being able to put down roots of any kind because it was too dangerous. We took a big risk revealing ourselves to you ten years ago, and everything we've done since then has been to protect the peace between two races." Gideon paused, a little furrow appearing between his eyebrows. "Perhaps the problem is that we were too rigid in our laws. We treated everything as black and white, and life is usually made up of shades of gray. In the future, things will be different. Vampires won't hide things from people. We won't live by separate rules."

"Lesley Brown, your daughter, Lucy, was a Belle Morte donor six years ago," Hari said, turning her attention to the woman sitting next to Jason. "What do you make of all this?"

"Lucy was a donor for several months, and I never once feared for her safety," Lesley said. "I'm not sure I'd feel the same if she was going into a Vampire House today."

"Any Vampire House or just Belle Morte?" Jason asked.

Lesley frowned, as if she hadn't considered that. "I suppose any."

"Over the last decade, thousands of donors have come and gone from the five Vampire Houses in the UK and Ireland, and none of them have suffered anything more than a broken nail. Why do you now think all houses are unsafe?" Jason said.

"Because when vampires fight each other, donors die," Lesley replied.

"You're talking like vampires fighting is a regular thing, when this is the first time in ten years that anything like this has happened."

"Do you think that changes the severity of it?" asked an older man in the second row of the audience.

"I didn't say that—"

"Are we supposed to believe that because this hasn't happened before, it won't ever happen again?"

"The system that vampires have lived by obviously needs reforming, and the vampires know that more than anyone. They want to work with humans to create a system for everyone, and surely that's better than tearing it all down and throwing vampires onto the streets," Jason said.

The man shook his head. "Your vampire friends let a lot of innocent people die."

"What happened was tragic, but it was not our doing," said Gideon quietly.

"We actually have a statement from Ysanne Moreau about this," Hari said.

She unfolded a piece of paper, and Jason caught a glimpse of crisp, small writing. He suppressed a smile. Of course Ysanne had sent it handwritten.

"'There is nothing that I wouldn't give to go back in time and change what happened, but that is beyond my power. I have nothing but remorse and regret for the lives that were lost during the power coup in this house, but the fact remains that the perpetrators of said coup are already dead. The vampires of Belle Morte fought and bled to stop Etienne and Jemima, and they deserve gratitude for that, not guilt by association,'" Hari read.

"It isn't just about them anymore. It's about Roger Schofield and the children that he murdered," the guy in the audience argued.

"None of us will ever forget what that man did," Gideon said, his voice cold. "Are you suggesting we should bear the blame for his crimes too? Despite him not even belonging to a Vampire House?"

"You realize Gideon's one of the people who stopped Schofield, right?" Jason said.

"People like Schofield are the very reason we have such strict rules about who can be turned and who cannot. Even Etienne didn't know what Schofield would do with his newfound immortality," Gideon added.

"I get that Schofield acted independently of Belle Morte, and you did everything you could to stop him. But that doesn't change the reality that vampires aren't human. You're dangerous," the man argued.

"If you're referring to the recent comments made by Karl Kendrick about vampires not being considered under the Human Rights Act, then we have a statement from the prime minister," Stuart said.

Jason held his breath, knotting his hands together.

Vampires were physically stronger than humans could ever be, but they were massively outnumbered by humans. Vampires couldn't afford to forget that.

"Prime Minister McGellan has stated that while she's aware of those comments, they are not representative of her cabinet, and if it turns out that said comments do have legal weight to them, then she'll do all she can to fight for the vampires' right to retain their homes," Stuart said.

Jason let out a quiet sigh of relief, though he wasn't sure if McGellan's words came from a place of justice or from the realization that it would be very difficult to work out what to do with vampires if they no longer had their mansions.

"So, where do you think we go from here?" Hari asked, looking from Jason to Gideon.

"The Houses need to modernize and the donor system needs to change," Jason said.

Out of the corner of his eye, he was aware of Gideon intently watching him, but he didn't dare look at the blond vampire. He couldn't afford the distraction right now.

"Assuming that donors ever go back," Lesley muttered.

"Don't you think that should be the choice of the donors?" Jason asked.

Lesley fixed him with a cool look. "I can tell you're not a parent."

"No, I'm not, but that doesn't mean I'm wrong."

The older woman's jaw tightened. "A parent's job is to protect their children from things that could harm them."

"When they're little kids, yeah, but once they're adults you have to let them make their own decisions," Jason said.

"You think that anyone would still *want* to be a donor after everything that's happened?" Lesley asked.

"I would," shouted a girl in the crowd, and another girl whooped in agreement.

"I hope that most people understand that what's happened recently is horrible and tragic, and no one's pretending otherwise, but it's hardly the norm," Jason said.

"Isn't it?" said another voice from the audience.

Jason looked up, squinting against the studio lights.

A man stood up, near the top of the tiered seats, and a shiver of trepidation ran through Jason. He recognized the guy, but he wasn't sure how.

"Of course it's not," he said.

The man tilted his head. "I disagree."

Jason studied him. The man was a little taller than average, probably around Jason's height, but bulkier, with sinewy muscle beneath his clothes. His reddish-blond hair was long enough to be tucked behind his ears, though not long enough to reach his shoulders, and a beard obscured the lower half of his face.

"Do you think the events we've seen recently should be considered the norm?" Stuart asked.

"I think people have forgotten what vampires really are," the guy said.

"And what are they?"

The bearded guy's eyebrows lowered, darkening his eyes. "Predators. While we're all gushing over them and groveling at their feet, we're forgetting they're a step above us on the food chain. Do you think vampires themselves have forgotten that?"

A hush fell over the studio.

Even the hosts looked perturbed.

"Vampires want to coexist with us, not hurt us," Jason said.

"All of them?" Beard looked around at the rest of the audience. "I think we've seen by now that that's not entirely true."

"Some humans want to hurt other people too," Jason said quietly.

"A human can't tear another human limb from limb with his or her bare hands."

Murmurs rippled through the audience, but Jason couldn't discern what anyone was saying.

"If vampires wanted to hurt humans, wouldn't they have done it long before now?" Jason asked.

"Vampires aren't stupid. They know that even with their superior strength and other attributes, they're still vastly outnumbered by humans," Beard said.

"You honestly think that if vampires had more numbers they'd just go out and slaughter people?" Jason shook his head.

"I think given the choice they'd do what comes naturally to predators."

"You're wrong," Jason said.

Beard tilted his head. "You think so?"

"I know so. Etienne and Jemima created their own army of newly turned vampires because they knew they couldn't get enough support among the existing vampires. And when those existing vampires found out what Etienne and Jemima had planned, they fought, bled, and died to stop them. They wouldn't have done that if they were all secretly longing for the day when they could just start killing people," Jason said.

Beard regarded him, his expression inscrutable, and suddenly Jason knew why he recognized the guy. He'd been one of the protestors in the video Walsh had shown at the meeting a few days ago. He'd said then that he'd only been at the protest to see what it was all about, but he'd obviously made up his mind about vampires now.

Lesley said something else and Stuart answered her, but Jason didn't hear what either of them had said. He couldn't take his eyes off Beard as the older man sat down, having apparently said his piece. But he didn't take his eyes off Jason, either, and something about that intense stare made Jason feel very cold.

CHAPTER FIVE

Gideon

He wished he'd never come.

At the same time, he was glad Jason wasn't alone on this stage.

He loved to listen to Jason talk, to see the way his eyes sparked with passion and defiance, to gaze at his artfully tousled hair and beautiful mouth.

"Let's get back to your suggestion of adapting the donor system," Stuart said to Jason. "Is this something that's being formally discussed among Vampire Houses?"

Jason hesitated. "I don't know exactly what discussions are happening between Houses, but Ysanne is aware that things need to change. I don't believe the old system is completely broken, but things won't exactly go back to how they were before," he said carefully.

"So you don't know what changes may be considered?" Hari asked.

Gideon heard Jason's heartbeat increase, as if he was bracing himself.

"You'll probably think it's outrageous," he said. "But we need to legalize turning humans."

Gideon had to clench his jaw to keep it from dropping. Next to him, Jason held himself too rigidly, his heart *thud-thud-thudding*.

Gideon didn't understand.

What did Jason possibly hope to achieve by this?

Vampires had rarely created other vampires on a whim, but having a law against it prevented them from turning possible friends or lovers. It meant that no one could make a rash or foolish decision when it came to handing out immortality. It meant that people like Schofield couldn't have this kind of power.

Ysanne wouldn't see this coming, and she did not like surprises.

"Why?" Hari asked. She sounded as puzzled as Gideon felt.

"The world has been fascinated with vampires ever since they revealed themselves." Jason glanced at Gideon. "They made us question everything we thought we knew and pushed us a big notch down the food chain. They changed *everything*."

As he spoke, Jason's nerves fell away. His posture straightened and his hands unknotted, and the passion that Gideon had come to associate with him crept back into his voice.

"I suppose none of us really see vampires as *people*, the same way we don't see superstars as *people*. We spent ten years building them into these godlike figures, but then we don't let people taste that for themselves," Jason said.

"Isn't that what the donor system was for?" Stuart said.

"And as a donor, I can say it wasn't enough. Yeah, we got to live with vampires, go to balls with them, feed them, yadda yadda yadda, but that all ends the moment the contract is up."

"I still don't see your point."

Gideon wasn't sure he did either.

"For ten years we accepted that new vampires don't get made anymore, and that no human would ever have what vampires have. But obviously a lot of people *didn't* accept it and were willing to do whatever Etienne and Jemima wanted if it meant they could become vampires. They knew there was no possible way for it to happen legally, so they threw their entire moral compass out the window. But we could introduce a new system that allows vampires to turn certain people. Would that be so terrible?" Jason said.

"If they're like Roger Schofield, yes," Lesley spoke up.

"He's the perfect example of why vampires shouldn't be allowed to turn anyone they like. But if we had a system where people could apply to become vampires, same as they once applied to become donors? It wouldn't be an overnight process—applicants would have to be over a certain age, for example. Their psychological state would have to be carefully evaluated. People with criminal records would be banned from the process."

Hari pursed her lips. "Putting people through tests to determine if they should be allowed to live forever sounds a little impractical, not to mention costly."

"Applicants can fund the process themselves. I'm not suggesting every Vladdict gets a set of fangs, but even having it as a possibility removes some of the mystery surrounding vampires. It makes them seem less unattainable. If a process like this already existed, I don't believe Etienne and Jemima would have found so many desperate volunteers, and then their plans would never have come close to succeeding."

"You're aware that people have to *die* to become a vampire?" Lesley snapped.

For just a moment Gideon's mind flashed into the past, to a dark room with a man he trusted, and the sudden sting of sharp fangs sinking into his neck. He pulled himself back to the present.

"I'm aware of that, but if vampires have taught us anything, it's that life and death isn't quite what we thought it was," Jason said. "Both my best friends, Renie and Roux, died, yet I still see them every day, and they're as real and beautiful and sassy as ever. Death changed them. Why can't it change other people?"

"If we legalized a temptation like immortality, a huge number of people would want to jump headfirst into something they don't understand," Stuart cautioned.

"Hence the vetting process. Every applicant would be carefully assessed—for years, if that's what it took. But it could be done," Jason insisted.

He was leaning forward now, his eyes blazing with passion. If Gideon had breath in his lungs, he would have caught it then.

"I'm afraid I still don't see the point," Stuart said.

"If one thing has been made clear by all this, it's that there's a distinct line between vampires and humans, and we're all supposed to stay on our separate sides. But maybe that's not good for any of us. Maybe it's time we took that line away," Jason said.

His eyes flicked to Gideon, blue as a spring sky, and a jolt went through Gideon that he struggled to conceal.

"Why are vampires forbidden from having relationships with humans?" Jason asked.

Everyone looked at Gideon, and he felt a flare of panic at being the center of attention.

"The Council believed it was irresponsible to allow the vampires in their Houses to become involved with humans. Since those humans would never be turned, those potential love affairs were doomed to fail, and it seemed kinder to simply not allow them," he said.

"But if vampires were allowed to turn humans, they'd be allowed to have relationships with them too," Jason said.

Gideon realized he was clenching his hands tightly.

Another woman stood up in the audience. "This kind of sounds like rewarding vampires for everything that's happened," she said.

"All I'm doing is pointing out that vampires and donors are all adults, and they should be trusted to make their own decisions. And when I talk about legalizing turning humans, I mean a tiny percentage. *Tiny.*" Jason held his thumb and forefinger close together and held them up so everyone could see.

"Then why do it at all?"

"It would stop vampires from being these otherworldly, untouchable creatures who refuse to ever share their immortality. Allowing humans and vampires to have relationships reminds the world that vampires are people, too, with feelings and needs and flaws. It's easier to forget that when we view them as completely different from us." Jason sighed and rubbed the back of his neck. "If we want to coexist again, we have to lower the pedestals we put vampires on to begin with. We have to remind people that vampires aren't all that different from the rest of us."

There was a strange feeling in Gideon's chest, almost as if he could feel the echo of his long-dead heart. He couldn't take his eyes off Jason.

"Gideon, your thoughts?" Stuart asked.

Gideon stared around at the audience watching him, the intrigued, adoring, cautious, hostile faces. For the last decade, he'd obeyed the rules of the Council and had stayed safe behind the walls of Belle Morte.

Safe, but static.

"I'm sure everyone here remembers the day that vampires revealed themselves to the world," he said. "You've all seen the footage of Ysanne saving people from those car crashes on the M3."

A few people murmured assent.

"Vampires have so many advantages over humans, and many of us have used them in the past to help people. But somehow when the donor system was set up, we lost sight of that. We shut ourselves away." Gideon paused, looking again at the faces around him. "Maybe we need to start helping again."

"How do you imagine that happening?" Stuart asked.

"I don't know yet." Gideon didn't even know if it was possible. When vampires had helped people before, no one had known they were vampires. They'd been able to slink back into the shadows once their good deeds were done, and no one was any the wiser. They wouldn't be able to do that now, and Gideon had no idea what impact that would have.

But maybe if they wanted to save their place in the human world, they needed to prove that they were more than pretty, immortal faces.

Well, they'd done it.

The show was over, and now he, Jason, and Seamus were preparing to leave London and return to Belle Morte. Gideon slumped in the back seat of the car, the cries of both fans and protestors still ringing in his ears, and a wave of tired relief washing over him.

"That went well, right?" Jason said, jiggling in the seat next to Gideon. "I think it went well."

Gideon opened his mouth, but a sudden wail of sirens cut his reply short.

An ambulance raced past, lights flashing, and drivers on the road ahead hurried to move out of the way. A police car quickly followed, and a moment later, another ambulance.

"Do you think there's been an accident?" Jason said, craning his neck so he could look through the windshield.

Everything inside Gideon went very still. He leaned forward, his eyes fixed on the second ambulance as it sped into the distance, his head clearer than it had been since they left the mansion that morning.

"Seamus," he said. "Go after them."

"Sorry?" Seamus glanced back.

"Something's going on."

"And?" Seamus said.

Gideon looked at Jason, but Jason's expression was as mystified as Seamus's. "What's wrong?" he said.

"In the studio, I said that maybe vampires needed to start helping people, and what better time to start than now?" Gideon said.

Jason chewed his lower lip, his confidence from the show fading into caution.

"I love the idea of vampires doing more to help people, but I'm not sure rushing into a situation we know nothing about is the best way to do it," he said.

"But we can help," Gideon insisted.

He stared at Jason, silently begging him to understand. This wasn't about polishing the vampires' image; it was Gideon's sudden *need* to remind himself that vampires could be more than they'd showed the world these last ten years. If things couldn't exactly go back to how they'd been before Etienne and Jemima kick-started this chain of events, then change might as well start here.

Jason took a deep breath and patted Seamus's shoulder. "Okay, let's do this."

While they drove, Jason took out his phone and tapped at the little glass screen.

"What are you doing?" Gideon asked.

"Traffic won't move out of the way for us like it will an ambulance, so we can't keep up with it. I'm seeing if there's any news about an accident so we can work out where to go," Jason explained.

Gideon eyed the phone in Jason's hands. Despite the ugliness he'd seen on those social media sites, the devices were beneficial too. All that information only a click away.

More sirens sounded, and three fire engines flashed by in a streak of red.

"Maybe a fire rather than an accident," Jason said, looking up.

Fire.

Unease rippled through Gideon.

Please don't let it be a fire.

"Firefighters are often called to car crashes too," Seamus said.

"It's a fire," Jason said a moment later, after tapping his phone a couple more times. "An apartment block in Shepherd's Bush."

He rattled off an address, and Seamus almost immediately took a left turn, but Gideon could barely focus. In his head he could already see the flames, smell the stench of the smoke and the reek of burning flesh. Decades had passed since *that* day, but the memories were scorched into Gideon's brain just as deeply as the flames had scorched his body. Being a vampire healed the wounds of the body, not of the mind.

Two more fire engines passed them, and a tight feeling slid through Gideon's chest, like it was hard to breathe, even though he didn't need to.

"You okay?" Jason asked.

Gideon dragged his eyes away from the window and struggled to focus on the boy sitting next to him. Jason's blue eyes were shadowed with worry, two small furrows between his eyebrows.

Gideon struggled to find words. He'd insisted on doing this; he couldn't back out now. Though something told him that Jason wouldn't judge him for a second if he did.

He looked away and said nothing.

The apartment block was on the corner of a street that Gideon didn't recognize. Seamus pulled up by the curb, a few feet from the fire engines, and they all scrambled out.

The block looked to have once been an old house, or something similar, now converted into what Gideon guessed were six apartments, three on the ground floor, three on the second. The ground floor apartments each had their own front door, with a fourth door on the right that likely led to a communal stairwell for the second floor.

That side of the building was a raging ball of fire already, thick black smoke pouring from the windows, and Gideon froze, icy terror gripping his chest.

He remembered another burning building he'd faced, so many years ago.

"Gideon?" He felt Jason's hand on the small of his back. "You okay?"

Gideon grasped Jason's sleeve. "I don't like fire," he whispered.

"Then let's go." Jason tried to steer Gideon away but Gideon resisted, his ears picking up what Seamus was saying to one of the spectators gathered in the area.

". . . happened?"

"No idea," the woman replied. "One second everything was normal, the next the place was an inferno." She shook her head. "Those poor people."

"There are still people inside?" Gideon said.

She nodded, apparently not noticing she was talking to a vampire. "The whole block has been vacant for months, but an estate agent from the place around the corner was showing a potential buyer around today. They never made it out."

Gideon swung in the direction of the fire engines, where the firefighters were donning protective clothing and breathing apparatuses. Two of them broke away from the main crew and headed around the back of the building—checking for other access points, if Gideon had heard correctly.

The man who seemed to be in charge—"Incident Commander," Gideon heard someone call him—issued orders in a calm, stern tone, too low for any bystanders to hear.

Unless that bystander happened to be a vampire.

It had already been ascertained that the estate agent and buyer weren't in any of the ground-floor flats, so they must be somewhere upstairs, but the thick black smoke billowing in the windows of the upper floor apartments was a real problem. Gideon had assumed that breaking one of the windows would have been the best choice, but according to what his vampire hearing picked up, that could worsen the fire and ignite the people trapped inside.

Assuming they weren't already dead.

Gideon stared at the leaping flames and thick plumes of smoke, his mind torn between what was happening now and what had happened decades ago.

He didn't want to be here.

He wanted to run—away from the fire, the memories, the fear. But this wasn't Brixton, and no one he cared about was in this building.

But two people were still trapped. Even if the firefighters could get to them in time, they'd be putting their own lives at risk.

Gideon didn't need to breathe.

He could heal from the burns.

Before he really knew what he was doing, Gideon walked toward the building.

"Gideon, no." Jason grabbed his shirt and hauled him back. "What the hell are you doing?"

"I have to do something," Gideon said.

"Are you crazy? That fire is out of control," Jason cried.

"I'm stronger and faster than any human, and smoke inhalation can't hurt me."

"The *fire* still can," Jason snapped, fear making his voice sharp.

Gideon knew that better than anyone. He knew exactly how it felt when flame seared flesh, melted clothes, ignited hair, and it wasn't an experience he was keen to repeat.

"I still have to try," Gideon said.

He shook off Jason's hands and raced toward the burning building.

CHAPTER SIX

Gideon

Several people shouted in alarm as he ran toward the block, and he heard the woman who'd been talking to Seamus say, "Wait, wasn't that . . ."

Two men peeled away from the fire crew and rushed to intercept him, but Gideon had vampire speed on his side; he easily dodged them. The door to the communal stairwell hung on its hinges, and Gideon kicked the rest of it aside as he plunged into the building.

The heat hit him like a wall, searing, scorching, the force of it almost driving him back. Even with their protective clothing, no firefighter could get through this blaze.

But, Gideon realized, he couldn't either.

The staircase had mostly collapsed, and though he could probably make the leap to the landing above, he doubted the floor was sturdy enough to hold him.

Sparks rained down from the ceiling, and Gideon swiped them from his clothes. There was a strange smell in the air, one he recognized but couldn't place.

The smoke made it almost impossible to see, but when he reached out with his left hand, he found a wall. The outer structure of the building was solid brick, but inside, where it had been divided into apartments, the walls felt like they were made of drywall. Eyes streaming from the smoke, Gideon slammed his shoulder against the wall, wielding his vampire strength to smash through it.

Bits of debris falling from his hair, he emerged in what looked like the living room of a ground floor apartment, barely visible through the smoke. A spark caught his sleeve, then another landed on his shoulder, and Gideon slapped them out before they could take hold.

He didn't trust the stability of the ceiling here either; it was too close to the blaze, and if there were any other exits, he couldn't see them. Even vampire vision was no match for this kind of smoke.

Gideon smashed through the farthest wall, landing in the middle apartment. The smoke was a little thinner here, and he swiped at his stinging eyes, trying to get his bearings, painfully aware of how little time he had. The fire was spreading so fast, faster than it had in Brixton that day, and the humans trapped here couldn't survive like Gideon could.

He needed to find them.

Gideon looked up at the ceiling. The floors were likely the originals rather than cheap additions like the drywall, but in an old building like this, they'd probably be wood. Strong, but not unbreakable.

He cast about the room. A small coffee table sat in the center; he dragged it closer. Thankfully, the ceiling was low, and he was tall. He climbed onto the table and reached up, testing the painted ceiling with both hands. It wouldn't be easy, but Gideon had once made a living from the power of his punches.

Now he could use that power to save two lives.

He slammed his fists against the ceiling, again and again, snarling with the effort, ignoring the pain that shot through his hands and up his arms, the blood smearing from his split knuckles. His fingers found a beam of wood and he wrenched it, widening the fist-sized hole he'd made.

The smoke in the room was thickening, the roar of the flames getting nearer.

Gideon punched up again, and this time his hand broke through. He tore at the edges of the hole, widening it, ripping open his fingers on nails and shards of wood, until it was big enough to fit his arms through. He gripped the edge of the hole and hauled himself up, forcing his shoulders through the narrow gap.

The apartment above was dark with smoke, burning Gideon's eyes.

"Hello?" he shouted, straining his ears over the hungry roar of the fire. "Can anyone hear me?"

No response.

Gideon crouched low, where the smoke wasn't as thick, and scanned the floor as best he could. There was no sign of anyone. That left only two apartments.

A door was in the opposite wall—it must lead to a communal hallway leading off from the staircase. Going through the doors would be easier than smashing through another wall.

How long had he already taken?

How much time did the trapped people have left?

Gideon ran to the door but a blast of heat drove him back before he reached it. The fire must already have spread along the hallway, cutting anyone off from escape. There was that smell again, but he still couldn't place it.

He turned to the wall on his left, gritting his teeth. His shoulder ached, but it looked like this was the only way.

Bracing himself, Gideon charged at the wall. He smashed through on the second attempt, falling hard on the floor in the farthest apartment. Something jabbed him in the head, and he could barely see through the smoke, but he fumbled around for whatever it was, and his bleeding fingers closed around a polished shoe.

Hope surged in his chest.

He felt his way along the shoe and up a leg, fumbling until he found a face—male, the jaw stubbled—and pressed his fingers to the man's neck. At first he thought he was too late, then he felt the faint thump of a pulse. Unconscious, but still alive.

On hands and knees, Gideon scrabbled about for the second victim. If the estate agent had been showing the buyer around, it was likely they'd been together when they'd collapsed, overcome by smoke.

Finally he found a hand, the fingers slack, and he groped his way up a woman's arm, shoulder, until he found her neck. She had a pulse, too, weak and thready, but there.

Through streaming eyes, Gideon looked around the room. After what he'd overheard from the incident commander outside, he couldn't risk breaking a window. It could kill them all. His only choice was to go down, through the floor.

He dragged the two bodies back through the hole in the wall—it was quicker to get them through an existing hole than to create a new one. The smoke was even thicker in the middle apartment, blinding, so suffocating that even Gideon thought he might choke on it.

Flames flickered at one end of the room—the door, he realized. It could only have taken him a couple of minutes to find the bodies, but the fire had rapidly spread in that time.

Frantically, he dropped into a crouch and felt around for the hole in the floor.

There.

But it wasn't wide enough. Perhaps he could drop both bodies through, but there was nothing to break their fall, and he hadn't come this far to save them only to injure them now.

Gideon tore at the floor, even as the fire spread farther into the room.

Raw fear pressed at the corners of his mind, making it hard to think, but he didn't stop.

A burning piece of wood fell from the ceiling, landing on Gideon's arm. He slapped it away but embers caught in his shirt, flames flickering to life, and he beat them out with one hand while tearing at the floor with the other.

He'd forgotten how loud fires were, the absolute *heat* of them. But he'd never forgotten the pain of the burns, and as more embers landed on him, his clothes caught fire for the second time in his life.

He'd run out of time.

It was now or never.

Gideon slung both limp bodies over his shoulders, one on each side, and leaped through the hole. Something ripped at his arm, and he snarled, but the pain felt distant, something he couldn't comprehend yet.

He landed in a crouch, the bodies on his shoulders jolting with the movement. The room felt like a furnace, the wallpaper curling and blackening around him, and he realized he couldn't go back the way he'd entered the building. The fire was devouring the building too fast; even Gideon couldn't walk through that and survive.

There were no floors left to punch through, nowhere else to go, and for a sickening heartbeat, he froze, convinced that he'd die here.

Perhaps it was a fitting end, after all, to be finally taken by the flames he'd escaped decades ago.

No.

He hadn't come here to die. He *wouldn't* die.

He could just glimpse a window through the smoke, a dull smear of gray through all that black. But smashing it could fuel the fire even more, incinerating him and the people he carried before he could get them to safety.

He tasted blood, and realized his fangs had slid out, pricking his lower lip.

He'd have to risk it. The two humans couldn't survive much longer in this, and if Gideon didn't get out now he'd burn to death with them. But he'd only get one shot.

Tightening his grip on the two bodies, Gideon backed up a couple of steps, then ran. He leaped into the air, hurling himself at the window, and as he smashed through, as he felt the blast of fresh air on his face, he wasn't here in Shepherd's Bush, he was back in Brixton, launching himself out of another window, another man held tightly in his arms.

Gideon hit the ground and rolled, trying to shield the two humans.

But there was no fireball, no explosion. They were out.

Bracing both hands on the pavement, Gideon pushed himself to his feet. The humans were sprawled like broken dolls on the ground, bleeding from the shards of glass all around them, but better some minor injuries than a painful, fiery death.

Someone screamed his name, and he looked up, blinking, trying to focus on the shape running toward him.

Jason.

"Oh my god, don't move," Jason cried.

He frantically slapped at Gideon's arms and chest, hissing and swearing, and it was only then that Gideon realized he was still on fire. Then the pain hit. He gasped and staggered, clutching blindly at Jason.

A man ran toward them, a blanket held in both hands, shouting at Jason to move, and Gideon lurched back, almost hiding behind Jason.

"It's okay," Jason said, reaching for Gideon.

But it wasn't; Jason didn't understand.

Gideon clutched Jason's arm. "Get me out of here," he whispered, feeling the prick of his fangs emerging again. *"Please."*

Jason stared at him, his forehead creased, his mouth slightly open, and Gideon tightened his grip on Jason's arm, silently begging him to listen before this all went wrong.

Jason snapped his mouth shut. "Come on," he said.

He hustled Gideon through the gathering crowd of onlookers, and Gideon kept his head low and his mouth closed, hiding his fangs and his reddening eyes. Someone shoved a camera in his face and Jason promptly smacked it away. People were barking questions, but Gideon couldn't focus on them, couldn't even hear them properly over the thundering heartbeats all around him. He didn't dare look at how bad the burns were, but relentless waves of pain were spreading through his body.

He needed blood.

Someone flung an arm around his shoulders, and a defensive snarl rose in his throat before he realized it was Seamus.

Between them, Seamus and Jason bundled him into the back of

the car, where the tinted windows would mostly hide him from the throng of spectators shouting questions and waving phones. Jason climbed in after him, slamming the door, while Seamus flung himself into the driver's seat.

"Time to go home, I think," he said, his voice full of a cheeriness that his face didn't reflect.

As they pulled away from the curb, Gideon dropped his head to his chest, struggling to calm the chaos in his head. His fangs pricked his lower lip; he tasted his own blood again.

There was a roaring in his chest, in his head, his stomach clenching with the need for blood, but he couldn't tell how much of that was due to his injuries and how much was due to the vivid memories of another fire.

Jason was frantically tapping at his phone, shooting little glances at Gideon, but Gideon kept his head down, trying to focus. The journey back to Belle Morte would likely take another two hours, and he had to stay in control every second.

Jason shuffled closer, until Gideon could smell the warmth of his skin, hear the thump of his heart. He squeezed his eyes shut, clenching his teeth until his jaw ached.

"You need to feed," Jason said.

"No," Gideon gritted out.

"But—"

"I said no!"

"Gideon—" Seamus started.

"Just get me back to the mansion," Gideon said. "Please."

Seamus didn't argue, and Gideon felt the car speed up.

It felt like forever until they were back in Winchester, and even longer until the familiar gates leading into Belle Morte appeared. The protestors were still there, still shouting, but Gideon could barely hear them over the noise in his head.

They parked and Gideon launched himself out of the car. Jason ran after him.

The front door opened and Gideon glimpsed Edmond's face before he pushed past the older vampire. He was almost at the staircase when he stumbled, fresh pain searing through him. Someone grabbed his arm, helping him upright, and he blinked, Jason's face swimming into view.

"I've got you," he said.

He guided Gideon up the stairs and down a hallway, and Gideon wanted to pull away—away from the smell of Jason's skin, the tantalizing rush of blood in his veins, the throb of his pulse—but somehow he couldn't.

It wasn't until Jason kicked a door shut behind them that Gideon realized Jason had taken him to his room in the donors' wing rather than the north wing where the vampires slept.

"Shit, sorry," Jason said, obviously coming to the same realization. "Force of habit."

Gideon's eyes were fixed on Jason's throat, the tiny rivers of blood running just below his skin.

"Here," Jason said, and handed him a pouch of bagged blood. Gideon realized that several more bags were poking out of Jason's pocket; someone must have handed them to him as soon as they arrived back at the mansion.

Gideon ripped open the pouch and turned around, not wanting Jason to watch him drinking.

"My offer still stands," said Jason quietly. "You can drink from me if you need to."

"I don't," Gideon said, wiping his mouth.

Drinking from a human could be an incredibly intimate experience, for both vampire and donor, but drinking cold blood from a bag like this felt somehow animalistic. Gideon didn't want Jason to see him like that.

"I don't understand why you won't let me help you," Jason said.

"Because I don't want to *hurt* you," Gideon shouted, whirling around.

Jason's expression was torn between confusion and determination. "Why do you think you'll hurt me?"

Gideon's throat closed up. "You don't know me."

"Maybe I'd like to."

Gideon searched for a reply, and while words failed him, Jason drew closer and took the first pouch from him before pushing a second into his hand.

"You're not healed yet," he said.

Gideon still didn't know how badly he'd been hurt. The waves of pain had faded, but beneath his ruined clothes patches of skin still felt raw. He could still smell the stench of charred flesh. He turned his back on Jason again, and drank.

That rawness disappeared as his injuries fully healed, and he closed his eyes, this time with relief. If it had only taken two bags to heal then he couldn't have been hurt as badly as last time. Maybe Jason had never been in danger from him.

Gideon set the empty pouch on the nearest surface, feeling calmer now, more in control.

"Why did you think you'd hurt me?" Jason asked, quiet but insistent.

Memories slammed into Gideon, the terrified faces of his friends as the flames raged higher through the place they'd called home, the feeling of his clothes and hair catching fire, the awful agony as his skin bubbled and burned. And the memory that scared him the most: the moment he'd lost control.

"Because I've done it before," he said, pulling back his lips to show his fangs, his eyes gleaming red. "I lost control once and I killed a man."

Jason's expression didn't flicker. "If you're trying to scare me off, it's not going to work."

Gideon let out a disbelieving huff of laughter.

Jason sat on his bed. "If you want to talk about it, I'm listening."

Gideon opened his mouth but before he could get words out, the stench of smoke hit him. He'd been so focused on blood that he'd managed to ignore it, but now it was all he could smell, wafting from his tattered clothes, still mixed with the lingering reek of burned flesh.

His hands trembled as he fumbled with the buttons on his shirt. He needed his burned, smoky clothes off. Now.

Jason jumped up and hurried over. Gideon recoiled, but Jason grabbed his shirt and held him still. "Let me help you," he said.

He unbuttoned what was left of Gideon's shirt, and as he peeled the smoky rags away from Gideon's freshly healed skin, his hands brushed Gideon's bare chest and Gideon jumped.

"Shit, sorry, did I hurt you?" Jason said.

"No," Gideon whispered, a knot forming in his throat. "It's just been a very long time since anyone touched me like that."

It had been a very long time since he'd even *wanted* anyone to.

Jason stared at him for a long moment, his forehead crumpled, then he lowered his eyes to Gideon's belt buckle. "Then I'm guessing I shouldn't . . ." He made a vague gesture with his hands.

"I don't need help taking off my own trousers," Gideon said.

Something flared in Jason's eyes, and Gideon's fangs reacted with a different sort of hunger this time.

He'd noticed Jason from the first moment he walked into this house, a spring in his step and a sparkle in his eyes, and the longer Jason stayed in Belle Morte, the more Gideon liked what he saw. It wasn't just that Jason was gorgeous. It was his determination to stand with his friends, no matter the risk to himself. It was his bravery. It was the passion with which he'd defended vampires today. It was how he'd listened to Gideon, how he'd used his own hands to beat out the flames on Gideon's clothes.

With a small jolt, Gideon realized how close Jason was standing, just a few inches of space between them.

Jason licked his lips, and Gideon's gaze dropped to his mouth.

Suddenly the room felt very small.

"Do you want to take a shower?" Jason asked.

"What?" Gideon stumbled back a couple of steps.

"To get rid of the smoke smell," Jason said. He looked puzzled again.

Of course that was what he meant. What had Gideon thought— that Jason was offering to take a shower *with* him?

"Right," Gideon mumbled.

"Towels and stuff are already in there. I'll find some clean clothes for when you're done," Jason said.

He stumbled into the shower, hoping Jason would be gone when he got out.

CHAPTER SEVEN

Jason

As soon as he heard water hitting the porcelain shower tray, Jason scooped up Gideon's ruined shirt and took it next door, to an empty room where donors no longer slept. He'd dispose of it properly later, but at least Gideon wouldn't have to see it when he came out.

Jason sniffed his own sleeve. He smelled pretty smoky too. He stripped off and showered, washing his hair twice to get rid of the smell, then helped himself to the clothes that had been left behind when the other donors had left. Fortunately, other guys had lived here.

He grabbed some clothes for Gideon, too, hoping the broad-shouldered vampire would fit into them, and hurried back to his room.

The shower was still running.

Jason knocked on the bathroom door. "I've got clean clothes for you. I'll leave them out here," he said.

A pause, then, "Thank you," Gideon said.

Jason ran his hands through his damp hair as he processed everything that had happened. The day had taken a turn he could never have predicted, but his experience on the *Daily Topic* had mostly been positive. It had felt like maybe he could make a difference, and he couldn't forget all that because of the fire.

The shower turned off, and as Jason heard movement from inside the bathroom, he turned his back. There was little in this world he'd love more than to see Gideon Hartwright fresh out of the shower in nothing but a towel—or preferably *without* the towel—but if Gideon had freaked out when Jason's hand had skimmed his bare chest, he'd hardly want Jason ogling him when he was half naked.

Behind him the door cracked open, and he pictured Gideon peeking out, checking that the coast was clear. There was a soft rustle as Gideon picked up the pile of clothes Jason had left, then the door closed again.

Jason sighed.

Gideon's fear of fire wasn't unusual, but his reaction to the fire, to the smoke, had been more than a garden-variety phobia. Something had happened to make him afraid, and even though his injuries were physically healed, Jason wasn't letting Gideon leave until he knew he was okay.

Finally, Gideon emerged.

Jason turned, and the breath caught in his lungs.

Gideon's hair was darker when it was wet, like shadowed gold, the slight curls damped down, casting his face into starker relief.

"Do the clothes fit okay?" Jason asked, though he could see they were too small, pulling too tightly across Gideon's chest and shoulders.

"They're fine," Gideon said. "Thank you," he added after a pause.

Jason ran his hand through his hair and winced.

"Are you hurt?" Gideon said.

"Oh," Jason said, surprised, then looked at his hands for the first time since they'd got back to the mansion. Red patches and small white blisters dotted his palms and fingers—he must have been running on too much adrenaline to notice.

"Let me see." Gideon approached him and took Jason's hands in his, lifting them higher so he could examine them.

Gideon's own hands were cooler than the average human's, but not cold.

"You slapped out the flames on my clothes," Gideon said, blinking as if he'd only just remembered it had happened.

Jason shrugged and tried to pull his hands back, but Gideon held them tight.

"You didn't have to do that," Gideon said.

"You were on *fire*," Jason said.

"I can heal from that."

"And I'll heal from this." Jason cracked a smile. "It'll just take a little longer."

"Unless I help," Gideon said.

"What do you mean?"

"Vampire saliva has healing qualities, remember?"

Jason's mouth turned to dust. It already felt like so long ago that he'd been a functioning donor that he'd forgotten that, and now it was all he could think about. Gideon had never bitten him, but he'd once sealed puncture marks left by another vampire by running his tongue over Jason's skin, and even though the encounter had lasted only seconds, it had formed the basis of every dirty dream since.

Gideon lifted Jason's hands, his fingers strong but gentle, and Jason's heart started to pound. He half expected to wake up any second.

Gideon ran his tongue over Jason's palm, and sensation flared up his whole arm. God, that felt good. Gideon licked Jason's palm again, then his fingertips, carefully healing each blister, then moved onto Jason's other hand.

Jason held his breath. His whole body felt like it was trembling, as if every single part of himself was focused on the feel of Gideon's tongue on his bare skin. If this was the closest he'd get to a kiss, he never wanted it to end.

But it did end.

Gideon pulled back suddenly. Red sparked in his eyes. "Is that better?" he said.

Jason examined his hands. Not a trace of redness or blisters remained. "Wow," he murmured, flexing his fingers. "That's amazing."

Gideon gave him a faint smile. "Being a vampire does have some advantages."

"More than just *some*. You saved two lives today," Jason said.

Gideon lowered his eyes.

Jason decided to take the plunge. "Do you want to talk about it?"

Gideon's head snapped up. "About what?"

"About whatever made you afraid of fire."

Gideon's mouth opened but nothing came out.

The air around them thickened with tension, but Jason couldn't tell what kind.

He realized that Gideon was still holding his hands.

Gideon realized it at the same time and snatched his hands back, letting Jason's drop to his sides.

"We should go and tell the others what happened," he said.

"Right." Jason tried to hide his disappointment.

They headed out of the south wing and toward the staircase, Gideon walking slightly ahead of Jason.

Their friends were still gathered in the lobby, clustered around Seamus. Renie and Roux both looked up as Jason came down the stairs, and Renie mouthed, *Are you okay?*

Jason nodded.

"I've just been bringing everyone up to speed," Seamus said.

"You're fully recovered?" Ysanne asked Gideon.

Gideon glanced at Jason. "I am."

"Good. What you did was very brave. A little foolish, perhaps, but still brave."

Renie beamed. "It was a hell of a middle finger to give to all the people who call us monsters."

Seamus was the only one who didn't look happy. "And very convenient timing," he said.

"What do you mean?" Renie asked.

"While Gideon was inside that building, I tried to get more information out of the eyewitnesses," Seamus said.

Jason felt a quick pang of guilt that he hadn't helped with that.

"According to three separate witnesses, the fire came out of nowhere. One second the apartments were fine, the next, they were a fireball. That doesn't seem normal to me, though I'll admit I'm hardly an expert," Seamus continued. "But one eyewitness, the woman working in the Laundromat across the street, swears she saw a man enter the block via the communal stairwell just a few seconds before the fire started. As far as she can tell, that guy never came out."

Gideon made a choked noise. "There was another person in there? And I didn't save him?"

"I don't know. None of the other witnesses saw this man. Did you see any trace of him when you went in?"

"No, but I didn't get the chance to look everywhere."

"Then it's possible the woman was mistaken. Eyewitness accounts are notoriously unreliable, and in stressful situations people's minds can easily mislead them," Seamus said.

"But?" Ysanne said.

"But what if she was right? What if this wasn't an accident, and the man she saw actually started the fire?"

Silence fell over the lobby.

"That smell," Gideon said, his eyes widening.

"What smell?" Ysanne asked.

But Gideon was looking at Jason. "When I first ran into the building, I could smell something, and I knew it was familiar, but I didn't have time to think about it."

"Okay?" Jason wasn't sure where Gideon was going with this.

"It was gasoline. I'm sure of it."

Silence fell again.

Jason swallowed the hard knot in his throat. "Let's say this *was* arson. Was it random or was it somehow connected to us?"

"I don't know," Seamus said again. "Perhaps I'm just being paranoid, but something about this doesn't feel right."

"Wait, are you suggesting someone started that fire and almost killed two people as some sort of 'gotcha' to vampires? And killed themselves in the process? That makes no sense," Renie said.

"When you put it like that, it doesn't," Seamus admitted.

Roux bit her lip. "Except people who hate vampires do have a history of arson." She gripped Ludovic's hand. "Remember what Iain Johnson and his thugs did to our hotel?"

It was Jason's turn to bite his lip. When Roux and Ludovic had left Belle Morte to hunt down some of Etienne and Jemima's escaped minions, they'd stayed at a small hotel in the city. They'd had several run-ins with a group who passionately hated vampires and anyone connected to them, culminating in the group attacking the hotel with Molotov cocktails in an attempt to kill Roux and Ludovic. They'd survived. Another guest at the hotel had not.

"Iain Johnson and his friends were all arrested," Jason gently reminded Roux.

"Their supporters weren't." Her voice was bitter. "A lot of people seem to think he did nothing wrong."

Ludovic's lip curled, showing off a hint of fang. "Perhaps this is where People Before Vampires started."

"And if they *are* responsible, they've seriously upped their game from protests and graffiti," Roux said. She looked around the group. "If they're willing to martyr themselves, they just became a far more serious threat."

"Hold on." Jason held up both hands. "Let's think logically for a second. Why would PBV do this? They couldn't possibly have known that Gideon would rush to the scene, or that he'd risk himself."

"The two people Gideon rescued—do we know who they are?" Ysanne asked Seamus.

"I don't, but I can find out. Why?"

"Walsh told us of attacks on former donors or anyone associated with donors. It's possible that these two fit into that category. It's also possible that the apartments might once have been home to donors, and any potential arsonists didn't know that the block was currently empty," Ysanne said. She tucked an errant strand of hair behind her ear. "I think it's time to call Walsh."

—

The group dispersed after that. Seamus accompanied Ysanne to her office to discuss the situation with Walsh, Isabeau drifted off into the mansion, and Roux and Renie dragged Jason to the bar to fix him a celebratory drink.

"Doesn't feel like there's as much to celebrate now," Jason said, climbing onto one of the chrome and leather stools that ringed the black marble bar.

"Nonsense," said Roux briskly. "We all watched the show this morning. You were fantastic."

She moved behind the bar. "Three cosmos?" she said, reaching for glasses.

"But you can't drink them," Jason protested.

Roux shrugged. "We can pretend."

She put the drinks together swiftly and efficiently, then slid one across the bar to Renie, who was making eager grabby hands.

Roux joined Renie on the other side of the bar, and patted Jason's shoulder. "Come on, smile," she said.

Jason pulled his drink closer. "Sorry. I'm pleased with how the show went, but this fire thing just shit all over that."

"Not *all* over," Renie said.

"Do you really think People Before Vampires could have done something like this?" Jason asked Roux.

She stared pensively at the bottles lining the shelves and the glass boxes that had once held sliced fruit and ice. Since the human staff—excluding a handful of guards—had been sent away with the donors, no one was restocking them now.

"If they're anything like Iain Johnson, yes," she said, then sighed. "But, objectively, we don't know that they *are* anything like him. I could be leaping to all kinds of conclusions."

"It does seem like a crazy coincidence if it was just a random arson attack, though," Renie said, toying with the stem of her glass. She sat up straighter and shook back her mass of auburn hair. "But until we know any more, let's not assume the worst."

"I can drink to that." Jason sipped his cocktail and made an appreciative noise. Roux sure knew how to mix a drink.

"By the way," he said to Renie. "Thanks for having those blood pouches ready for when we got back."

"Any time. I just wish Gideon hadn't needed them," she said.

"Me too." The memory of Gideon's ruined shirt, charred skin showing beneath, made Jason shiver. It could have been so much worse.

"Is he okay?" Roux asked.

"Yeah, he healed up fine."

"I didn't mean his physical injuries."

Jason looked down at the polished bar top.

"He seemed really freaked out when you guys got back. I figured he might tell you what was on his mind," Roux said.

"Why would he tell me?"

Renie and Roux exchanged amused looks.

"Because he likes you," Renie said.

Jason sighed and slumped across the bar. "Does he, though?"

"*Yes,*" the girls said in unison.

"Really? He barely lets me get close to him," Jason said.

"A vampire with emotional baggage? What a surprise," Renie dryly returned.

"Anyway, it's a moot point because humans and vampires still aren't allowed to date," Jason said.

"You literally just argued for it on national TV," Roux said.

"Yeah, but I wasn't doing it for *my* benefit. I was talking about general changes to the donor system."

"Besides," Renie chimed in, "I think Ysanne has more important things to worry about than whether or not a vampire and a human are boning."

Jason almost choked on his drink.

Renie smiled angelically at him.

"She's right," Roux said, turning her glass around and around on the bar top.

"Counterpoint: starting something with Gideon would make things worse for Ysanne," Jason said.

He liked Ysanne and, despite the mistakes she'd made, she genuinely wanted what was best for her people. So far she hadn't objected to his suggestion of abolishing the rule forbidding vampire/human relationships, but that might change once the dust settled. In the meantime, if Jason did attempt to start anything with Gideon, would that reflect badly on Ysanne? Would it be one more instance of her failing to enforce vampire law in her own House?

"Anyway, I'm the one who warned Renie against getting involved with vampires. Am I supposed to ignore my own advice?" Jason said.

"Why not? I did," Renie teased.

Jason managed a wan smile. "This would be much easier if Gideon was a normal human guy."

"But maybe then he wouldn't float your boat the same way," Renie pointed out.

Jason *did* have a particular yen for vampires, and in a sea of gorgeous, immortal faces, Gideon stood out. But it wasn't just about his physical looks. It was how he always acted quickly to protect others, even when it meant risking his own life. It was how he'd come on the show with Jason even though he clearly hadn't wanted to. It was how he seemed to hold himself so tightly together, as if he was afraid of ever showing anyone who he really was.

"*Anyway,*" he stressed. "It doesn't matter. People Before Vampires are potentially a serious threat now, and there's still a rogue vampire running around out there. That's a little more important than my crush."

Roux covered Jason's hand with hers. "Maybe so, but you deserve to be happy."

Jason sipped his drink and tried not to think too much about whether Gideon was the man who could make him happy.

Three cocktails later, Renie and Roux returned to the arms of their hot vampire men, while Jason wandered back to the south wing. As Renie had left, Jason had noticed that she wore only socks on her feet, and he'd felt a strange pang of envy. In many ways, Renie and Roux were still adjusting to their new lives here, but in other ways, they were completely at home in the vampire mansion.

He was almost at the top of the staircase when Gideon emerged from the north wing. His hair had dried, springing back into the slight curls and waves that Jason longed to run his fingers through, and he'd changed into his own clothes—dark trousers and a navy-blue sweater that hugged his muscular build.

They both paused, staring at each other.

"Thanks again for . . . you know," Jason said, waggling his healed hands at Gideon and wishing he had something wittier to say.

A long moment passed before Gideon spoke.

"It was 1977," he said. "Back then, it was considered acceptable for landlords to refuse to rent to gay men, leading many with no choice but to band together and squat in empty buildings. I never squatted, but the man I was seeing at the time did. Any time he met a man with nowhere to go, he took him under his wing and invited him to live in the squat. It wasn't an easy life, but they took care of each other. They were happy."

Gideon's face darkened. "Until the day someone decided that the squatters didn't deserve to live anymore, so they set fire to the building with everyone who lived there still inside."

"Jesus," Jason muttered.

"I arrived at the same time as the police, but they refused to do anything about it," Gideon said.

Pieces clicked together in Jason's head. "You weren't afraid of fire back then, were you?"

"Not like I am now."

"Because today wasn't the first time you ran into a burning building to save someone."

Gideon nodded. His hands were in loose fists at his sides.

"I went to save my friends," he said.

"And your boyfriend, I'm guessing," Jason said. He had a horrible feeling this story didn't end well.

"We never defined ourselves in those exact terms, but, yes," Gideon said. "I got nine men safely out via a makeshift rope through the window, and then part of the floor gave way. Jerry fell and I caught him, but as I hauled him to safety, the fire caught me instead. I lost the rope, and the rest of the floor wouldn't have lasted much longer—my only choice was to jump." Gideon paused, red flashing through his eyes, a muscle flexing in his jaw. "I was already badly burned from the fire, and the fall broke my ribs."

Jason winced.

"Those injuries were far more severe than anything I received today, and there were no convenient blood bags to hand. What do you think happened next?" Gideon asked, leaning forward slightly.

"You took it from a human," Jason said.

"I *killed* someone. I ran from the fire, and when he came after me, I ripped into his throat and drained him dry. I couldn't *stop*." Gideon's eyes were almost fully red now, burning with the pain of the memories.

Jason swallowed. "Your boyfriend?" he guessed.

Gideon shook his head. "It was one of the men who'd started the fire, but that doesn't change anything."

"Um, yeah, it does? He tried to kill you first," Jason said.

Gideon looked away. "You don't understand. I lost control. It could easily have been Jerry or one of our friends."

"That's why you were so desperate to get back to the mansion. You were afraid you'd lose control again," Jason said.

Gideon gave a jerky nod.

Jason took a step closer. "I wasn't."

Gideon's eyes flared wider. "How can you say that?"

"Easy. In the story you just told me, you ran from your friends before you could hurt them. If you'd been injured worse today, you'd have run before hurting me, Seamus, or anyone else," Jason said.

"You have no idea what vampires are capable of," Gideon whispered.

"Really? After everything I've seen since coming to Belle Morte?" Jason gave Gideon a wry look. "I know exactly what vampires are capable of, and as I've told you once today, if you think any of this will scare me away, you're wrong, so you might as well stop trying."

The corners of Gideon's mouth twitched.

Jason's conversation with Renie and Roux swirled in his head, and suddenly he wanted to pretend his objections hadn't happened. The attraction he felt to Gideon was stronger than anything he'd experienced with any guy. It was like a physical urge, a magnet reeling him in every time he tried to turn away.

But was he a fool for thinking there could be something between them?

Was he a fool for thinking it could ever work?

Or, when attraction burned this brightly, was it worth pursuing, no matter what happened?

CHAPTER EIGHT

Gideon

That night Gideon lay awake, staring at the ceiling, his head a tangled mess. Why had he told Jason about Jerry, about the fire? In the decades since it had happened, Isabeau had been the only person he'd told, but suddenly today the story had spilled out to a boy he barely knew, and he didn't understand why.

He couldn't stop thinking about Jason using his bare hands to slap out the flames on Gideon's clothes, or the blistered state of his palms afterward. Jason hadn't even hesitated.

Gideon felt like he'd been asleep for years—*decades*—and now Jason had come into his life and woken him up.

He pushed back the covers and climbed out of bed.

Maybe some fresh air would clear his head.

He made his way into the garden. The protestors must have packed up for the night—for once, he couldn't hear the angry roar of their voices. They'd be back in the morning, though; he was sure of that.

He hadn't expected to find anyone else out here, but as he turned a corner he saw Isabeau sitting on a stone bench, her face uplifted, her chestnut curls swaying in the breeze.

Isabeau tilted her head in his direction and smiled. "Couldn't sleep?"

"No."

"Me either." Isabeau patted the bench, and Gideon joined her. They sat quietly for a few minutes, looking up at the moon.

"What's on your mind?" Isabeau eventually asked.

"What's on yours?" Gideon returned.

Her expression darkened. "Ysanne."

"Why didn't you tell me about her?" Gideon said.

He'd known about Isabeau's history with Ysanne before he'd ever met Ysanne herself, but Isabeau had said nothing about them rekindling their relationship, and it stung that she'd kept this from him.

"She didn't want me to. She has to maintain a certain image as Lady of the House, and I suppose she thought a girlfriend would affect that."

"How did you cope with being with someone who was ashamed of you?"

Isabeau's eyes widened. "Ysanne was never *ashamed* of me, but Belle Morte had to come first. That's part of being a leader. I might not always have liked it, but I understood it."

"You never thought you deserved better?" Gideon asked.

Isabeau gave him a sad smile. "It's not that simple. Ysanne didn't force me into a relationship—I chose to stay, even though I knew she could never compromise her standing for my sake."

"Why *did* you stay?"

"Because I fell in love with her," Isabeau said, her voice quieter now.

Gideon's chest hitched. He'd believed himself in love before, more than once, and he'd felt the sharp sting of loss. But he wasn't sure he'd ever felt the depth of devotion that Isabeau so clearly had for Ysanne.

"What happens now?" he asked.

Isabeau offered a little shrug. "Sometimes love isn't enough."

"Would you ever give her another chance?"

"I'm not sure she wants one." Isabeau gave him a penetrating look. "Why so many questions?"

Words failed Gideon. He couldn't admit that discussing the collapse of someone else's relationship distracted him from thoughts of a certain blond ex-donor.

Isabeau's gaze sharpened, and Gideon looked away. He was telegraphing too much on his face, and Isabeau knew him too well.

"Our world is changing, and our rules are changing with it," she said.

"What do you mean?"

Isabeau placed a gentle hand over his. "None of us know what the future holds, so if there's something that you want, maybe you should go after it."

Gideon lowered his eyes, his head churning.

He was afraid. Jason was a road, something winding and unknowable, and Gideon was aching to take the first step. But he couldn't, because he didn't know where it would lead or what was waiting at the end.

"Don't you think we have more important things to worry about?" he asked.

Isabeau shrugged.

Gideon looked behind him, at the shadowed wall of Belle Morte stretching overhead. "I never appreciated how safe we were here," he said. "Until we weren't."

Isabeau gave a sad smile. "I know what you mean."

She and Gideon had lived together for a few years before Ysanne revealed vampires to the world, but even then, having his closest friend to rely on, Gideon had never felt secure like he did in Belle Morte. He and Isabeau had known that, sooner or later, they'd have to move on and find a new place to live. Vampires always did. And with the advancement of technology, staying hidden in the shadows would only have become harder and harder.

Belle Morte had changed that. Finally vampires had somewhere to call home, a place that they'd never have to leave. Gideon didn't know what he'd do if they lost that.

"Still," Isabeau said, straightening, "the prime minister has made it clear that we won't be evicted from our homes."

"For now. She won't be prime minister forever," Gideon said.

Isabeau didn't respond to that.

"We have a more immediate problem than the roof over our heads. Our blood supply won't last forever, and I'm afraid I haven't helped that," Gideon said.

"Don't you dare blame yourself for taking what you needed to heal. No one would have denied you that," said Isabeau fiercely.

"Yes, but now there's less for everyone else."

"We'll make do. Maybe this life has softened us, but we're still survivors, all of us. We'll find a way," Isabeau insisted.

"And the vampire children? Will they find a way too?"

Isabeau looked away. "I don't know," she said quietly. "But perhaps we need to focus on one problem at a time."

Gideon wasn't sure how they were supposed to do that. Even if People Before Vampires hadn't started that fire, they were still causing trouble across the city, and the tide of public favor was still shifting, with far too many people turning against them. And although he or she hadn't made any further attacks on people, a rogue vampire was still out there.

Isabeau rose to her feet. "I'm going to bed." She paused when Gideon didn't move. "You're staying?"

"A little longer," he said.

Isabeau patted his shoulder and walked away.

Gideon rested his weight on his palms and leaned back, looking at the star-sprinkled sky.

He wished he had the hope that Isabeau and Jason seemed to share. He *wanted* to have it. But he couldn't shake the fear that this time they were up against a threat they simply didn't know how to handle.

Jason

He'd switched his phone off overnight, and when morning came, he was glad he had. Turning it back on brought a barrage of notifications, texts, and missed calls, and he felt a stab of guilt when he realized several of them were from his parents.

He sent them a quick message apologizing for the delay and reassuring them that he was fine, though he didn't have time to talk yet. That made him feel guilty again—he didn't know what had gone public or how much they'd seen—but he couldn't face another call from his mum begging him to come home.

With no small amount of trepidation, he turned to the notifications. He hadn't noticed anyone filming yesterday, but of course they had been, because that's what people did these days. They saw a potential tragedy unfolding and whipped out their phones.

Jason had been tagged in multiple videos; he pressed Play on the first one.

His chest hitched. Yesterday he'd been *right there*, watching this unfold in real time, yet somehow it was worse seeing it like this. He saw the blazing building, saw himself try to stop Gideon from running into it, and heard the gasps from eyewitnesses when Gideon ran in anyway.

He was sure he heard Gideon's name off camera, but whoever was filming didn't seem to have noticed who Gideon was. It had felt as if Gideon had been inside for hours, and Jason hadn't been able to stop picturing all the hideous ways this could go wrong: Gideon burning to death, crushed beneath falling debris, trapped with no way out. Now he could see that Gideon had only been inside for a few minutes before he emerged, flinging himself through a lower window with two limp bodies slung across his shoulders. Jason saw himself running forward, frantically slapping at the flames on Gideon's clothes, and he winced, flexing his fingers, remembering the pain of the burns.

In hindsight, that hadn't been the smartest thing to do.

He watched another video, taken at a different angle. This one was breathlessly narrated by whoever was filming, and this guy definitely recognized Gideon.

Jason watched three more videos, some with commentary, some without, then searched for news headlines. Unsurprisingly, the fire was everywhere. If a famous vampire hadn't run into the blaze to save two strangers, it would probably have had a brief mention in the local news and not much more, but Gideon's involvement had made it national news.

In the sphere of social media, algorithms were dominated by the footage itself, or people reacting to or discussing it, and most people agreed that Gideon had done something amazing.

But not everyone viewed the events in such a positive light.

Jason clicked on a thumbnail showing a still of the fire, with the phrase *Hoax?* written across it.

A guy with slicked-back hair and glasses, who looked a few years older than Jason, appeared onscreen.

"Hey, it's your boy, Tommy," he said to the camera. "I'm back with the latest internet drama, and guys, this one is *juicy*. I'm sure you've all seen yesterday's footage going around, but in case you haven't, let's watch it real quick."

His face was replaced by the first video Jason had watched. Tommy let the video play in full before his face reappeared on the screen. "Yes, you saw that correctly. That's Gideon Hartwright running into that building, and Jason Grant trying to stop him. Both fresh off their *Daily Topic* appearance and miraculously doing what Gideon suggested and helping people." He raised an eyebrow. "Great timing, don't you think?"

He paused, as if giving that time to sink in. "All morning I've seen people gushing over this, calling Gideon a hero, saying how brave he was to risk his life, but can we pause the Vladdict shit for a minute and look at this critically? Vampires aren't like humans. Gideon didn't risk his *life*. He went into that building knowing he could walk out again." Tommy rolled his eyes. "Of course he didn't *walk* out, he did a dramatic Hollywood dive through a window. Real great for the people he was carrying, by the way. Don't worry about breaking their bones or slashing them up with broken glass, just make sure *you* look good."

Jason's hand tightened around his phone. Did this guy believe what he was saying?

"I don't want to sound paranoid, but I can't be the only one who thinks it's really weird that on the *Daily Topic,* Gideon *happened* to mention vampires helping humans, then the first thing he does when leaving the studio is *stumble* on two people trapped in a burning building." Tommy held up both hands and affected an apologetic expression. "I'm not saying the vampires started the fire to paint Gideon as a hero and give themselves some seriously good PR, but this looks a bit suspicious to me."

He rambled on a little longer, but Jason's attention turned to the comments. Tommy's video had racked up hundreds of thousands of views already, and hundreds of comments. Jason scrolled through them.

> I can't stand this guy, but he has a point.
>
> Are you crazy? Gideon was literally on fire—how is that not risking his life?
>
> Yeah, he probably fucked up those poor people by throwing them through the window. Should have let the professionals handle it.
>
> I know I'm weird as hell, but am I the only one who thinks Gideon looks sexy on fire?
>
> OMG, not to sound insensitive but there are SPARKS between Gideon and Jason!
>
> You're right, this doesn't add up.
>
> Suspicious as hell.
>
> They obviously started the fire.
>
> GIDEON!

The comments went on and on, but among those pointing out the holes in this theory and the gushing Vladdicts, far too many people agreed with Tommy.

Jason's stomach churned.

Another comment caught his eye.

> A few months ago I'd have laughed at the thought of vampires doing shit like starting fires to polish their image. But I just don't trust them now, especially not with one of them running around biting people. Check out Britney Allen's video on this.

Jason quickly searched the name and found a short video, which he played.

A young woman sat in front of the camera, her hair tucked behind her ears. She didn't look as comfortable as Tommy, which made Jason suspect she didn't do this regularly.

"I was asked to keep quiet about this until there was more information, but it doesn't look like I'll get answers, and I'm done being afraid. A few days ago, while jogging, I was attacked by a vampire. I thought I was going crazy, but Ysanne Moreau herself visited me, and it was confirmed that my injury was a vampire bite. She wouldn't say who the vampire was, and maybe she genuinely doesn't know, but if that vampire's still out there, other people are at risk. We all know what happened with Roger Schofield. Nine kids are *dead*, and it could have been more. Will Belle Morte let that happen again?"

Jason paused the video, feeling faintly sick.

He'd known the problem of the mystery vampire would have to be tackled sooner or later, but since no one else had been attacked and none of the bitten victims had been seriously hurt, it hadn't seemed as much of an immediate issue.

But this woman going public changed that, and it couldn't have come at a worse time.

Jason threw on some clothes and rushed out of the south wing, almost colliding with Renie at the staircase.

"I was just coming to get you," she said. "Ysanne's gathering everyone downstairs."

"A meeting?" Jason's heart sank.

Renie nodded.

"That's not good, is it? We never have meetings about anything good anymore," Jason said.

Renie sighed and took his hand. "Come on."

Edmond was already at the long table in the dining hall, with Ludovic and Roux to his left. Seamus sat opposite, while Ysanne and Walsh talked quietly at the head of the table.

Jason slid into the nearest chair, trying to calm his racing nerves. Maybe Ysanne was about to break the mold and give them some *good* news for a change. Though that seemed unlikely, judging by Walsh's grim expression.

Gideon entered the room and paused when he saw Jason, his eyes flicking around the table as if he was trying to decide where to sit.

For once, Jason was too nervous to care if Gideon sat near him or not.

Still, it was a welcome surprise when Gideon pulled out the chair next to him and stiffly sat down. Isabeau wasn't here, he noticed, but apparently Ysanne wasn't waiting for her.

"Walsh," she said, indicating the room with one hand.

"Right," he said, straightening and looking around. "I have a couple of updates about the fire. Since it happened in London, I'm not involved with the investigation, but I have some contacts, pulled a few strings, and I can tell you that the incident commander in charge of the scene has expressed that the cause of the fire is doubtful."

"What does that mean?" Jason said.

"At this stage he can't formally declare arson, but yeah, it's basically arson. You were right about the gasoline smell, Gideon, and the team found remnants from the plastic container the gasoline must have been in," Walsh said. "Obviously, at this stage there's no way to yet identify the arsonist."

"But PBV could still be responsible," Ludovic said, red flashing in his eyes.

"An investigation is being mounted, but at this stage there's nothing to suggest a connection," Walsh said.

"You said you had a couple of updates. What's the second one?" Gideon asked, leaning forward.

"There was no one else in the building."

"You're sure?" Gideon said, and Jason heard the hope in his voice.

"Absolutely. The eyewitness must have been mistaken," Walsh said.

Jason let out a soft sigh of relief. That was some good news, at least.

"I should probably also mention we're facing mounting pressure from groups concerned about the well-being of the vampire kids. We've always known some of their families aren't happy about them staying here, though they understand it's for the kids' safety, but if they change their minds, things could get very tricky," Walsh continued.

Jason deflated. Of course the good news hadn't lasted.

"Social Services have already established that they're happy with the children's living arrangements," Ysanne said.

"But the kids are only here because their parents consented. They wouldn't be safe going out into the world, but if the parents decide they want them back, you can't legally keep them," Walsh cautioned. "Three petitions to bring the kids home are taking off online, with thousands of signatures already collected." He sighed and ran a hand through his hair. "I'm sure the people behind them have good intentions, but they really don't know what the fuck they're fighting for."

"I hate to make things worse, but did you know one of the victims of the mystery vampire went public with that information this morning?" Jason asked.

Ysanne shot Walsh a sharp look, and he groaned.

"Shit, I didn't know that," he said.

"Why hasn't this vampire struck again?" Roux asked, resting her palms on the table.

"It's impossible to say, since we don't know who he or she is," Ysanne replied. "Walsh has a team mapping out anywhere a vampire could hide, but so far they haven't turned up any leads."

"Why haven't you asked us for help?" Ludovic said.

"Because at this stage, there's nothing you can do," Walsh answered.

Ludovic frowned. "Roux and I have already done this. We can do it again."

"We had leads then. We knew who we were looking for. Trying to track a vampire when no one knows what they even look like is like looking for a needle in a haystack."

Ludovic turned to Ysanne. "Let me visit the place where each victim was attacked. I might find things the police have missed."

"If you think it'll help."

Once Walsh might have taken that as a suggestion that the police didn't know how to do their jobs. He'd have balked at the notion of a vampire doing something the police couldn't. Jason liked this Walsh a lot more than the old one.

"I still don't get how it's possible that a vampire's been out there all this time without anyone knowing," Jason said.

"If we didn't have evidence, I'd have struggled to believe it myself," Ysanne admitted.

"Must be one hell of a vampire to stay hidden like this," Renie muttered.

Jason gave a weak chuckle. "Yeah, like Dracula or something."

No one spoke.

Jason's eyes widened. "Oh my god, it's not *Dracula*, is it?"

"Don't be absurd," Ysanne said, though there was no heat in her voice. "Dracula is nothing but a story."

"Oh, okay. Good."

Walsh cleared his throat. "Things are going to be a lot harder for us now that everyone knows about this vampire." He looked pointedly at Ysanne. "You'll be expected to have some answers, and we need to seriously think about how you're going to find and catch this vampire."

Ysanne lowered her eyes, and Jason realized she didn't *know* how. A chill ran through him.

If PBV *was* connected to the fire, no one in Belle Morte could do anything about it. It would be down to human police to sort. The safety of the kids depended on how long their families would let them stay. And they couldn't catch a vampire that they couldn't find.

For the first time, they were facing a series of threats that Jason wasn't sure they could handle. They were stuck here, inside these walls, helpless to do anything as it all closed in around them.

"Ludovic, if you're ready now, I'll take you to the site of each attack," Walsh said.

Roux opened her mouth but Ysanne held up one pale palm. "Before you ask, no, you can't go with him. You can't risk being out in daylight that long."

Roux's face fell but there was little point arguing. It would be decades before she'd built up the kind of tolerance that Ludovic had. Ludovic squeezed Roux's hand, and she leaned her head on his shoulder.

"You'd better be careful out there," she whispered.

Ludovic kissed her forehead. "Always."

When the meeting was over everyone drifted out of the dining hall and Jason followed, planning to go back to his room and bury his face in a pillow. He was almost at the vestibule when a prickling sensation spread across the back of his neck. He looked back.

Gideon was following close behind, his eyes intense, but he stopped when his gaze met Jason's. For a moment he stood there, looking so awkward that Jason half expected him to shuffle his feet.

"I didn't get a chance to tell you, but you were incredible yesterday." Gideon's words tumbled over each other.

Jason almost smiled.

Vampires were usually so cool and collected; it was refreshing to see one get a little flustered.

He gestured to the feeding room on his right. "You want to talk in there?"

He'd rather take Gideon upstairs to talk, but this was better than nothing.

Gideon hesitated, then followed Jason into the room.

Jason slumped onto the sofa, dislodging a tasseled cushion. "This has been a shitty day, and it's still only the morning." He raked his hands through his hair. "And the kids—fuck. What *will* happen to them? I can't even imagine what their poor families are going through."

"Do you have a family?" Gideon asked. A wry smile touched his lips. "Foolish question, of course you do."

"I've got the full package," Jason said. "Mum, dad, three siblings. Laura's seventeen, Shaun's fifteen, and Emily's eleven."

"Aren't they worried about you?"

Jason bit his lip, thinking of all those missed calls from his mum.

"They want me to come home," he admitted.

"Why don't you?"

"Because I'm needed here," Jason said, looking into Gideon's eyes.

They were such a lovely shade of gray, seeming to darken and lighten according to his mood. Right now they looked like early-morning mist in the countryside.

"But you'll go back eventually?" Gideon said.

Jason shrugged. "I have no idea what'll happen, but I'm not going anywhere until my friends are safe."

Gideon looked at the carpet.

"What about you? What was your family like?" Jason asked.

Gideon's head snapped up. "My family?" he said, as if the words sounded strange in his mouth.

"You must have had one once."

Gideon said nothing.

Jason held up his hands. "I get it. You don't want to talk about it."

"It's not—"

"Gideon, I'm used to vampires and their emotional baggage by now." He shrugged again. "Maybe one day you'll feel comfortable enough to talk to me, and maybe you won't. Either way, it's okay. It's your life and your choice."

"You don't think I'm rude for asking you questions that I'm not prepared to answer myself?"

Jason gave a little laugh. "You're many things, Gideon, but rude isn't one of them. You don't owe me anything."

If Gideon opened up to him, it would be because he trusted him.

Jason wanted to earn that trust.

Gideon

He almost hadn't followed Jason into this room.

Now his only concern was how he'd leave.

When he'd asked Jason about his family, he hadn't considered that Jason might ask the same questions in turn. That was how normal people carried out a conversation, but vampires weren't normal, and they often kept quiet about their pasts. There were too many ghosts, too many old wounds.

Jason understood that.

Almost without realizing it, Gideon sidled onto the sofa next to Jason. He swore he could feel the echo of his long-dead heartbeat again, thundering against his ribs.

He couldn't remember the last time someone had affected him like this, and it was both terrifying and exhilarating.

He'd noticed Jason from the moment he stepped into Belle Morte, but that had been a purely physical response. Jason was handsome. He put care into his appearance. It was enough to draw anyone's eye. Now, Gideon's attraction ran deeper than mere looks.

Jason was brave, willing to fight for the people he loved; he didn't walk away from difficult situations and he refused to back down in the face of threats. He was also compassionate and patient and understanding and honest and kind.

Every time Gideon thought Jason couldn't be any better, he did something that proved Gideon wrong.

It had been so long since Gideon had talked about his past to anyone but Isabeau, and part of him balked at the thought of opening up to Jason. But he already had. He'd told him about Jerry, about the fire in Brixton and the man he'd killed, and Jason had listened with an open mind and an open heart.

If Gideon had talked to him once, he could do it again.

"For most of my human life, I felt like I didn't fit in," he said.

He heard Jason's heartbeat quicken; obviously Jason hadn't expected Gideon to share anything.

"I was expected to marry a respectable woman and raise respectable children, but I always knew I wasn't attracted to women. When I was sixteen, my father caught me kissing another boy." He broke off and clenched his teeth. "I thought he'd kill me."

"Jesus," Jason muttered.

So many years had passed since that terrible night, but every detail was still etched into Gideon's brain—the way that rage had twisted his father's face, transforming him into a monster.

The flurry of his fists.

The rain hitting Gideon's face, washing away the blood.

The fact that no one came to help.

"After that I had to be careful not to even make eye contact with other boys when my father was around," Gideon said.

Jason's jaw was clenched, his mouth a hard line. "Telling you I'm sorry sounds kind of lame, but there aren't any other words. So, I'm sorry. Didn't you have support from *anyone*?"

That was when Gideon found words he hadn't spoken in a long time.

"My older brother," he said, the words like broken glass in his throat. "Godric."

A memory flashed into his head—sunlight gilding Godric's curls, so like Gideon's, his eyes crinkling at the corners as he squinted in the bright light, laughing at something Gideon had said or done. He was the eldest of the Hartwright children, and Gideon had looked up to Godric more than anyone in the world.

"He was four years older than me, but he was my dearest friend," Gideon said. "I even confided in him about my sexuality, because I thought he was the one person who wouldn't condemn me. And I was right. Godric was surprised, but he didn't turn on me or say there was something wrong with me. Life was hard, but it would have been much harder without him."

"He sounds like he was a good brother," Jason said.

Gideon snorted. "I thought so too. But when I turned twenty-one, I fell for someone. It made me careless. This time it was Godric who caught me. I thought he'd turn a blind eye, but he didn't."

Jason tensed.

"Godric told me that my nonsense had to stop, that I was too old for it. I didn't understand—he was the only person who'd shown me a single shred of support—and suddenly he was taking it away. But it had never been real. Godric had assumed that my sexuality was something I'd get out of my system before settling down with a nice little wife."

"But that was never going to happen," Jason said.

Gideon clenched his free hand. "I was so *angry*. All my life I'd thought that Godric accepted and loved me for who I was, but it was a lie."

"I'm sorry. I can't imagine how I'd feel if my brother turned on me like that."

"Shattering that trust hurt me more than my father's beatings ever had. We argued and we both said terrible things, burning the bonds we'd built over our lives." Gideon uncurled his fist and gazed down at his palm. "There were many things I could cope with, but Godric turning on me wasn't one of them. I knew then that I had to get out of that life."

"What did you do?"

"I left home that same night and never saw Godric or the rest of my family again."

"Did you ever regret that?" Jason asked, his voice soft.

That was a painful question, and a complicated one to answer.

"I regret never making amends," he admitted. "But he'd hurt me too deeply. It was as if our whole life, our whole relationship, was nothing but a lie, and I couldn't bear to see him again."

"I'm so sorry," Jason said.

Gideon smiled sadly. "I suppose I was also afraid that if I ever went back, he'd reject me. He wouldn't want to be reminded of the Hartwrights' black sheep. I preferred to live with the regret of not making amends than face the pain of him turning me away."

Jason's eyes were suspiciously bright. "I hate that you had to go through this."

"It's a drop in the ocean compared to what some vampires have been through."

"That doesn't make it any less painful."

"Once I became a vampire, I thought things would change, but I soon realized that I'd become a different kind of outcast," Gideon said. "Eventually I gave up on relationships entirely."

"So yesterday, when you said it had been a long time since anyone had touched you like that, how long are we actually talking?" Jason said.

"Since the night of that fire in 1977."

Jason's eyes bulged. "Holy shit." He clapped a hand over his mouth. "Sorry, that's not helpful."

Gideon found he could smile a little. "It's all right. Time moves differently for vampires."

"Still, that's a long time to be on your own," Jason said.

Gideon wasn't sure how to respond to that.

Jason looked him up and down. "And wasting your good looks being single all these years? Not cool."

Gideon blinked.

Jason bit his lip. "Wow, sorry, that sounded way less inappropriate in my head."

Gideon smiled again. "It's all right."

His gaze drifted to Jason's mouth, and the world faded for a moment. He wasn't strong enough to keep fighting; the pull was too intense.

Jason's heartbeat was a steady *thump thump thump*, increasing from the moment Gideon had sat down next to him. His eyes moved over Gideon's face, and the air between them was so charged it felt like lightning, crackling and surging and lighting everything up.

Jason swallowed, pulling Gideon's attention to the shape of his neck, the veins running beneath his skin. He'd tasted Jason's blood once before, very briefly. Gideon vividly remembered running his tongue over Jason's throat, that quick, sweet tang of his blood. It still came to him in his dreams sometimes, and he ached to repeat it.

He wanted to taste Jason in a different way, and he wanted it so badly that it blotted out all other thought.

Jason shifted position, leaning in slightly, and Gideon couldn't take it anymore.

He kissed him.

CHAPTER NINE

Jason

W hat?
What?

He was dreaming, right? He had to be dreaming.

But no, this was real. That was Gideon's mouth, soft against his, the featherlight brush of his tongue, the nervous tremor of his hand on Jason's knee.

Jason's heart sang with it.

He kissed Gideon gently but hungrily, cupping his cheek with one hand, and Gideon responded, his own hand moving along Jason's thigh. Blood surged in Jason's veins, and he grabbed the back of Gideon's neck, pulling the other man harder against him. His heart felt like it would beat right out of his chest, and the moment was so beautiful, so perfect that he never wanted it to end—

Gideon pulled back, blinking fast.

He looked so human, so vulnerable; there was fear in his eyes, and it stopped Jason in his tracks.

"Gideon?" he whispered, his voice ragged.

His mouth tingled, and he swore he could feel the imprint of Gideon's palm pressed against his thigh. Gideon's hands were in his lap now, and he wasn't looking at Jason.

Jason's heart sank.

For him, the kiss had been a moment of magic.

Maybe for Gideon, it had been a mistake.

"I'm sorry," Gideon whispered.

"For what?"

Jason put a hand on Gideon's knee, and Gideon flinched. It was a tiny flicker of expression, almost imperceptible, but a flinch nonetheless. Jason pulled his hand away.

Gideon climbed off the sofa, still not looking at Jason. "I should go," he said, his voice still so soft.

Jason wanted to protest, to ask him to stay, but he couldn't find the words. What had just happened?

Slowly, he got to his feet, watching Gideon go to the door. "Did I do something wrong?" he asked.

Finally, Gideon looked at him, and Jason had no idea how to read what was in the vampire's eyes. Gideon shook his head, and then he was gone, quietly closing the door.

For a brief, shining moment, dream had become beautiful reality.

Just as fast, it had fallen apart, and he didn't know why.

He traced his lips with a fingertip, as if that would somehow keep Gideon there.

What had gone wrong?

Could he fix it?

Jason left the feeding room and almost ran into Isabeau, who was standing outside. He smiled, but Isabeau's expression remained cool, and Jason's smile wilted.

"Everything okay?" he said.

"Don't hurt him," Isabeau said.

Jason's throat went dry. "Sorry?"

"I've known Gideon a long time, and he's more vulnerable than he looks."

At over six foot of solid muscle, Gideon was physically imposing, and Jason had learned in Fiaigh that he'd once been a champion boxer. Nothing about him *looked* vulnerable. But looks could be deceiving, and there was so much that Gideon kept hidden away.

Jason wet his lips. "I won't hurt him," he whispered. "I promise."

Isabeau's expression softened. "Good."

Gideon

He didn't know if he regretted that or not.

On the one hand, he'd fantasized about kissing Jason since he'd first seen him, and the reality had been better than every dream.

On the other, he couldn't see that he had any future with this human boy, and this *really* wasn't the time, not when the world vampires had built for themselves was teetering on a precipice.

He hurried through the lobby, pausing when he saw Ludovic, Edmond, and Walsh standing there. Walsh was showing them something on his phone, gesturing with one finger.

Gideon moved closer.

". . . depends how much time you need," Walsh said.

"Impossible to say until we're out there," Ludovic said.

"Are you going to the attack sites?" Gideon asked.

They all turned to him.

"Yeah." Walsh didn't sound enthusiastic that they'd find anything. Gideon wasn't, either, but they had to try. "Do you need help?"

"The extra backup couldn't hurt. In case we do find anything," Edmond said.

Ludovic nodded.

Walsh drove them away from Belle Morte and into the sprawling green lushness of the South Downs National Park. The woman who'd been bitten closest to the city had been walking her dog, and apparently she'd been too much in shock to pinpoint her exact location, though she knew the rough area.

Walsh took them to a vast meadow. Spring was still only stirring, winter reluctant to leave, but a few bold wildflowers had pushed up their heads, creating dots of color among the grass. Along the far edge of the meadow two people walked side by side, and the echo of a barking dog sounded from farther away.

Ludovic got straight to work tracking, prowling silently through the grass, head lowered. Walsh, Edmond, and Gideon stood back and watched.

"This is giving me serious déjà vu," Walsh called to Ludovic. "You?"

Gideon assumed Walsh was referring to when he'd worked with Roux and Ludovic to track down Roger Schofield and the rest of the Five.

Ludovic paused, looked up, then shook his head. "This is worse than tracking Schofield. We have nothing to work with."

Walsh sighed and shoved his hands in his pockets. "Yeah, I know. Just trying to lessen the tension."

Gideon thought that Jason would probably have done the same thing. It wasn't that he didn't understand the gravity of things; it was that he wanted to make it that little bit easier for everyone.

"I suppose it's too much to hope that either of you have any idea who our mystery vamp is," Walsh said to Edmond and Gideon.

"If we knew, we'd have a lead," Edmond pointed out.

Walsh sighed again. "Shit. Yeah." He pulled out a packet of cigarettes, passing the little box from hand to hand without opening it. "So you have no idea what we can expect from this, or how bad it might get."

Gideon and Edmond glanced at each other.

"Whoever this vampire is, he hasn't killed anyone or even taken a dangerous amount of blood from any of his victims," Edmond said. "Perhaps he took more than a vampire normally would from a donor, but not enough to put the average person in any danger."

"Still, we can't have vampires running around biting people," Walsh said.

"No," Edmond agreed.

"This vampire must secretly have been feeding from people all this time, and none of us were any the wiser. Why make himself known now? What changed?" Gideon asked.

"Everything," Edmond said.

"For us, yes, but for a vampire who hasn't been part of our modern world? He never used the donor system, so why would the collapse of it impact him in any way?"

"Maybe the timing's just coincidence?" Walsh suggested.

Gideon leveled him with a flat look. "You don't really believe that, do you?"

Walsh took out a cigarette and rolled it between his fingers. "No, but a guy can dream."

"Whoever this vampire is, he wants something," Edmond said, a few strands of dark hair blowing across his face.

"Yeah, but what?" Walsh still hadn't lit his cigarette.

"I don't know."

Across the field, Ludovic tensed and lifted his head, a predator sighting prey. A couple of seconds later a rabbit broke cover and darted across the grass, white scut bobbing. Ludovic's gaze followed it until the animal vanished into a thick patch of brambles.

"It won't be easy if we have to go back to that," Gideon remarked. "Hunting down prey won't exactly help our public image."

"It won't come to that," Edmond said, but his voice lacked conviction.

"It may, if we want to make sure there's enough bagged blood for Renie, Roux, and the children."

Edmond tensed. "We'll think of something."

"Let's hope we think of it soon, then," Gideon said. "If this mystery vampire does become a threat, we'll need all the blood we can get our hands on."

Jason

He only saw Gideon once more that day, when the blond vampire returned with Edmond and Ludovic. Apparently, Walsh had taken them to three of the four sites where the mystery vampire had bitten his victims, but Ludovic had found nothing. Tomorrow they'd visit the final site, though Jason doubted they'd find anything.

Still, he understood why they were trying. It was better than helplessly sitting around the mansion.

He'd hoped that he and Gideon might get a chance to talk, and strategically placed himself on the stairs so Gideon couldn't avoid him, but Gideon hurried past without a word.

It hurt.

Gideon had opened a door and invited him in, then just as quickly had slammed the door in Jason's face, leaving him in the cold.

The next morning, Jason lay in bed, texting his younger brother. Shaun might only have been fifteen, but he understood better than Jason's mum why Jason felt he had to stay.

There was a faint knock at the door.

Jason's heart skipped a beat.

The knock was too quiet to have come from Renie or Roux, and he couldn't think why anyone else would be here.

Except maybe Gideon.

He stared at the door, his phone still in his hand. He wore only boxers. He hadn't showered or brushed his teeth or done his hair.

Did he really want Gideon—if it was him—to see him like this?

Fuck it. If Gideon was the man Jason thought he was, he wouldn't care what Jason looked like first thing in the morning.

Rolling out of bed, Jason went to the door.

Gideon stood on the other side. He opened his mouth to say something, then stopped, staring.

Maybe Jason should have put on a T-shirt instead of flashing his bare chest at the man who'd been frightened off by a kiss.

Gideon blinked and dragged his gaze upward, focusing on Jason's face rather than his chest. "I owe you an apology."

"Do you want to come in?" Jason said.

He held the door open, and didn't miss the way Gideon's eyes lingered on his chest again as he walked into the room.

Suddenly Jason felt self-conscious. He wasn't shy about showing off the body he worked hard for in the gym, but there was something very intimate about standing in front of Gideon wearing practically nothing, when he had no idea how this would go.

"Do you mind if I grab a shower and throw on some clothes?" he said.

For a moment he thought Gideon *would* mind, and his skin heated at the thought of Gideon enjoying the view, but then Gideon said, "Not at all."

Jason grabbed the nearest clothes and hurried into the bathroom. Maybe a *cold* shower was in order.

He showered and dressed as fast as possible, keenly aware of the vampire waiting on the other side of that door.

Gideon had said he was here to apologize, but for what, exactly?

For ignoring Jason the rest of yesterday?

For kissing him in the first place?

Taking a deep breath, he went back into the bedroom. Gideon stood exactly where Jason had left him, halfway between the bed and the door.

"Okay." Jason perched on the footboard. "Obviously, we need to talk."

"I must apologize for my behavior yesterday," Gideon said.

"In what way?"

Please don't say the kiss.

Gideon lifted his chin and met Jason's eyes. "For leaving so abruptly. It was rude."

He sounded so formal that Jason couldn't help a smile. "Apology accepted," he said.

"When we have time, I'd still like you to teach me about the modern world. I fear I still have a lot to learn," Gideon said.

"Afraid so."

Gideon's eyes went to the phone that Jason had left on his bed. "You haven't been reading those lies about us again, have you?"

"Hell, no. I'm not in the mood for trolls today," Jason said.

Gideon frowned again. "Trolls? I understand that people didn't always believe in vampires, but I can assure you that trolls are nothing more than creatures of myth."

He was so freaking adorable that Jason wanted to kiss him, then and there.

"Not that kind of troll."

He tried explaining it to Gideon, but the vampire still looked puzzled.

"Why would anyone do that?" he said.

Jason shrugged. "Welcome to the internet. Home of people who talk tough while hiding behind fake names and avatars."

Gideon grabbed his hand. Red sparked in his eyes. "You're worth more than any of those bastards," he said fiercely.

Before he could think better of it, Jason kissed him.

Gideon froze, and Jason thought he'd made a horrible mistake, then Gideon made a soft noise in his throat and kissed Jason back.

A little voice in Jason's head warned him to take it slow, otherwise Gideon might panic again, but his hands hadn't got the memo. They clutched Gideon's shoulders, pulling him forward, and Gideon came eagerly, his weight pushing Jason back onto the mattress.

He was heavy and hard and tasted like everything Jason had ever wanted, and he couldn't see how he'd ever get enough of this. He slid a hand down Gideon's spine, and then lower.

Gideon broke the kiss and stared down at Jason with dazed eyes.

Jason almost couldn't breathe.

Gideon's thigh was wedged between his legs, their hip bones pressing against each other. Jason's blood raced and his skin felt electric, and his boxers were *way* too tight.

But Gideon had backed away again.

Jason tried to bring himself back to reality—not easy when he could still taste Gideon on his lips, still feel the delicious weight of the vampire spread across him.

"Are you okay?" Jason asked, his words breathless.

Gideon just stared at him, his eyes churning.

"I'm afraid," he admitted at last, his voice low.

"Of what?"

Gideon sat up and moved away from Jason, but he didn't run for the door. He still sat on the bed, his knee touching Jason's.

Jason sat up, too, trying to slow his racing heart. "Talk to me." He gave Gideon a little nudge. "I'm a great listener as well as a great kisser."

Gideon mustered a faint smile.

"Seriously, though," Jason said, after a few more beats of silence. "You can talk to me. You know that."

"I don't—" Gideon broke off with a frustrated noise. "It's been a long time since I've even been *close* to anyone who wasn't a friend. I don't know how to do any of this."

"Okay." Jason processed that. "Can I ask how old you are?"

"In vampire years or human?"

"Both."

"I was born in 1820, and I became a vampire in 1841, not long after my twenty-first birthday."

A shade under two hundred then—young compared to Edmond or Ludovic.

"Is it okay to admit that I've fancied the pants off you from the moment we met?" Jason said. Maybe that was too flippant. "I really like you, Gideon, and I think you like me too."

Gideon didn't deny it.

"I get that now's not the time, and I'm sure as hell not interested in pressuring you into something you're not ready for. But if we ever get a break from all this, maybe we could do something," Jason said.

"Something," Gideon repeated.

"Like . . . a date?" Jason was sure he wasn't normally this awkward. Then again, he'd never asked out a vampire before.

Gideon's face was unreadable. "Dating a vampire is very different from dating a human."

Jason considered that. He couldn't take Gideon out for a fancy dinner, or a cozy picnic, or make him a home-cooked meal. He couldn't take him to watch a romantic sunset or take long walks in the sunshine.

"Okay, so there're a few things we couldn't do, but that won't put me off," he declared.

But it did make him think.

So many Vladdicts would give anything to be where he was now, but Jason bet that none of them would have considered the reality of dating a vampire either.

They didn't realize the sacrifices that had to be made, even if it was only eating dinner together. Those little things could form the foundation of a solid relationship, and people couldn't appreciate the part those things played until they were in a relationship without them.

Which most people would never be.

"What sort of date would you want someone to plan for *you*?" Gideon asked.

"I'm easy, really. I like all the standard stuff, but there's one thing I've always wanted."

"What?"

Jason smiled wistfully. "I always wanted someone to get me flowers, but no one ever has. Apparently, having a dick means I'm not supposed to like them."

"I've never bought flowers for anyone," Gideon said.

"Never?"

Gideon shrugged.

"I bet no one's ever bought you flowers either," Jason said.

A faint smile touched Gideon's lips. "It never occurred to me to want them."

A pang went through Jason.

He wanted to treat Gideon the way he deserved to be treated, with tenderness and respect and appreciation—all the things that seemed to have been denied to him for most of his life.

But how was he supposed to do that?

Take Gideon for a romantic walk around the grounds?

The protestors were a bit of a mood killer.

Cook himself a romantic meal and then eat it while Gideon watched?

Maybe not.

There were more impracticalities involved with dating a vampire than Jason had ever realized, but he'd find a way around all that.

Gideon was worth it.

"You realize that it could be a while before I'm comfortable doing anything other than kissing," Gideon said.

"If you haven't kissed anyone since the '70s, I'm amazed you're even comfortable doing that," Jason teased, nudging him.

"I wasn't sure I would be," he said.

Jason grinned. "Just that irresistible, am I?"

"Something like that."

An idea took shape in Jason's head.

"How long until you head back out with Edmond and Ludovic?" he asked.

"Twenty minutes. Maybe thirty. Why?" Gideon said.

"I want to help you feel more comfortable. Do you trust me?"

Gideon studied him, looking so deeply into his eyes that it felt intimate, like kissing. "Yes."

"Take off your shirt."

Gideon hesitated, but it was a testament to how much he *did* trust Jason that he didn't question him. Climbing off the bed and taking a couple of steps back, he removed his shirt, folded it, and placed it on the nearest bed.

"What are you doing?" he asked, as Jason rummaged through the wardrobe.

Jason smiled in response.

A black velvet scarf hung at the back of the wardrobe. Neither Renie nor Roux had taken it when they moved out, so it was Jason's now.

Pulling it out, he approached Gideon.

Gideon still didn't question him, but he was starting to look apprehensive.

"Trust me," Jason said again.

"I do," Gideon murmured.

Gently, Jason tied the scarf around Gideon's eyes, knotting it behind his head, before kissing him softly on the lips. He ran his fingertips along the hard edge of Gideon's jaw, up behind his ears, and then down the lines of his neck.

He paused at the ridges of Gideon's collarbones, stroking the shape of them, and then flattened his palms on Gideon's chest, feeling the flex of pectoral muscles beneath pale skin, the faint dusting of golden hair against the pads of his fingers.

Gideon stood perfectly still, his face almost blank but for the compressed line of his mouth.

Jason swept his hands up Gideon's chest and along his shoulders, exploring every line of muscle; down his arms, squeezing the bulge of Gideon's biceps, and then back up to his shoulders.

Neither of them spoke; Jason's mouth was so dry he couldn't begin to find words. The silence only made it more intimate.

He smoothed his hands down Gideon's chest again, lower this time, and though he didn't want to break the beautiful silence, he had to ask: "Is this okay?"

Gideon nodded.

Jason explored the lines of Gideon's ribs. He traced the outline of the muscles in his stomach, stroking the soft, smooth skin that covered them, then carefully trailed his hands lower, touching the curve of Gideon's hip bones.

Gideon trembled slightly, and Jason took that as a sign not to go any lower.

He lost track of time as he read Gideon's body like braille, marveling in each touch, each new exploration of the beautiful male physique beneath his fingertips, and Gideon relaxed a little more each time Jason touched him, the hard line of his mouth softening until he was almost smiling.

Jason ached to use his tongue where his hands had been, tasting and exploring every inch of skin, but that was too much, too soon.

For now, he just wanted to remind Gideon how it felt to be touched.

Gideon's body was a work of art, all pale skin and hard muscle and golden hair—appearances weren't everything, but Jason felt it was a wonderful bonus that his vampire was the stuff wet dreams were made of.

Finally, when Gideon was putty in his hands, Jason slid one hand behind Gideon's neck, fingers tangling in his hair, and kissed him.

It was a chaste kiss, soft and gentle, but somehow more intimate than any they'd yet experienced.

Someone was trembling, and Jason couldn't tell if it was him or Gideon, or both of them.

He pulled off Gideon's blindfold.

Gideon stared back at him, his gray eyes so raw and vulnerable that Jason was afraid he'd gone too far.

But then Gideon kissed him again, slowly, as if he was trying to explore Jason's lips the way Jason had just explored him.

Before today, Jason would've said sex was the most intimate thing two people could share, but he was rapidly revising that opinion. Sex could be impersonal, meaningless, simply the scratching of a biological itch, but *this*?

This was different.

This was special.

Gideon

Kissing Jason for the first time had felt like a little piece of magic, and Gideon had worried that that magic would wear off, but each kiss still felt the same, eager but gentle, a moment taken out of time, when it was just him and Jason, and nothing else mattered.

Kisses were so simple, but so precious at the same time.

Jason abruptly stood up, pulling Gideon with him, and pressing the hard lines of his body against Gideon's in a way he hadn't been able to while they were sitting down.

Gideon's fangs slid out, the points pressing against Jason's tongue, and he pulled back.

Jason gazed at him, his eyes bright, lips parted. "What's wrong?" he said, slightly breathless.

"It's not always easy kissing a vampire. Sometimes the fangs get in the way."

Jason licked his lips. "Maybe you didn't realize this, but I get very turned on by vampire fangs."

A thrill raced through Gideon's blood.

Jason's gaze was fixed on Gideon's mouth, and Gideon smiled, showing off his fangs. Jason swallowed hard, his throat bobbing.

"They're beautiful," he whispered.

Gideon had been complimented on various aspects of his appearance over the years, but never his fangs. He liked it.

Jason swallowed again. "When I was still a donor, I was always waiting for you to bite me, but you never did."

Gideon had wanted to. From the moment he'd met Jason he'd dreamed of sinking his fangs into Jason's neck, but in his dreams the bite had led to something more. In real life, Gideon hadn't dared ask Jason to be his donor. He was afraid of what would happen if he did.

"You're not a donor anymore," he whispered.

"I'm not asking as a donor," Jason said. "Will you bite me?"

Vampires couldn't get goose bumps, but Gideon swore he felt them anyway.

"Are you sure?"

Jason nodded, his heart a thunderous beat in Gideon's ears. He tilted his head, exposing his neck and the exquisite veins beneath his skin.

Now it was Gideon's turn to swallow, though he didn't need to. Being around Jason seemed to reawaken some of the tics and habits he'd had as a human.

He'd dreamed of this for so long, and now it was actually happening.

He moved closer, inhaling the smell of Jason's skin and hair, counting his excited heartbeats.

Jason closed his eyes.

Gideon kissed his neck, a featherlight brush of his lips, and a little shudder rolled through Jason. Gideon slid his arm around Jason's back, supporting him, and gently bit down.

Jason gasped, clutching Gideon's arm.

His blood filled Gideon's mouth, and now it was Gideon's turn to close his eyes, because that taste he'd had before was nothing compared to this.

This was *bliss*.

He drew on Jason's vein with his mouth, and Jason responded with a moan, his hand traveling up Gideon's arm to the back of his neck, pulling him closer.

Jason hadn't shaved that morning, and Gideon could feel the slight roughness of bristle beneath his lips. It shot heat straight through him, and before he realized what he was doing, he was pushing Jason toward the bed.

Or maybe Jason was pulling him.

He couldn't tell anymore.

Jason's legs hit the edge of the bed and he folded, pulling Gideon down with him, Gideon's mouth still on his neck.

Gideon had long since stopped being aware of human heartbeats; it was part and parcel of being a vampire. But now, hearing Jason's heart pounding, knowing he was the one making Jason react that way, he felt a surge of pride.

He could have stayed this way forever, lying with Jason, drinking his blood while Jason clung to him like a lifeline in a storm.

But clarity cut through the fog of bliss in his head.

He had to stop before he took too much.

Gideon took his mouth from Jason's neck and ran his tongue over the bite marks, sealing them.

Jason gazed up at him, his eyes dazed and heavy lidded. His hand was still on the back of Gideon's neck, and he pulled him back down for a blistering kiss. Jason's mouth was as delicious as his blood, and Gideon sank into the kiss, winding his fingers through Jason's hair.

Jason suddenly pushed him away, and he pulled back, thinking he'd done something wrong, but Jason twisted his hands in Gideon's collar and turned him, pushing him down, switching position. The weight of him pressed on Gideon, muscles flexing in his arms. He was almost fierce in the way he kissed, and Gideon loved it.

And then Jason's hand moved down Gideon's chest, down the

planes of his stomach, heading farther south, and Gideon's whole body tensed.

Jason froze in response, his hand resting above the space between Gideon's hip bones.

"Too soon?" he whispered.

Gideon didn't know what to say. A deep-rooted hunger had woken in him, something he hadn't felt in decades, and suddenly the idea of taking things further didn't seem so intimidating.

But it still wasn't a good idea to rush things, especially when Edmond and Ludovic were probably already waiting for him downstairs.

"I should go," he murmured.

Disappointment flashed across Jason's face, then he smiled. "I'll see you when you get back?"

Gideon nodded.

Jason

While Gideon was out with the others, Jason spent the morning on social media, reading what people were saying about Belle Morte and vampires in general. He'd hoped that Gideon's heroic rescue of two people from a fire would have tipped public sentiment in their favor, and while lots of people still discussed that, there was a growing sense of unease about the nine vampire kids and what exactly the older vampires were doing by keeping them in Belle Morte and away from their families.

Some people raised genuine concerns about what was best for the kids.

Others shared speculations that made Jason feel sick.

He'd have chalked it up to people getting carried away online, except the numbers of protestors at the gate had been swelling all day, and it didn't sound as though any of them were here to support vampires.

Every so often someone took up the chant of "People Before Vampires."

Things were getting worse.

After Gideon had been gone for a couple of hours, Jason headed down to the vestibule. He wanted to be there when Gideon got back. Maybe they could—

Seamus raced out of a hallway, radio in hand, heading for the front door.

Jason's heart dropped into his shoes. "What's wrong?" he called, running after him.

Seamus didn't answer; he was already outside, running to the two guards who stood watch at the gate. Jason scanned the crowd, and his stomach lurched. A black Belle Morte car pulled slowly toward the gate, and even though Jason couldn't see through the tinted windows, he knew Gideon was inside. The crowd surrounded the car, shouting and banging on the windows, and even though Jason knew the vampires inside weren't in any real danger, his stomach still felt like he'd swallowed a rock.

The gates slid open to admit the car, Seamus and the other guards forming a line to fend off the bolder protestors who tried setting foot on Belle Morte soil. Jason ran forward to help.

When the gates were shut again and the vampires were getting out of the car, Jason turned to them, but something in his periphery made him look back. Someone was shoving their way through the crowd, their face covered by a dark hood. Why would someone hide their face unless they were about to do something they didn't want to get caught doing?

"Watch where you're going," someone snapped at the figure.

"Get the fuck out of my way, then," the hooded figure shot back, continuing to fight to the front.

"Wait," Jason said, narrowing his eyes.

He started forward, but Gideon caught his arm and held him back. "Don't get in the way," he said.

"But I know that voice," Jason said, pulling free.

He approached the gate, sure he was right, but hardly able to believe it.

The figure caught sight of him and threw back her hood, revealing a small, determined face, angry eyes, and a cloud of dark curls that seemed to bristle with the force of her fury. A gold locket hung around her neck.

"*Nikki?*" Jason said.

CHAPTER TEN

Jason

Dexter Flynn's daughter stared back at him, her chest heaving and her small hands balled into fists at her sides.

Jason gaped at her, words deserting him.

What the hell was she *doing* here?

Nikki wrapped a hand around the gate and gave it a shake. "You letting me in or what?"

Jason and Seamus traded looks, and Seamus pulled the key from his pocket.

"Vampire scum," someone yelled, and Nikki whirled around, eyes blazing.

"Fuck you," she yelled back.

Seamus unlocked the gate, holding it open just enough for Nikki. Another guy tried to push through, and Nikki promptly stomped on his foot. She slipped through the gap and Seamus quickly locked the gate again.

Jason knew that Nikki was a tough kid. She'd fought with them during the final battle for Belle Morte. She'd faced Jemima without flinching. She was fearless, determined, and brave, and right now she was also very angry.

But this was more than just anger. Her face was rigid but her lips trembled—however brave she'd been in the past, she was still only thirteen.

Something was affecting her badly enough that she'd come to Belle Morte.

Jason didn't know if this was to do with Dexter or if something else had happened, but if she needed their help, then Belle Morte owed her. Even if they didn't, they'd help anyway, because she was Dexter's daughter. She was their friend.

Jason put a tentative arm around her shoulders.

She tensed, then relaxed against him.

"Let's get you inside," he said.

Jason wasn't the only one shocked to see her.

Someone must've notified Ysanne of potential trouble; she was striding into the vestibule as Jason led Nikki inside. The Lady stopped, her eyes widening a fraction.

"Nikita," she said, recovering her composure in a blink. "What are you doing here?"

Nikki shrugged, but the anger from outside seemed to bleed away, and Jason was reminded how small she was. He held her a little tighter.

"I didn't know where else to go," she mumbled.

Ysanne gave Jason a look that was probably as close to baffled as she ever got. She had nothing but respect for Nikki, but she also wasn't the sort of person who got warm and fuzzy with kids.

Jason took pity on her.

"Why don't you come up to my room, Nikki? You can tell me what's going on," he said.

Nikki's curls bobbed as she nodded.

As he steered her toward the staircase, he met Seamus's eyes over Nikki's head.

Find Renie, he mouthed.

Having two younger sisters meant he wasn't unfamiliar with teenage girls, but Nikki might feel more comfortable with another girl around. And since Dexter had practically died in Renie's arms, and she'd kept his locket safe before giving it to Nikki, Jason reckoned she was the person Nikki would most want to see.

He'd barely got Nikki to his room before Renie, Roux, Edmond, and Ludovic turned up. Renie went straight to Nikki and hugged her.

"Hey, kid," she murmured. "What are you doing here?"

"Have you heard what's happening?" Nikki said.

"What do you mean?"

Pushing Renie away, Nikki fumbled for her phone. Her fingers skated over the screen, pulling something up. "Two days ago, twenty-three-year-old Jenny Riggs was assaulted while walking home after work. The gang who attacked her wore masks, so she couldn't identify them, but she reported one of them telling her she got what she deserved for helping vampires. They left her with a broken cheekbone. Earlier that morning, twenty-six-year-old Jake Glover reported a similar attack while he was jogging. The gang that went after him left him with three cracked ribs and a broken nose. Yesterday, nineteen-year-old Ada Brent posted to her socials that she was being stalked and harassed by a masked gang."

"Why do those names sound familiar?" Jason said, frowning.

"They're all former donors," Edmond said. "Jake and Jenny were donors here a few years ago. Ada was a donor at Midnight last year."

A heavy silence fell.

"Is this connected to People Before Vampires?" Ludovic's voice was as sharp as a blade.

"I didn't know if you guys knew about this, so I had to tell you," Nikki said.

"You came all this way to tell us that?" Jason said.

Something didn't add up.

Nikki's lip trembled, her defiant mask cracking. "Everything's just shit."

Renie put her arm around the younger girl again. "Tell us what's going on."

Nikki swiped a hand across her eyes. "They wouldn't let me live on my own," she said.

"Who wouldn't?" Edmond asked.

"Social services." Nikki practically spat the words.

"Oh, honey, of course they couldn't let you live on your own. You're only thirteen," said Roux.

Nikki glared up at her. "I can take care of myself."

"It's not that simple."

Nikki made a scoffing noise. "They sent me to live with my aunt. I haven't seen her in years, and suddenly I have to move nearly forty miles to Guildford. It's not like she even wants me."

Renie tightened her arm around Nikki. "Sweetie, no, don't think like that. Of course she wants you."

Nikki wriggled away. "Don't bullshit me. If she'd wanted a relationship, she could have visited in the last ten years. But she hasn't."

Jason frowned. "Okay, you need to start from the beginning."

Nikki sighed, blinking rapidly. "Diane is my dad's sister." She clenched her jaw. "*Was* his sister. They used to get on fine, at least that's what he always told me, but when vampires came out to the world, Diane was immediately against them, and when Dad started working at Belle Morte, he and Diane drifted apart. I barely know her, and now I have to move away from the only home I've ever known."

"She did choose to take you in now," said Roux carefully. "That has to count for something, right?"

Nikki snorted. She sat on Jason's bed, pulling up her knees and locking her arms tightly around them as if she was trying not to fall apart.

"Nikki," Roux said, her voice taking on a more serious note. "Does your aunt know you're here?"

Nikki nodded. "She didn't want me to come but screw her. She can't tell me what to do."

Roux and Jason exchanged uneasy looks.

"I don't want to live with her," Nikki whispered, her voice hoarse with unshed tears. "I don't want to leave Winchester. This is my home." A tear spilled over, and she brushed it away so roughly it was almost a slap.

There was a sharp pain in Jason's chest.

Living in Belle Morte, it was easy to see the damage that Etienne and Jemima had wrought, but sometimes he forgot the many ripple effects *out*side the house. So many lives had been destroyed. So many people still struggled to pick up the pieces.

"Why didn't you tell us you were coming?" Renie asked.

"Didn't think you'd let me," Nikki mumbled. She sat up straighter and squared her shoulders, a determined gleam creeping into her eyes. "Anyway, I'm here, and I'm not going anywhere."

"What do you mean?" Jason's heart sank.

"I'm not going back to that woman. I'm staying here."

Jason tried to find words, but nothing came. Nikki couldn't stay, even if it was legal. Belle Morte hadn't been built for kids. But telling her that would break her heart all over again.

Gideon

He'd followed Jason up from the vestibule, but then hung back in the hallway, both because he didn't want to crowd Nikki and because he had no idea what to say to a distressed teenage girl.

Now, Jason leaned against the wall opposite him, a few doors down from his room, where Nikki was curled up on his bed.

"I feel so guilty." Jason rubbed the back of his neck.

From the first time Gideon had laid eyes on him, Jason had stood out among the other donors. It wasn't just because he was gorgeous; it was because he had a sparkle. He was full of life and energy and color, like a ray of summer sunshine breaking through the clouds.

That sparkle was dimmed now. His face was tired and drawn.

"This isn't your fault," Gideon said.

"I know, but she came to us because she felt she had nowhere else to go, and we're going to send her back somewhere she's completely miserable."

"We don't have a choice."

"I *know*." Jason hung his head. "But that doesn't make it any easier. What if she never forgives us?"

Gideon moved closer to him. "She may be angry and hurt, but I don't believe she'll hold it against you. Not permanently. Make sure she knows you're still here for her, whenever she needs you. Perhaps once this is all over, she can come to visit."

"Yeah, maybe," Jason mumbled.

"I wish I knew what to say to make you feel better."

Jason lifted his head, a sad smile on his lips. "There *isn't* anything, but thank you for being here." His expression crumpled again. "It's not her fault, but she couldn't have picked a worse time to come, and I have no idea how to tell her she can't stay."

Gideon took his hand. "Come with me," he said.

He led Jason through the house and into the garden. No one stood guard on the back exits anymore; there were so few guards left that their energy was focused on monitoring the perimeter of the grounds.

"Where are we going?" he asked as Gideon led him across the lawn.

The ground wasn't frost hardened like it had been a week ago, but the air was still wintry, and Jason's breath came out in white clouds.

Gideon stopped in the middle of the garden and tipped back his head. The sky above them was so pale it was almost white, bleached by the watery light of the February sun.

Jason waited.

"Spring's coming." Gideon gazed around the garden. It was too early to see shoots on the trees, but here and there flowers emerged, the buttery-yellow heads of daffodils slowly unfurling. "Every year, winter kills everything, and every spring it comes back."

"Are you trying for a metaphor?" Jason said with a little smile.

"Possibly."

It was a clumsy attempt, but it had put a smile back on Jason's face, which was all that mattered.

Gideon was starting to realize there wasn't much he wouldn't do to put a smile on Jason's face.

"It wasn't the best metaphor, was it?" he said, and Jason chuckled.

"No, but I appreciate the effort."

A brisk wind picked up, carrying the din of the protestors closer. Jason shivered. "They sound so angry."

For the few minutes that he'd been out here with Jason, Gideon had barely noticed the noise.

"That's something we may have to get used to," he said.

Jason's chin came up. "I won't let that happen."

Gideon smiled a little. "You say it as if you have a choice. You can't change every mind, Jason. Maybe things will get better for vampires, but maybe we also need to understand that this damage may never fully be undone."

Jason's face fell, and before Gideon could stop himself, he traced the shape of Jason's mouth with his thumb, silently urging him to smile again.

"I just don't want you to have unrealistic expectations," he said.

Jason sighed and nodded, his eyes downcast. "I wish things *could* go back. I wish no one had died. I wish nothing had been turned upside down. I wish Belle Morte wasn't full of ghosts, and it still had fancy balls, and I could do what I always wanted, and ask you to dance."

Gideon's mouth tipped up. "You wanted to ask me to dance?"

"Of course."

"Why didn't you?"

Jason smiled wryly. "You weren't exactly giving me come-hither signals. I didn't think you were interested."

Gideon had always enjoyed the Belle Morte balls, but after years of them, they'd blurred into one long night. Until Jason came to his first one. Gideon would never forget how he'd looked, as elegant and beautiful as any vampire. In a sea of glittering faces, he'd stood out, the brightest of them all, as if he was lit up from the inside. He'd made Gideon's heart flip, and that in turn had made him afraid. He still couldn't remember the last time anyone had affected him as deeply and immediately as Jason, and he simply hadn't known what to do with those feelings. So he'd hidden from them and avoided Jason as much as he could.

"I was scared," he admitted.

Jason pressed his forehead to Gideon's. "I could ask you now," he said, his breath warm on Gideon's face.

"We're not at a ball," Gideon said.

"So?"

"There's no music."

Jason slid his arms around Gideon's waist, pulling him closer. "I don't care. Dance with me."

All those times when he could have asked Jason to dance but hadn't flashed through Gideon's head. He'd wasted those opportunities. He wouldn't waste this one.

"All right," he whispered.

He already knew Jason could dance—at every event, he'd quietly admired him from the corner of his eye—but he hadn't realized how good Jason was until they danced together.

At first they were slow, Jason's hand on Gideon's shoulder, Gideon's hand on Jason's back, their bodies close as their feet barely moved on the ground.

Then Jason's eyes gleamed, and he dropped his hand from Gideon's shoulder. He pulled Gideon in, deftly positioning his feet outside Gideon's, and moved his hand to Gideon's hip, leading him into a turn. A grin spread across Gideon's face. Jason wasn't the only one who could dance.

Slow dancing without music was no challenge. Salsa dancing without music was very different, and Gideon was surprised to find he relished the challenge. He also quickly realized he was out of practice. Isabeau had always been his salsa partner—dance classes were where they'd met—but they'd stopped going once vampires were revealed.

Jason moved with an easy confidence, his body flowing through the moves in a way that made Gideon aware of every inch of him. His posture and footing were flawless, and whenever Gideon missed a step or a cue, Jason smoothed it over as if nothing had happened.

"Where did you learn to dance like that?" he asked.

"My parents go to salsa classes every week. It looked like fun, so a couple of years back my sister and I started going too. She got bored of it pretty quick, I didn't," Jason explained.

He executed a little bow.

"Where did you learn?" he asked, straightening up.

"Isabeau and I used to dance together, but clearly I'm rusty," Gideon said.

Why hadn't they continued dancing once they got to Belle Morte? Maybe it hadn't quite fit the aesthetic that vampires had crafted for themselves. Until now, Gideon hadn't realized how much he missed it.

"You might have to help me polish my technique," he said.

"Any time."

As they stood in the garden, Jason's breath puffing white and his nose turning slightly pink from the cold, Gideon allowed himself a small glimpse into a possible future—one in which vampires were accepted again, where Jason and Gideon could be together and happy, and the only thing Gideon had to worry about was whether he was picking up enough salsa tips from the guy he liked.

Was that future possible?

Jason shivered, and Gideon snapped back to the present. He took off his jacket and draped it around Jason's shoulders.

The smile Jason gave him, soft and small, made Gideon's heart clench.

How could someone affect him like this with nothing more than a smile?

How could any smile be that beautiful?

Suddenly his ears pricked, his attention going to the wall.

"Do you hear that?" he said.

Jason tilted his head, listening.

"Something's wrong," Gideon said. "The people outside, they sound panicked."

Jason's reply was drowned out by the sudden crash of metal on metal.

Something had just hit the gates.

Jason

He jumped and grabbed Gideon's arm. "What the hell was *that*?"

The crash came again.

Seamus jogged over, his cheeks flushed from the cold. "Someone's ramming the front gates," he said.

"*What?*" Jason heard the words but they didn't sink in. This couldn't be happening, not after everything. Belle Morte deserved a fucking *break* already.

"Is anyone hurt?" Gideon asked, his voice as dark as his expression.

"No, everyone got out of the way in time. I think this is bluster rather than a serious attack, but it's still a good idea for you two to get inside," Seamus said.

He was off before Jason or Gideon could say anything, heading back in the direction of the gate.

Jason shivered again, and this time it had nothing to do with the cold. "Back to reality, I guess."

Gideon was looking past him, head slightly tilted, brow furrowed.

"What's wrong?" Jason said.

"I thought I heard—"

Gideon's next words were lost as a loud crash rocked the garden, and Jason whipped around to see a section of the wall behind him disappear in a cloud of brick dust.

The red dust spread outward, settling on the grass, and a dark shape appeared through the gap. A figure in black, with a balaclava covering his face.

"Oh my god," Jason whispered, fear pulsing through his chest. "The car, the gates—it's a diversion."

The figure advanced, and Gideon stepped in front of Jason, shielding him. He was as tense and coiled as a snake.

"Get out," he growled, and the man froze.

Swallowing hard, he pulled a wooden crucifix from his pocket and brandished it in Gideon's face.

"Get back," he declared, and there was a fierce certainty in his voice, the fervor of a man who believed he was in no danger.

Gideon just stared at him.

"*Back*," the man cried, thrusting the crucifix forward, almost hitting Gideon's nose.

"Oh for god's sake," Gideon snapped, and snatched the crucifix. He crushed it with one hand and threw the pieces in the man's face. "Get out of my home or I'll throw you out," he said, his eyes shining red.

Jason's instincts prickled.

The car ramming the gates was a diversion. But a diversion for one man who didn't even know what he was doing? That didn't add up.

He turned.

His throat turned to dust.

More figures in black were spilling through the hole in the wall.

The first man pulled out a small bottle and tossed the contents in Gideon's face, and Jason was seized with white-hot terror.

Walsh had used liquid silver against Schofield, and it had just about melted off his face. If there was silver in that bottle—

Gideon wiped water off his face.

Not silver, then.

Jason's relief was short-lived; the black-clad figures were still coming, too many for him to count.

The first man laughed, and Gideon promptly punched him, laying him out cold on the ground, surrounded by pieces of his crushed crucifix.

"Get inside, now," he ordered Jason, as the other intruders moved toward them, slowly but steadily.

Jason didn't want to leave him, but if Gideon had to look out for him then he'd be distracted, vulnerable. He turned and ran for the back door.

He was almost there when something hard hit his back, knocking him to the ground. Jason's attacker tried to pin him down, but he fought, jabbing his elbows back until he connected with what felt like someone's stomach. His attacker let out a soft *oof*.

Jason threw him off and scrambled to his feet, but another man had almost reached the back door. Jason tackled his legs, throwing him down. He clambered up the man's back, using his knees to pin his arms down, but he'd forgotten his first attacker.

Something cracked against his head, and the world went sideways. He hit the ground before he realized he'd fallen. His attacker stood over him, fists balled, eyes narrow slits of hatred. He drew his foot back, ready to kick, but the second man grabbed his arm.

"We don't have time for this. Get the kids and get out. That's the plan," he snapped.

The kids?

Ice-cold horror washed over Jason, numbing the ache in his head. These people weren't here to kill vampires. They'd come for the *kids*.

"*No*," he cried, launching himself to his feet.

He got in a couple of decent punches, but then, as he drew back his fist for a third, someone grabbed his wrist and yanked his arm back. A shard of pain sliced into Jason's shoulder, and he twisted his body, trying to relieve the pressure on his arm.

The blood drained from his face as he saw who'd grabbed him.

"You," he breathed.

The bearded man from the *Daily Topic* stood there, his face impassive. He was the only one not wearing a balaclava.

"What are *you* doing here?" Jason cried, trying to pull free, but the guy was *strong*.

He said nothing, just stared at him with cool eyes, and a shiver rolled down Jason's spine.

The man let him go at last, so suddenly that Jason stumbled and almost lost his footing.

"I'm going into that house now," he said. "Don't try to stop me."

"I'm not afraid of you," Jason said.

Something dark slid through the man's eyes. "You will be."

His fist blurred, and when it hit Jason's jaw, it felt like a sledgehammer.

Everything went fuzzy and white.

His face was cold.

He was on the ground again, his cheek pressed to the grass, his thoughts rattling loose in his skull.

"Ow," he mumbled.

What happened . . . people had come over the walls, and . . .

The kids.

That was a lightning bolt of clarity to his battered brain, and he scrambled to his feet. The world spun again, and he almost went back to his knees.

How long had he been on the ground?

The world slid properly into focus, and Jason's blood ran cold.

The back door hung open.

His attackers were inside Belle Morte.

CHAPTER ELEVEN

Jason

Closer to the wall, Gideon was fighting off more attackers; several men lay at his feet—dead or unconscious, Jason couldn't tell. He wanted to rush over and protect Gideon, but the kids needed help more than he did.

"Gideon," he yelled. "They're in the house."

He didn't wait for a reply but charged through the back door and into Belle Morte.

"Intruders," he shouted. "Intruders in the house!"

He ran as he shouted, his jaw aching like holy hell, fear racing through his veins.

Those men couldn't possibly know the kids were in the west wing, and even if they *did*, they couldn't reach them without running into a vampire or two.

Jason raced around the corner and almost collided with the bearded man who'd hit him. At the same time, his first two attackers rounded the corner up ahead. One of them dragged a small figure with him, and Jason recognized the red hair and waiflike build of Chloe Hegerty, one of the vampire kids. The guy had his hand clamped tightly over Chloe's mouth, and her small frame sagged against him like she was a rag doll.

Jason clenched his fists. "Let her go."

Chloe looked up at Jason, reddish tears trickling down her face.

"I won't let them hurt you, Chloe," he said, watching her would-be kidnappers, trying to decide which of them would attack first.

The bearded guy appeared to be the strongest, but he was staring at Chloe with a look of disbelief. "It's true, then," he whispered.

Feet thumped behind Jason, and every instinct warned him that more enemies were coming. Gideon hadn't been able to hold them all off, and they were flooding into the house, too many for Jason to handle.

Fuck, was Gideon okay?

Tears stung Jason's eyes.

He swung around as two more men in balaclavas appeared. "Where are the others?" the shorter of the two snapped.

"Start with this one," said Chloe's captor, giving her a shake.

"Easy," the other guy shot back. "We're not here to hurt them."

The guy sneered. "*You* might not be."

The bearded man slowly reached for Chloe.

A loud yell echoed through the corridor, a yell of pure rage and defiance, and suddenly one of the men was on the floor, clutching his knee. Standing over him, her hands curled into furious fists, was Nikki Flynn.

As the man tried to stand, Nikki grabbed a nearby vase from a pedestal and smashed it over his head. He went limp.

His friend gaped at Nikki, so taken by surprise that he let Chloe go, and as soon as the small vampire slipped from his hands, Nikki let out another yell and kicked the guy squarely between the legs.

He let out a noise like a wounded animal and folded, clutching both hands to his crotch.

Another man shoved past Jason and grabbed Chloe, but she suddenly sparked to life and sank her fangs into his hand. He yelped and snatched his hand back. Nikki seized Chloe's wrist and dragged her out of the way, using her own body to shield the other girl.

The man shook his hand, splattering blood on the floor, and then clenched his fists. He drew his arm back, ready to attack, and Jason was about to charge to Nikki's defense when a pale hand grabbed the man's wrist and sharply twisted.

Bone cracked and the man screamed.

Edmond stood over him, his eyes like fire.

Renie, Roux, and Ludovic fanned out behind him, and behind them, Jason glimpsed other Belle Morte vampires, coming to protect their home.

"Gideon's outside. He needs help," Jason cried.

Ludovic flashed past, punching a path through the black-clad figures filling the hallway.

The man Nikki had kicked groaned and tried to climb to his feet, but Renie promptly knocked him back down, putting one foot on his chest to pin him in place.

There was a flurry of confusion as fists flew and people shouted, and Jason pressed himself against the wall because even though he could handle himself in a fight, he wasn't jumping in if the vampires could sort things. It didn't take them long. A handful of men broke away from the group, running back the way they'd come, as if the spirit had gone out of them; the others quickly followed. Within seconds there were only a few unconscious bodies lying here and there, and the conscious man still trying to twist out of Edmond's grasp.

"Why are you here?" he growled.

"They came for the kids," Jason said, his heart hammering with adrenaline.

Edmond glanced at Nikki and Chloe, and Nikki stood straighter as his eyes touched her.

"They're not hurting anyone in this house," she said.

Edmond nodded, his face expressionless.

The man he held was several inches taller and several pounds heavier than him; he'd have towered over the vampire if he'd stood upright. But Edmond easily held him with one hand.

Chloe whimpered, and Edmond's gaze swung to her. She cowered behind Nikki, her arms wrapped around her middle. Blood was smeared across her mouth from where she'd bitten her attacker, and Jason's stomach twisted.

"Nikki, can you take Chloe upstairs?" he said.

"No," Chloe cried, darting from behind Nikki and throwing her arms around him. "I want to stay with you."

Jason looked helplessly at Edmond, then at Renie and Roux.

"Take them upstairs," Edmond said. "We're going to find out who these people are, and the children don't need to be around for that."

"But the others—" Jason started to say.

"We'll handle it." Edmond looked at Chloe and his eyes softened, the blazing red dying down. "Jason, if you want to help, this is the best thing you can do."

Edmond was right.

"Come on, sweetie. Let's get you cleaned up," Jason said to Chloe.

He stepped over the man Nikki had knocked out, his arm around Chloe, pressing her face against his chest. It didn't make much difference now—she'd already seen more than her share of violence—but he didn't know what else to do.

"Nikki?" he said, turning back to her.

She stuck out her bottom lip, looking from him to Edmond. Her hands were still in tight little fists, her chest heaving. When it came to fighting, Nikki was fearless, but there was something fragile in her, too, and it peeked out through the cracks in her defenses.

Jason held out a hand, and Nikki looked at it for a long moment. Then she hung her head and sighed. She didn't take his hand, but she followed him as he led Chloe to the stairs.

It was only after they started climbing that Jason realized he had no idea what had happened to the bearded man.

"Who the fuck *are* those guys?" Nikki exploded as soon as they were in Jason's room.

"I don't know," he replied, leading Chloe to the bathroom.

She shuffled along, her face blank, white except for the trail of bloody tears and the smear of red on her mouth.

Inside the bathroom, Jason sat her on the closed toilet and ran a washcloth under the tap. Nikki stood in the doorway, rage pouring off her.

Jason wrung out the cloth and carefully dabbed at Chloe's face, cleaning away the blood. She stared mechanically ahead, fresh tears cutting red paths down her cheeks.

Was it easier for vampire kids to cry than it was for adults?

They'd probably find out over the next few years.

"Who were they?" Chloe said. Her eyes were unfocused, staring at a spot on the wall, over Jason's head.

"I don't know, but the others will find out. They've got this under control." He wiped away her tears.

The diversion had worked, as had the initial show of numbers, but these were people who thought that crucifixes and holy water worked on vampires. Jason's friends could handle idiots like that.

"They shouldn't *have* to have it under control," Nikki snapped, eyes flashing. "This is their home."

"You can smash something if it'll make you feel better," Jason offered. "I'm sure there are breakables in my room."

One side of Nikki's mouth tipped up in a reluctant smile. "Maybe later. I don't want to upset her." She nodded at Chloe.

Jason mouthed his thanks, but Nikki didn't smile.

There was a lot of anger in the girl, and it worried him. Sooner or later it needed addressing, and he didn't think she'd get that help living with her aunt.

But one problem at a time.

He had to take care of Chloe first.

"Can you get up?" he asked, placing the bloodied cloth in the basin.

She'd stopped crying, but the blank way she still stared at the wall was almost as bad.

"Chloe?" he said.

Nothing.

Jason looked at Nikki, who shrugged.

"Okay," he muttered.

Moving slowly so as not to startle the vampire kid who could tear him in two if she wanted to, Jason slid one arm under Chloe's legs then the other around her shoulders, and lifted her.

She felt like a bundle of twigs, and he shook his head. It seemed impossible that this fragile, traumatized girl could be capable of the strength and speed he'd seen from his vampire friends.

Nikki moved aside, and Jason carried Chloe to the bed that had been Renie's. Without needing to be asked, Nikki pulled the covers back, and Jason laid Chloe down.

She gasped, her eyes finally focusing.

"You're okay," Jason soothed her, tucking strands of hair behind her ears. "No one's going to hurt you."

She nodded, letting him draw the covers up.

His own eyes prickled. She was so young, and Schofield had ensured that she'd be trapped at this age forever.

Gideon's concerns about what they'd do with these kids had never seemed so stark.

If only her parents were here. That was who she really needed. But it wasn't safe for her to leave the house, or to bring her family here. But after what had happened today, maybe it wasn't safe here either.

Jason closed his eyes, gritting his teeth against the frustration building into a shout on the back of his tongue.

This was such a mess, and it didn't seem like there'd ever be a way out.

"I'm sorry," Chloe mumbled, looking up at him.

"You've got nothing to be sorry for," Jason told her.

Chloe's eyes started tearing again. "What did they want?"

"Edmond will find out," Nikki said.

It wasn't an explanation, but Chloe was so burned out that she accepted it. Within minutes she was asleep.

Jason moved away.

Nikki watched him, and Jason fought the urge to sag against his own bed. Nikki was one tough little cookie, but as the only adult in the room, he felt he had to stay strong for them all.

"You were amazing down there. Dexter would have been proud," he told her.

Pride sparked in her eyes. "Dad always told me to go for the balls."

"Good advice. But I wasn't talking about the fighting. I was talking about the way you protected Chloe. That's what he'd really have been proud of."

Nikki shrugged like it was nothing, but her hand stole to her locket and clutched it tight.

She was smaller than Chloe, and now that Chloe was a vampire, even Nikki's ball-kicking wouldn't put them on a level playing field, but Nikki hadn't hesitated to place herself in front of Chloe. She'd have taken a punch for the girl, too, or worse.

"Nikki," Jason said, then stopped, struggling to find the words. He settled for a question instead. "How did you get there before the others? I thought you were with Renie and Roux."

She shook her head. "I wanted some alone time to . . ." She lowered her eyes, her throat working.

"To what?" asked Jason gently.

Nikki's lips trembled and she turned her head away, but not before Jason saw tears in her eyes.

"I wanted to see the place . . . where my dad died. But I didn't know where it was."

Jason heart had been wrung out so much lately that it almost seemed impossible it could twist any harder, but Nikki's words proved him wrong.

"I won't pretend I know what you're going through," he said. "I've never lost anyone. But I can see how much anger and grief you're trying to hold in, and that's not healthy. It's okay to let it out."

Nikki snorted.

"It is," Jason insisted.

"Do you think they wanted to hurt the kids?" Nikki asked, changing the subject.

"I don't know."

Nikki was quiet for a moment, then she said, "Dad always told me that if anyone tried to take me somewhere against my will, I should fight with everything I had, even if they threatened to hurt me. He said that whatever they threatened to do, if I fought back it wouldn't be as bad as what they planned once they'd got me where they wanted me."

"You think those guys wanted to take the kids somewhere so they could do something worse to them?" That made Jason's chest hurt.

He rubbed his jaw, feeling the bone-deep ache from the punch he'd taken.

"It's something to consider," Nikki said.

Jason looked at her. Nikki's head was tilted, her expression thoughtful. She shouldn't be thinking about shit like this. She was *thirteen years old*, for god's sake. She should be thinking about school and boys—or girls—and her friends, not pondering the motives behind the attempted kidnapping of nine traumatized vampire children.

"What will happen to those guys?" Nikki asked.

"Hopefully they'll be arrested."

With any luck, Jason's friends had the situation under control by now and someone was already on the phone to Walsh. Maybe the police were even on their way.

"What the hell did they think would happen?"

"Not everyone agrees with us keeping the kids here. Maybe these guys thought they were rescuing them."

"Excuse me while I roll my eyes right out of my head."

Jason shrugged. "People have thought stranger things."

Nikki leaned against the wall, wrapping her arms around herself. "This is messed up," she mumbled.

"Everything that's happened since Jemima and Etienne made their move has been messed up."

"And this isn't the end of it, is it?"

Jason couldn't bring himself to answer that.

Gideon

Once Ludovic had burst onto the grounds, joined swiftly by Ysanne and Isabeau, the attempted invasion of Belle Morte was over in seconds.

If Gideon had been allowed to kill his attackers, he wouldn't have needed help. They weren't trained fighters, and though a couple had slipped past his defenses with their knives, the wounds had been glancing, no real power behind them.

But he hadn't killed anyone. There were bruises and concussions, maybe even some broken bones, but nothing life-threatening.

Once the intruders had been disarmed, Seamus and his team bound their wrists and ankles with black cable ties and sat them against a wall to wait for the police. They left the weapons where they'd fallen, glinting in the grass.

With everything under control, Gideon went to find Jason.

The immediate threat might be over, but his chest was still tight with fear. Someone would have told him if Jason had been hurt, but all he could think about were those men and their knives, trying to get past Jason and into the house.

Jason was in his bedroom, sitting on the edge of the bed with his hands clasped in his lap. Nikki lay behind him, hugging a pillow. Chloe Hegerty slept on the other bed, her red hair fanned out around her bone-white face.

As soon as Gideon walked in, Jason jumped up and threw his arms around him.

"Thank god you're okay," he said.

For the briefest moment, Gideon stiffened. He'd gone so long without this kind of casual contact that doing it in public—even if that public consisted of just one other person—still came as a surprise. But the moment was gone in an instant and then he hugged Jason back, pressing his face into the side of his neck and listening to the reassuring thump of his heart.

Jason pulled back, his eyes narrowing as he spotted the blood on Gideon's shirt.

"You're hurt," he said.

"Hardly," Gideon said. There was a slash on his forearm and another across his shoulder blade, but they'd close as soon as he drank some blood. He was barely even aware of them.

Jason turned him around to inspect the shoulder slash.

"I'm fine," Gideon insisted, turning back. He narrowed his eyes, looking Jason over. There was a reddish swelling on one side of his jaw—someone had hit him.

Gideon had seen Jason hurt before, though never seriously, and though it wasn't serious this time, anger was a hot flare in his chest. He should have broken a few more bones out in the garden.

Jason touched his jaw. "It's just a bruise," he said.

"I kicked one of them in the balls," Nikki piped up.

"Good girl," Gideon told her, and a smile spread across her face.

"Do we know who they are yet?" Jason asked.

Gideon shook his head. "The police have been called. For now, Ysanne, Ludovic, and Edmond are keeping an eye on them."

"Just keeping an eye?" Jason asked.

"Tempting though it is, Ysanne has forbidden anyone from interrogating them. They'll have to be arrested and tried according to human laws, and if we're supposed to be playing by those same laws, we have no right to question anyone. We have to leave that to the proper authorities."

"Did you find the bearded guy?" Jason asked.

Gideon frowned. "Who?"

Jason gestured with his hand. "About yay tall, red hair and beard? He was in the audience when we appeared on the *Daily Topic*."

Gideon's eyes darkened. "And he was here? With that group?"

"Yeah. I have no idea what happened to him."

"Ysanne's organized a thorough search of the mansion in case anyone slipped past, so if he's hiding somewhere, we'll find him. Although I think it's far more likely he ran away in the chaos," Gideon said.

Jason nodded, relieved.

"How's Chloe doing?" Gideon asked, looking at the girl as she slept, a fragile shape curled under the covers.

Edmond had given him a brief rundown of what had happened, and it made Gideon's blood boil.

Anger flickered in Jason's eyes. "Not great."

"Thank goodness for you." Gideon gripped his hand.

"And me," Nikki said, kneeling on the bed.

"And you." He squeezed Jason's hand. "Can we talk outside?"

Jason frowned slightly, but he didn't object as Gideon led him out of the room.

As soon as the door was closed and they were away from inquisitive young eyes, Gideon pushed Jason against the wall and kissed him, threading his fingers in Jason's hair.

Jason's hips ground against his in a way that made the blood in his veins rush, and the only thing that stopped him from pulling Jason back into the bedroom and pushing him onto the bed was the two young girls in there.

"I'll make sure to get punched more often if that's the reaction I get," Jason teased when they broke apart. His voice was breathless, his eyes bright.

Gideon scowled. "That's not funny. You could have been really hurt." His fingertips traced the air in front of Jason's jaw, not quite touching the bruise. "I was worried about you," he said, cupping the unbruised side of Jason's face.

The laughter faded from Jason's eyes. "I was worried about you too. I hated leaving you."

"I'm glad you did. It was safer for you."

"What happens now?" Jason asked.

"That depends on the police. I'm really not sure what normal protocol is in this situation."

Jason frowned. Gideon wanted to kiss the tiny grooves that appeared between his eyebrows when he was deep in thought.

"They should be charged with trespassing, breaking and entering, attempted kidnapping, and assault." His eyes went to the gash on Gideon's forearm. "Really, that should include assault with a deadly weapon, but your injuries will heal before anyone can charge them."

"Yours won't," Gideon pointed out, feeling that hot flare of anger again.

"They didn't come after me with knives," Jason said. He slid his hands up Gideon's arms and squeezed his biceps. "Though I may need a hot vampire to kiss my bruises better later."

Gideon's blood heated. He kissed Jason again, gentler this time, tasting the soft curve of his lips, a delicious contrast to the hard lines of his body.

"Do me a favor?" Jason said.

"Anything."

"Can you get some blood from the kitchen? It might make Chloe feel better when she wakes up, but I don't want to leave her just yet."

Gideon stepped back and appraised Jason. Even bruised and beaten, his first thought was for the well-being of other people. "I can do that."

"Thank you."

Gideon hurried off, trying to process the warm, full feeling in his heart.

Jason

He'd suspected Chloe wouldn't sleep long, and he was right. By the time Gideon returned, carrying a pouch of blood, Chloe was stirring. When Gideon walked in, her eyes flew open and she scrambled back, clutching the covers.

"It's okay, it's just Gideon," Jason said soothingly, holding out his hands.

Chloe hung her head, a curtain of straggly red hair hiding her face.

Jason took the pouch from Gideon and opened it. "Drink this. It'll make you feel better."

Chloe hesitated, her eyes scanning his face.

"I'm an ex-donor, honey. I've seen vampires feed before," he told her.

She took the blood, but stared at it for a long moment before lifting it to her mouth.

"I hate this," she said, when she'd drunk half the bag.

"The blood drinking?"

"*Everything*," she burst out, her voice thin and shaky. "I don't want to be a vampire." She threw the bag to the floor and blood spilled out, puddling on the carpet. "I want to go home."

Her words were so like Nikki's.

And just like Nikki's, Chloe's old life was over.

"I'm so sorry, but that isn't an option right now. We have to keep you safe," he said.

"For how long? Are we supposed to stay here forever?"

Words failed Jason. Chloe might be a vampire, but she was also a kid, and Belle Morte hadn't been built for her any more than it had been built for Nikki.

"I promise we're doing everything we can to clear this mess up," he said.

"But nothing will ever be normal for us again," said Chloe quietly.

"I'm sorry." Jason wished he had something useful to say.

Roux came into the room. "Chloe? Ysanne thinks it's best if you go back to the west wing, with the others."

Chloe shot Jason a panicked look. "I'll take her," he said.

"You sure?" Roux asked.

Jason nodded.

—

He really didn't want to be in this part of the mansion. Although he'd never visited the west wing, never seen June Mayfield rabid and chained up here, it was the place where everything had started going wrong.

But the vampire kids knew none of this—to them, it was still just the guest wing of the house.

Of course, Gideon came with him. Jason wanted to take the vampire's hand, but Gideon didn't offer it, and Jason didn't ask. They quietly returned Chloe to her room, and three of the other vampire kids immediately took care of her. As bleak as today had been, that lifted Jason's spirits. At least the kids had each other.

That feeling didn't last.

"Fuck," he muttered, when they reached the short staircase that led out of the west wing. His chest felt heavy. "I hate that I can't *help* her."

"You just did," Gideon told him.

Jason slumped against the wall and buried his face in his hands. "Hardly. You saw the state of the poor kid."

"But that's not your fault." Gideon put his hand on Jason's shoulder. "You can't fix the whole world, however much you might want to. Don't put so much pressure on yourself."

Jason gave a long sigh.

Gideon was right.

If he put that much pressure on himself, he'd always end up disappointed.

"For what it's worth," Gideon said, "I love that you do try to save the world."

"Yeah, I'm a regular superhero," Jason muttered.

Gideon looked intently at him. "To some people, you are."

"Where's my cape then?"

A smile touched Gideon's lips. "I can get you a cape."

Jason managed a smile. "Edging into role-play territory, aren't we?"

Gideon's eyes heated, and Jason was suddenly very aware of him, the way Gideon was standing so close, his body almost touching Jason's. His lips were parted, and when Jason turned toward him, the hard shape of Gideon nudged his hip. "Maybe one day," Gideon said, his voice low in his throat.

Jason swallowed and saw Gideon's eyes follow the movement.

Gideon leaned in to kiss him, and Jason eagerly responded, sliding his hands around Gideon's waist. Gideon moved closer, pressing his body against Jason's.

"I like being able to do this," he whispered.

"Me too."

Gideon slid his hand through Jason's hair, pulling him close, and as their tongues brushed against each other, Jason thought he might combust from that alone. Gideon nipped his lower lip, and he felt the slight pressure of fangs.

Other people might have found that intimidating.

Jason loved it.

Fangs were *hot*.

Gideon pushed Jason against the wall, and everything faded away until it was only him and Gideon—

Someone cleared their throat.

Gideon's eyes flared open and he stepped back, pressing his lips together. Jason couldn't tell if he was amused or mortified.

Seamus stood at the foot of the stairs, a knowing twinkle in his eyes. "Sorry to interrupt."

Jason gestured in the direction of the hallway that led to the guest rooms. "We were just taking Chloe back."

"So I see," Seamus said. "Ysanne wants you downstairs. The police are on their way, and you'll both have to give statements."

"Right." Jason smoothed his clothes.

Seamus turned to lead the way, and Jason hurried after him and caught his wrist.

Seamus lifted a questioning eyebrow.

"What you just saw—me and Gideon—please don't tell anyone," Jason whispered.

Maybe his girls were right, and Ysanne had bigger things to worry about than whether a human and a vampire were dating, but maybe she'd still consider it a transgression.

Seamus made a zipping motion across his mouth. "My lips are sealed."

The police arrived quickly, arrested the intruders—those the vampires had captured, at least—and everyone gave statements, except for Nikki and Chloe, who had no legal guardians present.

Despite Nikki's protests, Ysanne instructed Seamus to contact Nikki's aunt so Diane could collect her.

Jason squeezed her small shoulder. "I'm really sorry that you can't stay. If I had my way, you'd be able to."

Nikki gave him a brief smile. "Yeah, I know. You're pretty awesome, Jason Grant." She lifted her chin as she met Ysanne's eyes. "I'm guessing since we've just had a major security breach, you won't want Diane waltzing up to your front door."

Ysanne's lips thinned. "It's not ideal, but I have little choice."

"I could meet her outside," Nikki offered.

"Absolutely not. As long as you are under my roof, I consider you my responsibility."

"If I go outside, I won't *be* under your roof," Nikki pointed out.

That earned her a subtle glare. "Please don't waste my time with semantics," Ysanne said.

Nikki nodded, looking lost and deflated suddenly. It was one thing to know that she couldn't stay, but another to realize how little time she had left.

"Before I go, and before I talk to the police," she said, "there's something I need to do."

Ysanne and Jason waited.

Nikki touched her locket, stroking the curved edges with her thumb. "I need to see where my dad died."

Jason and Renie took Nikki to a hallway, not far from the staircase, and stood back, giving her some space.

"Here?" Nikki said.

Renie nodded, her eyes fixed on the patch of carpet where Dexter had taken his last breath. There was no blood left—at least none that Jason could see—but he wondered if Renie could still smell traces of it.

Nikki stared at the spot for the longest time, then her knees buckled.

Renie started forward but Jason held her back. *Don't*, he mouthed.

Nikki was fierce and vulnerable by turn, and Jason's instincts told him that, right now, the last thing she wanted was to be hugged. Some battles she needed to fight on her own.

A shudder ran through Nikki's body; she opened her mouth but all that came out was a soundless gasp.

"He died fighting?" she said, clutching her locket.

"Yes," Renie said.

"And you were with him?" Nikki looked back at her.

She nodded, her eyes bright with emotion. "I stayed with him until the end."

Nikki blinked rapidly. "Good. He wouldn't have wanted to be on his own."

"You were his last thought," Renie said.

Nikki's face blanched with sudden rage. "If he'd been home more often, we would have had more time together. But he was always working. He said it was so he could put aside money for me, so I could have whatever future I wanted, but this is the one future he didn't think about, isn't it? One without him. All that money, all the opportunities, it means nothing now."

"I'm sorry," Renie whispered, her voice hoarse with unshed tears.

"Not as sorry as me."

There was nothing Jason or Renie could say to that, because it was true.

"I know it's not much comfort, but I've put my number and Renie's into your phone. You can call either of us whenever you want," Jason said.

Nikki reached out a shaking hand to touch the carpet, then snatched it back. "I just want him back," she whispered, her face crumpling.

She folded over, hugging her waist, rocking back and forth.

This time when Renie moved forward, Jason didn't stop her.

But Nikki scrambled to her feet before Renie could hug her.

"Don't," she whispered, her eyes glassy. "Please, just . . . not right now."

"Okay." Renie took a couple of steps back.

Nikki turned fully to face them. "Will you always be here?"

"In this house?" Jason said.

He and Renie exchanged glances.

"Honey, I really don't know. No one knows what the future will—"

"No." Nikki impatiently cut him off, slashing the air with her hand. "I mean, will you always be here for me?" She didn't look at either of them now, as if she was afraid of what she'd see in their expressions.

"Always and forever," said Renie at once.

"What she said," Jason added.

This time, when Renie moved in for a hug, Nikki didn't pull away.

Diane Flynn arrived forty-five minutes later, and Ysanne showed her and Nikki to an empty feeding room so Nikki could make her statement to the police. Then it was time for her to leave. She flung her arms around Jason once more, while her aunt waited impatiently by the front door.

"We'll talk soon, yeah?" Jason said.

Nikki nodded, her cloud of curls tickling his chin.

"Let's go, Nikita," Diane said, reaching for her arm.

Nikki neatly dodged.

Seamus opened the front door and Nikki marched through it without another word, her small chin lifted in the air. All Diane could do was hurry after her.

"This sucks," Renie mumbled, shoving her hands in her pockets.

Jason pulled her close with one arm and kissed the top of her head.

"If everyone could gather in the dining hall, we have some things to discuss," said Ysanne quietly.

Jason was starting to wish he'd never have to set foot in that room again. But he went with Renie and Gideon, and the others who were already there, and took a seat at the table, bracing himself for whatever was coming now.

"Do we know who attacked Belle Morte?" Edmond asked. He reclined in his chair, graceful as a cat, but Jason didn't miss the coiled tension in his body.

"I'm sure none of you will be surprised to hear they're all from the group calling themselves People Before Vampires," Ysanne said.

"Bastards," Renie muttered.

"The group appear to have come with different priorities—some of them genuinely believe they came to rescue the children and return them to their families. Others intended to kill them, and potentially any other vampires they could," Ysanne continued.

"So even if they weren't responsible for that fire at the block of flats, they've still upped their game to become a very serious threat," Ludovic said. His voice was sharp and hard. Roux squeezed his hand.

"It appears so."

"What happens now?" Renie asked.

"The intruders will be dealt with according to human laws and human courts. But the children cannot stay here anymore. Clearly, it isn't safe for them," Ysanne said.

"Are you sure?" Renie asked.

"I cannot take the risk. They'll be better off in Houses that aren't the epicenter of this catastrophe."

"You're moving them to another Vampire House?" Jason said.

The kids didn't necessarily want to be here, but over the days they *had* been at Belle Morte, it had become familiar to them. They knew who lived here. They knew the layout of the mansion. Now Ysanne was proposing to ship them off to Houses that they didn't know, away from the city they'd been born and raised in.

"It's for the best. We brought them here to protect them, yet we almost failed in that," Ysanne replied. "I'll begin making arrangements with other Houses as soon as this meeting concludes."

She looked around the table, her eyes sharp. "For the time being, I must ask that no one else leaves the mansion, not even to go onto the grounds. Until we can repair the damage to the wall, it simply isn't safe."

Jason had expected extra security measures, but his heart still plummeted. Belle Morte was a huge building, and lack of privacy wasn't a problem, but it still felt like being locked in a cage.

"What exactly did they do to the wall, anyway?" Jason asked. It looked like a bomb had gone off, but he hadn't heard an explosion as such.

Ysanne's mouth hardened. "We're not entirely sure. Seamus's initial conclusion was that a vehicle of some sort must have been involved, but further examination has revealed no such evidence, nor was there any evidence of tools or explosive devices."

"So, what, someone knocked it down with their bare hands?" Renie muttered.

Ysanne didn't respond.

"Did anyone catch the bearded guy?" Jason asked. "The one who was at the *Daily Topic*?"

He received blank looks in return.

"No one else saw him?" Jason said. "He was the only one not wearing a balaclava."

"About this tall?" Edmond gestured with his hand. "Reddish beard."

"That's him."

"I saw him, but I didn't realize it was the same person."

"I think he might have been the ringleader," Jason said. "He keeps turning up everywhere."

Roux frowned. "Why was he the only one not wearing a balaclava?"

"Because I have no need to hide my face," said a voice behind her, and everyone at the table spun around.

The bearded man stood in the dining hall entryway, his arms loose at his sides, his jaw set.

Alarm bells clanged in Jason's head.

"How the fuck did you get in?" Renie exclaimed.

He gave her a dismissive look. "I never left."

"But we searched the mansion."

He just smiled.

He moved farther into the room, and the alarms in Jason's head got louder. Something about him felt wrong, dangerous, like Jason's most primal instincts were warning him to run from this threat.

Ysanne opened her mouth, and the guy fixed her with a cold look. "Don't bother calling for your guards. I had to kill the one by the front door, and I don't think you can afford to lose any more."

Ysanne's eyes blazed red. "Who are you?" she said, her voice like breaking ice.

The guy pulled out a chair at the end of the table and sat down, like he wasn't facing a room of furious vampires. "My name is Ivar Haldorsen."

"You have no right to be in my house."

He tilted his head, eyeing her with amusement. "You're welcome to try to remove me, but it might not go the way you think."

In his periphery, Jason saw Edmond tense, ready to leap up if Ysanne needed him. But a change had come over Ysanne's face. The Lady of Belle Morte stared back at Ivar, her lips slightly parted and her brow furrowed, and while it wasn't exactly *fear* Jason saw in her eyes, it was too close to that for comfort.

"Who are you?" she said again.

"I have lived so much longer than you, Ysanne Moreau," Ivar said, and his voice was lower than before, harsher. "I know more of this world than you ever will."

"You—" Ysanne got no further.

Ivar surged to his feet and slammed his fist on the table—*through* the table. Wood crunched, splinters flew, and absolute silence fell on the dining hall. There wasn't a single mark on Ivar's hand.

When he raised his eyes again, they burned blood red, and a chunk of ice dropped into Jason's stomach as he finally joined the dots.

"Now," Ivar said, taking his seat again as if nothing had happened. "We have a lot to talk about."

CHAPTER TWELVE

Gideon

The tension in the room was so thick that Gideon could practically feel it.

His instincts warned him that a threat was in his home, one that needed to be dealt with. Other instincts, deeper and older, warned him that Ivar Haldorsen was the most dangerous thing in this room, and they needed to tread very carefully.

Jason broke the silence. "You're a vampire," he said, sounding as stunned as Gideon felt.

"I am," Ivar said.

"You're the one who's been feeding on people."

Ivar gave a small shrug. "I have to eat."

"Where the hell have you been all this time?" Renie demanded.

"Anywhere I want."

"That's not an answer."

Ivar's eyes hardened, and the temperature in the room seemed to drop.

"Are you under the impression that I'm required to answer you?" he said.

Red sparked in Edmond's eyes.

"I think what Renie means is, why have you stayed hidden?" Jason said.

Ivar's eyes flicked to him. "I've lived a very long time, and I've seen far too much of humans already. When I first heard of Ysanne's plan to reveal our existence, I believed it would end in disaster. I kept to the shadows to watch it play out, and at first I was pleasantly surprised. After the initial shock, humans appeared to be far more welcoming of our kind than I'd thought." A sneer curled his lip. "And then they turned vampires into their playthings, and you not only let it happen, you *facilitated* it. We are among the greatest predators this world has ever known, and you let our prey turn us into their *pets*."

Ivar looked around the dining hall, his stare red and hard. "And look how they've now turned on us. We've shown our teeth, and humans don't like that, so, like rabid dogs, they want to put us down."

"That's not true," Jason said.

"No?" Ivar's gaze pinned him in place, and Gideon's hackles rose.

Jason swallowed, but didn't back down. "No. A lot of people are scared and confused, and that's making some of them lash out, but they don't all want vampires dead."

"That's very easy for a human boy with no experience of the real world to say." A growl crept into Ivar's voice. "You are a child, a single heartbeat in the span of existence. What do you know of suffering, of loss, of war? What have you seen of the darkest sides of human nature?"

Jason opened his mouth, but nothing came out.

"He might not, but we have." Gideon indicated the other vampires around the table.

Ivar turned to him. "Then you should know better."

"Better than what?"

"Better than to trust them," Ivar snarled.

"You supported what Etienne and Jemima wanted?" Renie asked.

Ivar snorted. "Their ambitions were laughable. They may have wanted to remind humans that vampires are more than pretty faces, but they still intended to preserve this system you built. They were still happy as puppets, dancing for human approval."

"Okay, I'm so confused right now." Jason held up both hands. "You seem to hate humans, but you were at a protest *against* vampires. When you came to the *Daily Topic*, you didn't sound like vampires' biggest fan either."

"I was honest about my motivations in attending that protest. I did want to see what it was all about," Ivar said.

"And?"

"I realized that humans are the same mindless, savage animals they've always been."

"You were human once," Jason said quietly.

Gideon tensed, not knowing how Ivar would react.

But Ivar didn't acknowledge Jason's words.

"Why did you come to Belle Morte with that gang today?" Roux asked.

"To see how you'd react. To see if you'd defend yourselves." Ivar's lip curled again, this time showing a gleaming hint of fang. "I'm more than a little disappointed. Those men broke into your home, threatened your lives, and you let them walk away."

"Uh, they were *arrested*," Renie said.

"You should have torn them to pieces," Ivar said.

"Wouldn't that make *us* the mindless, savage animals?"

Ivar's face darkened. Edmond leaned forward, shielding Renie from the older vampire's cold stare.

"Why have you come forward now, after so long?" Roux asked, her soft voice diffusing the rising tension.

"Because it's clear that humans and vampires cannot peacefully coexist."

"We managed it for ten years," Edmond said.

Ivar gave him a withering look. "What you call peaceful coexistence, I call submission. You bowed to them and let them control you and look where it's got you. The novelty has worn off, and they don't want to play with you anymore."

"You're wrong about this," Jason said.

"Human nature doesn't change. I've seen over a thousand years of it, and humans are irredeemable," Ivar said.

"A thousand years." Jason faintly echoed Ivar's words.

Even Gideon was taken aback. Ysanne had always been the oldest vampire in Belle Morte—one of the oldest in the world, and even she was only around six hundred. At barely two hundred himself, Gideon couldn't fathom the things that Ivar must have seen.

Ivar turned his stare on Ysanne. She lifted her chin and met his eyes. "It was your decision to reveal us. Do you regret it?" he asked.

"No. In this modern world we could never have stayed hidden forever, not all of us," she replied.

Ivar tilted his head, eyeing her like prey. "Agnes always spoke highly of you. I wonder what she'd think if she could see what you've become."

Ysanne stiffened, her eyes flaring wide with shock, her fingers gripping the edge of the table.

"You knew Agnes?" she said.

Gideon glanced around the table, but only Edmond didn't look surprised. Clearly no one else knew who Agnes was or what she meant to Ysanne.

"A long time ago. She never spoke of me?" Ivar said.

Ysanne took a long moment to reply, emotions churning across her face. "Not by name, but I believe now that she did mention you. Her red-haired Viking."

"Holy fucking shit, you're a *Viking*?" Jason blurted.

Everyone stared at him.

"Sorry," he mumbled. "That's just really cool."

Ivar smiled a little. "It's been a long time since anyone called me that, but yes, it's how my people were once known."

Jason might be excited by the revelation, and Gideon himself might have been fascinated by it under different circumstances, but all he could think of was how much older and stronger Ivar was than them. How the hell could they stop him if things turned ugly?

"Why are you here now? What do you want?" Ludovic asked.

"I want to know what you're going to do about this growing human threat," Ivar replied.

For a few heartbeats, no one spoke.

"How do you mean?" Jason asked cautiously.

"The humans are proposing to strip you of your rights and evict you from your houses. Even you can't all have grown soft enough to allow that."

"Hold on, those aren't official proposals. That's just what *some* people have suggested," Jason said.

Ivar made a dismissive gesture with one pale hand. "Even if this hadn't happened, you couldn't have imagined that this gilded lifestyle would last forever. Humans are mercurial creatures, and sooner or later they'd have got bored with you."

"We're working on reforming the donor system to ensure a better and more stable future for everyone," Jason said, glancing at Ysanne.

Ivar chuckled, and it wasn't a nice sound. "Perhaps you are that soft, after all. Even as humans turn on you, you still wish to remain their pets."

"You have a very strange view of our lifestyle," Ysanne said.

That earned her another chuckle. "I know what we are. You seem to have forgotten."

"I think it's you who's forgotten. We've never been remorseless killers."

"You weren't born until hundreds of years after I became a vampire. What would you know of our nature?" Ivar said.

"I know enough," Ysanne replied.

The air felt suffocating again, as if the power coming from the two older vampires was forming a physical weight that pressed down on the table.

"I don't get it. Are you suggesting we should abandon the donor system?" Roux said.

Ivar smiled, showing off his fangs. "You believe humans should worship us as celebrities. I believe they should worship us as gods."

That wasn't an answer, but something warned Gideon not to point that out. There was a gleam in Ivar's eyes that he really didn't like, an edge of something barely controlled.

"And how do you plan to enforce that?" Ysanne asked.

"I haven't decided yet."

Ysanne flattened her palms on the tabletop. "It sounds as if you're suggesting some sort of war with the human world, and I should warn you, we would consider that, and you, a threat to our way of life. We've fought to protect ourselves before, and we will do so again, if necessary."

"You've never fought someone like me." Ivar showed his fangs again.

"Be that as it may, we won't cower from you or anyone else," Ysanne said crisply.

"If only you possessed that same spirit when it came to humans."

Ysanne rose smoothly to her feet. "I'll ask that you leave my house now. We don't have to be enemies, but I will not be threatened by you."

Ivar rose too. "Ysanne Moreau," he said, a mocking edge to his words. He moved so suddenly that in the blink of an eye he stood before her. "You've grown so used to people fearing you."

"I do not wish to inspire fear in my people," Ysanne said, and Gideon thought her eyes flicked to Renie.

Ivar smiled thinly, his fangs gleaming like knives. "I do," he said.

His hands were a pale flash through the air as he snapped Ysanne's neck.

CHAPTER THIRTEEN

Jason

Jason felt like his heart had stopped beating.

Ysanne crumpled to the floor like a broken doll, her blond hair fanning around her, and Jason wanted to run to her, but he couldn't move. He became aware of pressure on his knee, and he looked down to see Gideon's hand there, tightly squeezing. Gideon's face was rigid, his eyes shining red.

On the other side of the table, Edmond launched himself forward, only to be pulled back by Ludovic and Renie.

"Oh, stop looking at me like that," Ivar said. "If I wanted her dead, she would be."

A fragile flame of hope sparked in Jason's chest.

Ivar adjusted his sleeves at the wrist. "This conversation didn't go the way I'd hoped. Maybe next time it will."

He moved back with inhuman grace, flowing out of the room as quickly as he'd come, and no one followed him. Jason didn't know if it was because they knew it was pointless, or if everyone was frozen in shock.

Then Isabeau gave a soft cry and rushed to Ysanne's side. "We need blood," she cried.

Jason rolled up his sleeve, but Gideon put a hand on his shoulder and turned him around. "Get it from the kitchen," he ordered.

"But—"

"With an injury like that she might not be able to stop herself," Gideon said.

Jason didn't think Ysanne would hurt him, but there was no time to argue. He ran to the kitchen. When he came back, his arms brimming with blood pouches, someone had carefully arranged Ysanne's head so she was looking up at the ceiling.

Jason tore open a pouch, his hands trembling so much that he spilled half its contents. "Fuck, sorry," he said.

Isabeau took the pouch, and Jason opened another, this time without spilling any. Isabeau bent over Ysanne, her thick chestnut curls spilling around her shoulders, blocking Jason's view. When she reached back behind her, Jason placed another pouch into her hand, then opened a fourth, ready for when she needed it.

The dining hall was deathly quiet; Jason's breathing seemed too loud. He'd never been so aware that he was the only person here who needed to breathe.

After another pouch and what felt like a fucking eternity, Ysanne made a soft noise and, with Isabeau's help, sat up.

"I think we may be in trouble," she said.

Jason almost laughed, both from relief and because only Ysanne could be so matter-of-fact after having her neck literally broken.

Ysanne braced one hand on Isabeau's knee as she slowly climbed to her feet, and a look passed between the two vampires, full of emotion but completely unreadable. At least to Jason.

Ysanne smoothed her dress and flicked a few strands of hair over her shoulder as if nothing had happened, but her mouth was a bloodless line, and she blinked more than normal. Ivar's attack had shaken her, whether she wanted to admit it or not.

"I'll have to contact the other Houses in Europe and inform them what's going on," Ysanne said.

"And ask them for help," Edmond put in.

Ysanne glanced at him, but she didn't disagree.

"Arrangements must also be made for the children. Clearly, they can't stay here," she said.

Chloe's face flashed into Jason's head, her fragility, her tearstained exhaustion. "Let me go with them," he said impulsively.

Gideon shot him a startled look.

"Not permanently," Jason added. "Just while they get settled."

"They'll all go to different Houses," Ysanne reminded him. She no longer leaned on Isabeau for support, and Jason wasn't sure, but he thought Isabeau had taken a step back, deliberately putting space between herself and Ysanne.

"Then at least let me go with Chloe. I really think she needs it," Jason said.

Ysanne gave him a short nod.

Gideon's hand slid into Jason's. "If you're going, so am I," he murmured.

Jason squeezed his hand.

Gideon

Ysanne had initially planned to send the children to different Houses across the UK that same day, but caution stayed her hand. If Ivar or anyone from the earlier attack was still watching Belle Morte, it was better that they didn't know the children were leaving.

After another twenty-four hours had passed, Ysanne decided that the dust had settled enough for them to begin the move, and nine vampire children gathered up the meager belongings that had been dropped off by their families when it became clear they couldn't come home any time soon and were divided among a series of black Belle Morte vehicles, to be ferried across the country.

No one knew when they could come back to Winchester.

Chloe was headed for Lamia, which meant Jason and Gideon were too.

Police had cleared everyone from the gates—protestors, supporters, and press alike—and though the silence should have been welcome, Gideon found it a little unnerving. He certainly didn't *miss* the noise, but everything seemed so quiet now, as if the house was holding its breath. It was as if now, without all those voices on the outside, he was aware how many voices *in*side had been silenced.

When Chloe approached the car that would take her away, Jason and Gideon flanking her, she stopped and grabbed Jason's hand. He winced.

"Honey? Not so hard," he said.

Chloe dropped his hand like it was red hot.

Gideon felt for the girl.

He'd been where she was now.

Some vampires relished their strength and healing ability, but few did immediately. Most vampires struggled in those early weeks, overwhelmed by the power they now wielded. Humans were so fragile, and they didn't realize it until they became vampires.

Chloe had forgotten how strong she was. A simple thing like holding someone's hand was potentially dangerous—if she wanted to, Chloe could have crushed every bone in Jason's hand. It was no surprise that some vampires grew to enjoy this kind of power, but before the enjoyment came the fear. Vampires had to learn to be careful around humans, learn to control their strength, and that wasn't always easy. It took time.

Chloe wrapped her arms around herself. She seemed so much younger than fourteen. "I'm scared," she whispered.

"We're right here with you, and we won't let anything happen," Jason said.

Chloe nodded, but her expression was desolate. She climbed into the car.

Jason was about to follow her, but Gideon suddenly pulled him back and kissed him. He stumbled, catching Gideon's shoulders for support, but his kiss didn't falter.

"Take me by surprise, why don't you?" he said, but a little sparkle was back in his eyes.

"I like surprising you," Gideon said.

"I've noticed."

The bright moon highlighted strands of Jason's hair and played along the edge of his jaw, and Gideon wanted to kiss everywhere the light touched.

Jason *was* his light.

Gideon had never realized how gray his world was until Jason came along and broke through the clouds.

He'd been so afraid of getting close to someone that he'd locked his heart away, and, before Gideon even realized it was happening, Jason had unlocked that door.

It shouldn't be possible to fall for someone this fast, but Gideon couldn't pretend it wasn't happening.

He *was* falling, hard and fast, and he had no idea what that meant, or if Jason felt the same way. He didn't dare ask.

Lamia was in Bristol, a little over ninety miles from Winchester, and even with the traffic they ran into, it only took a couple of hours to get there.

It felt like much longer.

Chloe stayed as close to Jason as her seat belt would allow, and though Gideon didn't mind letting the girl hog Jason's attention, it gnawed at him that this was necessary.

They'd brought Chloe and the others to Belle Morte because they'd thought the children would be safe there. Now they had to send them away.

Nobody spoke much; what was there to say?

When they arrived outside the gates of Lamia, two women were waiting for them. Gideon recognized the tall woman with the dark hair cut in a severe bob—Kara Braun, a German vampire who'd come over to England around fifty years ago if memory served correctly. Ysanne had mentioned that Kara was currently acting as Lady of the House, though no permanent appointments had been made. Choosing a new Council would require careful consideration, and with one crisis after another hitting the vampire world, neither Ysanne nor Caoimhe had time to address the issue.

Gideon didn't recognize the solid woman standing with Kara, but based on her uniform, he assumed she was Lamia's head of security.

The gates swung open, admitting the car. They parked on the wide, paved driveway and climbed out as Kara strode forward. She shook Gideon's hand first, then Jason's, with brisk professionalism. She didn't quite seem to know what to make of Chloe and the other two children who'd come from Belle Morte.

"Follow me," she said, turning.

Like all the vampire houses, Lamia was beautiful, all weathered gray stone, the darker slate roof punctuated by chimney stacks. The driveway led up to the house, interrupted only by a circular stone fountain. Three wide, shallow steps swept up to the front door, the grayness of the stone broken up by potted plants.

As with Belle Morte, the name of the House was spelled out on a stone bas-relief above the door.

Kara led them into a large, marble-floored foyer and up a curving staircase of wrought iron. Gideon had never been inside Lamia, and under different circumstances he might have liked to look around.

"The children will stay in the rooms that previously belonged to our donors," Kara informed them, glancing back.

Unlike Belle Morte, whose separate wings were accessed via one main staircase, Lamia's donor wing appeared to be completely separate from anywhere else in the house. Kara opened the first door on the left and ushered them inside.

The room was done all in cream, from the carpet to the subtle pattern of roses on the walls to the corniced ceiling overhead. A double bed dominated the middle of the space, and to the left of it was a white marble fireplace topped with a gilt-framed mirror.

"This is great," Jason said with false cheer, looking around.

Chloe took a few steps forward. Her red hair seemed even brighter against all that cream. "I don't want to be on my own," she whispered.

Jason crouched in front of her, both hands on her shoulders.

"You're not alone. You've got Lindsay and Leonard," he said, glancing at the other children standing silently nearby. "You'll be safe here."

Lindsay walked over and put an arm around Chloe. "I'll take care of her," she said.

He smiled, but it was shadowed with sadness. "I know you will." He straightened up, one hand still on Chloe's shoulder. "This is only temporary," he reminded her.

He didn't say anything about bringing her home when this was all over, because Belle Morte *wasn't* home.

Gideon wasn't sure if anywhere was really home for these children anymore.

"Gideon and I are staying overnight, so we'll be right here if you need us," Jason said.

After the children were settled, Kara led Jason and Gideon farther down the hall and gestured at the two doors in front of them. "We put you next to each other," she said. "Sleep well."

"Thanks," Jason mumbled.

He opened the closest door, then shot Gideon a surprised look when Gideon followed him in.

The room looked much the same as the first, though accented with shades of palest gray. It was a warm, inviting room, but somehow it made Gideon uncomfortable. It wasn't Belle Morte. It wasn't home.

Jason made a beeline for the bed and flopped onto it face-first, sending cushions flying.

"I wish we didn't have to do this," he said.

Gideon edged closer. If he was braver, he'd climb onto the bed next to Jason. Maybe even stay the night. But that still felt like a step too far.

"You can't fix all problems, remember?" he said, gazing at the back of Jason's artfully tousled hair.

"I know, but I really wish I could fix *this* one." Jason rolled over. "But I have no idea how anyone can. Even if we can stop Ivar, and that's a fucking big if, what then? The kids come back to Belle Morte?"

"They can't stay here permanently. Their families are all back in Winchester," Gideon said.

"But they can't go home," Jason said. "Even if regular houses were vampire-proofed, there's no system for feeding them. Are donors supposed to go to their houses? Are we supposed to arrange deliveries of bagged blood? Would it even be safe for them? The groups who see vampires as a threat and are willing to act against them will probably always exist now. They're not much threat to older vampires, but the kids are an easier target. So are their families."

He covered his face and groaned.

Gently, Gideon pulled his hands away. "Stop panicking when we don't know what's going to happen."

"I'm not panicking. I'm . . . *fretting*," Jason replied. "And it's completely justified. Are you sure this has never happened before?"

"Vampire children?" Gideon shook his head. "Not that I know of. It's hard enough for an adult to adjust to being a vampire, but a child? There's a reason we don't ever turn them."

"I want to fight for a better future for them, but *what* future?" Jason said. "I know you'll never get older, either, but can you imagine being forever stuck at their age? Even if they live for hundreds of years, in the eyes of the law they'll always be kids. They can't go back to school or go to college, university, or get a job, which means kissing goodbye to any dreams or aspirations they might have had. How do you think they'll handle that?"

"I don't know," Gideon admitted, lowering his eyes. Jason bit his lip, and Gideon immediately wanted to kiss the spot.

"Can I ask you something?" he said.

Jason smiled. "You just did."

Gideon didn't smile back, and Jason straightened as he realized Gideon was serious.

"What's wrong?" he said.

Gideon wrestled with the question that was burning a hole in his tongue. Maybe it was a bad time to ask, but he'd started now.

"Do you ever think about children? I mean, do you want them?"

Even if things eventually stabilized, Gideon could never offer Jason *normal*, but what if that was what Jason wanted?

Jason frowned. "Where's this coming from?"

Gideon lifted one shoulder in a shrug. "When I was human, the thought of them filled me with dread. It meant sleeping with a wife I didn't love and wouldn't want to touch in that way. After I became a vampire, I stopped thinking about it. Vampires can't have children, and I never considered it a great loss."

Jason sat up, his forehead scrunched in the most adorable way. "To be honest, Gid, I've never cared much about kids."

Gideon's heart fluttered at the nickname.

"I mean, I *like* them, but I also like giving them back to their parents when they become annoying," Jason went on. "I always imagined I'd be the fun uncle, rather than anyone's dad."

"What if you change your mind?" Gideon had to ask.

Jason's frown deepened.

"It's just, you're only nineteen," Gideon said.

There were only a couple of years between them, but Gideon had already lived lifetimes. Jason hadn't. It was easy for him to say he didn't want children at this young age, but that could change.

Then he wondered if he was looking too hard for problems that didn't exist, so it would give him an excuse not to get too close.

"I'll admit you have a point. I *don't* know how I'll feel in the future, but if you're worrying about this because you're a vampire and I'm a human, then stop. Plenty of humans don't want kids either. Right now, I'm not interested, and if that changes further down the line, we'll deal with it," Jason said.

Further down the line . . .

Gideon swallowed.

Without even realizing it, Jason had made it very clear that he thought they had a future, regardless of what happened to vampires. For the first time, that didn't make Gideon uneasy.

"Anyway, Ivar's the main problem we need to deal with. Everything else will have to wait," Jason said. His expression turned troubled, and he ran his hand along the edge of his jaw, wincing as he touched the swollen bruise. "What if we *can't* deal with him?"

"We've dealt with every other threat," Gideon reminded him.

"But none of them were a threat quite like this. Etienne and Jemima were cunning and clever, and Schofield was a slippery bastard, but none of them had Ivar's raw power. Have you ever met a vampire that old?"

"No," Gideon admitted.

Jason frowned. "Do you know who Agnes was? She seemed like a big deal to Ysanne."

Gideon shook his head. "I've never heard of her."

He joined Jason on the bed, and they lay quietly for a few minutes.

"Do you have any idea how we can stop Ivar?" Jason's voice was smaller than normal.

"We don't even really know what he wants yet," Gideon pointed out.

"No, but he's obviously not on our side, is he? Look what he did to Ysanne."

"I don't think he's on any *side*," Gideon said. "He did hurt her, but he was right in saying he could easily have killed her if he'd wanted to."

"So why didn't he?"

"Maybe he doesn't want to make complete enemies of us."

"But are we even any threat to him? He's got a good thousand years on most vampires in Belle Morte, and I can't imagine how much stronger that makes him," Jason said, gnawing his lip again.

"But he's still only one man. No vampire is completely invulnerable," Gideon said.

Jason's throat bobbed as he swallowed, and Gideon heard his heartbeat quicken. "But even if we beat him, it won't be without a cost, will it? We won't all walk away from a fight with a vampire like that."

It was something that Gideon had been trying not to think about, but Jason was right. They'd seen so much death lately. Gideon was tired of it.

He leaned over and placed a soft kiss on Jason's lips. "Somehow we'll find a way," he said.

Jason smiled, but it didn't reach his eyes, and Gideon wasn't surprised. He didn't believe his own words.

Shuffling down the bed a little, Jason nudged Gideon with his foot. "Distract me."

Mild panic flashed through Gideon, followed by intrigue. "How?" he asked.

"I don't know." Jason thought for a moment. "Tell me how you became a vampire."

Gideon's mind traveled back to that night, when his whole world had collapsed and been reshaped into something new. "I haven't thought about that in a long time."

"You don't have to tell me if you don't want to," Jason said, half sitting up. "We can talk about something else."

"No, it's all right." Gideon sat up, too, resting his hands on his knees, palms up. "The man Godric caught me with was called Nicholas. After I left home that final time, I went straight to him and told him what had happened, how trapped I felt, and how afraid I was of the future that was being forced on me. I told him I wanted to leave it all behind and be with him. He asked if I'd take an entirely new life if I could. I said yes."

"Nicholas was a vampire?" Jason guessed, his eyes widening.

Gideon nodded. "I wanted an escape, and he said he could give me that. I accepted his offer, even though I didn't know what I was agreeing to. He turned me that night."

"Wait, sorry, Nicholas didn't explain any of this to you?" Jason said, holding up a hand.

"No. Until he bit me, I'd never even heard of a vampire."

"Why the hell wouldn't he tell you?" Jason demanded.

"Maybe he thought I wouldn't believe him," Gideon said. "Or maybe he thought I'd say no if I knew what was really going on."

"Please tell me you can see how messed up that is. He tricked you into something that you didn't fully understand and couldn't properly agree to."

"When I first woke up as a vampire, I was furious with him," Gideon said. "But I still stayed."

Jason lay back on the bed. "Why?"

"Because I loved him, and I didn't know what else to do. I suddenly had a new life that I could never have imagined, and I didn't want to face it alone. Nicholas was the only other vampire I'd ever met, and I simply didn't know where I'd be without him."

"What happened to him?" Jason asked, tucking one arm behind his head. Muscles flexed in his arm, drawing Gideon's gaze.

"Over time I came to realize that I didn't *truly* love Nicholas. Or at least, I'd fallen *out* of love. I had forever to live, but I couldn't imagine spending it with him." Gideon lifted one shoulder in a shrug. "If I'd stayed with him, it wouldn't have been much different from being trapped in a relationship with Eleanor. He'd taught me how to survive as a vampire, but when I knew I was ready to face the world alone, I left him and never saw him again. I don't even think he's still alive, but if he is, he doesn't live in any House that I know of."

"I'm glad you never saw him again," Jason said.

Gideon smiled. "Is that jealousy I hear?"

"Actually, no. That relationship wasn't healthy, Gideon. He *lied* to you. He tricked you. You deserve better than that."

"I never forgot that he'd lied, but he'd also given me a new life, a *future*. Just as I couldn't forget the lies, I couldn't forget the good he'd done me."

Jason frowned. "Being a good boyfriend after lying to you shouldn't excuse the lies."

Gideon smiled sadly. "People are complicated. You'll never understand how difficult and lonely a vampire's life could be back then, and in some ways I can't blame Nicholas for being so desperate for companionship that he lied to someone he loved."

Jason lowered his eyes. "Fair point. Also, who's Eleanor?"

Gideon blinked. "Sorry?"

"You mentioned being trapped in a relationship with her?"

"Did I?" He hadn't realized her name had slipped out, but that was Jason's fault for making him so comfortable.

Jason nodded.

"I was engaged to her, when I was human. Our parents arranged the match, and though we were good friends, she didn't want to marry me any more than I wanted her. But I was afraid of what my father would do if I broke off the engagement," Gideon said.

Jason took his hand, rubbing his thumb along Gideon's knuckles.

"In the end, Eleanor eloped to Scotland with her secret lover. I never heard from her again, but I like to think they had a good life together," Gideon said.

"I'm glad you didn't have to go through with it," Jason said.

"Me too." Gideon gazed down at their entwined hands. "Has anyone ever pressured you to do something you didn't want to?"

"Not in any major way. Some people roll their eyes at the hairdresser thing, but no one's ever told me not to do it. Not to my face, anyway," Jason said.

"I don't understand."

"I studied hairdressing at college because I'd love to have my own salon one day."

"And some people don't like that?"

"It's not that they don't like it, as such. It's just . . ." Jason searched for words. Then he made dramatic jazz hands. "Gay hairdresser! Such a cliché! You know?"

Gideon frowned. "There's nothing wrong with your career."

"Not sure I can call it a career when I've never even worked at a salon, but I appreciate the sentiment," Jason said. "I'll never feel ashamed for doing what I love, and I love hair. The right cut can make anyone beautiful, and I love helping people find it. It's like creating art."

Gideon reached out and slid his fingers through Jason's hair, his fingertips gentle as they ghosted along Jason's scalp. Jason's breathing hitched.

"Perhaps you can practice on me sometime," Gideon suggested.

Jason's face lit up. "Um, yes, please."

Gideon tilted his head to one side. "Really?"

"Why not? You've got great hair, and I'd love to play with it." There was a heated note in his voice that suggested he wanted to play with more than just hair.

Gideon's hand was still in Jason's hair, their faces so close that Jason's breath warmed Gideon's face. Even without kissing, there was something incredibly intimate about the moment.

"Do you want to cut it?" Gideon wasn't sure how he felt about that. Contrary to what some people believed, vampire hair did grow, just very slowly. That was why most of them never experimented with haircuts—if it went wrong, it could take years to grow out.

Jason swallowed, licked his lips, and tried to meet Gideon's eyes, but his gaze kept dropping to Gideon's mouth. "Not if you don't want me to."

Gideon shook his head. "I like it the length it is." He gave Jason a mischievous smile. "Unless you think this isn't the right cut for me."

Jason stroked Gideon's cheek. "I said that the right cut can make anyone beautiful. You're already beautiful. Your hair doesn't need to change."

Gideon dropped his voice to a husky whisper. "But you'd still like to play with it?"

Jason had to visibly try twice to get words out. "Yes."

"Then let's do that."

It wasn't just that he thought it would be fun for Jason to practice on his hair, or that he was curious to see what he'd do.

It was that he couldn't shake the memory of Jason's hands gliding over his body, touching him with the gentleness and reverence he'd never thought he'd get.

Gideon wanted more, but he was too nervous to say that.

"Wait here," Jason said, and scrambled off the bed. He disappeared into the bathroom at the other end of the room, and through the half-closed door, Gideon heard rustling and faint banging.

"What are you doing?" he asked.

"Looking for the stuff I need," Jason called. A couple of minutes later, he emerged and looked around the room.

His eyes sparkled with excitement, and his hands were eager and expressive; Gideon felt he could have watched him forever. He didn't know what it was to be passionate about something like this. A padded chair sat in one corner; Jason carried it into the bathroom, then beckoned Gideon in.

He hesitated, still sitting on the bed. A flutter of nerves started in his stomach, before moving lower, and the strangeness of it made him pause.

Humans seemed to view vampires as sexually dominant creatures, always slick and confident, which, considering the image vampires projected, was no surprise.

Gideon was used to being the powerful, strong, handsome vampire that the country knew and loved. *Had* loved, anyway. He wasn't used to a human boy making him feel so young and unsure of himself.

Jason poked his head around the bathroom door. "Hurry up. I want to start playing."

Gideon went in.

Jason had positioned the chair in front of the basin. Various containers and bottles of products were lined up on one side of the basin, and two small towels were on the other. A hair dryer lay on top of the towels.

Whenever a vampire *did* want a cut, a hairdresser was discreetly hired to come to the mansion. The cut itself was always done as quickly as possible, and the hairdressers were never allowed to make conversation.

At the time, Gideon had been glad of that rule.

Now the perfunctory nature of it seemed cold, and he looked forward to Jason's style.

Jason patted the back of the chair. "Don't make me wrestle you into this, because I will."

Gideon sat down, and Jason draped a towel around his shoulders. He dislocated the showerhead, pulling the attachment over to the basin.

"Are you sure you know what you're doing?" Gideon teased.

It felt good to tease.

Jason clutched his chest in mock-horror. "How dare you! I styled Renie and Roux's hair for house events, and they always looked fantastic."

He gently tipped Gideon's head back over the basin. "I'm an artist," he said. "And tonight you're my canvas."

He turned on the shower, and warm water cascaded over Gideon's head, followed by the gentle touch of Jason's fingers. He heard the *snick* of an bottle opening, then Jason massaged shampoo through his hair, filling the room with the smell of citrus.

Gideon wasn't used to this.

Any hairdresser visiting a vampire house was expected to do their job as quickly as possible, which for Gideon meant a dry cut. He didn't like strangers getting too close, especially when he was in a vulnerable position.

But now he'd put himself in Jason's hands in a way that he hadn't done with anyone a very long time. The intimacy that Jason showed him, in so many ways that didn't involve sex, was new and beautiful.

Jason rinsed away the shampoo, then applied conditioner, before turning off the shower. He squeezed excess water from Gideon's hair, then lifted the towel from his shoulders and wrapped it around his head.

"I could get used to being pampered like this," Gideon remarked, standing up so Jason could shuffle the chair around to face the mirror. He sat back down.

Warm light came into Jason's eyes. "Oh, honey, you haven't been pampered yet."

The memory of Jason's hands running over his chest, gently learning the shape of him, coupled with the gleam in his eyes, the promise in his voice—Gideon shifted in his chair.

He tried to think about something else as Jason set to work, but it was impossible. Jason was beautiful. Even when he wasn't teasing, even when there was nothing even remotely sexual about the situation, Gideon couldn't take his eyes off him. Jason was completely engrossed in his work, engaging combs and sprays and bottles of things Gideon didn't recognize, and the combination of passion and concentration on his face made Gideon want to leap up and kiss him.

So many of the countless Vladdicts who'd passed through Belle Morte's doors had made him grind his fangs with frustration.

They didn't see vampires as people, or understand how hard their lives had been.

They simply saw pretty celebrities—mannequins, almost.

Vampires were things they looked up to and admired, but at the same time, vampires weren't quite real to them.

Gideon had never been comfortable with that.

Jason was a Vladdict—or at least he had been when he first came to Belle Morte—and maybe being a vampire was what had initially drawn him to Gideon, but he'd stayed for much more than that. He could see past the vampire to the man inside.

"There," Jason said, unmistakable pride in his voice. He stepped back from the chair.

Gideon had been so lost in his thoughts, and so busy watching Jason's face, that he hadn't focused on what Jason was actually doing, and he couldn't help a small sound of surprise as he saw himself in the mirror.

Jason hadn't done anything drastic, just arranged his hair in a way that looked both carefully styled and casually mussed, but it was different to how he normally looked, more modern, and for a moment Gideon felt like he was looking at a human version of himself.

"You okay?" Jason said.

Gideon couldn't reply. Seeing himself like this was like glimpsing a world in which he'd never become a vampire, in which he and Jason were just two ordinary people falling for each other, free from all the terrible things that had happened recently. The fact that if he hadn't become a vampire, he'd have died long before Jason was born didn't matter. The glimpse of a life that could never be cut him to the core.

"Gideon?" Jason sounded worried now. "Oh god, you hate it. I'll change it."

He reached for Gideon's hair, but Gideon ducked. "No, I love it. It just surprised me. You're good."

Jason grinned. "Did you doubt me?"

"No. But I didn't realize *how* good you were."

"Nothing like a firsthand demonstration," Jason said. His grin widened.

Gideon hooked his finger through the belt loop on Jason's jeans and pulled him closer. Jason eagerly pressed himself between Gideon's thighs and kissed him until Gideon's head spun from the sweet warmth of Jason's mouth.

But suddenly it was all too much, and Gideon broke the kiss, gently pushing Jason away.

"Sorry," he muttered.

Jason moved back a little more, smoothing his hair. "Hey, don't apologize. We'll move at whatever pace is comfortable for you."

"Have you ever had to move slowly before?"

"That doesn't matter." Jason took Gideon's hand and gave it a little tug. "I'm okay with this."

"I'm sure I'm not the first man you've been with, but . . ." Gideon trailed off, feeling monumentally awkward.

Jason took pity on him. "How many boyfriends have I had?"

Gideon lowered his eyes. "I shouldn't have asked."

"I don't mind."

"I was just curious, I suppose." Gideon frowned, searching for the words. "I haven't had many relationships, and most of them had to be kept secret. You're so much younger than me, but it feels like you've probably had more experience?"

Jason gasped and clutched his chest. "Are you slut-shaming me?"

"What?"

Jason laughed. "God, you're cute when you're confused. Come on."

He tugged Gideon's hand again, urging him out of the padded chair and back into the bedroom. He climbed onto the bed, leaning against the headboard. Gideon sat closer to the foot of the bed.

"Okay, previous boyfriends," Jason said, crossing his feet at the ankle. "I was thirteen when I had my first kiss, and it was bloody awful, to be honest. Neither of us knew what we were doing. It was all awkward tongues and banging teeth."

That brought a smile to Gideon's lips, and Jason mirrored it, his eyes warming.

"So obviously that doesn't count, but we tried again when we were fifteen. At the time it felt like a proper relationship, but it fizzled out after a month, so . . ." Jason shrugged.

"Since then I've had three boyfriends, a couple of one-night stands during college, and a handful of slightly drunken fumbles." Jason spread his arms. "And that's it. My entire sordid history."

He nudged Gideon with his foot. "How does it compare to yours? A couple of hundred years is plenty of time to put some notches in your bedpost."

Gideon smiled again. "My bedpost is surprisingly un-notched. Dating can be very difficult as a vampire, remember?"

Jason slowly nodded. "I was only nine when vampires revealed themselves, and I barely remember when you *weren't* public. It's easy to forget how hard your lives were for the centuries before."

"If vampires ever *are* allowed to turn humans, those humans would need to think very seriously about what they'd be giving up," Gideon said.

"That's why the application process should be slow and careful. I'd never approve of a system that allowed anyone to be turned just because they felt like it. Only the people who could prove this was really, truly in their best interests would be eligible," Jason said.

"They'd also have to understand they would, in a sense, be giving up their friends and families, because they'd outlive them all," said Gideon somberly.

"That happens to humans too," Jason pointed out.

"Children generally outlive their parents, yes, but when parents outlive their child, or friends or partners die young, it's usually due to accidents or illnesses. Becoming a vampire means you *know* you'll outlive the people you love. You'll also have to watch them grow old, while you never change. Your children, or your nieces and nephews, growing old and having children of their own, and then dying, and their children having children, growing old and dying, and the whole painful process going on and on. Most people can't comprehend how difficult that is."

"Did you have nieces or nephews?" Jason asked.

Gideon's chest filled with shadows. "I don't know," he said quietly. "Godric was courting a woman when I left—I think her name was

Dorothy—and he'd mentioned that she'd make a good wife, so I like to think they got married and had children." Gideon shook his head. "Not that it matters now. Any children they might have had are long dead too."

"But their descendants might not be. You could have living relatives, Gideon." Jason straightened, almost bouncing on the bed in excitement.

Gideon shook his head again. "Anything's possible, but I left that part of my life behind."

"Were you ever temped to check in with Godric? See how he was doing?"

Gideon was silent for a while, his heart aching with old grief. "I couldn't," he said at last, struggling with the words. "When he turned on me, it felt like he'd cut my heart out of my chest. I couldn't go back after that."

"I can't imagine the position you were in. The thought of never seeing my brother and sisters again—" Jason shuddered.

"Sometimes I told myself that it wasn't too late to track Godric down and repair what was broken, but I was never strong enough. I couldn't put myself in a position where he might hurt me again." Gideon swallowed, picking at the bedcovers. "I wish our last words hadn't been angry, but it's far too late to change now."

Jason leaned forward and took his hand, rubbing soothing circles with his thumb. "I'm sure he knew you loved him and forgave him, even if you never got a chance to tell him."

Gideon flinched. "I don't know if I ever *did* forgive him, though, even after all this time."

Jason was quiet, his face pensive.

"You think I should have made more effort to reconcile?" Gideon said.

"Not my place to say. I've never been in that situation," Jason replied.

"But you don't understand?"

"How could I? My family have always accepted and loved me, but Godric was your only rock in what was probably a very deep, cold ocean, and suddenly he took that rock away and left you to drown."

"You don't think I'm a bad person for not giving him another chance?" Gideon said.

"What?" Jason's eyes widened. "Of course not. You were a scared young man in a horrible situation, and the only person who'd ever supported you, the only person you thought had ever really loved you, had suddenly thrown you to the wolves. I don't see how anyone could blame you for running and not looking back."

Gideon said nothing, and Jason cupped his cheek with one hand.

"Hey," he said softly, and Gideon raised his eyes. "You're not a bad person. You're *not*. You're kind and compassionate and honest. You risked your life to save Roux, and I know you'd do the same for any of us. I'm so sorry that this happened, but it wasn't, in any way, your fault. No one can change what happened with your old family, but don't forget everyone you have in Belle Morte. We're your family now."

Jason

He'd half entertained a fantasy of sharing a room with Gideon now they were out of Belle Morte, especially after such a bonding moment, but his hopes were dashed when Gideon eventually left and went to his own room next door.

Still, the beds were comfy, and Gideon *had* helped distract him from the growing mountain of shit that threatened to rain down on them. He'd get a good night's sleep if nothing else.

The next morning, he was woken by a ringing phone. Bleary eyed, he fumbled, knocked it onto the floor, then stretched over the side of the bed to pick it up. Belle Morte's number flashed onscreen, and suddenly Jason was wide awake, his stomach knotting.

He and Gideon had only been gone overnight; what else could have gone wrong in that time?

"Hello?" he said.

"Hi!" Renie's voice was too cheerful; it sounded forced.

Jason sighed. "What's wrong?"

"Have you heard from Nikki?"

Jason sat up, his heart thumping. "No, why?"

Renie hesitated. "Her aunt contacted the mansion this morning. Apparently she's run away again."

"Fuck," Jason said.

"Yeah," Renie agreed.

"We haven't heard from her."

Renie made a frustrated noise. "Okay. I'll let you know if we hear anything."

She ended the call.

The phone dropped from Jason's hand, making a soft thud as it hit the bedcovers.

"Fuck," he said again, raking one hand through his hair.

He ran next door to Gideon's room. The vampire was still sleeping, one arm flung above his head on the pillow. Jason shook him, and Gideon jerked awake, red flaring in his eyes.

"It's okay, it's me," Jason said.

"What's wrong?" Gideon asked.

Jason told him.

Shadows gathered in Gideon's eyes.

"We have to find her," Jason cried.

Gideon caught his wrist. "There's nothing we can do."

Jason gaped at him, his heart pounding too fast. "What are you talking about? Nikki's *missing*."

"Jason." Gideon's voice was calm and firm. "How can we find her when we don't even know if she's still in Guildford?"

"Don't you think it's likely she's running back to Belle Morte?"

"Possibly, but we're not there, remember? We're in Bristol," Gideon said.

Jason's mouth hung open as he stared at the vampire. He *had* forgotten.

"If, when we get back, Nikki turns up at the mansion, we can decide what to do next," Gideon continued.

"But what if something happens to her? The groups attacking donors could go after her too," Jason said.

Nikki's involvement with saving Belle Morte from Etienne and Jemima wasn't public knowledge because she'd never told anyone about it, but enough people knew she'd organized the crowd who'd descended on Belle Morte to back Etienne and Jemima into a corner, and people had to know that her dad had been head of security too. If former donors were at risk, Nikki could be too.

Gideon took Jason's hand. "I know," he said, kissing his knuckles. "But there's still nothing we can do."

"You're right." Jason sighed. "It's just hard."

"It's hard because you care."

It was Jason's turn to kiss Gideon's knuckles.

"I still think we should head back to Winchester as soon as we can," he said.

Gideon didn't argue.

Gideon

The journey back passed in relative silence, but it wasn't the tense quiet from the night before when they'd been packed into a car with three scared vampire kids. This was the comfortable quiet of two people who didn't need to talk to fill the space.

As soon as they reached Winchester, Jason craned his neck to peer through the tinted windows, scanning each street that they passed. He didn't say anything, but Gideon knew he was looking for a small figure with a cloud of dark curls and a gold locket around her neck.

But there was nothing.

At one point, Jason received a text from Renie informing him that reinforcements had arrived from Vampire Houses overseas, and Caoimhe had traveled from Ireland to help with Ivar. The news seemed to lift Jason's spirits, though it didn't chase the shadows from his eyes.

When they arrived back at the house, Seamus was waiting outside.

His face was grave, and Gideon's chest tightened. Something was wrong.

Jason shot Gideon a panicked look, coming to the same conclusion, and Gideon gave him what he hoped was a reassuring smile.

"Gideon," Seamus said as soon as they climbed out of the car.

Jason clutched his hand tightly. "Whatever's going on, we'll get through it," he whispered.

Gideon tried to smile again but his face felt like it was frozen. Why was Seamus looking at him like that, his face both grave and pitying?

"What's going on?" he said.

"There's someone here to see you," Seamus said.

Gideon blinked, caught off guard.

"A visitor? For Gideon?" Jason sounded as surprised as Gideon felt.

"I think you should come inside," Seamus said.

They followed him into Belle Morte.

A man was waiting in the vestibule, his back to them. A dark suit covered broad shoulders, and the chandelier light gilded his neat blond hair.

Gideon frowned.

There was something about the way the man stood, something familiar . . .

The man turned around.

The world spun sideways. There was a dull roaring in Gideon's ears. His bones felt like they'd turned to water.

He was aware of Jason saying his name, but he couldn't speak.

And then his tongue started working again, but he could only manage one word.

"Godric?"

The blond man smiled, showing off his fangs. "Hello, little brother. It's been a long time."

CHAPTER FOURTEEN

Jason

What?
What?

Surely he'd misheard—

Gideon reeled, and Jason put both hands on his shoulders, steadying him. Gideon clutched Jason's shirtfront, his eyes fixed on Godric, his face bone white.

"I don't understand," Gideon said, and his voice sounded more lost than Jason had ever heard it.

He was almost overcome with the urge to leap in front of Gideon and shield him. Godric had badly hurt Gideon all those years ago, and Jason wouldn't let him do it again.

"Is there somewhere we can talk privately?" Godric asked.

His calmness made Jason furious. How could he be so fucking calm when Gideon was shattering into pieces?

"You can use my office if you need some privacy," said Ysanne from behind Godric, and Jason jumped. He'd been so focused on the brothers that he hadn't noticed her standing there.

"Thank you," Godric said, smiling graciously.

He looked like Gideon—they had the same eyes and hair, though Godric's was shorter, with no hint of curls, and he was at least ten years older—but he carried himself with a confidence Gideon had never had. That only made Jason angrier. Godric was one of the reasons Gideon had struggled with his confidence all these years. He had no right to stand here, all perfect and composed, as if nothing had ever happened, as if Gideon hadn't thought he was dead all these years.

"Follow me," Ysanne said.

Her eyes flicked toward Gideon, and that brief look was full of pity.

She led them to her office, leaving Seamus to get back to his duties, and even opened the door for them. "Take as much time as you need." She touched Gideon's arm before she walked away, the briefest brush of fingertips, but from Ysanne, it was practically a hug.

Godric indicated the open doorway. "Shall we?"

Gideon hadn't let go of Jason's hand, and as he moved toward the office, Jason went with him.

Until Godric placed a hand on his chest.

"My brother and I need some time alone," he said, and though his voice was kind, Jason felt the sudden urge to punch him.

Who the fuck did Godric think he was, to come in here after all this time and think he could shove Jason aside?

"Take your hands off him," Gideon said, low and deadly.

Godric immediately removed his hand.

"I merely thought—" he started.

"Jason's with me. Where I go, he goes," Gideon stated, still in that low voice.

Godric's congenial mask slipped, then he smiled again, a fixed one that didn't quite reach his eyes. He had faint laughter lines, Jason noticed, and it was a jarring sight on a vampire. Most of them were turned long before they'd had a chance to develop laughter lines.

It was like seeing the man Gideon might have grown into if he'd lived past twenty-one.

Gideon marched into the office, still holding Jason's hand so hard it was almost painful. Unlike with Chloe, Jason didn't ask him to ease up.

Gideon

Godric closed the door behind him and perched on one corner of Ysanne's polished black desk.

Gideon simply couldn't believe he was here—that he was *alive*.

As alive as a vampire could be, anyway.

He'd aged since Gideon had last seen him, but that was hardly surprising. He'd only been twenty-five when they'd had that last fight, the one that had torn a rift between them.

A rift that had never fully healed.

A rift that had opened again, larger than ever, now that Godric was here.

"So," Godric said, clasping his hands. "You're probably wondering why—and how—I'm here."

Gideon stared stonily back. "It had crossed my mind."

The world still felt like it was askew, as if the sheer force of shock had knocked it off its axis, but something else was building inside him now—pure, utter rage.

All these long years Gideon had thought his brother was dead. He'd grappled with the memories—both positive and negative—and he'd been eaten up with guilt and regret, anger and exhaustion, and the whole time Godric had actually been out there, a vampire too.

And Gideon had never known.

"How long have you been a vampire?" he said.

"Since I was thirty-five," Godric replied.

"How? *How* did this happen?"

He realized he was shaking, and he squeezed Jason's hand, trying to anchor himself.

"I suppose I should start from the beginning," Godric said. His confident mask faltered, and he looked at the floor, twisting his hands. "Do you remember the last time we spoke?"

Gideon wondered if it was Jason's presence that was making Godric so uncomfortable, or his own memories of that day.

"Do you think I could forget?" he said, his voice as sharp and bitter as the pain in his chest.

Godric pressed his lips together. "I suppose not."

Silence dominated the room. Gideon clung to Jason's hand with both of his. Jason was his rock—without Jason, he'd be swept away.

Godric rubbed the back of his neck. "That was the night you left."

"That was the night I realized I no longer had any reason to stay," Gideon countered.

Godric didn't dispute it. "I waited for you to come home. But you never did," he said.

That rage inside Gideon grew and grew, and finally he had to let go of Jason's hand or he'd hurt him. He clenched his hands instead, until they ached, but it was better than hurting Jason.

"How could I come home? I had *nothing* to come back to."

"You still had me," Godric offered, and Gideon's temper slipped free.

He kicked one of the chairs in front of the desk, sending it shooting across the room.

"No, I *didn't*. Everything I thought I knew about you, about us, had been a lie."

"I didn't see it that way," Godric said quietly.

"I did," Gideon snapped.

It felt like there was a hot, hard ball in his chest pushing against his rib cage, making him want to lash out. If he'd still been human, he'd have stopped breathing.

"I know we left things in a bad way, but I fully expected you to come home that night. When you didn't, I assumed you were getting drunk somewhere and you'd stumble home in the morning. Instead, you just disappeared."

"Did our father worry?" Gideon asked.

He had little love left for the man, but part of him still wanted to believe his father had cared about him, had missed him when he was gone.

Godric said nothing for another long moment, and that was all the answer Gideon needed.

"I looked for you, for months," Godric said. "I even delayed my wedding because I thought something awful must have happened to you."

Gideon let out a short laugh. "Well, I did die."

"After a while I stopped looking," Godric went on. "I didn't want to believe you'd died, so I told myself that you'd simply gone into the world to make your fortune. But I never gave up hope. Every day I found myself scanning the streets, hoping to see you. When Dorothy and I married, I hoped with everything I had that I'd see you in the church, but of course I didn't."

Something twisted hard in Gideon's chest.

He'd always assumed that Godric had married Dorothy and had had a family with her, but actually hearing it? That was harder than he'd expected.

"When Dorothy announced her first pregnancy, I hoped you'd somehow hear about it and come home. I hoped to see you at the christening. I hoped to see you when each of our children was born, and every time my hopes were dashed."

Gideon could have pointed out how badly Godric had dashed his own hopes, but what came out of his mouth was, "How many children did you have?"

"Four," Godric said, pride creeping around the edges of his mouth. Pride, tinged with sadness. "Elizabeth, Thomas, Matthew, and Beatrice."

Gideon knew without needing to be told that none of those children had been turned into vampires. They might have grown up and lived long, happy lives, but they were dead now, and dust in their graves.

And Godric was still here, remembering them.

Suddenly Gideon's throat felt like it was full of thorns.

He'd never met his nieces and nephews. Maybe it didn't make sense to care about people he'd never met, but his eyes burned with the loss of them, the loss of a life that might have been.

"I didn't think you'd want to see me if I came back," he said.

"Of course I would. You're my brother," Godric said.

The anger rushed back.

"That's right, your wretched younger brother who couldn't just fit in, who couldn't just marry a nice girl and have children like everyone else. Your brother, who blackened the family name by being born a certain way. What would you and Dorothy have done if I'd visited you and brought my lover, another man?"

Godric folded his lips into a hard line.

"Exactly. Your love has always been conditional, Godric, and I deserve better."

Out of the corner of his eye Gideon saw Jason smile. It was soft and warm and full of pride.

Godric said nothing.

"How did you become a vampire?" Jason asked.

Gideon wasn't sure Godric would reply, since he clearly wasn't happy about Jason being here. But Godric squared his shoulders. "There was a woman," he said, his voice hard. "Amelia."

"A vampire?" Jason guessed.

Godric gave a single curt nod. "I didn't know at first. She wasn't a local woman, she simply appeared in town one day. She was strange and distant, and she never fitted in."

Gideon narrowed his eyes.

"Amelia wanted me." Godric seemed faintly uncomfortable saying it. "But I was a happily married husband and father, and I didn't return her affections." He paused, his eyes flickering with anger and sadness. "She didn't take rejection well."

Suddenly Gideon realized where this was going, and it was not what he'd wished for his brother, despite the bad blood between them.

"When she understood that she couldn't have me in life, she made sure to have me in death." Godric's voice was flat and even, but there was so much anger there too. "Amelia turned me against my will."

Gideon didn't know what to say. He'd been angry with Nicholas for not being honest with him about the new life he was offering, but what had happened to Godric was far worse. His vampire life had been *forced* on him. Gideon wouldn't wish that on anyone.

"I'm sorry," Jason offered.

Godric nodded, his eyes fixed on the carpet.

"Did Dorothy ever know?" Gideon asked.

"No. How could I tell her? Staying with my family would have put them in danger. I had no choice but to leave."

Gideon struggled to absorb this. Ever since becoming a vampire he'd assumed that Godric had lived a happy, normal human life with a happy, normal human family. Never in his wildest dreams had he imagined this.

"I still provided for them anonymously, and made sure they never went without, but I could never go back to them." Now Godric met Gideon's eyes, and it struck him how similar their paths had become, though very different circumstances had led them there.

If he'd ever gone back to visit Godric, he'd have known that his brother had become a vampire. Maybe they could have spent all those decades together, healing the wounds they'd caused each other. Instead, they were almost strangers.

"What happened to them?" he asked.

"They lived long, fruitful lives. I watched over them until Dorothy died, and our children had children, and so on. I spent the years watching my descendants, until finally losing track of our bloodline sixty years ago when an only child emigrated and I couldn't follow him."

"What happened to Amelia?" said Jason quietly.

"She attracted the attention of the wrong people, and they cut off her head for it."

It sounded as though Godric couldn't care less, and Gideon couldn't blame him. Amelia had taken everything from Godric. He still carried around so much hurt and anger when it came to his brother, but he was glad that Amelia was dead.

"Where have you been all this time?" he asked.

"Like most vampires, I traveled a lot, but for the past forty years I've been in America," Godric said.

"Why?"

"Why not? I'd grown tired of Europe, and I no longer had any family to watch. The thing that had kept me going all that time had abruptly ended, and I didn't know what to do with myself."

How different things would have been if Godric and Gideon had each known the other's fate.

"Our last descendant emigrated via air travel, which I couldn't use, but crossing the ocean in a ship was a different matter. I decided to abandon my old life and start again on the other side of the world."

"And you've been there ever since," Jason said.

"Yes."

"In a Vampire House."

Godric's expression tightened. "For the last ten years, yes."

"Which House?" Gideon asked.

"Does it matter?"

"Humor me."

"I settled in Fallen Night, under the leadership of Joseph Miller. I thought about visiting you, many times, but—"

"Wait." Gideon cut him off, the blood hammering at his temples. "You knew I was here? You knew I was a vampire?"

Guilt flashed across Godric's face. "Yes."

"For how long?"

Now Godric couldn't meet his eyes again. "Since the Houses were first established. The United Kingdom was foremost in bringing vampires to the public eye, and Joseph kept close watch on the English and Irish Houses, and everyone inside them. In those early days, many Lords and Ladies were in constant contact with each other, via human staff, smoothing out various wrinkles in the donor system."

"Ten years." Gideon's chest ached. "For ten years you've known I was here, and you never said a word."

"I thought it was better this way. When I found out you'd been a vampire all this time . . ." He shook his head. "I didn't know how to process it."

Gideon knew that feeling. It hurt.

"At first I was determined to travel to the UK to find you. But I had no idea what to say after all this time."

"*Sorry* would have been a good start," Gideon snarled.

"Perhaps." Godric fiddled with the lapels of his suit. "The more I thought about it, the more I remembered our last fight, and the more I convinced myself that you wouldn't want to see me."

He wasn't entirely wrong about that. Gideon was so *angry.*

Godric helplessly spread his palms. "Eventually the months turned into years. I kept track of you as much as I could, though. I wanted to know you were safe and happy."

"Did Ysanne know about this?" Jason asked, his voice hard.

That hadn't even occurred to Gideon.

Surely she wouldn't have kept something like this from him. Then again, it wasn't her responsibility to share other people's secrets, and she'd kept things from them before, when she thought it was for the best.

"She didn't know," Godric said, and Gideon closed his eyes in relief. "Belle Morte was formed before any of the American Houses, so we knew who lived in each English House before you even knew who we were. Ysanne asked Joseph to furnish her with a list of all the vampires who'd be living in Fallen Night, the same as the Council was asking of all burgeoning Houses. That included me. But by then I knew you were here, and I didn't know how I felt about it. So I begged Joseph to give Ysanne a false name instead of my real one. Which he did."

"Ysanne'll be pissed when she finds out," Jason muttered.

"I told her everything as soon as I arrived. I believe she understood, she's given me permission to stay as long as necessary."

"Why did Joseph lie for you?" Jason asked.

"Because he understood my situation. He pitied me. Besides, do you think I'm the only vampire who's assumed a false name over the decades? As far as anyone aside from Joseph knew, I was Gordon Harrod, not Godric Hartwright. It's the name I chose, and the name I've lived under ever since."

"What changed? Why are you here now?" Gideon said.

"Belle Morte has been the center of so much trouble lately—"

"If that's what you were concerned about, you'd have been here after we reclaimed the House from Jemima and Etienne."

"I came because of the attention brought on by the rogue vampires," Godric said. "Belle Morte needs help. *You* need help. But that wasn't the only reason." He gazed at Gideon. "I saw you on that talk show. Your appearance wasn't only important in England—vampires in countries all over the world have been affected by what happened here. Suddenly I was reminded that, even though you're an adult and you've been a vampire longer than me, you're still my little brother. I hadn't realized how tangled up in this you were, and I suddenly felt that I needed to protect you."

"Protect me?" Gideon repeated, his head throbbing. "I needed your protection when I was human, but you weren't there for me. What makes you think I need it now?"

Godric's eyes flicked to Jason.

A horrible suspicion stirred inside Gideon, and he almost couldn't put it into words because he was afraid of the answer.

"Is this because of Jason?" he said.

Jason gave a little start.

Godric licked his lips, looking like he was carefully selecting his words. "Like many others, I've seen the footage of you running into that burning building. I saw Jason try to stop you, and I saw him use his own hands to put out your burning clothes. Am I wrong in thinking there's more than friendship between you?"

Gideon and Jason glanced at each other; too late, Gideon realized that was as much of an answer as anything.

"If you've kept track of me this last decade, you'll know I've never had a boyfriend while living in Belle Morte. It seems terribly coincidental that you only decide to visit once I have one," he said.

Jason smiled, soft and warm, and squeezed Gideon's hand.

"What exactly are you accusing me of?" Godric said, his voice carefully neutral.

"Coming to let me know disappointed you still are."

Godric said nothing, and Gideon's bones heated with rage. For an entire decade Godric had kept his existence hidden, and if he'd only broken that because he wanted to opine on this relationship, Gideon would drag his brother from the house and hurl him into the street.

"I won't lie to you, Gideon. I did assume that your interest in men was a phase, but if you think I've come to condemn your relationship with Jason, you're wrong."

"Good, because if you had, you'd have killed any chance you have of seeing me again," Gideon said.

"Seeing him on television—"

"His name is Jason," Gideon snapped.

"My apologies," Godric said, finally meeting Jason's eyes.

Jason nodded, his face expressionless.

"When I saw Jason on television, speaking in defense of vampires, I realized I'd been a coward. I told myself that you wouldn't want to see me, and perhaps I was afraid of the rejection, but I also realized that your life was moving forward, and I should be a part of it. Assuming you wanted me to be," Godric said.

Gideon took a long pause to digest that.

"I don't know," he said at last.

Godric nodded, his expression rigid.

"I don't think you realize how badly you hurt me," Gideon said. "I've carried that anger and hurt and that feeling of betrayal all this time, and I can't let that go just because you're here now. Just because you're sorry for what happened."

He paused then, because Godric actually hadn't apologized for that terrible day.

"*Are* you sorry?" he asked.

"I never meant to hurt you," Godric said.

It wasn't an answer, and it certainly didn't put Gideon's fears to rest, but he was too exhausted to press him now.

"I don't know if I'm ready to let you back into my life," he said. "I need time to think."

Taking Jason's hand, he walked out of the office.

They went to Jason's room, where they were unlikely to be disturbed.

"Are you okay?" Jason said.

"I have no idea," Gideon replied, slumping against the wall and scrubbing his hands over his face. "I can't believe this is happening." He closed his eyes, resting his head on the wall. "Tell me what to do."

"I wish I could." Jason leaned against his bed.

Everything Gideon had felt about his brother had been at a distance because he'd believed Godric was dead. But now . . . now it had all resurfaced.

"If he wants forgiveness, I don't know how to give it. Especially when I'm still not sure he's sorry."

"You think he has a problem with me?" Jason said.

"Not you, *us*."

Jason slowly nodded. "Maybe he's still struggling with the fact that his little brother is with another man."

"That's not something he should struggle with."

"Maybe not, but you've struggled with it yourself. I'm not defending Godric, but you were both raised a certain way, and maybe he's still adjusting, same as you had to."

There was truth in his words, but Gideon still had difficulty processing them.

Seeing Godric again had unleashed a chaos of emotion inside him, so twisted and tangled that he couldn't begin to sort out how he really felt.

"I remember when we were children," Gideon said. "Even though he was four years older than me, he was always willing to play toy soldiers or marbles, or whatever I wanted. I looked up to him. I wanted to *be* him when I grew up. I know that what happened between us was because people couldn't just be gay back then, and Godric reacted like most people would have done. But that didn't make his betrayal hurt any less."

"You're worried he'll hurt you again," Jason said.

Gideon swallowed. His throat ached, and his face felt like the skin was drawn too tight over the bones.

"It could happen, if I let him back in," he whispered.

"You're not alone this time. You've got me. You've got your friends. We're all here for you, whatever you decide."

"Last time, it felt like Godric smashed me into a million pieces."

Jason cupped Gideon's face, sliding his hands into Gideon's hair. "I won't let that happen this time," he said, his voice fierce.

Gideon stared back at him, at this beautiful man who, in the short time they'd been together, had made him feel brighter and more alive than anyone else ever had.

"What did I do to deserve you?" he whispered.

Jason grinned, and the sight of it ignited Gideon, made him feel like he was full of fire. But it was a good kind of fire.

"You just got lucky, I guess." Jason kissed the tip of Gideon's nose.

"Why have you been prepared to put up with so much for me?" Gideon asked.

"Well, you're smoking hot," Jason teased.

There was a strange feeling in Gideon's chest, something soft and warm and powerful, something he hadn't felt in so long. But he had no idea how to put it into words.

It seemed impossible that he could care this much about someone he'd known for such a short length of time, but if he'd still been human, Jason would have made his heart pound and his breath catch.

From the moment Gideon had laid eyes on him, he'd known Jason was special, though he couldn't have said exactly how or why. The more he got to know him, the more right he realized that first impression had been.

Suddenly words didn't seem necessary, not when Gideon could *show* him how much he cared.

Slowly, he dropped to his knees.

Jason

One moment Gideon was standing in front of him, his face conflicted; the next, he was sinking to his knees, his eyes storm-dark with emotion.

Jason's heart gave a huge thump in his chest.

"What are you doing?" he whispered.

In response, Gideon ran his hands up Jason's legs, squeezing his thighs.

Jason's breath hitched.

This had to be a dream.

It looked like Gideon was about to . . . but he couldn't be—they weren't at that stage yet.

"Gideon?" he said, a husky rasp.

Gideon still didn't answer. His hands traveled higher, to Jason's belt buckle, and Jason almost forgot how to breathe. This was really happening.

"This isn't too soon?" he said, his heart beating so hard it was almost painful.

Gideon looked up him, and the gleam of red in his eyes made Jason weak at the knees. "Does it look like it's too soon?" he said, and undid Jason's belt.

Jason grabbed the footboard with both hands, gazing down at Gideon as he slowly pulled down Jason's zipper and freed him.

He'd been in this position before, but he'd never seen anything as beautiful as Gideon on his knees, his eyes shining red as he touched Jason for the first time, his hand gently stroking up and down.

"Fuck," Jason said.

And then Gideon leaned in, closing his mouth around Jason, and Jason's whole body jerked.

"*Fuck.*"

The heat of Gideon's mouth was like magic. At first he was hesitant, looking up at Jason with a hint of question in his eyes, like he wasn't sure he was doing it well enough, but as Jason responded by groaning his name, he grew more confident.

Jason grabbed his head with one hand, his fingers tangling in the vampire's hair, and squeezed his eyes shut as sweet pressure built deep inside.

Before Gideon, he'd have confidently said he knew what good oral sex felt like. Now he couldn't remember anyone before Gideon. He couldn't remember anything ever feeling this good.

He was lost in sensation, drowning in it, and inside him a wave of pure pleasure was building higher and higher, and he couldn't get enough air in his lungs, and the wave was about to break . . .

"Gideon," he gasped. "I . . ."

At the slight pressure of Gideon's fangs, Jason saw stars. He came with a hoarse cry, but Gideon didn't pull back. He stayed on his knees, his mouth still gently working Jason until the scorching blast of pleasure faded and there were only delicious, pulsing aftershocks.

Jason opened his eyes.

He felt drunk, lightheaded and fuzzy. When he let go of the foot-board, his legs weren't strong enough to hold him, and he slid to the floor.

Gideon gazed back at him, his eyes still red.

"Holy shit," Jason breathed when he found his voice. "That was . . . *holy shit*. That was incredible."

A smile curved Gideon's lips, smug and bashful at the same time.

Jason reached for him, for the hard shape jutting beneath his trousers, but Gideon stopped him.

"No," he said.

"What?" Jason struggled to think straight.

"I want this to be a gift, something I've given to you."

"It is. Now I want to give you something back."

Gideon shook his head. "And you will, but not today. I wanted to do something just for you, and I don't want anything in return."

It wasn't just returning the favor—Jason *wanted* to make Gideon feel as good as he'd just done—but he also wouldn't push this. Gideon had come so far in such a short space of time, but if this was how he wanted things, Jason would respect that.

But he couldn't wait to make Gideon feel that good too.

Gideon had helped him forget for a little while, but Jason's glow soon faded, and reality rushed back.

Ivar was still out there.

Nikki was still missing.

Jason should be *doing* something instead of getting cozy with Gideon. He called Nikki, he texted, but the calls went unanswered and the texts unread.

But a couple of hours after he and Gideon returned to Belle Morte, notifications started flooding his phone, and he felt the now-familiar stirrings of dread. He almost didn't look; he couldn't handle much more bad news right now.

But he had to.

Several people had tagged him in a video, and he held his breath before clicking Play. Winchester Cathedral came into view, shaking slightly—whoever was filming had an unsteady hand. It was common to see tourists and locals milling about, sitting on the grassy areas around the cathedral, or with phones and cameras raised, gazing up at the soaring Gothic structure. But today no one was looking at the cathedral.

A young guy was hunched over nearby, clutching his neck, while other people gathered around him, several talking anxiously, though Jason couldn't hear what they were saying, others on their phones.

"He fucking *bit* me," the guy yelled.

"Where did he go?" someone said in the background.

The camera panned wildly around, and whoever was filming gasped as a figure slipped into view. He glanced briefly at the camera, and it was Jason's turn to gasp. He knew that red hair and beard, and those cold eyes.

Ivar stared at the camera a split second longer, then ran into the cathedral, people scattering to get out of his way.

Jason almost couldn't breathe. Ivar's lithe grace and speed reminded him of something, but he couldn't work it out. He watched the video again, and then it hit him. Ivar moved the way Gideon had when he ran into that burning building.

The way only a vampire could move.

One of the eyewitnesses at the time had said she'd seen a third figure go into that building before the fire started, but when no body had been found, they'd all assumed she'd been mistaken.

But what if she hadn't been?

What if *Ivar* had set that fire?

A vampire as old as him could have got in, started the blaze, then escaped without anyone seeing.

Was he about the do the same thing? To the *cathedral*?

Jason raced to find the others.

CHAPTER FIFTEEN

Gideon

"We have to stop him," Ludovic said.

Jason had run into him, Gideon, and Isabeau on the way to Ysanne's office, and he'd blurted everything out on the way.

Now they were crowded in the office, Jason showing them the video.

"How long since that was filmed?" Ysanne asked, her pale eyes fixed on the screen.

"About five minutes," Jason said.

His fingers flew over the screen, and Gideon had no idea what he was doing, but then he looked up and said, "I can't find any reports of a fire at the cathedral."

"But he still attacked someone," Ludovic said. "We can't risk it."

"He's right," Ysanne said, her voice heavy.

"No offence, but how are you planning to stop him? I've seen how strong that guy is," Jason said.

"Force of numbers," Ysanne replied. "Ludovic, round up the oldest vampires under this roof and bring them to the vestibule. I'll fetch Seamus and make transport arrangements."

"I'm coming with you," Gideon said.

He might not be one of the oldest vampires, but he was big, and he was strong, and he wasn't afraid of a fight.

Jason sidled closer to him, his face taut with worry. "This could be a trap. To do this in such a public place meant he knew we'd see it. He *wants* us to," he said.

"Agreed, but what choice do we have?" Ysanne said. "Even if human bystanders weren't at risk, we can't sit behind our walls and do nothing while another vampire runs wild."

Ludovic and Ysanne left the office, and Gideon turned to Jason.

"This is dangerous," Jason said.

"I'm still going," Gideon said.

Jason brushed his knuckles along Gideon's cheek. "I know. Just be careful, okay?"

Gideon kissed him. "I will."

Gideon had never learned to drive a modern car, and he knew he wasn't the only one, so he was surprised to learn that several of the vampires he'd shared a home with for the last decade *did* know how.

Benjamin, Fadime, and Phoebe could all drive, though Phoebe was one of Belle Morte's younger vampires, so Ysanne insisted on her staying behind. They couldn't leave the mansion undefended.

Ten vampires headed out to the cathedral, Benjamin and Fadime each driving one of Belle Morte's black cars—Ysanne hadn't let the surviving guards come either. They could do nothing against Ivar.

She'd also refused to allow Godric to come, though he'd offered.

As they approached the cathedral, Gideon, flanked by Edmond and Ludovic, had to remind himself not to charge in. In the car, Ysanne had warned them to approach the situation with absolute calmness. They had no idea what they were walking into, no idea what Ivar had planned for them, but it was imperative that the human bystanders thought that they had this under control.

But there was a hard knot in his chest.

If Ivar *had* started that fire, why?

What had he hoped to achieve?

What was he doing at the cathedral?

Murmurs broke out as the people around the cathedral realized they'd arrived, and dozens of phones shot up. Gideon marveled that, even with a potentially dangerous vampire on the loose, they were still more interested in filming everything than getting themselves to safety.

Edmond looked expectantly at Ysanne, waiting for her to issue a command. Ysanne studied the cathedral for a prolonged moment, her face hard.

"Fadime, Alexandra, check the perimeter of the building. It seems likely that he wants us inside, but it doesn't hurt to be cautious," she said.

The two women peeled off the main group, splitting up and heading around the cathedral in a pincer movement.

"Hugh, keep an eye on things out here," Ysanne instructed. "Make sure there are no nasty surprises hiding among the spectators. Everyone else with me. I'm sure some of you already know, but this is the longest medieval cathedral in the world, which means there are a lot of places Ivar could be hiding."

Gideon wished they'd had time to organize reinforcements from other Houses, but no one could have got here in time. Ivar probably knew that.

They headed to the cathedral, still moving quietly and calmly, as if nothing was wrong, though Gideon was sure he wasn't the only one who felt horribly on edge. Ivar could be anywhere inside, and he hadn't brought them here to talk.

But as he stepped into the ancient building, thoughts of Ivar briefly fled, and all he could do was stare. The soaring roof, the colossal stained-glass windows scattering light across the medieval tiled floor, the smell of candles, the sense of time and history that perhaps shouldn't have been so impressive to a vampire, but somehow still was.

Edmond moved to the welcome desk, where visitors purchased tickets, and talked quietly to the woman working there. Even though she looked like she was in her sixties, she batted her lashes at him like any other Vladdict.

He rejoined the others.

"She says Ivar did come in, but he bought a ticket like anyone else. She hasn't seen him since," he reported.

Ludovic frowned. "Why would he bother buying a ticket?"

"I'd have said it was because he was trying to blend in, but why would he do that?" Edmond said.

"Spread out. Find him," Ysanne ordered.

They split into pairs and fanned out through the chapel. Gideon and Isabeau moved side by side down the length of the nave, and Gideon tried to focus on their task instead of gazing in wonder around the cathedral, where the bones of ancient kings rested and the stones were older than any vampire walking through.

Except perhaps Ivar.

But they didn't find him.

Between them they searched every transept and chapel, the

choir and the presbytery, and the flooded crypt, where still water surrounded a dark statue. They questioned other visitors, none of whom seemed to realize that anything had happened outside, but as they hit dead end after dead end, a dark pit of unease opened in Gideon's stomach.

"Something's wrong," he said. "Why would Ivar bring us out here only to disappear?"

"Maybe we just haven't found him yet," Isabeau reasoned.

"We've looked everywhere."

"We thought we'd looked everywhere at Belle Morte, but somehow he was still there."

A faint alarm sounded in Gideon's head.

Jason's words from earlier came back to him, and suddenly he felt like he'd been plunged into ice water.

"My god," he breathed. "It *is* a trap. But not for us."

Isabeau's forehead furrowed before awful clarity slid across her face. "This is a diversion."

Gideon was already running, calling to the others as he went, his voice echoing around the cathedral.

"Ivar never planned to confront us here. He just wanted to get us away from the mansion. He's going to Belle Morte."

They'd emptied the mansion of their strongest vampires, leaving only a few behind, none of whom were strong enough to stand against Ivar.

Gideon's heart leaped into his throat, making him feel like he was choking on thorns.

Jason.

Jason

Belle Morte had never felt so empty. The atmosphere had changed once the donors left, but even though vampires didn't fill the space with the same noise as humans, it was obvious that so few of them were left in the house.

There was a heavy ball of dread in Jason's chest. No one knew what Ivar had planned, which meant the vampires of Belle Morte had no idea what they were walking into.

Gideon had no idea.

Jason had seen him fight and knew he could handle himself, but Ivar was unlike any vampire they'd faced before. None of them knew what he was capable of.

But whatever worry he felt about his boyfriend, Renie and Roux were feeling it a hundred times worse.

Jason was following them downstairs, racking his brain for a way to distract them, when his phone rang. It was an unfamiliar number, and normally he'd have rejected the call immediately, but some instinct made him pause.

"I'll catch up with you guys," he said.

"We'll be in the library," Roux said.

They continued down the stairs, while Jason answered the phone. "Hello?"

"Jason?"

"Nikki?" Jason gripped the banister with one hand and closed his eyes. "Thank god. Where are you?"

"It doesn't matter," Nikki said.

"Yes the hell it does," Jason said. "Tell me where you are, and I'll come get you."

"No. And I'm calling from a pay phone, so you won't be able to find me."

"Those still exist?" Jason blurted, then mentally kicked himself. Not the time.

Nikki laughed a little. "Here and there, yeah. Listen, I just wanted to let you know I'm safe, but I'm not going back to Guildford."

"You're in Winchester, then?" Jason said.

A pause.

"No," Nikki said, but Jason heard the lie in that single word.

It wouldn't help him find her, but at least he could narrow down her location to the city, which was better than nothing.

"Nikki—"

"I've got to go. I'll be fine, Jason, don't worry about me."

"No, wait—"

Nikki hung up.

"Shit," Jason breathed, staring at his phone.

Nikki had to know that he couldn't leave things there. She *had* to know that he'd have to call the police or Walsh—had do whatever he could to help them find her. Or maybe she *didn't* know that. She was a thirteen-year-old girl in a horrible situation, who probably wasn't thinking clearly.

Jason hurried the rest of the way down the staircase. Roux was good with situations like this. She'd know what to do.

When he reached the library, it was empty. Jason wandered up and down the length of the room and called their names a couple of times, but his girls weren't here. He frowned. He'd only been on the phone to Nikki for a couple of minutes; why hadn't Renie and Roux waited for him?

Jason walked back to the door. They couldn't have got far in that time—

He froze.

A few feet away, in front of a sofa, was a smear of red on the plush carpet.

Jason approached it.

It wasn't blood.

It couldn't be.

But even as Jason crouched in front of it, he knew. The blood was fresh and wet, and though there wasn't much of it, someone had been hurt here. Very recently.

Jason's stomach felt like it was climbing into his throat. His heart pounded against his ribs. There was a prickling feeling on the back of his neck, like insects crawling across his skin.

Slowly, he straightened up and turned.

Ivar stood behind him, his head slightly tilted, red sparking in his eyes.

"Oh," was all Jason managed to say.

Ivar regarded him. There was a couple of feet between them, and though he knew it wasn't enough, Jason still tried to dart past the vampire.

Ivar's hand shot out and grabbed Jason's jaw, holding him still. Jason could feel the sheer fucking *strength* in those pale fingers, and fear swamped his mind until he almost couldn't think. Ivar could crush his skull like an egg without even trying.

The library door opened, and Phoebe, a Belle Morte vampire Jason had fed once or twice, came into the room.

Letting Jason go, Ivar moved so fast he was almost a blur, lunging across the room and flinging Phoebe like a rag doll. She crashed into the bookshelves hard enough to splinter the wood. She fell to the floor, books raining down on her, and Ivar stalked over. He gripped a handful of her hair and slammed her head against the floor, once, twice, until she went limp.

Sick, dizzy adrenaline flooded Jason's body. He couldn't tell if Phoebe was dead, but even if she wasn't, she couldn't help him. He looked at the door, which suddenly seemed a million miles away.

"If you're wondering whether you're fast enough, you're not," Ivar said.

Jason swallowed, but he couldn't dislodge the lump in his throat.

"Where are Renie and Roux?" he said. "What have you done to them?"

Ivar tilted his head again, like an animal sizing up prey.

Tears stung Jason's eyes. "Have you killed them?" He almost couldn't get the words out.

Ivar didn't respond.

Jason tried to control his panicked thoughts. The smear of blood was small, and though that didn't mean it couldn't have come from a fatal, or even life-threatening injury, some instinct told him his girls were still alive. Or undead.

"What are you doing here? What do you *want*?" he said.

Maybe if he kept Ivar talking he could buy himself some time, hoping the others had realized the cathedral was a diversion and were on their way home.

"You know what I want," Ivar said.

"I don't, not really." Jason struggled to get his pounding heart under control, as if that mattered to the vampire who could hear every beat. "The fire at that apartment block in Shepherd's Bush—that was you, wasn't it?"

Ivar looked faintly amused. "How did you guess?"

"An eyewitness saw a third person enter the building shortly before the fire. Since that person never came out, and no body was found, I'm thinking vampire, and only someone as old as you could have got out without anyone seeing," Jason said.

"I do hope that's not your attempt at flattery."

"It's not, and I know vampires can tell when someone's lying. I'm just pointing out facts."

After a moment, Ivar nodded.

"You wanted Gideon to go into that building, didn't you?" Jason said.

"Why would I want that?" Ivar asked.

"I don't know, but you didn't start the fire for the fun of it."

Amusement crossed Ivar's face again. "How do you know? You don't know me."

"No, but you're not stupid, and you haven't come out of hiding after all these centuries to cause random chaos," Jason said. "When you came to Belle Morte before, you said you wanted to remind vampires of who they really were, but I can't work out what committing arson has to do with that."

"How do you think I knew you and Gideon would go to that building?" Ivar asked.

Jason tried to think.

How long had he kept the Viking talking?

How far away from Belle Morte was the cathedral?

"You couldn't have *known*," he said. "But after what Gideon said about helping people, you accurately guessed that if you created a life-or-death situation close to the studio, Gideon would see an opportunity to practice what he preached."

"Very good." Ivar sounded only a little patronizing.

Jason's mind raced. Gideon had never spoken publicly about his fear of fire, so Ivar couldn't possibly have known that. It must have been coincidence. After all, arson was quick to commit, and fires spread devastatingly fast.

"I still don't get it, though. You said you wanted the world to remember how dangerous vampires could be, but then you set Gideon up to rescue those people from a fire. That shows him as a good guy, not the killer you seem to think he can be," Jason said.

"He *can* be. All vampires can," Ivar said.

Jason couldn't exactly argue with that. Gideon himself had admitted how he'd once lost control and killed someone, and statistically, he was unlikely to be the only vampire in Belle Morte to have been in such a situation.

"But that's what you were trying to prove?" he said.

Ivar silently watched him. He seemed to be enjoying this.

A light bulb went off in Jason's head.

"You knew there was no way Gideon could get in and out of that building unscathed. You knew he'd be hurt. That's why you started such a big fire. You *wanted* him to be injured because you hoped he'd lose control and attack the people around him." He thought for a moment. "Or me."

"I'd rather hoped you," Ivar said.

"I'll try not to take that personally," Jason muttered.

Ivar laughed. "There would have been a vicious irony in it, no? You and Gideon appearing on national TV, preaching about vampires and humans living in harmony, and then Gideon turning on you in front of everyone. He wouldn't even have had to kill you for it to have an effect."

"But it didn't work."

"I must admit, Gideon had more control than I expected."

"Or you're just wrong about him."

The Viking's smile was cold, showing the dagger-sharp tips of his fangs.

Jason's eyes slid to Phoebe, still lying in a heap at the foot of the bookshelves.

"Your faith in him is admirable, if foolish," Ivar said.

Ivar took a step closer, and Jason forced himself to hold his ground. "Why are you here now?" he said.

Ivar gave another cold smile. "The horse's head."

Jason's heart was racing again. Throughout parts of their conversation, Ivar had seemed almost reasonable, but the way he was looking at Jason now, like a pure predator, made him remember exactly who he was alone with.

"I don't understand," he said.

"You're a smart boy. You'll figure it out," Ivar said.

Jason didn't see the blow coming. Something hit the side of this head, and the world went black before he even hit the floor.

CHAPTER SIXTEEN

Gideon

The first thing he saw was Belle Morte's front door, torn clean off its hinges and lying on the path outside. The gates were untouched, but no one came to let them in. Protestors still thronged the road outside, but for once they were more focused on what had happened to the mansion than on the vampires returning.

Edmond jumped out of the car and ran to unlock the gates. Several people tried talking to him but he brushed them off. Maybe later they'd have time to question the eyewitnesses, but now they needed to get inside.

They hadn't beaten Ivar here.

Gideon's veins felt like they'd frozen over. His heart was a chunk of ice.

For the first time, he really didn't want to go inside Belle Morte. He was too afraid of what they'd find.

Edmond opened the gates and the cars pulled through. Gideon climbed out, his feet faltering as he drew closer to that front door.

Ludovic shoved past him and ran into the house, shouting Roux's name.

Gideon stepped into Belle Morte.

The marble plinths that usually bracketed the doorway had been tipped over, their flower-filled bowls smashed on the floor. Burgundy fabric was pooled in heaps where the drapes at the window had been torn down, though at least the UV-blocking shades were still intact. The crystal-drop chandelier lay in the middle of the vestibule, the branches raised among a sea of broken glass.

Near the entryway to the left-hand parlor, a black-uniformed guard lay on his side, and Gideon's nostrils flared at the scent of fresh blood.

"Jason," he whispered.

Ludovic and Edmond raced upstairs, no doubt heading for their rooms in the north wing, where they obviously hoped Renie and Roux would be. Isabeau vanished down one of the hallways leading off from the vestibule, and a couple of seconds later, she shouted Gideon's name.

He ran.

Another fallen guard blocked his path, and though he felt a sharp stab of guilt, Gideon leaped over the man. Jason was his priority.

He found him lying outside the library, Isabeau crouched over him. A purple bruise was spreading across his right cheek, but he was conscious, blinking slowly as Isabeau untied the ropes around his hands and feet.

"Gid," he whispered. He tried to stand but his legs weren't steady enough, and he pitched forward. Gideon caught him, one hand instinctively cupping the back of Jason's head, holding him close.

Watching them, Isabeau managed a soft smile.

"What happened?" Gideon asked.

"You have to find Renie and Roux. He did something to them," Jason mumbled.

Gideon caught the scent of blood again—*Jason's* blood—and he felt something damp against his shirt. He looked down. There were small slashes running up both Jason's forearms, not deep enough to require medical treatment, but enough to still bleed.

A soft snarl slipped between Gideon's lips, and he lifted Jason's hand so he could get a better look at the injuries. Jason blinked, staring at them as if noticing them for the first time. Then he shook his head. "We have to find the girls."

Faint footsteps sounded from the staircase, and then Ludovic and Edmond rushed down the hallway.

"Did you find them?" Jason said.

"No." Edmond's voice was like ice, his fangs fully extended.

Jason grabbed Gideon's arm. "He'll want to hurt them. The quickest way to hurt new vampires is sunlight."

Horrified understanding dawned on Edmond's face. "They're outside," he said.

He tore down the hallway, Ludovic hot on his heels. Jason pulled out of Gideon's arms and ran after them, and Gideon followed.

They passed another unconscious guard—Gideon noticed that she had slashes on her arms, too, the same as Jason's—as well as the tangled, unconscious bodies of Deepika and Rebecca. It looked like they'd gone down protecting each other.

Gideon caught up with Edmond and Ludovic as they burst into the garden, Jason lagging behind.

Renie and Roux had been gagged and chained with silver to a pair of slender trees by the wall, close to the area that Ivar had torn down. Roux's eyes were closed, her head hanging on her chest, but Renie was conscious, fighting to break free. Her eyes widened when she saw them, desperate sounds falling from her gagged mouth.

Ivar had shredded the girls' clothes—not sexually, but in a way that exposed their skin to the sun, and though it was an overcast day, that made little difference to vampires as young as Renie and Roux. Raw red patches bloomed on their pale skin, and Renie's eyes burned red with fear and pain.

Edmond and Ludovic ran to them. Roux stirred as Ludovic ripped the chains apart with his hands, hissing as the silver burned his palms. He scooped her into his arms, Edmond doing the same with Renie, and they raced back to the house.

Gideon and Jason followed them.

Gideon felt wound tight, on edge, his blood racing. Was Ivar still here? Was he watching them even now?

Inside, they found that the fallen guards and vampires had been moved. Edmond and Ludovic made a beeline for the vestibule, no doubt intending to veer off to the kitchen, where the bagged blood was stored, but as they passed the staircase, Isabeau blocked their path.

"The blood's all gone," she said.

"*What?*" Edmond growled.

Isabeau ran her hand through her thick curls. Gideon couldn't remember the last time he'd seen her look so tired.

"It's gone. Ivar took it. Every drop."

"I can feed them," Jason blurted.

"Not after having been knocked unconscious," Gideon said.

Ludovic rounded on him. "They need blood."

Gideon stared the older vampire down. "We'll find another way."

"It's okay," Roux mumbled. She wriggled out of Ludovic's arms, and leaned against him, her palms wrapped around his biceps. "Neither of us want Jason to risk himself."

Renie nodded.

Jason started to protest, but Gideon shot him a stern look.

"We've gathered everyone in the library," Isabeau said.

Edmond and Ludovic exchanged wordless looks, and Edmond shook his head. "I'm taking Renie upstairs."

"Join us when you can," Isabeau said.

The library was a mess. One section of the bookshelves had caved in, as if something heavy had been thrown at it, and several others had been stripped of their books. Fadime was quietly moving around the room, separating the books that could be salvaged from the ones that had been torn apart.

"Shit." Jason sighed, looking around. "Looks like Ivar had fun."

Every sofa was occupied by either a guard or a vampire, some still unconscious, others in various stages of recovery. Ysanne moved among them, speaking quietly to her people.

"Who did we lose?" Gideon asked, dreading the answer.

"No one," Isabeau replied.

Gideon frowned, sure he'd misheard.

He looked around the room again. It looked as though Ivar had taken out everyone who'd been left in the mansion, and every guard bore the same cuts on their arms as Jason.

Why had Ivar done that?

"He broke in, trashed the place, and didn't kill anyone," Jason murmured, processing everything.

"He could have killed us all," said Phoebe, propped on one of the sofas. She sounded shaken, and Gideon wasn't surprised. Ivar had damn near cracked her skull, and there was no blood to heal her.

"But why didn't he?" he said.

"Because we got here in time," Edmond growled, coming back into the room with Ludovic. Blood speckled their clothes, and Gideon saw Jason wince, knowing it wasn't their own.

"How are they?" he asked.

"Resting. But they need blood," Ludovic said.

"I'll contact the other Houses and see what they can spare," Ysanne said.

"Assuming Ivar hasn't got to them too," Gideon muttered darkly.

Jason had lowered his head to study the cuts on his arms, picking at dried spots of blood, but now he looked up, frowning.

"The horse's head," he said.

"What?" Gideon moved closer to him.

"The horse's head," Jason repeated, as if Gideon should understand.

Gideon cast a worried look at Isabeau, who seemed just as mystified.

"Maybe you should sit down," he said, taking Jason's elbow and steering him to a sofa.

Jason pulled free. "That's what Ivar said to me. I didn't understand it at the time, but I think I do now." He looked around at the vampires and guards. "Hello? *The Godfather*?"

"If you have a point, please make it." Ysanne's voice was clipped.

"The scene in *The Godfather* where the Corleones put a horse's severed head in that guy's bed. That's what Ivar was doing. He was showing us what he was capable of, but he never intended to kill anyone. Not yet, anyway. It's a display of power. He was showing us that he can come and go from Belle Morte whenever he wants, and there's nothing we can do to stop him," Jason explained.

"Then why trick half of us into leaving the house first?" Gideon asked.

"Maybe even a vampire as old as Ivar doesn't want to take on the entire house," Jason mused. "Or maybe he just enjoyed playing with us. Who knows what a guy like that finds entertaining?"

Gideon grasped Jason's wrist and gently raised his arm. "Why would he do this?" he asked, indicating the lines of cuts.

Jason sighed. "He confirmed that he started that fire. He'd hoped that you'd get injured badly enough that you'd turn on me, or any other human close by, but obviously that didn't happen."

Gideon flinched. It *could* have happened.

"Ivar is convinced that vampires are primarily predators, and they need to start acting like it. He's trying to force you all to lose control. He's injured every vampire left in the house and taken the blood supply so you can't heal." Jason looked past Gideon to Edmond and Ludovic. "I don't think he ever intended to kill Renie and Roux."

"He chained them in the *sun*. With *silver*," Ludovic snapped.

Jason winced. "I know. But if he'd wanted them dead, he could have killed them a thousand ways before you got back to Belle Morte. He could have slaughtered us all. But he can't manipulate you if you're all dead." Jason held up both arms, showing the bloody marks. "He's done this to every human in the house, but all the wounds are shallow. He wants us to bleed around you, at a point when so many of you are weakened. He's hoping you'll turn on us."

"And maybe there's another facet to this," Isabeau said. "If he's hoping to manipulate us, then he still needs leverage, which means keeping people we care about alive."

Jason nodded. "Good point. At this stage, he's just showing us what he *can* do, flexing his muscles."

"What happens when his plan doesn't work?" Fadime asked. She glanced around the library. "I think I speak for us all when I say that we'll never turn on the humans in this house."

"Then Ivar ups his game and does something worse," Jason said bleakly.

"Unless we kill him first," Gideon said.

"If anyone has any suggestions about that, I'm all ears."

No one spoke.

"Who's Agnes?" Jason asked.

Ysanne stiffened. "Excuse me?"

"You and Ivar both know her, so I'm guessing she's a vampire. Is there any chance she knows something we don't? Some weakness he has?"

Ysanne's mouth was a tight line. "Agnes is the woman who turned me, and I can assure you, she's been dead for a very long time. She can't help us."

Seamus rose to his feet from a sofa farther into the room. His jaw was set, blood drying on the slashes on his arms. "First things first. I'll get a first aid kit and patch everyone up."

"I'll contact the other Houses and warn them to be on their guard, as well as ask them for spare blood," Ysanne said. Her expression hardened. "Though they can ill afford to spare it either."

"Maybe that's part of Ivar's plan too. Why bother attacking the other Houses when he can put pressure on their already limited blood supply?" Gideon said.

Another somber pause.

Ivar was slowly backing them into a corner, and still no one had a clue how to stop him.

Godric, standing at the back of the library nursing a bruised jaw, spoke up. "Perhaps the Houses are no longer safe. Ivar's already proven that he can come and go at will, so could we lessen his advantage by relocating? Somewhere he doesn't know about?"

A shard of suspicion slid between Gideon's ribs, and he took a couple of steps toward his brother.

"It's very coincidental that Ivar only showed up shortly before you did," he said.

Godric's eyes widened. "What?"

"Just an observation."

"It sounded more like an accusation." Godric sounded genuinely hurt, and Gideon faltered. "Do you really think I would do something like that?"

"I don't know. I don't know you anymore."

"Gid." Jason's soft voice cut through the confusion in Gideon's head. He blinked, focusing on his brother's wounded expression.

Isabeau touched Gideon's arm, her face sympathetic. "This has been a hard day for everyone, and emotions are clearly running high."

He heard the words she didn't say. *Don't say something you'll regret.*

"For now, let's focus on getting blood to those who need it most," Isabeau said. "Then we can discuss how to tackle Ivar."

As soon as she contacted them, all three Houses agreed to send as much as they could spare, though Nox and Midnight were much further away, and their supply would take hours to reach Belle Morte.

In the meantime, a small group of uninjured vampires headed out to hunt wild animals. It was nothing compared to human blood, but animal blood was better than nothing.

The crowd outside the gates had doubled in size, though it seemed they were mostly press this time, rather than protestors. Ysanne had calmly picked up the front door, but the hinges were destroyed, so all she could do for the time being was lean it against the wall. The open space allowed the voices of the press, their cacophony of barked questions, into the house.

When the blood eventually arrived, there was precious little of it, and since so much was needed to heal the various injuries that Ivar had inflicted, Belle Morte would quickly run out again.

That, Gideon wearily told himself, was a problem for another day.

He went to the south wing. Jason had disappeared an hour ago, mumbling about wanting a shower, while Gideon had stayed to help get everyone fed.

He knocked on Jason's door, and was greeted by a subdued "Come in."

Jason was just climbing off the bed when Gideon went in. His hair was damp, unstyled, and bandages covered his forearms. He grimaced a little, raising his arms.

"I know it seems like overkill, but I wanted to visit Renie and Roux," he said.

"How are they?" Gideon asked, closing the door.

"Physically they've healed up, but . . ." Jason trailed off, his blue eyes sad. "Roux was unconscious for most of it but Renie thought they were going to burn alive out there. She's pretty fucking shaken."

"I know the feeling," Gideon muttered. "When we realized the cathedral was a diversion, when we got back to Belle Morte and saw the front door torn off . . ." It was his turn to trail off. He couldn't find words to explain the terror he'd felt.

Jason slumped back onto the bed, burying his head in his hands.

"Fuck," he whispered.

Gideon moved closer. "It's all right. You're safe now."

Jason gave a wobbly laugh. "I wasn't worried about me. I was worried about my friends."

"*I* was worried about you," Gideon said.

Jason lifted his head. Tears gleamed in his eyes, and Gideon's heart twisted. "Really?" he said.

"More than I can describe." He brushed his fingers against Jason's cheek, catching a tear as it fell.

"This has been a shitty, shitty day," Jason said. He breathed out, trying to compose himself, but his eyes were still shiny. "Will you stay with me tonight?" he blurted. "I don't want to be alone."

It almost shouldn't have seemed like a big ask, especially considering what Gideon had already done for Jason that morning, but he still hesitated. It had been so long since someone had shared his bed; he almost couldn't imagine it now.

But the word *yes* automatically tumbled from his lips.

He couldn't imagine refusing Jason anything when he looked so vulnerable and teary-eyed, but as a relieved smile crossed Jason's face, Gideon realized it was more than that.

He *wanted* this, for himself as much as Jason.

Today he'd crossed lines with Jason that he'd thought would take much longer to even approach, and he had no regrets.

The memory of Jason standing above him, his eyes bright with desire, his whole body trembling, was imprinted on Gideon's brain, something he'd never get tired of mentally replaying.

Gideon touched his mouth, remembering the feel and taste of Jason on his tongue. He was looking forward to repeating that.

Hearing Jason cry his name, knowing that he was solely responsible for making Jason feel that good, turned him on in a way he hadn't felt for a long time.

That didn't mean anything would happen tonight.

Everything had moved much faster than Gideon had expected, but that didn't mean he was ready to abandon all caution.

Sharing someone's bed, even if it was for nothing more than sleeping, could still be extremely intimate, especially when the memory of this morning was still so fresh.

But he liked the thought of sharing a bed with Jason. He wanted to know what it was like to wake up with him, what it felt like to see him in the morning.

Gideon was starting to realize he wanted far more from this beautiful boy with his sparkling eyes and generous heart than he had ever imagined.

CHAPTER SEVENTEEN

Jason

He spent the next couple of hours fielding calls and texts from friends and family. Footage of the man Ivar had bitten, along with the Belle Morte vampires arriving at the cathedral, had been going viral even while Ivar was inside the mansion, methodically taking out everyone he found. No one gathered at the gates had known what was happening inside, but it hadn't taken long for photos and footage of the torn-off front door to go viral, too, and speculation was rampant.

Ysanne had assured everyone in the house that she would make a public statement, letting the world know what was going on, but she hadn't done it yet, and Jason had no idea what she'd say when she did.

Providing more details about the Ivar situation meant publicly admitting that he was still running wild and none of the other vampires had any idea how to stop him. But part of the current backlash against vampires was how they'd lied to people, and if vampires wanted to repair those social bonds, they needed to be honest.

Right now, it felt like they were damned if they did and damned if they didn't.

Was that what Ivar had wanted, or was this just playing in his favor?

People Before Vampires was trending across several platforms, but Jason didn't dare look any deeper into that. He'd seen enough ugliness for one day.

He felt useless, restless. He'd always known that being human meant he couldn't contribute in the same way as a vampire, but he couldn't stand just *sitting* in his room, unable to do anything.

He picked at his bandages, thinking about how much blood it had taken to heal the damage Ivar had caused, and how little there was left, and an idea struck him. Maybe there *was* something he could do to help.

He fetched his phone.

After tossing a pillow on the floor, Jason sat with his back against the side of the bed, resting his wrists on his knees as he held up his phone at face level. Taking a deep breath, he started recording.

"Hi, guys," he said, waving to the camera. "I'm sure some of you already know who I am, but for those of you who don't, my name is Jason Grant, and I'm currently the last donor in any UK Vampire House. Although I don't actually *donate* anymore. And that's why I'm making this video."

He paused for effect.

"After everything that happened with Etienne Banville and Jemima Sutton, all donors excluding me were sent home, but vampires still need blood to survive, so each House was provided with a supply of bagged blood. But after protestors attacked Belle Morte's deliveries, we were told we wouldn't get anymore. Hospitals and blood banks can't afford to send blood to vampires if it's just going to get destroyed by misguided protestors."

He hesitated, unsure whether he should mention Ivar. Probably not if Ysanne hadn't yet issued a statement.

"Basically, the situation in Belle Morte isn't great, guys. Even if I was an active donor, I can't feed everyone. I'm sure some of you are wondering why vampires can't just drink animal blood, and the older ones can, for a while. But they can't survive on it forever. And younger vampires like Renie Mayfield, Roux Hayes, and the nine kids Roger Schofield turned *need* human blood. None of them chose this, so even if you're mad at vampires in general, don't punish the youngest and most vulnerable. Please."

Jason ran his hand through his hair.

"I don't know what I'm hoping to achieve with this, except just letting people know how serious things are. If you've ever cared about vampires, please share this video. Help me spread the word, and maybe between us, we can come up with a solution."

He ended the video and sagged against the bed with a sigh.

Maybe this wouldn't make any difference, but at least he'd *tried*.

He avoided social media for the rest of the day. Maybe his video was getting a positive response, and maybe people were tearing it to shreds. Either way, he needed a break.

By the time evening came he'd managed to put everything to the back of his head and focus on the one thing he had to look forward to.

Spending the night with Gideon.

If only he wasn't so nervous.

"This is ridiculous," he told himself, staring down his reflection in the bathroom mirror. "He literally had your dick in his mouth earlier, and now you're nervous about sharing a bed with him? Come on."

The pep talk didn't help.

He hadn't told anyone else about tonight; it was something he wanted to keep between himself and Gideon for now. At the same time, he kind of wished he *had* told someone, because then they could have talked it over with him.

But with no help from his friends forthcoming, Jason turned to a little Dutch courage. He swiped a bottle of whiskey from the bar and took it to his room, swigging periodically as he cleaned and tidied the place.

Gideon had seen it all before, so making sure every speck of dust was banished was a bit silly, but tonight felt special, even if they did nothing but sleep. If nothing else, it was a brief reprieve from the chaos that had engulfed the vampire world.

In Jason's head, the memory of Gideon's mouth on him played in a constant loop, and three times he almost stopped for a cold shower.

A knock sounded at the door, and already Jason recognized it as Gideon's.

"Crap," he muttered, looking around the room.

Was everything okay?

No boxers or socks on the floor?

The only thing out of place was the whiskey, standing on the nightstand that had once been Renie's. Jason blinked, staring at it. He'd only meant to bolster his courage with a few sips, but the level in the bottle had dipped a lot lower than that.

"Crap," he repeated.

That fuzzy feeling in his chest wasn't just nerves.

Gideon knocked again and Jason hurried to fling the door open, almost tripping over his bed on the way.

"Hi," he said breathlessly, then winced as the door hit the wall.

Gideon looked curiously at him, and his nostrils flared slightly. "Whiskey?" he said.

Jason held up both hands. "Okay, I'm a little tipsy, but it was an accident, I swear. I was nervous."

"Nervous?" Gideon asked, walking into the room.

"Well, yeah. This is kind of a big deal."

Gideon closed the door and leaned against it, his expression inscrutable. He had one arm behind his back, like he was hiding something.

"Not because I think we're going to do anything," Jason hurried to add. "But just because—I don't know. I really like you and it makes me anxious sometimes. And now I'm babbling. I'll stop."

Abruptly he shut his mouth.

Stupid whiskey.

Gideon's lips twitched into a smile. "I don't mind that you've been drinking. In fact, I think it's adorable."

"No, it's not," Jason muttered, scuffing the carpet with one socked foot.

Gideon's smile grew, and there was a definite twinkle in his eyes. "Yes, it is."

"What if you'd turned up and I'd been falling-down drunk?" Jason asked.

"Then I'd have put you to bed, helped you deal with your hangover in the morning, and still thought it was adorable."

Well.

Okay, then.

"Are you hiding something?" Jason asked, curiously eyeing the arm that Gideon still had behind his back.

Gideon looked at the floor, his shoulders rigid with awkwardness, then brought out his arm to reveal a bunch of daffodils, obviously picked from the spring flowers that had braved the chill February weather in the grounds. As bouquets went, it was small and a bit sad—several stems were broken where Gideon had clutched them too hard—but they were the most beautiful flowers Jason had ever seen.

"You said that no one had ever bought you flowers," Gideon said, his voice a little gruff. "So, um . . ." He thrust them at Jason.

Some people dreamed of lilies or orchids, or huge arrangements of roses, but this floppy bunch of quickly picked daffodils was more perfect than anything.

"Thank you," Jason whispered, taking them.

There were no vases in the room, so he used the ceramic pot that normally held his toothbrush. The little yellow bouquet lifted his spirits more than words ever could.

He set it on the nightstand so eagerly that he knocked over the whiskey. Gideon caught it with one hand.

"Nice reflexes," Jason said.

Gideon smiled.

Jason took the bottle and jiggled it. "I wish I could be a good host and offer you some, but . . ." How to finish that without seeming insensitive? "Did you like drinking?" he said instead. "When you were human?"

"I could take it or leave it," Gideon replied.

"Do you miss it?"

"Not as much as food."

Intrigued now, Jason moved to his bed. He left the whiskey on the nightstand; he didn't need any more of that.

After a moment's hesitation, Gideon joined him.

"You still miss food then?" Jason said. "I suppose I thought vampires got used to not being able to eat."

"Most of the time we do. But I don't think any vampire can go their whole life without ever missing food."

Jason settled against the pillows, getting comfortable. "Did you have a favorite food?" he asked.

Gideon's face softened as he cast his mind back. "I miss bacon."

"Even *I* miss bacon, and it hasn't been that long since I had it," Jason said.

Literal lifetimes without bacon?

That was almost a fate worse than death.

"Mince pies," Gideon said, a faraway gleam in his eyes. "We always had them at Christmas, and I used to get so excited."

"I've never been that into mince pies," Jason said.

"What do you look forward to at Christmas?"

"I do love a gingerbread man," Jason admitted. "But you can get those all year now, so I don't think of them as a Christmas food anymore."

"I've never had one." Gideon sighed. "There are a lot of things I've never had."

"Is that difficult? Do you ever get bored of blood?"

"We don't have a choice. We'll die without it."

Jason gave him a little nudge. "That's not what I asked."

"I've never got tired of blood, and I don't know any vampires who have. It doesn't all taste the same."

"How does that work?" Jason asked, propping himself on one

elbow so he could look up at Gideon. "Is it to do with blood groups? Does A taste better than B?"

Gideon shook his head, and a blond curl fell across his forehead. Jason wanted to wrap it around his finger.

"It's difficult to explain. Sometimes it's down to individual taste, the same as with humans and their food. Some vampires think male blood tastes better than female, and vice versa. Some prefer the blood of blonds or brunets."

"Do *you* have a favorite type?" Jason asked.

Heat darkened Gideon's gray eyes. "I'm very partial to blond boys named Jason."

"Good to hear, because I'm very partial to blond vampires named Gideon."

A smile touched Gideon's lips. "What was it you called me that first night? A gorgeous piece, I believe?"

Color crept into Jason's cheeks. "You heard that?"

"I'm a vampire."

"Sometimes I forget you guys have crazy-good hearing. I'm not ashamed I said it, though. You *are* gorgeous."

Gideon toyed with Jason's fingers.

"You don't really think Godric had anything to do with this, do you?" Jason asked.

Gideon stiffened. But he didn't stop playing with Jason's fingers. "I considered Jemima a friend since before the formation of the Vampire Houses, and I'd never have thought she was capable of betraying us all. But I was wrong. I could easily be wrong again."

"Yeah, but—"

"Can we not talk about that now?" Gideon said.

"Sure." Jason snuggled against him. "But whatever happens, don't forget you'll always have everyone in this house. We're your family, and we all love you."

Gideon

Long after Jason had fallen asleep, Gideon lay awake, staring at the ceiling. Nothing about Jason had been as he'd expected. He'd mentioned Godric to previous boyfriends, but none of them had been as understanding. Even if they hadn't said it out loud, he'd seen the glimmer of judgment in their eyes. Not in Jason's. He might never have been in that situation, but he'd empathized with Gideon rather than condemning the choices he'd made.

He'd always carried a measure of guilt in his heart for how things had ended with Godric, but even if his brother had never returned, Gideon was sure that weight of guilt had eased, and that was down to Jason.

It wasn't just that he didn't judge either.

He'd said that the people of Belle Morte were Gideon's family now, and he was right. Everyone under this roof accepted him and cared about him.

They were more than friends now. They *were* his family. Or maybe they always had been, and he hadn't fully realized.

Most importantly, Jason was also a part of that family, and that was what kept Gideon's mind going around and around.

We're your family, and we all love you.

Jason had no idea how deeply his words had sunk in, and Gideon wasn't even sure Jason had noticed he'd used the *L* word.

But Gideon had noticed.

Jason hadn't used it in the sense that he was declaring his love for Gideon, but it had rocked him nonetheless.

It seemed impossible that he'd known Jason for such a short time, because everything about this felt so *right*. Before Jason he could never have imagined being this comfortable with someone this quickly.

He ghosted his fingertips along Jason's shoulder. Jason slept on his back, his face turned slightly away, the covers bunched around his waist. His chest was beautiful, all tanned skin and hard muscle, a faint dusting of blond hair between his pectorals. Gideon wanted to explore every muscle and every inch of skin, the way Jason had done for him. He wanted to know every secret of Jason's body.

His fingers moved from Jason's shoulder, trailing down the side of his chest. He stirred but didn't wake up. Gideon pressed his palm against Jason's warm skin, listening to the soft thump of his heart and the rhythm of his breathing.

He mumbled something in his sleep, and Gideon smiled.

He didn't believe in love at first sight. Lust at first sight, yes, but that was a very different thing. He'd wanted Jason from the moment Jason stepped through the doors of Belle Morte, all tousled blond hair and sparkling blue eyes, but he'd never imagined lying in a bed with him like this. He'd never imagined that he could feel this comfortable with someone he still barely knew.

This wasn't love.

But it was turning into something much more than lust.

Jason

He woke up with a heavy weight across his chest and looked down to see Gideon's arm draped there. He must have rolled over in the night.

Jason smiled.

Gideon looked adorable asleep, his face pressed against the pillow, his hair mussed, the muscles in his shoulders bunched.

His arm was almost too heavy lying across Jason's chest like that, but he refused to move it. He didn't know how often he'd get moments like this, so he wanted to enjoy it while it lasted.

Gideon shifted and cracked open an eye.

"Morning," Jason said, though he didn't have a clue what time it was.

Gideon gave him a sleepy smile, and Jason had to resist the urge to pounce on him.

The facade that vampires had always presented to the world was one of polished perfection. They were always groomed and made-up and stylishly dressed, and that was yet another reason why they'd always seemed like something more than human. They were always flawless.

Gideon first thing in the morning was still a beautiful sight, but it was also more *real* somehow. His hair was mussed on one side, flattened on the other where it had been squashed against the pillow, and his eyes were heavy lidded with sleep.

The intimacy of that moment, seeing the vulnerable person behind the vampire facade, made Jason's heart flutter.

Yeah, he could definitely get used to this.

Gideon rolled over, taking half the covers with him, and Jason's mouth went dry at the sight of his bare chest: ridges of muscles beneath smooth, pale skin, broad and hard and completely lickable. That was a sight he could never get bored of. Gideon stretched, and Jason couldn't help himself.

He leaned over and licked his nipple.

Gideon froze, midstretch.

Jason looked up at him, worried he'd gone too far, but there was no fear in Gideon's eyes, only desire.

Growing bolder, Jason licked his nipple again, pressing one hand to the play of muscles in his stomach. He wanted to go lower, but one step at a time.

Gideon slid his hand up Jason's arm, along his shoulder, into his hair.

"Is this okay?" Jason whispered, pressing kisses on his chest.

Gideon just nodded.

Jason leaned across him, aiming for his other nipple, and then Gideon grabbed him and pulled him on top, hard chest against hard chest.

Jason's heart felt like it was going to explode.

Under the covers, they both wore only thin pajama trousers, and Jason could feel the solidness of Gideon's muscular thighs, the edges of his hips, the shape of *everything*. He could feel exactly how much Gideon enjoyed having him here.

Maybe it was time to return that favor.

He sat up, intending to slide down the delicious length of his body, but Gideon moved first.

He reared up, his hands sliding along Jason's back, his mouth pressing against the curve between his neck and shoulder. His lips were gentle, but when Gideon kissed him again, Jason felt the scrape of fangs, and a shiver rolled through him.

"I want to bite you," Gideon whispered, his tongue flicking against Jason's skin.

Jason nodded, his throat too dry to speak.

Gideon licked his neck again, sending sensation skittering along his skin, and then he bit down.

Sparks danced in Jason's eyes and he clutched Gideon's shoulders, unable to hold back a little gasp.

The first time Gideon had bitten him had been sweet bliss, but this? This was a hundred times better. This time he was straddling Gideon, aware of every single part of him. One hand tangled in his hair, and the other clung to his shoulders. His hips rocked gently against Gideon's.

Gideon abruptly pulled back and Jason let out a little whimper of protest. Gideon cocked his head to one side, listening. A tiny bead of blood glistened on his lower lip.

"What's wrong?" Jason whispered.

Gideon gave him a small smile and licked away that bead of blood. "We're not alone."

"What?" Jason twisted around, scanning the room.

"Not here. Outside," Gideon said. "I can hear them."

Jason slid off his lap and went to the door.

Renie and Roux stood outside, whispering; they stopped as soon as the door opened.

"Um, hi." Renie waggled her fingers at him. Her eyes zeroed in on his neck, and a grin spread across her face.

Too late, Jason realized that Gideon hadn't sealed the bite. And Renie and Roux had probably heard what was going on.

His face heated.

"What's going on?" he said.

A smile like sunshine lit up Roux's face. "Look," she said and shoved her phone in Jason's face.

"'Fangs and Friends,'" he read aloud. "I don't understand, what is this?"

"It's a volunteer group set up to arrange blood donations for vampires," Roux explained.

Renie's eyes gleamed with excitement. "They've already got more than two hundred people signed up. Do you see what this means? People do still want to be donors."

Jason stared at the online page, his heart starting to thump. This was a ray of light breaking through a storm. "This is amazing."

Roux's expression dimmed slightly. "It is, but we need to be careful not to get too ahead of ourselves. These volunteers are helping us now because we're in a crisis, but they may not be this generous forever, not for free, anyway. That's why the donor system was set up the way it was—so the donors got something in return."

"Even if we don't get donors anymore, we can still pay for blood donations, can't we?" Renie said.

"Yes, but I don't know how much of the Houses' funding comes from magazines and fashion shoots and TV deals. I doubt any of them are jumping to fund us right now," Roux replied.

It occurred to Jason that all those magazine and TV deals were part of the mythology—that gilded, fairy-tale lifestyle that had put vampires on the pedestals he was now proposing to take them down from. Stripping away some of the glitz and gloss would make the vampires seem more real, more human, but it might also negatively affect their income.

Still, he wasn't sure they had much choice. Things had changed too much for it all to just go back to how it was before.

"The Houses must have other sources of income, otherwise who'd still be paying the guards, providing food, and covering the bills?" Jason pointed out. "For now, let's just enjoy this victory."

"There's something else," Renie said. "The people at the gates have doubled, but now most of them are here to *support* us. Maybe the tide's turning at last."

From the south wing, Jason couldn't hear anything outside, but if Renie was right, he wanted to see it for himself. It almost seemed too good to be true.

He also wanted to go back into his bedroom and finish what he'd started with Gideon.

After an internal struggle, he stifled a sigh. As delicious as Gideon was, if Jason went back to bed with him now, his mind would only be half there. He needed to see what was happening at the gates with his own eyes. Gideon deserved his full attention.

"Uh, I need a moment," he said.

Roux stifled a smile.

Renie didn't.

Jason pressed both hands to her face. "Honey, if you keep grinning like that, your face will split open."

"I'm a vampire. I'll heal," she said.

Jason squished her cheeks together so she couldn't talk, but he couldn't smush away her grin.

"Take as long as you want," Roux said. "We just thought you'd want to know."

Jason let Renie go. "Thanks," he said.

Roux gestured to Jason's neck. "Don't forget to get that sealed up. Unless you like it that way."

Jason's hand shot to his neck, and the tiny beads of blood still wet at the puncture points of Gideon's fangs. He was starting to understand why some donors had refused to seal their bites, wearing them proudly, like tattoos. He loved the sight of Gideon's fangs, loved the feel of them sliding into his throat, but leaving bites unsealed meant holes like track marks, and drug addict wasn't a good look for anyone.

"I'll catch up with you later," he said.

As he shut the door, it occurred to him that while he and the girls had been teasing each other, Gideon was still in bed, possibly feeling very uncomfortable.

"Sorry about that," he said, turning around.

Gideon leaned against the pillows, a faint smile on his lips. He'd run his hands through his hair, teasing out the flattened bits, and Jason had to take a moment to admire him. He was just so damn scrummy.

"They probably heard more than we wanted them to, didn't they?" Jason said.

"Probably," Gideon agreed.

"Do you mind?"

"It's too late even if I did. Besides, vampires learn to mostly block out background noise." That faint smile returned to Gideon's lips. "Otherwise we'd never stop hearing people having sex."

Jason climbed back onto the bed and tilted his head, exposing his bite. "You mind closing this?"

Gideon leaned forward and ran his tongue over the punctures. A shudder ran through Jason's whole body.

"You need to go and see what's happening outside," Gideon said, sitting back against the headboard.

"How did I know you were going to say that?"

Gideon smiled again. "Perhaps we already know each other too well."

His tone was lighthearted, but the reality of the statement hit Jason square in the chest.

Sometimes the depth of his feelings for Gideon made him uneasy, because it seemed so fast, and he couldn't believe that Gideon possibly felt the same way.

But maybe he did.

Jason slid off the bed. This was too much to think about right now, even for him.

"I'm going to grab a quick shower," he said, gesturing at the bathroom.

He left the door open while he showered, in case Gideon wanted to join him, but apparently that was another step too far.

For now, anyway.

Jason bounded down the stairs, feeling a real sense of hope for the first time in days, but his steps faltered when he found Ysanne waiting for him at the bottom, pale arms folded.

"Um, hi?" he said.

Ysanne coolly regarded him. "I've been made aware of a certain video posted online by a certain ex-donor," she said.

"Oh. Yeah. About that." Jason bit his lip.

Ysanne raised one eyebrow. "You didn't think to run something like that past me first?"

Jason felt like a mouse crouched in front of a cat. An immensely strong, frosty-eyed cat.

"Honestly, no," he admitted. "I didn't say anything in the video that I thought you'd have a problem with, and I was trying to help. Which I've done, haven't I?"

Ysanne's expression softened. "I have also been notified of this Fangs and Friends movement, and arrangements for blood donations are currently underway, so, yes, you've made a difference, and we're all grateful for that. But please remember that I am Lady of this House, and I need to know these things."

"Right. Sorry."

Ysanne stood to one side, indicating that Jason could pass, and as he did, something slammed into him, and he whirled around with a gasp.

"Nikki!" he cried.

"Excuse me?" Ysanne said.

"She called me yesterday. With everything that's been going on, I completely forgot." Jason wanted to kick himself. How could he have forgotten something like that? Almost a whole day had passed since he'd received that call, and he'd spent most of it in bed with Gideon, while Nikki was *still missing*.

"What did she say?" Ysanne asked.

"Not much. She doesn't want to go home, but she's in Winchester somewhere. That's all I know. Will you tell Walsh?"

"Of course."

Walsh—or someone in his department—would get on the case as soon as possible, but that still didn't make Jason feel better. It didn't excuse the fact that he'd forgotten Nikki.

But there was nothing he could do about it now.

He continued outside, stepping through the gaping opening where the front door had been. Sudden cheers rose up, and Jason looked around, almost expecting to see a vampire behind him, but there was no one. Then he realized: the crowd was cheering for *him*.

Suddenly feeling awkward, he waved, then ducked back into the house.

"Wow," he whispered.

Roux's words came back to him, and he sobered. As positive as this development was, they couldn't afford to become complacent. Ivar could easily destroy all this goodwill.

He checked his phone.

It came as little surprise that not all the news was good. Just as people had speculated that vampires had deliberately started the Shepherd's Bush fire to paint Gideon as a hero, people now suspected that vampires were trying to paint themselves as victims, and they urged their followers not to listen.

But the good far outweighed the bad.

Jason's video wasn't the only one that had gone viral.

The footage of Gideon's dramatic dash into the fire was making the rounds again, and this time the comment sections had nothing but praise for how he'd risked himself.

And the video that had started it all was everywhere again— Ysanne revealing vampires by using her incredible strength to save humans trapped in their cars after a devastating highway crash. Jason hadn't seen that video in a while, and he'd forgotten how iconic it was: Ysanne dressed as elegantly as ever, stilettos adding several inches to her petite frame, lifting a motorcycle over her head as if it weighed nothing.

It was strange to look at those images now and realize that Ysanne was someone he considered a friend.

Jason listened again to the people outside, cheering for him, cheering for vampires, then he bounded back upstairs, feeling like his heart had wings.

Gideon

He'd showered in Jason's room rather than returning to his own, washing his hair with the rose-scented shampoo that was probably left over from when Renie and Roux had lived here. Jason must have started using it when he moved in—he smelled like roses too.

Gideon couldn't help smiling at the thought that he'd smell like Jason.

Sharing products like this was something a couple did, when they had their own bathroom. Surprisingly, Gideon didn't recoil at that.

He heard Jason's footsteps before he came into the room, and there was a spring in his step that hadn't been there recently.

"Good news?" Gideon said.

"*Great* news," Jason declared. "Ysanne's making arrangements for this Fangs and Friends thing, so at least that's one problem sorted. Hopefully it will mean a fresh blood supply very soon."

There was a funny feeling in Gideon's chest, something soft and warm and powerful, and it wasn't until then that he realized what it was.

Pride.

"Because of you," he said.

Jason grinned bashfully. "Not *just* me."

Gideon continued to stare at him, the world shifting inside his head and beneath his feet. This handsome, passionate, beautiful boy really was his.

Jason's eyes softened, and suddenly that smile felt like it was just for Gideon.

It was the loveliest smile he'd ever seen.

Something else stirred in his chest, an emotion that he wasn't sure how to identify. It swelled, making him feel like it was hard to breathe even though he didn't need to.

As he stared at Jason, he felt that last shred of his old fears fall away. He'd wanted to take things slowly, but now he was hard and aching, and his bones were on fire, and he needed Jason more than he'd never needed anyone.

He didn't want to wait anymore.

CHAPTER EIGHTEEN

Jason

The air around them changed suddenly, becoming charged with heat. The way Gideon looked at him was like he wanted to devour him, in the best possible way.

Gideon kissed him, sliding his tongue into Jason's mouth and winding his hand in his hair. They'd kissed plenty before, but never with this edge of urgency, of *need*. Gideon's fangs pricked his lip, and he tasted the faint tang of his own blood.

"Sorry." Gideon pulled back.

Jason licked his lip, and Gideon's eyes tracked the movement, flaring red. "Nothing to be sorry for," Jason said, and kissed him again.

Gideon propelled him backward, but he didn't realize they were at the bed until he was falling back on it. Gideon's weight stretched out on top of him, hard and heavy.

"Is this too much?" Jason said, looking up at him.

The feel of Gideon wedged between his thighs, the weight of Gideon pressing against him, the red gleam in his eyes—Jason didn't want any of it to end. But if it was moving too fast for Gideon, then he'd put the brakes on.

And then take the world's longest, coldest shower.

Lowering his head, Gideon nipped Jason's lower lip, not hard enough to break skin, but hard enough that Jason could feel the pressure of his fangs. A shiver of delight rolled through him.

"It's not too much," Gideon whispered. "Nothing is too much."

Jason frowned and started to sit up. "But—"

Gideon put a hand on his chest and gently pushed him back onto the bed. "*Nothing* is too much," he repeated, looking into Jason's eyes.

His heart almost stopped beating, because if Gideon was saying what he thought he was saying—

Gideon kissed him again, moving his hips against Jason's in a way that made it very clear what he wanted.

The rest of the world melted away.

Keeping his eyes locked on Gideon's face, Jason unbuttoned the vampire's shirt, his throat growing drier with each inch of hard, pale chest that was revealed.

"You should go around shirtless more often," he teased, running one hand up and down Gideon's chest, feeling the play of muscle, the scattering of golden hair across his pecs.

"Should I?"

"This," Jason said, rearing up to kiss his nipple, "is a work of art, and it's almost criminal that the whole world doesn't get to see it."

Gideon ran his tongue down Jason's neck, lingering over his pulse, and Jason almost forgot to breathe.

"I don't really think you want to share me," he said.

"You're right, I really don't," Jason said, amazed that he could even get the words out.

He hadn't imagined that Gideon would be ready for sex so soon. He certainly hadn't imagined that, even when the time came, Gideon would be so relaxed, so teasing.

He wanted more of it.

He pushed Gideon back, shifting position so the vampire lay beneath him, and tugged at his own shirt, almost tearing it in his excitement. Gideon watched, his eyes shining red.

"You're so fucking gorgeous," Jason told him.

His hand moved to Gideon's belt, then lower, and Gideon made a small noise, pushing his hips against Jason's hand.

Jason had been dreaming about this ever since he laid eyes on Gideon; he wasn't about to rush it.

He unbuckled Gideon's belt and drew down his zipper. Gideon's whole body was tense, but it was a good kind of tense. His eyes were locked on Jason's, and the sheer level of trust and intimacy there took his breath away.

He hooked his thumbs into the belt loops of Gideon's trousers and slowly pulled them down. Gideon lifted his hips, helping.

When Gideon was naked at last, Jason sat back on his heels and just looked at him.

"Gorgeous," he said again.

But looking wasn't enough.

He moved up Gideon's body and kissed him, pushing his pelvis against Gideon's, making Gideon clutch his shoulders. Then he abruptly broke the kiss. Gideon made a noise of protest, but Jason was already kissing his way down his chest, tracing the muscles in his stomach with the tip of his tongue before finally settling where they both wanted him to be. He closed his mouth around Gideon, and Gideon responded with a sharp gasp.

Nestled between Gideon's thighs, Jason never took his eyes off his face. He always wanted to know that his partners were enjoying things as much as he was, but with Gideon it felt like so much more than that.

Every noise he made, every movement of his hips, each time he curled his fists in the covers made Jason glow.

Seeing him completely vulnerable like this, seeing him come apart, hearing him moan Jason's name, was as intimate as the sex itself, and Jason wanted to treasure every second of it.

He planned as many repeat performances of this as possible, but he would only see it the first time once.

Gideon stiffened and shattered, and the sound of Jason's name on his lips was the most beautiful thing Jason had ever heard.

He wanted to hear it again.

Hands shaking slightly, he peeled off his jeans. He reached over to the nightstand, opened the drawer, and pulled out the bottle of massage oil that he'd kept there since he moved into the room. He *had* dreamed of Gideon a lot, and it felt faintly surreal to pour oil into his palm this time, knowing this was the real thing.

Gideon didn't resist when Jason gently rolled him over and put his hands on Gideon's hips, pulling him onto all fours.

His heart felt like a balloon, light and bright and buoyed up, and full of something he wanted to name but couldn't quite manage.

"Are you okay?" he whispered, pressing a kiss to Gideon's shoulder.

Gideon nodded, his hair falling in his eyes.

Jason moved back, pressing one hand to Gideon's hip and the other to the base of his spine to hold him in place while he gently pushed inside.

Sheer.

Bliss.

Aware of how long it had been since Gideon had slept with anyone, Jason moved in short, shallow strokes, giving the other man time to get used to him, and each careful thrust took him closer to heaven.

Gideon was saying his name over and over and over, but Jason had to bite his own tongue because the only words that wanted to come out were that he had completely fallen for Gideon.

Too soon.

But he couldn't pretend he didn't feel it.

From the moment he'd walked into Belle Morte and seen Gideon, it was like he had seen his own future.

His blond, broad-shouldered, six-foot-tall future.

He slid a hand up Gideon's back, relishing the flex of hard muscle beneath pale skin, and grasped his shoulder. Gideon grabbed his hand, squeezing it tight while he gasped Jason's name.

He was moving faster now, gripping Gideon's hip with one hand, his shoulder with the other, and everything inside him was tense and vibrating, a wave of pure pleasure building and building and building.

The world exploded.

Stars flashed in Jason's eyes. He was weightless, boneless, floating free, and those waves kept coming, rolling over his whole body and making him shake.

He heard Gideon shout his name one more time, and then the strength drained out of him, and they slumped onto the bed together. Jason buried his face in the soft spot between Gideon's neck and shoulder, the breath shuddering in and out of him.

It had never been that good.

Jason always enjoyed sex, but it was always better when it was with someone he truly cared about.

With Gideon, he felt attuned to the other man's body in the most incredible way, like they were joined in ways other than physical. Jason wasn't sure he believed in souls, but if they were real, then his had brushed against Gideon's in that moment.

Lying in bed with Gideon, little aftershocks of bliss still rippling through him, he *knew*. There was something special here, something that people searched for all their lives, and he'd do anything to keep it.

Gideon

He felt like he was floating on a cloud, his body still pulsing deliciously. Jason lay on his back next to him, his chest rising and falling with heavy breaths, his face soft and relaxed.

He was so beautiful that it made Gideon's chest hurt—and it wasn't just physical beauty. Jason's heart, his soul, the very core and essence of him were beautiful.

That was what Gideon was falling for.

"Jason," he said, propping himself on one elbow.

Jason looked up at him, his eyes drowsy and glazed.

Gideon linked his fingers with Jason's, running his eyes down the naked length of Jason's body.

"Thank you," Gideon whispered.

Jason's breathing hitched, then he smiled, his eyes glittering with emotion.

"You've made me feel so much stronger than I ever thought I could be," Gideon said.

People marveled at the physical strength of a vampire, but that wasn't the only kind of strength that mattered. Jason had helped Gideon find a different kind, one that was even more important.

"This is about Godric, isn't it?" Jason said, studying his face.

Gideon had to smile. Of course Jason knew what was on his mind.

"Yes." He used his thumb to draw small circles on Jason's chest. "I don't know if I can let him back into my life, but I can give him the chance to try. Even if it doesn't work, he won't break me again. Not now I have you."

A fiercely protective light came into Jason's eyes as he nodded.

If Gideon fell, Jason would catch him.

If he broke into pieces, Jason would put him back together.

Gideon had nothing to fear, as long as Jason was with him.

CHAPTER NINETEEN

Jason

Waking up with someone had never felt so good.

After a long and emotional day, Jason still felt drained, but he was happy, too, and that outweighed everything else for now.

Gideon slept beside him, one arm flung out, his hand dangling off the edge of the bed.

He was so adorable when he slept that Jason wanted to kiss him all over.

But there was something he needed to do.

Sliding out of bed, he walked to the jeans he'd tossed onto the floor yesterday and retrieved his phone. On the way he caught a glimpse of his reflection in the mirror, and he couldn't help a smile. His eyes were full of stars.

Yesterday he'd called and texted Nikki about a dozen times, but she'd never responded, though he could see that she'd read his messages. This morning, when he checked, there was still no response, and concern speared him.

He slipped into the bathroom, hoping not to wake Gideon, and tried calling again, but there was no answer. He texted, begging her to tell him where she was and if she was okay. This time the message went unread.

Unease twisted in Jason's chest.

Maybe Ysanne or Walsh would have some news.

When he went back into the bedroom, Gideon was awake, his chin propped on one hand.

Jason stopped, heat creeping into his face. Seeing Gideon like that, drowsy and tousled and probably still naked, made Jason want to forget everything and rush over there to ravish him.

Gideon's eyes heated, as if he sensed the direction of Jason's thoughts. He pulled the covers away, a wicked grin playing on his lips.

Yup. Definitely still naked.

"Feel free to greet me like that every morning," Jason said, savoring the view.

There was still a lot they needed to discuss. If they were going to start spending nights together, in whose room? Gideon had lived in his north wing bedroom for ten years, so it didn't seem fair to expect him to give it up, but this bedroom held so many memories for Jason. It represented so much.

And, if he was honest, he quite liked the idea of them having the whole wing to themselves, for now at least.

"Come here." Gideon beckoned Jason with one finger.

He didn't need telling twice.

He jumped into bed with his boyfriend, pulling the covers up around them. "I seem to be wearing too many clothes," he said, looking down at himself.

"Yes, you do. Maybe you can rectify that."

Jason grinned and stripped.

Gideon's skin was always cool to the touch, but here in the little cocoon of bedding, the warmth from Jason's body seemed like it was enough for both of them.

Gideon's hand slid down, cupping Jason beneath the sheets, and he caught his breath.

"I like starting mornings like this," Gideon said, gently pumping his fist.

"Me too," Jason managed.

Gideon's hand slowed, his expression suddenly serious. "There's something I need to ask you."

"Okay."

"I know you didn't suggest legalizing turning humans for your own benefit, but have you thought about it?" Gideon said.

Jason shifted position, resting his weight on his elbow so he could look Gideon in the face.

Gideon's hand still lay beneath the covers, but he wasn't touching Jason anymore, which was good because if he had been, Jason would have struggled to form a coherent thought beyond *more*.

"What do *you* think about it?" he asked.

"There are a lot of benefits to being a vampire, but a lot of negatives too," Gideon replied.

That was true.

"I know all that already. I know what I'd be getting into." Jason paused.

"But you're not sure you want to get into it," Gideon guessed.

"It's complicated," said Jason truthfully. "I've loved vampires for as long as I've known about them, and if you'd asked me this before I came to Belle Morte then I'd have said yes in a heartbeat. But that would have been based on an illusion. I didn't *know* vampires then, only their celebrity facade. Now I'm very aware of what a person would have to give up to become a vampire."

He trailed a finger along the bulge of Gideon's bicep. "I want to live with you. If that means living here, then I'll do it. But I still want a life outside this house. It's not healthy to be cooped up the way you've all been for the last ten years."

"You may be right about that," Gideon admitted.

Jason thought about it, *really* thought. "The thing is, I'm only nineteen, and I don't think I'm ready to make a change like that. There's still so much I want to do that I wouldn't be able to as a vampire. I'm not saying I'd never want to turn, but I don't want to now."

Gideon was quiet, looking down at the sheets.

"Are you okay?" Jason said.

Gideon smiled, his eyes gentle. "Of course I am. I won't pretend I wouldn't want you to turn, but I'd never pressure you into it. You have to make the choice yourself."

"And if I decide I never want to?"

Gideon didn't stop smiling. He took Jason's hand, squeezing it. "I'll accept that, same as you've always accepted me."

"Thank you," Jason said.

Gideon's grin widened, and red sparked in the depths of his eyes. His hand moved to Jason's thigh. "Weren't we in the middle of something?"

Jason could only nod, his body thrumming with anticipation.

Gideon wriggled under the covers, his eyes locked on Jason's as he slid down the length of Jason's body.

When he felt the warm heat of Gideon's mouth close around him, he closed his eyes and went to heaven.

Gideon

After Jason had gone to take a shower, Gideon lay in bed, thinking. He couldn't pretend Jason's answer was the one he'd hoped for, but it was an answer he would respect.

He reached for Jason's phone, still lying on the pillow, and checked to see if there was any word from Nikki. Jason hadn't mentioned it, but Gideon had heard him calling someone from the bathroom, and it could only be her.

Still no response.

Unease spiked in Gideon's chest.

"What are you up to?" Jason said, coming out of the bathroom with just a towel wrapped around his waist. Beads of hot water glistened on his chest, and Gideon licked his lips.

By the way Jason grinned it was clear he'd caught the movement.

"I was just seeing if you'd heard from Nikki," Gideon said.

Jason's grin faded. "Anything?"

"No."

Gideon patted the bed and Jason joined him.

"I'm really worried about her," Jason said.

Gideon watched a droplet of water slide down Jason's spine and disappear into his towel. "Maybe this is a good sign. If she'd run into trouble, she would have called for help by now."

"Unless she can't," said Jason morosely. "Or unless she lost her phone."

Gideon wanted to believe that even the people who passionately hated vampires wouldn't take that out on a child, but he'd seen too much of the darkness of human nature.

"I don't understand why she won't answer my calls," Jason said.

"Last time she came here, we sent her home again. Or not *home*, but to her aunt's house." Gideon caught another drop of water with his thumb.

"We didn't have a choice," Jason said.

"I know. But Nikki's only thirteen, she's still grieving for her father, and she's lost her home. It's hardly surprising she's not thinking clearly," Gideon said.

Jason swore under his breath. "I just want to *help* her."

"I know. You caring so much about other people is one of the things I love about you."

This time when Jason smiled, it was warm and real and sparkling. It made Gideon's heart feel like it was full of light.

"Then is this a good time for me to nudge you about Godric?" Jason said.

"What do you mean?"

"If you're serious about giving him a chance, you need to start doing that."

Gideon lowered his eyes. He knew Jason was right, but that didn't make it any easier. Today almost felt too soon.

But if he balked, it was only delaying the inevitable, and the longer he did that, the harder it would be. It was why Godric had spent ten years on the other side of the ocean, wanting to visit Gideon but unable to bring himself to do so.

He slid one arm around Jason's waist, his hand landing on the place where his towel was knotted.

Jason grabbed his wrist, laughter in his eyes. "Nuh-uh. Don't change the subject."

"But I like this subject much more."

"It is a very good subject," Jason agreed. "But that doesn't mean you can wriggle out of this."

"It does mean I can help you wriggle out of this towel," Gideon countered, tugging it.

Jason laughed, and it was like sweet music.

This time he didn't resist, and Gideon pulled the towel away. His sexual appetites had fluctuated over the years, but he'd never felt like he couldn't get enough of someone.

But Jason had lit a fire under his skin, deep inside him.

"I guess you can talk to Godric later," Jason said, and pulled Gideon down on top of him.

CHAPTER TWENTY

Gideon

Ysanne had given Godric a room in the north wing, and Gideon couldn't help wondering if she'd rescind that offer if he asked her to. She wasn't under any obligation to let Godric stay; she was doing this because she thought it was best for Gideon.

She was right, of course.

Whatever had happened between them, however angry and hurt Gideon still was about that night, he would never forgive himself if he didn't try to fix things.

He went to his brother's room.

Inside, Godric already seemed completely at home in his new surroundings, and that only irritated Gideon further. Godric had always been popular and charming, at ease with everyone he met—it was one of the reasons Gideon had idolized him so much when they were human.

Now he wanted some sign that Godric was out of his depth here, that this was even half as hard for him as it was for Gideon.

"I wasn't sure you'd come," Godric said, getting up from where he'd been lounging on the bed.

"Neither was I," Gideon admitted.

Godric smiled, and Gideon was struck again by the faint signs of aging on his brother's face. He hadn't had any of those faint lines when Gideon had left home.

Was he still the older brother? They'd been born four years apart, but ten years separated the times they'd been turned into vampires. Godric had aged. Gideon hadn't. In human years, Godric was still older. In vampire years, Gideon was.

It was enough to make his head hurt.

"This isn't how I expected our reunion to go," Godric said, leaning against the bedpost.

"What did you expect?"

Godric spread his palms. "I suppose I thought you'd be happy to see me."

In some ways he was, but he didn't quite know how to put that into words.

Godric's expression dimmed. "You really do blame me for what happened when we were younger, don't you?"

"I don't think you have any idea how hard it was for me," Gideon said.

"You think I don't know how ironfisted our father was? You think I've never felt the weight of his expectations?"

"Not in the same way. You *wanted* to get married and have a family. You *accepted* that there was a place for you in society, and you were happy with that. But I didn't have a place. I was supposed to change everything about myself."

"Not *every*thing," Godric said.

Gideon glared at him. "I'm gay, Godric. That's who I am. So when someone expects me to pretend I'm not, then they're expecting me to change everything. You have no clue how that feels."

"You're right, I don't," Godric admitted.

"Then don't try to tell me that I'm wrong in how I feel."

They were silent for a few moments.

Gideon had known this wouldn't be easy, but he hated how hard it was. Once he wouldn't have hesitated to tell Godric exactly what was on his mind. Once, Godric had been the man he'd looked up to, the brother he'd loved and trusted.

Now he didn't know what Godric was.

That hurt.

"I could have coped with Father being disappointed in me. I could have coped with him trying to push me toward marriage. But he hated me, Godric."

Godric started to protest, but Gideon silenced him with a slash of his hand.

"Don't. Maybe you never saw the look in his eyes, but I did. If I'd been the one to end the engagement with Eleanor, he'd probably have killed me," he snapped.

"You think I would have let that happen?" Godric said.

"You never intervened when he beat me, you never stood up to him, so you'll forgive me if I wouldn't have put my life in your hands."

Godric's lips were pressed so hard together they were white, bloodless lines. "I'm sorry," he said.

They were words that Gideon had longed to hear for so many years, but now they didn't change much, because he still wasn't sure how Godric felt about him. If Godric still couldn't accept him then his apologies were meaningless.

"I need to know how you feel about me now," Gideon said, everything inside him clenching tight as he waited.

Seeing Godric had only exacerbated his anger and grief—but he still loved Godric too. He'd known that he'd missed his brother, but he hadn't realized just how much until he was standing in front of him.

The combination of fear and anger and hope and love felt like a lead weight in his chest, suffocating him.

"You're my brother," Godric said, as if that answered everything.

But it didn't.

"That's not what I asked," Gideon said.

"All I ever wanted was for you to be happy, and I assumed that the things that made me happy would do the same for you. I didn't understand, and I've spent a long time since then regretting that. I can't pretend that I don't find it odd that two men can feel that way about each other, but I accept that they can."

His facade crumbled suddenly, and he squeezed his eyes shut.

"I missed you," he said.

Gideon swallowed. "I missed you too."

The anger had never left him, even when he'd pushed it so deep down that he almost couldn't feel it anymore, but that didn't mean he hadn't missed his brother.

"I don't care that you're gay, Gideon." Godric's voice hardened. "But I think this relationship with Jason is a mistake."

The bottom dropped out of Gideon's world. For a shining moment, it had seemed like everything would be all right.

"What?" he said, halfway between shock and anger.

"You don't think that being with him is putting him in danger?" Godric said.

The walls seemed to close in on Gideon. His brain turned to water.

"I don't . . ." His words faltered.

Godric's eyes were sympathetic and his words were gentle, but it felt like they'd opened a black pit beneath Gideon, and he was struggling not to fall.

He wanted to deny it, but what if Godric had a point? Gideon knew about the abuse that Jason had faced online. He knew about the bottle that had been thrown at Jason's head on the way into the television studio. He'd seen the ugly bruises courtesy of Ivar's fists.

He couldn't pretend that Jason wasn't in danger. He'd worried about it, but he'd never thought that *he* was the one putting Jason in harm's way.

Now the thought was in his head, and it felt like being punched in the heart.

"I just think it's something you need to consider," Godric said.

He reached out to pat Gideon's shoulder, but Gideon jerked away, his eyes burning. He'd been so afraid that Godric's refusal to accept Gideon would destroy any love left between them, but he'd never imagined that Godric would hurt him like this. He'd never imagined that Godric could make him doubt his relationship with Jason.

But the doubt was there now, a horrible little seed burrowing into his mind and growing twisted black roots.

He needed to get out of this room.

He fumbled for the doorknob, unable to tear his eyes away from Godric's pitying expression.

The worst part was that Godric wasn't *trying* to hurt him. He just didn't seem to realize the damage his words had caused.

Gideon threw open the door and stumbled out of the room, his mind squeezing into a tight, painful ball.

Godric called after him but Gideon didn't look back.

Jason

While Gideon hopefully started the healing process with Godric, Jason headed downstairs in search of a late breakfast. Maybe once he'd eaten he'd pester Ysanne to see if she'd heard anything about Nikki.

He was almost at the kitchen when the door flew open and Renie rushed out, auburn hair flying.

"There you are!" she exclaimed.

Jason stopped dead. "What's going on?"

"Ivar," Renie said grimly.

Jason's stomach plunged.

Footsteps sounded behind him, and he turned to see Roux hurrying through the ballroom, her phone clutched tight in one hand. "Has he seen it?" she said.

"Not yet," Renie replied.

"Seen what?" Jason asked.

Roux held up her phone so Jason could see it and played the video onscreen. He found himself looking at a huge stretch of highway, cars scattered across the road like broken toys. There was something weirdly familiar about it.

"—a situation unfolding on the M3 just outside Winchester," said a crisp voice off-screen. "Reports have been flooding in, along with video recordings from the scene."

The images onscreen changed, becoming a jerky clip of the road from a different angle, the picture shaking as if whoever was filming couldn't hold their camera steady. It wasn't just cars, Jason realized. A motorcycle lay on the side of the road, the paintwork scratched to hell. There was no sign of the rider. Farther down, a van had tipped onto its side, the windshield a web of cracked glass. Jason couldn't tell if the driver was still inside.

The picture changed again, this time zooming in on a man standing on the hood of a car that was skewed across the road.

Jason's mouth went dry.

The first time he'd seen Ivar, the guy had blended in with everyone around him. Now he looked less human than any vampire Jason had ever seen.

Ivar had abandoned his normal clothes for a blue tunic over loose-fitting gray-brown trousers, with a darker gray cloak pinned at his shoulders, fluttering behind him like a sail.

His hair was loose, glinting reddish-gold in the sunlight, fluttering like his cloak.

It wasn't just his clothing that made him look so different. Something about his presence had changed. For the first time Jason truly felt that he was looking at Ivar Haldorsen, the Viking vampire, someone far older and more dangerous than anyone he'd ever met.

The clip ended and another took its place, focusing on a car that had crumpled against the metal barrier dividing the highway lanes. Inside, someone was screaming.

"Jesus," Jason whispered. "Did Ivar cause this accident?"

"We think so," Renie said.

"Why?"

"Isn't it obvious?" said Roux. "He's re-creating the day that Ysanne revealed vampires to the world. Ten years ago she saved innocent people from a pileup, and now Ivar's going to undo all that by *killing* innocent people."

CHAPTER TWENTY-ONE

Jason

Within minutes Ysanne had assembled everyone in the vestibule, Caoimhe and Godric with them. This time they had to risk leaving Belle Morte unguarded.

"This is crazy, we don't even have a plan," Renie cried.

"I think the plan is to go to that section of the M3 and kick Ivar's ass," Roux said, but the tremor in her voice betrayed her lack of confidence.

"You're not coming," Edmond said.

Renie's eyes flashed red. "The hell I'm not."

"No arguments. It's broad daylight out there."

Renie's mouth snapped shut.

"But you still don't have a plan," Roux said.

"We also don't have a choice," Ysanne said. "If we don't stop Ivar, a lot of innocent people may die."

Roux didn't argue with Ludovic; she just pulled him down for a kiss and whispered, "Come back safe."

"I will," he said.

Watching them, watching everyone getting ready to go and fight someone they might not be able to beat, Jason's chest felt like it was going to explode. He was sick with fear for Gideon and stricken with frustration that he was getting left behind. Again.

He reached for Gideon's hand, but there was already too much space between them and Gideon wasn't looking at him. Jason searched for words, but he had no idea what to say, so he just stood there, watching as the vampires trooped out of the mansion to go and confront Ivar, while he had to stay behind with Renie and Roux.

"Fuck." Renie tucked her hair behind her ear with a shaking hand. "What if they can't do this?"

None of them said it, but Jason was sure they were all thinking of how quickly Ivar had rampaged through Belle Morte, and how quickly he'd taken down Ysanne, the oldest and strongest among them. What chance did any of them have, really?

"I'm going upstairs," Renie mumbled, to no one in particular.

Roux put her arm around Renie's shoulder as they turned toward the staircase. "They'll be okay. Our guys are tough."

"So's Ivar."

Roux glanced back at Jason. "You coming?"

"I'll catch you up," he said.

Roux nodded, and she and Renie continued up the stairs.

Frustration knotted inside Jason. He couldn't fight Ivar, but surely he could still help. All those people trapped in their cars, the vampires would be too busy fighting Ivar to help them. Would emergency services be able to reach them, or would Ivar stop those too?

Alone in the vestibule, Jason made a crazy, impulsive decision.

He ran up the stairs and headed for his bedroom. Inside, he went to the wardrobe and pulled out the black cap lying on the wooden floor. He'd worn this only once before—after they had traveled back from Ireland to reclaim Belle Morte, relying on caps and scarves for anonymity.

Now Jason needed that anonymity again.

Pocketing his phone, he hurried back downstairs and went to the nearest of the two exits at the back of the mansion.

Jason slipped onto the grounds. The air was cool, but not as cold as it had been during most of his time at Belle Morte, like spring was finally waking up. Here and there freshly unfurled daffodils created splashes of color against all the green, and Jason smiled, thinking of the flowers that Gideon had given him, still in their little pot in his room.

When he reached the broken section of wall he paused, staring at the crumbled bricks and settled orange dust. Yellow tape had been rigged across the gap, but that wouldn't keep anything out. Jason strode forward, fragments of rubble crunching underfoot.

"What are you doing?" said a voice, and Jason spun to see a guard whose name he didn't remember standing behind him, one hand on the radio at her hip.

He silently swore, but he should have known it wouldn't be this easy.

"There's something I need to do," he said.

"You can't leave," said the guard.

"Actually, I can."

"Ysanne said—"

"Ysanne's not here." Jason didn't have time for this. "If I want to leave, you can't physically stop me."

That made her hesitate. When Ysanne had decreed that no one was to leave the mansion, she hadn't mentioned what might happen if someone did, most likely because she'd assumed that everyone would respect her orders. If Jason had still been just another donor, the guard would have had more authority over him, but he wasn't, and he suspected she didn't view him like that either.

While she wrestled with the dilemma, Jason ducked under the tape and left the grounds.

She didn't come after him.

He jogged a couple of streets away from the mansion before calling a taxi. Within two minutes it had pulled up next to the curb. If Jason was going to change his mind, now was the time to do it. He paused with one hand on the door, glancing back in the direction of Belle Morte, then climbed into the car and drove away.

He didn't know which bit of the M3 Ivar had attacked, and he couldn't ask his driver to drive around looking for it, so he'd picked a roadside café as his drop-off spot, hoping it wasn't too far from the scene.

His phone hadn't rung yet, so he assumed no one at Belle Morte had realized he was gone. That wouldn't last, but he'd deal with the fallout later.

"You meeting someone here?" the driver asked as he pulled up outside the café.

"Uh, yeah," Jason lied.

"I hope they're not coming from the other direction. I think there's been a bad crash farther down."

"Do you know how much farther down?" Jason asked.

"A couple of miles?" The driver twisted in his seat and gave Jason a speculative look. "Do I know you? You look kind of familiar."

Jason shrugged, hoping the guy wouldn't suddenly place him. "Just got one of those faces, I guess. Thanks for the ride."

He hopped out of the car.

He waited until the taxi had pulled away before breaking into a steady jog along the verge next to the road.

It wasn't long until he heard the screams. He picked up the pace, trying to keep his breathing steady and his rising panic under control. Suddenly he was there, and he skidded to a halt, his heart thumping like a hammer.

It was worse than it had looked on the news.

Cars were strewn everywhere; crumpled and gouged metal bodywork glinted dully under the winter sun. Black tire tracks crisscrossed the tarmac where vehicles had desperately swerved. Jason could see the motorcycle still on its side on the edge of the road, still without any sign of its rider.

Ivar stood in the middle of the wreckage, and Jason was struck again by how completely not human the Viking vampire looked. It was nothing to do with his clothing, which Jason now guessed was a homage to his historical roots, and everything to do with the presence of him, as if the weight of the millennia that he'd lived was so heavy everyone could feel it.

Jason saw a flash of blond curls—Caoimhe—as she lunged at Ivar. He flicked his hand as if he was swatting a fly, and Caoimhe was hurled against a nearby car. The door buckled under the impact and Caoimhe fell into the road with a pained snarl.

Almost faster than Jason could see, three more vampires rushed Ivar. Jason glimpsed Edmond's raven hair among them. Ivar batted them away with a sweep of his arm.

Hugh lay motionless a few feet from the fight, and Ludovic was crouched over someone Jason couldn't see.

"Please," he whispered. "Don't be Gideon."

But no, there was Gideon, running at Ivar from behind. He leaped at him, a knife in one hand, and Ivar spun, catching Gideon by the throat in midleap. He threw him, and Gideon landed on the roof of a nearby car before rolling off and landing in a crouch.

He didn't appear to be injured, but that didn't ease the knot of absolute terror in Jason's chest, because Ivar could so easily kill Gideon. He was toying with them.

Jason realized he was moving forward, his feet automatically heading toward Gideon, and he braced one hand on an abandoned car to physically stop himself. Ivar might be toying with the other vampires, but a single blow from the Viking could break his neck.

No matter how difficult it was, and how fucking useless it made him feel, this was one fight he couldn't be a part of.

Jason gave himself a shake. He hadn't come to fight; he'd come to help the people still trapped in their cars.

Dozens of people milled around, either having already escaped their cars or having stopped before reaching the scene, but none of them were rushing to help. Maybe they were too scared to get close to a vampire fight. Jason couldn't blame them for that.

But he couldn't stand and watch.

Taking a bolstering breath, he dashed forward. A red car sat at an angle across the road, the taillights smashed and the side dented where another car must have sideswiped it. A young woman was in the driver's seat, tears streaming down her face as she tried and failed to open her door. The metal beneath the handle bore a deep indent, as if someone had punched it—most likely Ivar.

Jason had seen vampires exert their incredible strength in many ways, but he couldn't comprehend the power of a single punch crumpling a car like this and sending it spinning.

He reached the car and knocked on the window. The woman jumped.

"Can you get out the other side?" Jason said.

She frantically shook her head. "My baby. Please help her," she cried.

Baby? Jason peered through the back window. "Oh shit," he whispered.

He hadn't noticed the baby strapped into the back seat, somehow still asleep despite everything.

"Help her," the woman cried again, shrill with desperation.

"I will," Jason said.

He grabbed the door handle and gave it an experimental tug, but whatever damage Ivar had caused had it stuck fast. The only other option he could think of was to smash the window.

Frantically he scanned the road, looking for something to use, and suddenly he heard running feet. He looked up and his heart almost jumped out of his throat.

"Nikki?" he gasped. "What the fuck are you *doing* here?"

CHAPTER TWENTY-TWO

Jason

"Helping," Nikki replied. A thin black band pushed her curls off her face, and in one hand she clutched the baseball bat that she'd brought when they broke into Belle Morte to stop Etienne and Jemima.

"But—"

"No time to argue." Nikki pushed past him.

She examined the car, her jaw set with determination. "Looks like we're going through the window." She rapped on the glass with her knuckles. "Can you get into the passenger seat and cover your face? I'm going to break in."

The woman gaped at her, then scrambled into the adjacent seat, as far from the driver's window as possible, and wrapped her arms around her head.

Nikki took a step back, eyed the window, then swung the baseball bat at the center of it. The bat bounced off the reinforced glass, the impact knocking Nikki back a pace.

"Ow," she muttered.

"Let me," Jason said. He took the bat, aimed, and swung. The window shattered, glass spraying into the car, and the woman shrieked. In the back seat, her baby woke up and started crying.

Jason used the end of the bat to knock away shards of glass still in the frame. "Can you reach the baby?" he said.

The woman scrambled between the seats to unfasten the belt around the baby's car seat, then she lifted the seat into the front.

"Pass her to me," Jason said, leaning through the window.

She did, and Jason carefully lifted the car seat to safety and handed it to Nikki.

"Okay, your turn," he said, holding out his arms again.

Glass crunched under the woman's boots as she climbed across the seats, and Jason saw a streak of blood on her palm where a shard must have caught her. He pulled her through the window, supporting her weight until her feet touched the road.

"Thank you," she breathed, clinging to him a moment longer before rushing to her baby.

"There's a café a couple of miles up the road. Go there if you can," Jason said.

He hated to turn away from them now, but they were safe; they didn't need him anymore. Other people were still trapped.

He and Nikki worked quickly, and after a few minutes some of the spectators watching from a safe distance came to help. In the background Jason could hear sirens approaching rapidly, and he felt a flash of panic—maybe he and Nikki should have left this to the professionals. But they couldn't have known when help would arrive, or what Ivar would do next.

A low groan reached Jason's ears, and he spun around. A small green car had crashed into the central barrier, and at first glance Jason had thought it was empty. But when he looked closer he realized that the driver had slumped sideways across the passenger seat.

The hood of the car had buckled, driving the dashboard forward and trapping the man's legs.

He groaned again, feebly raising one hand.

Jason looked behind him. Two ambulances had arrived and, judging from the distant sirens, more were on the way, but they already had their hands full dealing with other casualties, and paramedics didn't have the experience or equipment to rescue someone from this kind of wreckage. That was the job of the fire department, and they hadn't arrived yet.

"Nikki, help me," Jason cried.

She raced to his side, bat in hand.

Jason wrenched open the driver's door and half climbed into the car. "Can you hear me?" he said.

Another groan.

"We're going to get you out of here, okay?" Jason said.

That time there was no response.

Jason ran his hands over the bulging mass of the dashboard, trying to work out how badly the man was pinned and how severe his injuries were. Blood soaked the left side of his jeans, but Jason couldn't see where it was coming from.

He braced one hand on the dashboard and pushed, though he knew it was futile. No human would shift that without help.

Maybe he could try to ease the man's legs out?

He touched the man's thigh, the only part of his legs that he could reach, and his eyes flew open, a strangled scream breaking from his lips.

"Fuck," Jason whispered. "I don't know what to do."

Nikki silently watched him.

Jason tried again to shift the dashboard, planting both feet on it and pushing, but nothing budged.

"*Fuck*," he yelled.

He had no idea who this guy was, but the red patch on his jeans was spreading, and Jason could hear blood dripping onto the floor. He was losing too much—if someone couldn't get him out soon he was going to die.

Gideon

Blood ran down his arm from a deep gouge caused when Ivar had slung him along the road, but Gideon couldn't feel it. All he could focus on was the vampire in the middle of the road, the impossibly strong, impossibly ancient vampire who they could barely touch.

A familiar shout cut through the fighting haze in his head.

Gideon whipped around, frantically scanning the road. It was impossible . . . he couldn't be here—the blood drained from his face. Jason was just feet away, climbing out of a wrecked car, his hair disheveled, a smear of blood on one arm, and standing in front of him was Nikki Flynn.

Gideon forgot about everything and raced to his boyfriend.

"What are you doing?" he demanded, grabbing Jason's arm.

Jason flapped one hand at the car. "Help him."

Gideon's nostrils flared, catching the scent of freshly spilled blood—far too much of it. Someone was still in the car.

Ducking his head inside, Gideon assessed the situation. He could hear the man's heart fluttering, struggling to cope, could smell the blood as it pumped from his injuries. He needed help, now.

Gideon planted both hands on the ruined dashboard and pushed. Crushed metal groaned, then shrieked, and he thought he heard the man gasp, but he couldn't tell if it was from pain or from relief as the pressure eased on his legs.

"We need help over here," Jason yelled.

Through the fractured windshield Gideon glimpsed the bright shapes of ambulances nearby, and someone jogging toward them. He pushed harder, gritting his teeth with the effort. Something sharp sliced the edge of his palm but he ignored the sudden sting and pushed harder, forcing the twisted bulk of metal back. He wasn't strong enough to move it much, not on his own, but he only needed to ease it so that the injured man could be pulled to safety. When he'd created a gap, he shifted position, climbing over the man to get out of the car. The man had lost consciousness, but Gideon could still hear the flutter of his heart.

Carefully, trying to jolt him as little as possible, Gideon pulled him across the seats, freeing his injured legs from the wreckage. Hands grabbed his shoulders, pulling him aside—a pair of paramedics, he realized.

Gideon stepped back, giving them space to work.

Jason flung his arms around Gideon's neck, squeezing him tightly. "Thank you," he whispered.

Gideon pulled free of the embrace. "You shouldn't be here," he said, anger sparking in his veins. "You should be back at the mansion, where you're safe."

"I couldn't sit around when people needed help," Jason argued.

"Me either," Nikki chimed in, hefting her bat.

"Hey," someone shouted, and Gideon looked up to see another

paramedic standing by a car farther down the road. "Can you help?"

Gideon ran to her.

"The door's stuck," she said, gesturing.

Her face was young and pale, and Gideon wondered how long she'd been in this job, and whether this accident was the worst she'd seen.

He wrenched open the door, giving the paramedic access to the passengers inside.

"Thanks," she said.

Ivar roared suddenly with pain, and Gideon spun around.

Edmond had managed to land a blow, driving a shard of metal deep into Ivar's shoulder. He twisted it, tearing through flesh and muscle, and Ivar backhanded him, knocking Edmond off his feet. Gideon heard something crack as Edmond hit the hood of a car farther down the road and crumpled to the ground. Ludovic was at his side in a flash.

Ivar ripped the tire off another car and advanced on Edmond and Ludovic, and ice rushed through Gideon's veins. So far Ivar had been toying with them, but that could change at any second.

"Ivar!" Jason shouted.

The Viking paused, tire in hand, and slowly turned.

"Jason—" Gideon started to say, reaching for Jason's sleeve, but his boyfriend neatly sidestepped and walked toward Ivar.

Thick, heavy dread rose in Gideon's chest.

"Why are you doing this?" Jason asked.

Ivar lowered the tire, but didn't let it go.

"All these people," Jason said, gesturing to the cars, the survivors, the paramedics. "What did they ever do to you?"

Ivar spared the spectators a brief glance. "Nothing."

"Then why are you hurting them?"

Ivar cocked his head, his brow furrowing as if he'd only just realized that was what he was doing. "Hurting them?" he repeated.

"Don't you even care?" Jason said.

"No more so than if a human cared about stepping on a bug," Ivar replied.

"People aren't bugs."

Ivar smiled, cold and sharp. "Your short, insignificant lives mean little to me, boy."

"My name's Jason, and you know it," Jason said.

Gideon felt a flash of equal parts fear and pride—fear that Jason had put himself in this dangerous situation, and pride that he was refusing to let Ivar see how scared he was. Because he *was* scared. Gideon could hear it in the frantic thump of his heart.

Ivar regarded him, his head still tilted, but his smile had softened slightly, making him look amused rather than murderous.

"You all see me as the villain, don't you?" he said, looking at the vampires gathered around.

"Can you blame us?" Gideon stepped up next to Jason and took his hand.

Ivar's gaze dropped to their clasped fingers, and his expression turned brittle.

"You think you're so different from me?" he said.

"Yes. We aren't the monsters that you want us to be, and nothing that you do will change that," Edmond said, climbing to his feet. His voice was tight with pain, and he cradled one arm to his chest. "When Etienne and Jemima started hurting people, we all fought to stop them, and no matter how much you beat us, terrorize us, or injure us, we won't turn on the people around us."

Ivar didn't bother to look at him. "In another thousand years, you'll see the world differently. You'll realize how little humans matter."

"We will never be like you," Gideon said.

Ivar's eyes sharpened, again dropping to Gideon's and Jason's clasped hands.

"You think your little human romance will save you from the realities of immortality?" he said.

"I know what immortality is," Gideon said.

Ivar laughed harshly. "You? You've lived a couple of centuries, Gideon Hartwright, the blink of an eye compared to me. You have no idea of the weight of time—*real* time. Do you truly believe that this human can save you from that?"

He took a step closer, and Jason's grip tightened on Gideon's hand.

"How long do you think your human boy will live? Another sixty years? Seventy? A heartbeat in eternity. Before you know it, he'll be gone," Ivar said.

Gideon tried to harden himself against the words, but they slipped past his defenses, sharp as broken glass.

"And centuries from now, when that boy is nothing but dust and memories, you'll wonder how you ever cared about him at all," Ivar continued.

"I'm sorry," Jason said.

That threw Ivar off guard; he blinked and paused. "What?"

"I'm sorry for whatever happened in your life to make you this way. I can't imagine what you've been through to make you see only the worst in people, but I pity you."

Ivar's eyes flashed red. "You pity me?" he said, his voice thick with scorn. "You, an insignificant *human*, pity *me*?"

Jason didn't flinch. "Yes."

A spell seemed to have fallen on the scene. Gideon could hear voices behind him: humans talking, the paramedics continuing to work. But the vampires were absolutely still. The tension stretched out, thick as tar, and Gideon felt like everything was teetering on a knife edge.

Sirens split the air, heralding the arrival of fire engines, and suddenly the spell was shattered.

Ivar hefted the tire, turned, and flung it at Ludovic and Edmond. Fast as lightning, Ysanne launched herself in front of them and knocked the tire from the air. It rolled down the road.

Gideon scanned the area, looking for something to use as a weapon.

In the second that he'd taken his eyes off the scene, Ivar had thrown Isabeau to the ground and was raising his foot to kick her in the head. Ysanne moved like a blur again, throwing herself across Isabeau and taking the kick to her side instead. From the sharp gasp she let out, Ivar had probably broken a couple of her ribs.

Caoimhe and Godric rushed at Ivar from behind, distracting him.

Isabeau shoved Ysanne away and scrambled up. Ysanne was slower to find her feet, one hand pressed to her ribs. She moved in front of Isabeau, as if trying to shield her from Ivar even though his attention was no longer on them, and Isabeau shoved her again.

"What are you doing?" she snapped.

Ysanne stared back at her, apparently lost for words.

"I don't need your protection," Isabeau said.

Jason grabbed Gideon's arm. "What about a car?" he said.

"What?"

"Could we run him over?"

Gideon looked back at Ivar just in time to see him toss Godric against the dividing barrier in the middle of the road. Despite the tension still lingering between them, Gideon had to fight not to leap to his brother's defense.

"A car won't kill him," Gideon said.

"How about a van?" Jason said.

Gideon followed his gaze up the road to where a dark-blue van had pulled over by the verge. No one sat in the driver's seat, but the lack of damage suggested it had stopped voluntarily rather than being forced off the road.

He shook his head. "It still won't kill him."

"But could it subdue him enough to take him out of the fight?" Jason said.

"I don't know."

"It has to be worth trying," Jason insisted.

Gideon looked at Ivar again, then back at the blue van. "He'll see it coming. Unless he's distracted."

Jason's eyes widened. "No way. You're not being the distraction."

Gideon winced as Caoimhe sailed through the air and vanished into the trees lining the edge of the highway. "It won't just be me."

"But he's so much stronger than you," Jason said.

Gideon brushed his hand against Jason's cheek. "I was once a champion boxer. I know how to throw a punch, and how to take one too."

"But you've never boxed someone over a thousand years older and stronger than you."

Gideon kissed him. "I'll be okay," he said. "Go get that van."

Jason ran.

Gideon strode toward Ivar, pausing only to pick up a long shard of glass lying in the road. He slid it into his pocket. Despite his confident words, there was a cold pit of fear in his stomach. Physically, he was bigger than Ivar, but that meant little in the vampire world.

"Haldorsen," he roared, and Ivar turned.

Gideon punched him. It was a good punch, landing squarely on Ivar's face, drenching Gideon's knuckles with blood, and it rocked Ivar back a pace. Gideon felt a spark of triumph. He followed with a second punch but Ivar was ready this time; he sidestepped, grabbed Gideon's wrist and sharply twisted. Pain shot up Gideon's arm and he gasped, trying to turn his body into the twist to ease the pressure. Ivar grinned, but he'd left himself unguarded. Gideon aimed a kick at Ivar's knee. Ivar turned, taking the impact on his thigh instead, and then Godric, Ysanne, and Benjamin were there, grabbing Ivar and hauling him away from Gideon. Ivar let go of Gideon's wrist, and he gasped again as feeling rushed back into his arm, then he delivered another crushing punch to the Viking's face, this time feeling Ivar's nose crunch under his fist. Fresh blood sprayed down Ivar's face, and he laughed, baring red-stained fangs.

Ivar threw his head back, butting Benjamin with the back of his skull, and it was Benjamin's turn to clutch a broken nose. Ivar tossed Ysanne against Godric as if she weighed nothing, and Godric promptly let Ivar go so he could catch her.

Ivar grabbed Gideon by the throat and lifted him off his feet. Even though Ivar couldn't strangle him, Gideon instinctively grabbed Ivar's wrist to ease the pressure on his neck. He reached into his pocket, pulled out the shard of glass, and slashed it up the inside of Ivar's wrist.

Blood sprayed, spattering Gideon's face, and Ivar snarled and dropped him.

Gideon heard the sudden revving of an engine, and threw himself backward. He expected to see the blue van; instead, a white truck shot down the road, a bearded man behind the wheel, Jason in the passenger seat. The truck was fast, but Ivar was still almost faster. Gideon hoped that the opened veins in his wrist had slowed him down just that little bit.

Ivar tried to dodge, but the truck clipped his hip, and Gideon heard the satisfying crunch of breaking bones. Ivar rolled across the road with a roar, and for the first time since the vampires of Belle Morte had come to challenge him, Gideon felt a spark of hope. Ivar wasn't dead, but they'd just landed a serious blow. If they all rallied together, perhaps they could take him down for good—

The Viking vampire shoved himself to his feet, his face twisted with pain, and ran. He bolted across the road and the grassy verge, and into the thickly clustered trees beyond.

Gideon heard a female yelp, and then Caoimhe staggered out, blond curls disheveled, expression bemused.

Ludovic, Ysanne, and several others immediately gave chase, and Edmond looked like he was about to follow, but then fell back against the nearest car, still cradling his injured arm.

Farther down the road, the truck screeched to a stop, and Jason jumped out. He ran to Gideon as Gideon was running to Edmond.

"Are you okay?" Gideon asked.

"Yeah," Jason said.

"I'm fine," Edmond said at the same time.

They both glanced at each other.

Jason eyed Edmond's arm. "Is it broken?"

"Dislocated, I think," Edmond replied.

"We'd better relocate it, then," Gideon said.

Jason backed off, raising both hands. "I don't think it's as easy as that. We need a paramedic."

"Why?" Gideon asked.

"If you don't know what you're doing, you can cause more damage. Muscles, ligaments, that sort of thing," Jason said.

"I'm a vampire," Edmond reminded him. "None of that is a threat to me."

"Oh, right."

Gideon took a firm hold of Edmond's wrist with one hand, his other steadying Edmond's elbow. "You ready?" he said.

Edmond nodded.

Gideon rotated Edmond's arm, trying to maneuver his shoulder back into place, and although Edmond didn't make a sound, his face was drawn tight with pain. Finally Gideon felt the pop as Edmond's shoulder slid back into place, and Edmond sagged against the car again, his eyes closed.

"Are you okay?" Jason asked.

"Absolutely," Edmond said through gritted fangs.

They didn't find Ivar. Even Ludovic's tracking skills weren't much help; the Viking had simply vanished.

As they regrouped in the middle of the road, assessing their various injuries, Ysanne reached for Isabeau, but she sharply pulled away.

"Isabeau—" Ysanne started.

"Please stop pretending that you care. It isn't fair," Isabeau said.

Ysanne recoiled a little. "I do care."

Isabeau snorted.

Ysanne stared at her, both of them seeming to forget that they had an audience.

"I owe you an apology, don't I?" she said.

Isabeau cocked an eyebrow.

"I couldn't have stopped the Council from arresting you, but I should have fought harder on your behalf," Ysanne said.

Finally Gideon understood why there'd been so much tension between the two women. Before Etienne and Jemima had launched their coup against Belle Morte, they'd attempted to frame Isabeau for the murder of June Mayfield. The Council had removed Isabeau for questioning, and she hadn't been released until the mansion had been reclaimed.

It seemed that Isabeau was still raw about Ysanne's inability to stop her detainment in the first place.

Isabeau's eyes flashed. "*That's* what you think this is about?" she said, her voice harsh with rage.

"I . . ." Ysanne actually seemed lost for words. "Isn't it?"

Isabeau made a disgusted noise and stalked off.

Jason cleared his throat. "We should probably get back to the mansion. You guys need blood."

"You can take some from me," Nikki offered, striding over, her baseball bat tucked under one arm.

"Absolutely not," Ysanne said, recovering her composure. "We do not drink from children."

"Will you drink from me?" asked another voice.

A young man had approached them, twisting a knitted hat between his fingers.

"You stopped that crazy bastard right before he was about to flip my car," the man continued. "Me and my girlfriend could both have been killed." He gestured to a dark-haired woman standing a few feet behind him.

"You can drink from me too," called another voice. The bearded man who'd driven the truck with Jason was jogging up the road toward them.

"And me," said a middle-aged woman, peeling away from the spectators.

As more and more people volunteered, Jason rested his head on Gideon's shoulder. "If Ivar was hoping to further sever the bonds between humans and vampires, then he really screwed up. It looks like all he's done is made them stronger."

Gideon wanted to reply but the words stuck in his throat. They'd beaten Ivar this time, but he wouldn't have changed his mind about what he was doing.

Sooner or later, he'd be back.

CHAPTER TWENTY-THREE

Jason

Even after Ivar had fled, Jason couldn't fully relax until they were inside the grounds of Belle Morte. Maybe that didn't make sense—Ivar had broken in before, he could easily do it again—but this mansion had become Jason's home, and despite all the bad shit that had happened there, he felt safe there somehow.

Isabeau was first into the house, stalking ahead as if she couldn't wait to be away from everyone. Ysanne was quick to follow her, and Jason thought they'd find somewhere private to talk, but apparently whatever Isabeau had been bottling up was too big to contain anymore, because as soon as they were inside the vestibule, she whipped around in a blaze of chestnut curls.

"I never blamed you for what happened with the Council," she snapped at Ysanne. "Even if you'd fought harder, you'd have been outvoted. I've always known you can't be biased in my favor, and I've never *expected* you to be. When the Council took me away, I was scared and angry, but I also knew I was innocent, and I had complete faith that you would prove that, and then you'd come and get me." The anger in Isabeau's voice faltered. "But you didn't."

Ysanne looked completely bewildered. "I sent a team—"

"Exactly." Isabeau cut her off. "While I was imprisoned, I had no idea what would happen to me, how long I'd be there, or what was happening to anyone I cared about, and I coped by reminding myself that you wouldn't leave me there. I imagined how it would play out—you breaking down the prison door and taking me in your arms—but you never fucking *came*. You sent a team to free me, but you couldn't be bothered to come yourself."

Jason glanced back at the doorway, wondering if he and the rest of the group should slip back outside and let Ysanne and Isabeau have this moment in private. Movement caught his eye, and he looked up to see Roux and Renie at the top of the stairs.

What the hell? Renie mouthed.

Jason didn't know if she was referring to the fight unfolding in the vestibule or the fact that he'd left the mansion, so he offered a helpless shrug.

Ysanne stared at Isabeau, her mouth slightly open. "I didn't think you'd have wanted to see me," she said.

Jason had never heard the Lady of Belle Morte sound so uncertain.

"You didn't even try." Isabeau's voice cracked.

"I thought you were angry with me," Ysanne said.

"Then you don't know me at all. I've always understood how important your duty to this house is. I'd never have kept our relationship secret all these years if I didn't understand, but the time when I needed you more than I *ever* have, you weren't there. You never even tried to make amends for it. You put your own pride and hurt feelings above me—above *us*. How exactly am I supposed to react to that?"

Ysanne continued to stare at Isabeau, apparently lost for words.

"I needed you," Isabeau continued, quieter now. "I needed you, and you weren't there, and you never reached out to me. You just stood and watched as this gulf grew between us."

Still, Ysanne said nothing, and Jason's chest ached in sympathy.

Ysanne had lived a long and probably difficult life, and she was no stranger to physical pain. Before now, Jason would have bet that she'd dismiss the possibility of words hurting her. But Jason could see her expression now, the pain on her face. Isabeau's words were tiny weapons, and each of them had found their mark.

Isabeau made a disgusted noise. "There's nothing more to be said here, is there?"

Ysanne sank her teeth into her lower lip, her eyes burning. "Yes," she said. "Isabeau Aguillon, *ma belle*, I love you."

Isabeau's expression barely changed.

There was a flutter of emotion in her eyes, gone in a blink.

"What difference does that make?" she said, and her voice was strange, as if she was fighting back tears.

"I can't lose you," Ysanne said.

Isabeau turned away. "Maybe you already have."

Ysanne caught her arm, and Isabeau looked at her with sad eyes. Ysanne glanced behind her, at everyone gathered in the vestibule, and there was a flash of surprise in her eyes, as if she'd forgotten they had an audience. But she didn't ask Isabeau to move this discussion somewhere else, and when her eyes landed on Jason, he gave her an encouraging smile.

Ysanne turned back to Isabeau. "I have been so blind, so unforgivably stupid," she said. "I thought you blamed me for not protecting you, and I wasn't strong enough to face your condemnation. So I ran and hid, and I never considered how that would hurt you. Now that I see it, I cannot believe my own selfishness."

Isabeau said nothing, but she was listening; she hadn't left yet.

"I know that nothing I can say will change what's happened, and I don't deserve your forgiveness, but I've never loved anyone like I love you," Ysanne went on.

Jason realized now why Ysanne was doing this publicly. For once, she was putting her relationship with Isabeau above Belle Morte, and she wanted everyone to see it.

"I should never have kept you a secret all these years, and if you give me another chance, I'll never keep you a secret again. I'll spend the rest of our lives making amends for this, as long as I know that you *will* be a part of my life," Ysanne said.

She was still holding Isabeau's arm, and now her hand slid lower, to clasp Isabeau's. Still, Isabeau didn't pull away.

This relationship had nothing to do with Jason, but he found himself holding his breath, willing Isabeau to give Ysanne another chance, because despite her icy exterior, Ysanne was a woman who still *felt* as deeply as anyone. She deserved to be happy. They both did.

"I've made so many mistakes, but I'm learning from them," Ysanne said. "I don't deserve your forgiveness, but I'm begging you for it anyway."

And then Ysanne did something that Jason had never thought he'd see. She got down on her knees in front of everyone and clasped her arms around Isabeau's legs.

Isabeau gazed down at her, lips parted, eyes wide with astonishment.

"I love you," Ysanne said again. "I am old, Isabeau, and set in my ways, and stubborn and prideful and arrogant, but you are the only woman in the world who will ever own my heart. I may not be able to fix everything that's gone wrong in our world, but please let me fix this relationship. Please tell me it's not too late."

Isabeau swallowed and brushed her knuckles along Ysanne's cheek. "It's not too late," she whispered.

Hope soared in Jason's chest, and he saw that hope reflected on Ysanne's face.

Isabeau grabbed the front of Ysanne's dress, pulled her to her feet, then dragged her closer until their lips met in a passionate kiss.

Jason clapped before he could stop himself, but neither vampire seemed to notice.

"I will never keep you a secret again," Ysanne murmured against Isabeau's lips.

Isabeau murmured something back in French. Jason didn't understand it, but he saw Edmond suppress a smile.

"This is so sweet I'm getting diabetes," muttered a small voice by Jason's shoulder, and he looked down to see Nikki standing there. Her baseball bat was conspicuously absent, and suddenly all the bravery and fire from earlier had faded, and she was a thirteen-year-old runaway again.

Jason's inner happy faded.

"Come with me," he said, and steered her into a parlor on one side of the vestibule. Nikki didn't resist, but her head was lowered; Jason couldn't see her face.

When they were away from everyone, Nikki sighed and leaned against the wall. "Are you going to yell at me?"

Jason shook his head. "Nikki, you were amazing today, and your dad would have been so goddamn proud, but, sweetie, you can't keep running away. If you seriously want to work as security for a Vampire House one day, you need to learn to follow orders."

"I helped save lives today by *not* following orders," Nikki said, scuffing her heel along the parquet floor.

"Fair point," Jason conceded. "But you can't keep doing this, and you know that."

"Yeah," Nikki mumbled, not meeting his eyes. "Diane and I got into a big fight, and I just snapped. I found myself jumping on a train back to Winchester before I knew what I was doing."

"How did you know to come to the M3?" Jason asked.

"It was all over the news. I realized some shady shit was going on, so I headed over there to see if I could help."

Jason smiled and shook his head. "You're so ridiculously brave, do you know that?"

Nikki shrugged, but she was smiling too. "It's not that big a deal."

"Yes, it is." Jason put his hands on her shoulders. Nikki stared up at him, all wild curls and young eyes. "You're going to do amazing things one day, Nikki Flynn, and I'll be there to see all of them. When you're older, any Vampire House will be lucky to have you, but for now, you're still a kid."

Nikki nodded. "I'll call Diane and tell her where I am."

There was a good chance that Nikki's aunt had already seen her splashed across the media after what had happened today, but Jason didn't mention that.

"Do you want me to do it?" he said. He didn't envy Nikki the trouble she'd be in.

"Thanks, but I have to face the music myself," Nikki said, and pulled out her phone.

"Hey," Jason said, and Nikki looked up again. "I'm so fucking proud of you," he said, and hugged her.

Gideon

As everyone dispersed throughout the mansion, Godric caught up with Gideon as he climbed the main staircase.

"Are you all right?" he asked.

"Why wouldn't I be?" Gideon replied.

"When Ivar had his hands on you—" Godric shook his head. "That really scared me."

Gideon's throat knotted.

Everything he'd just witnessed between Isabeau and Ysanne was a reminder that some relationships were worth fighting for, but the love he'd had for his brother was still so tangled up with hurt and anger.

"I'm fine," he said.

Godric nodded, but his eyes were shadowed with worry. "Jason was very brave today," he said.

Gideon couldn't keep a smile from his lips. "Yes, he was. And also very foolish for rushing in like that."

"He obviously cares about you a great deal."

"But?" Gideon said, because there was clearly a *but* coming.

"Do you think Ivar had a point in what he said to you?" Godric asked.

Gideon stiffened. "You think Jason and I have no future?"

"I think that Jason is human, and humans have very short lives compared to ours," said Godric carefully. "I think that one day he'll leave you, whether he wants to or not."

"Jason cares about me."

"But he'll die, and you won't. That is one of the curses of immortality." Godric blinked, pain spreading through his eyes. "I loved my wife, and I still lost her. I loved my children, my grandchildren, my great-grandchildren, and I lost them too. You're all I have left, and I can't bear the thought of you suffering like I have."

Gideon had nothing to say that.

He walked away from his brother and headed to the south wing, to Jason's bedroom. There, he sat on Jason's bed and quietly waited for his boyfriend to join him, which he knew he inevitably would.

It was another thirty minutes before Jason entered the room, rubbing his jaw. "Nikki's aunt is coming to pick her up. Again," he reported.

"Let's hope this is the last time," Gideon said. Unless Nikki could forge some kind of bond with her aunt, the next few years of her life would be very difficult.

"Maybe when this is all over, we can go and visit her in Guildford," Jason suggested.

Gideon made a noncommittal noise. What if this wasn't *ever* over? Every time they dealt with one threat, another sprang up in its place, a hydra of crises. Would they ever be able to stop fighting and just live their lives, like they had before?

"I'm not happy that you came today," he told Jason.

"Oh no, you might have to spank me," Jason replied.

Gideon gave him a stern look, and Jason sighed and approached the bed.

"Okay, I know it was reckless and dangerous, but you don't know how it feels to always sit on the sidelines and never be able to help," he said.

"You don't know how it feels to watch your human boyfriend facing up to the strongest vampire any of us have ever met," Gideon countered.

Jason winced.

"But," Gideon continued, stroking Jason's hair, "I'm also incredibly proud of you."

Jason laughed. "I just had this conversation with Nikki."

"That doesn't make it any less true."

"It just feels weird to be on the receiving end of it."

Jason lay back on the bed, his palms under his head, his feet still on the floor. "Today could have gone worse," he said.

"It could have gone better too," Gideon said, his mood souring as he pictured Ivar disappearing among the trees. "If we'd caught him, this would all be over. Instead, he'll be recuperating somewhere, ready to come back when he's at full strength, and that won't take long."

"I know, but can't we enjoy this victory while we have it?" Jason said.

It seemed a little pointless enjoying something they likely wouldn't have for long, but saying that would dim Jason's mood too. Gideon didn't want to do that.

"Did you mean what you said to him?" he asked.

"About pitying him?"

Gideon nodded.

"Yeah," Jason said. "He's lived so long and seen so much, and that could have been amazing, but instead it's turned him into *that*. That's fucking tragic, isn't it?"

"I hadn't thought about it like that," Gideon admitted.

"You just saw him as a bad guy?"

"Considering the threat he poses to us, and the people he hurt today, yes," Gideon said.

Jason rolled over, gazing up at Gideon. "You know that all that stuff he said was crap, don't you? Not every vampire ends up like Ivar."

"Maybe they do when they get to a certain age. Maybe that's why none of us have seen a vampire that old in a long time, if ever."

Jason reached up and caught Gideon's chin with his fingers. "He was wrong," he said firmly. "You're not going to become like Ivar. None of you are."

Gideon smiled, closed his fingers around Jason's, and didn't argue the point anymore.

But later that night, after Jason had fallen asleep, Gideon lay awake, his mind going over and over Ivar's words. He hadn't told Jason that Godric had expressed his own concerns, or that both Ivar and Godric had got into his head, that the things they'd said had burrowed under his skin and curled around his bones, making him feel all wrong inside.

No matter how hard he tried, he couldn't shake the fear that there was a grain of truth to what they'd said.

CHAPTER TWENTY-FOUR

Jason

A further two days passed with no news of Ivar. Jason learned that Walsh had immediately sent armed teams to scour the area, but they hadn't been able to track him down any more than Ludovic had.

Even though he knew that, sooner or later, Ivar would be back, Jason treasured every second of those two days, because in that time things felt normal. As normal as life ever was inside Belle Morte, anyway.

But of course, it couldn't last.

When his mum called one Friday afternoon, Jason didn't expect it to be anything other than a check-in. With everything that had happened lately, she was unhappier than ever about him staying at Belle Morte, but she'd stopped pressuring him to come home—though she still called regularly to see how things were going.

"Hi, Mum," he said, ducking into a nearby feeding room.

"Hi, honey."

Her voice was subdued, and Jason's chest squeezed with dread.

"What's wrong? Are you okay?" he said.

"I'm fine, it's not me."

"Is it Dad?" Jason grabbed the back of a nearby chair for support.

"No one's hurt, if that's what you're thinking," she said. "Well, not really."

That didn't ease the tightness in Jason's chest. "What does that mean?"

"Your brother's been suspended from school for fighting."

Jason blinked. "I'm sorry, what?"

Shaun was a good kid. He didn't get into fights.

"I think you need to talk to him."

"Me?" Now Jason was thoroughly confused. "No offence, Mum, but isn't that something the parents should do?"

His mum was quiet for a moment. Then she said, "The fight was about you."

Jason sat down. Hard. "What?"

"You need to talk to him, Jason."

"Is he there now? Does he know you're calling me?"

"Yes, he's here. No, he doesn't know I'm calling."

"Does he even *want* to talk to me?"

Jason was close with all his siblings, but this was so out of character for Shaun that he had no idea what to think or how to react.

"Of course he does. He's your brother."

Jason bit his lip. Gideon and Godric were brothers, but there still seemed to be a hell of a rift between them.

"Put Shaun on the phone," he said.

He waited while his mum fetched his little brother, listening to the muffled sounds as she made her way upstairs.

When Shaun came on the phone, he sounded as subdued as their mum. "Hey."

"Hey, kid. Is there something you want to tell me?" Jason said.

Shaun was silent.

"Okay, I'll start," Jason said. "You got suspended today. Do you want to talk about that?"

There was a noise on the other end of the phone that he thought might have been a shrug.

"What was the fight about?"

Shaun sighed down the phone, and it was a thin, sad sound. "You remember when I had trouble with that Greg Wilson guy?"

A wave of protective anger crept over Jason. It didn't matter that Shaun wasn't a nervous eleven-year-old anymore; he was still Jason's little brother. "That snotty little dickweed who used to hassle you when you first started high school?"

"Yeah."

"I thought he left you alone after you didn't react to him."

"He did. Until now." Shaun fell silent.

"What's he doing now?" Jason said.

"Saying shit about you."

"Me? Like what?"

Shaun didn't answer.

"C'mon, kid, I'm not going to get my feelings hurt by some petty schoolboy," Jason said.

"He was going on about you and Gideon, okay? He kept getting in my face and saying how you were a pervert, how you were sick and wrong."

Jason rolled his eyes. "So he's a boring little homophobe—"

"You don't get it. It wasn't about you being gay, it was about Gideon being a vampire. *That's* what he thinks is sick. He kept saying that Gideon was dead, so you were basically screwing a corpse."

Jason's throat tightened. Okay, that stung more than he'd expected.

"He said our parents must have raised you to think that fucking dead people was okay, so we probably all did it. Then he started laughing and saying that I wouldn't have to try hard to get a date for prom. I'd just have to go to the graveyard with a shovel."

"So you hit him," Jason guessed.

"Yeah," Shaun mumbled.

"And then what?"

"Then he hit me back."

"Are you okay?"

The thought of someone hurting his little brother made Jason want to throw a punch or two of his own.

"I'll have a black eye by tomorrow, but I'm fine." There was a proud note in Shaun's voice. "He looks worse than I do."

Jason sighed. "Look, I love that you wanted to defend me, but you can't go throwing punches just because someone said something stupid."

"You don't think that was more than stupid?" Shaun demanded.

"Even if it was, it's not worth picking a fight over, and risking getting kicked out of school."

"I'm not getting kicked out. We both got three-day suspensions, and then we're back," Shaun said.

"And what if Greg runs his mouth again?" Jason asked.

Shaun didn't reply.

"You walk the hell away," Jason said. "Seriously. No matter how much of a dick he is, it's just words. I'm not getting upset over it, so neither should you."

"So I'm just supposed to ignore it?" Shaun said.

"If he brings it up again, you can always tell him that even screwing a corpse is more action than he'll ever get, but otherwise, yeah. Just ignore it. People like that aren't worth anything more, and if you spend your life getting upset over other people's opinions, you're going to be very miserable."

It was Shaun's turn to sigh. "Yeah, you're probably right. It's just hard sometimes."

"Only if you let it be," Jason said.

"Hey, are you coming to the march on Sunday?" Shaun changed the subject.

"What march?" Jason asked.

"Haven't you heard? You've probably been tagged in it a billion times."

"I haven't been on social media lately."

"There's a big march at the high street on Sunday. People want to show their support for Belle Morte," Shaun said.

"Really?" Excitement flared inside Jason, followed just as quickly by an icy wave of panic.

Shaun chattered about details, but Jason could no longer hear him. The quiet comfort of the last two days was gone.

The last time Ivar had launched an attack, it had been on a busy public road, with the intention of undoing what Ysanne had done a decade earlier. He wouldn't repeat the same thing, but any further attacks would almost certainly be in public places. Ivar wanted spectacle.

That was why he hadn't resurfaced these past couple of days. He'd been biding his time, waiting for the right opportunity to strike, and now it was here.

Ivar was going to attack the march.

CHAPTER TWENTY-FIVE

Jason

He ran to Ysanne's office like a fire was spreading behind him. He knocked on the smoked glass of the door because bursting into Ysanne's office unannounced was still a big no-no, but rather than Ysanne's crisp voice, he heard what sounded like furniture being jolted.

Then there was silence for a moment or two.

"Ysanne? I really need to talk to you," he said.

When she eventually came to the door, something about her was different. Jason couldn't put his finger on it. Her clothing was the same, her hair was the same, her marble expression was the same.

Then he looked closer, and little details came into focus—very un-Ysanne-like details. There was a small but distinct crease on one side of her fitted dress. A few strands of pale blond hair were slightly out of place, which for Ysanne was practically a bedhead. Most noticeable were her eyes. They sparkled in a way Jason wasn't sure he'd seen before.

Then she moved fractionally, allowing an inadvertent peek into the office, and Jason caught a glimpse of curly auburn hair.

Oh.

It took everything he had to keep his face neutral.

A lot of unexpected things had happened to him since arriving at Belle Morte, and in some ways, interrupting Ysanne and Isabeau while they were having fun, was one of the strangest.

Ysanne lifted a perfectly arched eyebrow. "Yes?" she said, a touch impatiently.

"I think I know where Ivar will attack next," Jason said.

Ysanne glanced over her shoulder, then looked back at Jason. "We'll meet in the library in three minutes," she said.

Jason went straight there and spent the next few minutes agitatedly pacing the floor, his mind churning. Finally, Ysanne and Isabeau arrived, both looking as immaculately tidy as ever, no sign of whatever Jason had interrupted.

"Tell us what's going on," Isabeau said.

Jason did.

"But you don't *know* anything for certain," Isabeau said.

Jason looked pleadingly at Ysanne. "Ivar found out about the early protests against vampires, he can find out about this one. Especially if it's as big as my brother thinks it will be. If he's going to attack anywhere, it'll be there."

"I agree," Ysanne said. "I think we need to call Walsh."

"Use my phone," Jason said and handed it over. "Put it on speaker," he added.

Ysanne shot him an awkward look, and didn't say anything for a long moment. Something clicked in his brain.

"Here. I'll show you how," he said.

"Thank you," Ysanne said stiffly.

She called Walsh, and as she relayed to him what Jason had told her, Jason joined Isabeau on a nearby sofa, quietly listening.

Walsh exhaled, his voice sounding rougher than ever. "You don't have anything more concrete?"

"Just gut instinct and common sense," Jason piped up.

"Ivar wishes to make a statement, of sorts. He believes that vampires and humans can't truly live in harmony, and he seems determined to prove that through violence and possibly even murder," Ysanne said.

"For fuck's sake," Walsh muttered. "I thought we were done with this once we nailed that Schofield bastard."

"Inspector, after all your years as a policeman, you should be aware that there's never an end to people who wish to harm others."

Walsh responded with another rough sigh. "Yeah, you're right."

"So what do we do about this?" Jason asked.

"I'm not sure what you want me *to* do. No one's found a single trace of Haldorsen, and we can't stop him if we can't find him."

"But we can't let him attack the march," Jason said.

"Agreed. Shutting the whole thing down is probably the best option."

Disappointment sat heavily in Jason's stomach. "Really?"

"You have another suggestion?" Walsh asked.

"It's worth pointing out that the march would bring Ivar out of hiding, which is surely what we want," Isabeau suggested.

"It is, but not at the risk to innocent human life," Ysanne said. Isabeau nodded.

Jason twisted his hands together because he didn't know what else to do with them. Isabeau had a point—to stop Ivar, they had to lure him into the open. A vampire that old wouldn't fall for cheap tricks, so the march would have been the perfect place to get him where they wanted. But Ysanne was right too. They couldn't sacrifice people to get to him. They'd have to find another way. Jason just didn't have a clue what that was.

"Leave the march to me, I'll make sure it gets shut down safely. You just focus on finding and stopping that bastard," Walsh said.

"This is so unfair," Jason mumbled after Walsh had hung up. "All those people were going to come out to show their support for vampires, and Ivar's already ruined it."

"It's better that he ruins it through cancellation than turning up and hurting people," Ysanne said.

"I know, I know, but it still sucks."

"Perhaps it can be reorganized at a later date, after Ivar's been stopped for good."

Her words were optimistic, but even she couldn't hide the hollow note in her voice. Clearly, she had no idea how to stop him either.

The weekend slid past, and even though the march had been cancelled, Jason felt tense and on edge. He wasn't the only one; there was a strange atmosphere inside Belle Morte, like the mansion was holding its breath, like it, too, knew that something would happen soon.

Sunday came and Jason tried to keep himself busy, tried not to think about how the day should have gone and how Ivar had ruined it without even needing to do anything.

It was midafternoon when his phone pinged with a text from Shaun. *Don't be mad*, it read. There was an attached photo. Jason opened it and found himself staring at Shaun and their older sister, Laura, their faces pressed together to fit in the frame, both wearing matching grins. Behind them was a blur of other faces, and Jason's blood turned to ice as he realized that, despite Walsh's efforts, the march had gone ahead anyway.

The police could come to shut it down since it was no longer authorized, but that wouldn't stop Ivar.

Jason made a choked noise, and in a flash Gideon was at his side. "What's wrong?"

Jason showed him the photo. "The march," he whispered.

"It's still happening?" Horror dawned on Gideon's face. "Walsh said it had been shut down."

"I guess people decided to break the law and do it anyway. *Fuck.*"

All those people thought they were helping, but they'd put themselves in the worst kind of danger.

"Find the others," Jason said. "We need to get there."

Everyone assembled, armed themselves, and left the mansion in record time. Once again, Renie and Roux had to stay behind, but this time Jason insisted on coming.

"My family are at that march," he said fiercely, when Gideon tried to make him stay with the girls. "I'm going, with or without the rest of you."

They made it there in just a few minutes and parked a short distance away. The long, pedestrianized road that made up the high street was packed with people, some waving placards and banners; Jason even spotted one woman wearing a T-shirt with Edmond's face on it.

He couldn't help himself from nudging the tall vampire. "Do you think Renie would like one of those?"

Edmond gave him a lethal look. "Don't even think about it," he growled.

Jason patted his shoulder. "I make no promises."

He looked over the crowd again. Neither Shaun nor Laura had responded to his texts, and there was no way he'd spot them among this many people.

"If Ivar is here, he hasn't made a move yet," Ludovic said.

"No, but we don't know how long these people have been here," Edmond said.

Jason leaned closer to Gideon. "Is there any chance that I'm wrong and he's not going to try anything?"

"There's always a chance," Gideon replied.

"But you don't believe it."

Gideon's voice was too flat, too tense.

"No. I think your gut instinct was right. If Ivar's not here yet, he soon will be."

Ysanne, Edmond, Ludovic, Caoimhe, and Gideon all wore black caps like Jason's, while the other vampires had raided the erstwhile donors' rooms for hats, scarves, and bandanas—anything they could use to make themselves less recognizable.

Looking at them now, though, Jason wasn't sure it had been worth bothering with. They'd got away with the meager disguises last time because it had been dark, raining, and crowded. Now it was just as crowded—more so—but it was also broad daylight. No one who looked twice at any of the vampires here would mistake them for anyone other than who they really were.

Still, it wasn't like they'd had much choice.

Walsh had been notified, and the police were undoubtedly on their way, but they couldn't do much against even a regular vampire, let alone one with Ivar's power.

On Ysanne's command, they split into four groups, spreading around the outskirts of the march as it moved down the street in the direction of Winchester Cathedral. Jason wondered what they'd do once they ran out of ground. Turn around and go back the other way?

He stuck close to Gideon as they skirted the crowd, their backs to the shops and cafés that lined the street.

"I know this could go wrong at any second, but it's still amazing, isn't it? All these people?" Jason said.

Gideon's mouth was a tense line. "All I can see is how many people Ivar can hurt."

Jason brushed his fingers along Gideon's hand, and Gideon responded with a wan smile.

Minutes slid past and nothing happened, and a desperate hope settled in Jason's bones. Maybe, just maybe, he *had* been wrong. Maybe they all had.

And then someone screamed.

Jason and Gideon exchanged looks and ran toward the sound, shoving through the tightly packed crowd. Farther down the street Jason glimpsed a flash of familiar blue, and his stomach plunged.

"That was Ivar's tunic," he said.

Then crowd shifted and he spotted the vampire, still wearing his Viking regalia, his hair glinting red-gold under the sun, looking as ancient and terrifying as the last time Jason saw him. His injuries from the fight on the highway had long since healed.

In one hand Ivar held an iron bar, twisted at one end, and when Jason stood on his tiptoes, trying to see over the heads of the crowd, he spotted a painted wooden sign lying on its side near the vampire.

He looked up.

Winchester was an old city, parts of it dating back to medieval times, and to maintain that aesthetic some of the shops still used wooden boards hung from metal bars to show what they were selling.

Ivar had torn one down and discarded the board so he could use the thick bar as a weapon.

He swung it and shattered the windows of the nearest shop front. Screams rang out, and Jason glimpsed staff inside the shop rushing for the farthest wall, away from the flying glass.

Ivar strode forward and smashed another window. A woman's head jerked, a line of red appearing on her cheek where a shard of flying glass had hit her. The man with her rushed forward, yelling at Ivar, and Jason wanted to scream at him to get back, but the words stuck in his throat.

The Viking cocked his head, the movement almost animalistic, then he cracked the bar against the man's head. The man crumpled to the ground and didn't move.

Panic threatened to choke Jason. He hadn't realized how many people would be here, or how packed together they'd be. This wasn't like the highway, where the vampires had had space to fight and Jason and Nikki had had space to rescue people. Here, there was no room to do anything.

People jostled him as the crowd shuffled back, putting distance between them and Ivar, and though a full panic hadn't erupted yet, it was probably only a matter of time. If that happened, Ivar wouldn't need to do anything else. He could just sit back and watch as people trampled each other in their desperation to get away.

Jason turned to Gideon, but he wasn't there. Somehow, they'd got separated in the movement of the crowd, and now Jason couldn't even see him.

His gaze fell on the Butter Cross of Winchester, an ancient cross monument with carved pinnacles sitting on top of five octagonal steps in the street, just in front of a black-and-white Tudor-fronted building. Several people had already clustered on those steps, but there was still some breathing room, and before Jason could think twice, he was shoving through the throng to reach the cross.

He clambered up the steps until he was higher than everyone else and could clearly see Ivar at the front of the march, still swinging that twisted iron bar, broken glass forming shining patterns on the ground all around him.

Ivar's eyes gleamed red, and for the first time it occurred to Jason that the Viking vampire wasn't entirely stable.

"Ivar," he shouted.

Gideon would kill him for this.

Ivar turned his head in Jason's direction, and surprise briefly flared in his eyes. "Back again?" he said. "Such a loyal pet to the vampires of Belle Morte."

"Not a pet, just a friend," Jason said. "And boyfriend to one of them."

Someone in the crowd giggled, and the heavy atmosphere lightened, just a fraction.

"Ivar," Jason said again, softer this time. "I know we've been in this position before and—"

"And once again you're going to express your pity and your belief that I'm wrong," Ivar said.

"You *are* wrong." Jason spread his arms wide. "Look at all these people."

Ivar gave the crowd a dismissive glance.

"They're here today for vampires, because they've shared their world with us for the last ten years and they want to continue doing that," Jason said.

"*Their* world? Vampires like me were around long before any of them," Ivar growled.

"Okay, well, they're here now and they're not going anyway."

"Neither am I."

"You don't *have* to," Jason cried, flinging up his hands.

In his periphery he spotted Gideon at last, moving silently toward the Butter Cross.

"Ivar, you've been around for over a millennium, and you've shared the world with humans all that time. Why are you turning on them now?" Jason said.

"Because they turned on *us*," the vampire spat.

"But they *didn't*." Jason threw his arms wide again, indicating the crowd. "Look at them! They haven't turned on us. The people you attacked on the M3? They didn't turn on us either. They lined up to feed us, to help us heal our injuries."

"Us?" A strange look crossed Ivar's face. "I think you've forgotten, boy, you're not a vampire."

"I haven't forgotten anything. I just don't view vampires and humans as two different species," Jason said coolly.

Ivar laughed, a harsh sound that rang out across the street. "We are as different as night and day."

"Night and day are two sides of the same coin. One can't exist without the other," Jason countered.

"You think vampires and humans need each other to survive?" Ivar sounded amused.

"Vampires certainly need humans."

Irritation flared in Ivar's eyes; clearly he didn't like being reminded of that.

"A lot of shit has happened lately, a lot of bloody, tragic, horrible shit, and it's screwed up a lot of lives, and, yes, that's made some people turn against us, but not everyone. I don't blame you for only seeing the worst in people, and I can't imagine what you've been through in your life, but the world isn't as bleak as you think, and people aren't as bad," Jason said.

Ivar's eyes were fixed on his face, but the red had faded from them. "You really think all these people came because they care about vampires? We're just *entertainment* to them," he said.

"Excuse me." A hesitant voice spoke up, and a young blond woman carefully pushed through the crowd. "I can't speak for everyone, but if Ysanne Moreau is here, I came for her."

Jason searched the crowd but he couldn't see Ysanne. She'd be listening, though. The young woman's voice rose into the air, clear as a bell.

"Ten years ago, Ysanne Moreau pulled me out of my car when I got into a major crash, on the day that we learned vampires existed. She saved my life." The woman paused, looking around. "I didn't know it at the time, but I was pregnant." The woman glanced back, and Jason realized she wasn't alone. She held the hand of a young boy. "Ysanne didn't just save me, she saved my unborn son."

"My great-grandmother's family was left nearly destitute after her husband was killed at the Somme. Ysanne secretly gave them enough money to keep going," called another voice.

Another woman pushed forward. She was old, bent almost double as she leaned on a wooden cane, her gray hair neatly styled and glasses perched on her nose, but when she spoke, her voice was as clear as anyone's.

"I was a little girl living in London when the Blitz came. My father had gone off to fight, and my mother and I were staying with her sister when a bomb hit our house. My aunt was killed, and I was trapped under the rubble. My mother tried desperately to dig me out, but she wasn't strong enough." The old woman lifted her voice even more. "Isabeau Aguillon dug me out. If she's here today, thank you."

"My granddad was killed fighting on the Western Front," shouted another voice. "In letters that he wrote to my gran, he talked about Edmond Dantès and Ludovic de Vauban, and how they fought together, and all the people they helped save."

More and more voices joined in.

"Hugh Daven saved my boy from drowning."

"Fadime Shah rescued my sister from an abusive boyfriend."

"Gideon Hartwright saved me and my friends from a burning building."

That last one caught Jason's attention more than the others. He looked down, trying to catch Gideon's eye, but Gideon was frantically looking around, trying to find the speaker.

Still the voices continued.

"Caoimhe Ó Duinnín carried my mum three miles to a hospital."

"Isabeau Aguillon helped women get the vote."

"Jemima Sutton pulled my granny out of the way of a speeding car."

Jason blinked at Jemima's name, but maybe he shouldn't have been surprised. Jemima hadn't always been a villain.

Throughout the revelations, Ivar hadn't said a word.

"Don't you see?" Jason called to him, and the Viking blinked as if coming out of a trance. "Most of these people are strangers, but their lives are still tangled up with vampires, and there'll be people all over the world with stories like this, going back centuries. We've all lived in harmony since vampires revealed themselves: Jemima and Etienne couldn't destroy that, nor could Roger Schofield. You won't do it either."

Ivar suddenly lunged, plowing toward the Butter Cross, and despite the icy wave of fear that crashed over him, Jason stood his ground and waited for the Viking to reach him.

Ivar leaped up the stone steps to where Jason stood and grabbed him by the throat. He saw Gideon rush forward, but Godric was faster, throwing both arms around Gideon and dragging him back.

Jason stared into Ivar's burning red eyes and swallowed against the vampire's iron grip.

"I'm not afraid of you," he said, though that wasn't exactly true. "You can kill me, kill my friends, kill everyone here, and it still won't achieve what you think it will. The world isn't a cold, cruel place, and people aren't all monsters. We've built a world together, and you could be a part of that, if you wanted to."

Ivar's fingers loosened. His eyes were still red, but less fiery than they'd been a moment ago.

"Please can we just end this?" Jason said.

Ivar's hand dropped from Jason's throat and hung loosely by his side. He took a step back, and suddenly he looked lost, like he'd found himself in a world that he didn't understand and couldn't navigate.

He gazed over the crowd, at the vampires and all the people they'd helped over the years, and his eyes settled on Gideon.

"It still won't work," he said, and Gideon stiffened. "You still don't realize it, but one day you'll wake up and understand my view of the world." He glanced back at Jason. "Maybe it won't be until the boy dies, but it will happen. You have no future with him."

Jason didn't argue. It wasn't worth it.

"Maybe I can't make you see the truth, but one day you will," Ivar said, looking at the crowd again, but Jason wasn't sure if he was addressing them or the vampires mingled among them. "Ask yourselves why you haven't seen a vampire as old as me in such a long time. Ysanne, ask yourself why you never saw Agnes again. The weight of time becomes too much. We go mad from it. You'll see. Eventually."

Ivar dropped the iron bar, and it clattered down the steps before coming to rest on the cobbled street.

No one tried to stop him as he walked away.

CHAPTER TWENTY-SIX

Gideon

No one moved until Ivar had disappeared, even though Gideon's very bones ached with the need to run after him and beat him to a pulp for putting his hands on Jason.

Ivar was still a threat.

Last time they'd faced him, he'd fled to heal his injuries.

This time he'd chosen to walk away unscathed, but how long would that last?

How long until he came back?

Godric still had both arms wrapped around Gideon's chest, holding him back, but his grip had relaxed, and Gideon irritably shook him off.

"We have to go after him," he said.

"Not a chance," said a familiar voice at his elbow, and Gideon realized Isabeau had slipped through the throng to join them. "We came here to prevent human casualties, and Ivar walking away accomplishes that. If we go after him now, if we goad him into a fight, then people could die."

Gideon knew she was right, but there was a tight heaviness in his chest, making him feel wrong and full of broken edges.

"Was he wrong?" he asked.

Isabeau frowned. "What do you mean?"

"Will we end up like him one day?"

"No." Isabeau's reply was confident and immediate.

"But there *aren't* any vampires as old as him, at least not that we know of. There were once, because vampires have always existed. Where are the other old ones?"

Isabeau's frown deepened, but before she could respond, Jason had shoved his way toward them and was flinging his arms around Gideon's neck.

"Fuck, that was intense," he cried.

Gideon hugged him back, but he couldn't dislodge the heavy feeling pressing against his ribs, weighing on his heart.

It wasn't just because the potential truth in Ivar's words chilled him to his core.

He couldn't shake the image of Jason standing up on the Butter Cross, Ivar's hand wrapped around his neck. Jason had come to Belle Morte to be a donor, nothing more. He was supposed to have left the mansion and gone back to his normal human life by now. Instead, he was still here, tangled up in the vampires' mess, and Gideon couldn't see a light at the end of the tunnel.

How much danger had Jason been in since coming to Belle Morte? And how much of that danger was because of their relationship?

Jason

He felt like he was full of sunshine as he and Gideon broke away from the crowd and headed up to the street to where the vans were parked.

For the first time in a long time, it felt like things were going to be okay.

"Fuck vampires," someone yelled, breaking Jason's happy spell.

A small group stood on the opposite street, a mix of men and women of different ages, but all of them sharing similar expressions of disgust and dislike.

"People before vampires," a woman shouted, and hurled something.

Jason flinched, and felt Gideon instinctively grab him, ready to pull him out of harm's way.

But it was just an egg, and not a very well-thrown one. It cracked on the pavement several feet short of them, and a laugh bubbled in Jason's throat.

"You'll have to try harder than that," he said.

The woman gave him the finger. Jason returned it with a smile.

Gideon said nothing.

"Hey." Jason nudged him. "You okay?"

Gideon smiled, but it was tight and forced, an imitation of the beautiful one Jason had come to know so well. Ever since Ivar had left, Gideon had been giving off a strange vibe, one that Jason couldn't interpret.

Gideon didn't speak on the journey home, and Jason tried not to read too much into that because the trip *was* only a few minutes. But something felt wrong.

When they were safely inside the mansion's grounds and climbing out of the van, Jason grabbed Gideon's arm. "Are you going to tell me what's wrong?"

Gideon looked back at him, and Jason had no idea how to read what he saw in his eyes. He'd come to know the vampire so well, and suddenly it seemed as if everything he knew and loved had retreated back inside Gideon, leaving something cold, remote.

"Nothing," Gideon said.

He pulled away from Jason and strode inside, leaving him standing outside, his heart twisting into a knot. Their relationship had been built on a foundation of trust and honesty.

Gideon had just lied to him.

Jason followed him inside.

Renie and Roux were waiting in the vestibule, sitting on the bottom step of the staircase, huddled over a phone; Jason guessed they'd been following the events as best they could from news reports.

They both jumped up when he came in and ran to hug him.

"Are you okay?" Roux asked, looking at Jason's neck.

He touched the place where Ivar had grabbed him. If he had bruises, he was too distracted to feel them.

"I'm fine, but Gideon's been in a weird mood since Ivar left," he said.

"We noticed," Renie said.

"You did?" Jason's heart twisted. Part of him had hoped that it was all in his head.

"As soon as he got in he made a beeline for the north wing, didn't even speak to us," Roux said.

"Go talk to him. In my experience, most relationship problems are caused by miscommunication," Renie advised.

"Right," Jason said.

He was halfway up the stairs when another voice called his name, and he turned to see a handsome blond vampire heading his way—just not the one he was looking for.

"Are you looking for my brother?" Godric's voice was as neutral as his expression. Jason didn't like it.

"Yeah."

Godric quickened his pace, putting himself ahead of Jason on the stairs. Jason tried to sidestep him, but Godric quickly moved to block him.

Jason set his jaw. "Look, I know you don't like me, and to be honest, I really don't care, so if you've got something to say then just spit it out. I'm not in the mood for games."

"I don't dislike you," Godric said.

"Oh."

"I just don't think you should be with my brother."

Jason's temper sparked. "What the fuck are you talking about?" he said. "Are you seriously telling me that after everything you put Gideon through, you're going to try screwing things up for him now he's finally happy?"

Surprise registered in Godric's eyes, but he still didn't move. "That's not what I'm trying to do."

Jason folded his arms. "Enlighten me."

"You're human, Jason. You're human and fragile and short-lived. Gideon isn't any of those things."

"This may shock you, but I already know that," Jason snapped.

"I don't think you fully realize why this is a problem. You claim that you're making Gideon happy, but it won't last, will it? Humans have such short lives—that's why their relationships with vampires don't work."

Any other time Jason might have felt sorry for Godric. Not only had he been turned against his will by a demented admirer, he'd had to let his family think he was dead. This issue was personal to him because he'd been forced to watch his wife and children and all their descendants grow old and die, while he'd stayed the same. It was no wonder he didn't approve of human/vampire relationships.

But today Jason had no patience for Godric. "You know what?" he snapped. "This is Gideon's life and Gideon's decision. You haven't been there for most of his life, so you don't get to start controlling it now."

Shoving past Godric, he continued up the stairs, and this time Godric didn't try to stop him.

Jason knew which bedroom was Gideon's, but this was the first time he'd actually visited it, and as he opened the door a little tremor ran through him. Maybe he should have checked out the place sooner, but it had always suited them both to have the south wing to themselves.

Gideon's room was charcoal gray, the wallpaper bearing the faint impression of darker gray trees, as if a nighttime forest was trying to push through the walls, and the carpet was the color of a rain-washed pebble. The furniture was dark wood, like Edmond's, and everything looked too neat, too organized, almost as if no one actually lived here.

Gideon *did* spend more time in Jason's room than his own these days.

Jason tore his gaze away from the decor and focused on the vampire sitting quietly on the edge of his bed.

"Gid?" he said, taking another couple of steps forward.

Gideon didn't look up.

"Okay, I have no idea what's going on with you, but I'm seriously worried. You're not fine. We've always been honest with each other, so please don't start lying to me now," Jason said.

Finally Gideon lifted his head. His face was more remote than Jason had ever seen it, even before they were together, back in the days when Jason had been languishing in the throes of unrequited lust, hoping against hope that tight T-shirts and good hair would get Gideon's attention.

It was as if a wall had suddenly sprung up between them, and Jason had no idea where it had come from.

Or how to get over it.

Gideon studied Jason's face for a long time. "You could have died today."

"He didn't even hurt me," Jason said.

"He could have."

"But he didn't."

Jason hated the distant way Gideon looked at him, as if he was a stranger.

"Everything turned out okay," he said.

"Until next time."

Jason balled his fists in frustration. "Who even says there'll be a next time?"

"Every time we think we've dealt with a threat, another one arrives. There's always a next time," Gideon said.

"Then we'll deal with that when the time comes. *Together*," Jason insisted.

Gideon looked away.

"What if Ivar was right?" he said.

"About what?"

"Us."

Jason swallowed, feeling suddenly shaky. "What do you mean?"

"I struggled to adjust to this world and this relationship, and I'm only a fraction of Ivar's age. What kind of person will I be in another five hundred years? A millennium? Will I lose my grip on reality, driven mad by the sheer weight of time?"

Jason started to answer, but Gideon interrupted.

"I know of vampires who ended their own lives before we were revealed to the world because they could no longer cope with living as long as they had. There are vampires living in this very building who attempted suicide because it seemed a better alternative than struggling on with the weight of everything. There are Vampire Houses across the world now, but we don't know of a single other vampire as old as Ivar. What does that tell you?" He didn't give Jason a chance to respond. "It tells me that he had a point."

"So, what, you think the future's completely hopeless? You think all vampires will eventually go mad and either kill themselves or try to kill innocent people? That's ridiculous," Jason said, his heart pounding.

"No one knows what the future holds."

"Exactly," Jason cried. "No one *knows*. Not you, not Ivar, not anyone. And if everyone was too scared to try anything because of what might happen in a thousand years, then mankind would never have left their caves."

Gideon surged to his feet. "Do you honestly think that we have a future together?"

"*Yes*. Don't you?"

Gideon didn't reply.

There was a funny feeling in Jason's chest, like he wasn't getting enough air into his lungs. "What are you trying to say, Gideon? That it's over?"

"Maybe that's for the best."

Jason felt like he'd been punched again, only this time it hurt much more, a sledgehammer of utter disbelief crashing into him. "Are you actually breaking up with me right now?"

Gideon said nothing.

"You can't be serious." Jason's breath came quick and fast, sawing in and out of his lungs. "I know how we feel about each other—are you saying you're going to throw all that away?"

"I'm trying to do what's best for you."

"That's bullshit," Jason snapped. "Being with you is *my* decision. *Mine.* If that puts me in danger then I'll accept it, because you're worth it."

He stared at Gideon, waiting for him to say something, to smile and say that Jason was right, and he had no idea why he'd even suggested breaking up.

But Gideon didn't.

When he lifted his eyes to Jason's face, they were dark with pain, but they were also resolute.

"I'm sorry," he said.

Tears burned Jason's eyes as he felt his heart crack. "Gid," he whispered. "I love you."

Gideon pressed his lips together and said nothing.

Jason stumbled back, fumbling for the door handle.

He couldn't believe this was happening, but it was. Gideon wasn't backing down. He wasn't changing his mind. He was watching Jason's heart break in front of him, and he *wasn't changing his mind.*

Jason stumbled out of the room and braced one hand on the wall.

Everything inside him was splintering. His heart was full of broken glass. He had to get away from here.

He broke into a run, racing out of the north wing and back to the safety of his own bedroom.

And Gideon let him go.

CHAPTER TWENTY-SEVEN

Gideon

Not so long ago, a desperate vampire had stabbed Gideon in the chest with a pitchfork.

That didn't even compare to the pain he felt now.

How could his heart hurt so much when it didn't even beat?

What the fuck had he just done?

His legs ached to run after Jason, but instead his knees buckled, and he found himself crumpling to the floor.

"You have to protect him," he whispered, clenching his fists until they hurt.

As long as Jason was with Gideon, he was in danger. Gideon couldn't have that. He couldn't see Jason die because of him.

He loved Jason, and that was why he had to give him up. So Jason would be safe.

Gideon pressed a fist to his forehead, a low groan trickling between his lips.

He wanted to rage at Godric for planting that awful seed of doubt in his head, but how could he blame his brother when Godric had been right all along?

He'd do whatever it took to protect Jason.

Even if that means shattering both your hearts? asked a little voice inside.

Gideon hesitated. He was trying to keep anyone from hurting

Jason, but hadn't he done just that? The awful look in Jason's eyes, the shock and pain and betrayal, was burned into Gideon's mind.

He'd hurt the person he loved more than anyone.

But however bad Jason was feeling, it could be worse. Who knew what the next crisis would be, or how they'd handle it? Even now, complete strangers felt bold enough to shout at him in the street and throw things. Ex-donors were being attacked in the streets—that could happen to Jason, too, any time he left Belle Morte.

Iain Johnson and his gang of thugs had tried to kill Roux and Ludovic, more than once. Just because they'd been caught didn't mean others wouldn't try the same thing.

If Jason stayed with Gideon, he'd always be in danger.

Gideon would do whatever it took to stop that from happening.

But it *hurt* so much.

Jason was the best thing that had ever happened to him.

If he lived another hundred years, or even a thousand, he'd never find another Jason.

"This is the right thing to do," Gideon whispered to himself.

Something slid down his cheek, and when he touched his face, his fingertips came away red.

It was the first time he'd ever cried as a vampire.

He had a feeling it wouldn't be the last.

Jason

When he was still a donor—it felt like a lifetime ago now—Jason had warned Renie not to fall for Edmond, or any other vampire. He'd warned her that it couldn't end well.

He hadn't taken his own advice.

He had fallen for Gideon, completely and utterly, and now Gideon had broken his heart.

No, not broken it—*shattered* it. Everything inside him was in pieces, so small and sharp he doubted they would ever fit back together. Even if he could reassemble them, there would always be holes. He'd given too much of himself to Gideon to get all those pieces back.

How could Gideon possibly think that breaking up with Jason would protect him?

Jason sat on the floor and buried his face in his hands.

He loved Gideon. He'd hoped to spend the rest of his life with the man, and just like that he'd lost him.

Wrapping his arms around his knees, Jason started to cry.

Jason cracked open an eye, wincing at the bright artificial light over-head. He'd fallen asleep, curled into a ball. His side ached from lying on the floor.

His heart ached worse.

He pushed himself upright and leaned against the bed.

How long had he been asleep?

He was so exhausted and heartsick that it took him a few more moments to realize that someone had draped a blanket over him. He hadn't even heard anyone come in.

For a wild moment he was sure it had been Gideon, but he deflated just as quickly when he realized it must have been Renie or Roux.

If it had been Gideon, coming to fix things, he'd have woken Jason up. He would at least have stayed in the room, not covered him up and then slunk off.

Jason fumbled for his phone. His eyes were dry and gritty, sore from crying, and his head pounded. It was like the hangover from hell.

His phone told him it was ten. He'd slept through the night.

Grasping the edge of the bed, he hauled himself to his feet.

This was real, then. Yesterday really had happened. He'd lost Gideon. Where did he go from here?

First things first, he needed to tell Renie and Roux. They must have guessed that things hadn't gone well after finding him on the floor, but he didn't know if he could face seeing anyone yet.

He texted them a brief explanation, then dropped his phone onto the bed.

A few minutes later a knock came at his door.

"It's us," Renie said.

Jason dithered. He wanted to be alone to grieve the loss of his relationship with Gideon. He wanted to be with people who loved him. The latter won out. He opened the door.

"Oh, honey," Roux said and hugged him.

Jason didn't want to cry again, but the tears came before he could stop them, soaking into Roux's shirt. Renie joined the hug, trying to stretch her arms around them both.

Eventually, they moved to the bed, Jason sitting against the headboard with Roux next to him, Renie sprawled on her back at their feet.

"If you'd had a real choice about being turned into a vampire, would you still have done it?" Jason asked.

Both girls considered it.

"I think I'd still have wanted to be turned, sooner or later," Renie said. "Edmond's the love of my life, I want forever with him."

Roux nodded.

"Would you have wanted to be turned straightaway? Or would you rather have been human a little longer?" Jason said.

"I'd have spent at least a week gorging on all my favorite foods," Renie said.

"Given the choice I wouldn't have been turned straightaway," Roux said. "I'd have wanted a few more years of sunbathing and holidaying and seeing more of the world. I might have got a couple more tattoos or piercings. I just would have done everything that I knew I wouldn't be able to anymore."

"I often thought about getting a tattoo, but I always chickened out," Renie said. "Now I don't have the option. I know it's such a small thing, but it's one of many that vampires can't do."

Jason absorbed that.

"Had you and Gideon talked about you becoming a vampire one day?" Roux asked.

"A bit. Not that it matters now," he said.

"If you had to make the choice right now, what would you want?" Roux asked.

"To be with Gideon," Jason said.

"But as a human or a vampire?" Roux's voice was gentle.

"I don't know. Gideon can't give up his vampire life for me, so would I give up my human life for him?"

He gazed at his best friends. They were both vampires. His boyfriend—*ex*-boyfriend—was a vampire. If he never turned, could he cope with aging when everyone around him stayed so young? But becoming a vampire required a lot of sacrifices. What if he turned and realized the price was too high? There was no coming back from something like that. Once someone became a vampire, the only way out was death.

Then he thought of Gideon—lying in bed beside him, his hair mussed, his smile sleepy, and everything they'd found together.

"I'd become a vampire for him, but only when I was ready," he said. Then he shook his head. "But I have no idea how long it would take me to *feel* ready. What if I changed my mind and realized I didn't want to turn after all?"

"Then that's the choice you'd make," Renie said.

"But would that have been fair to Gideon?" Speaking about their relationship in the past tense hurt.

"What do you mean?" Roux said.

"If I stayed human forever, then I'd get old and wrinkly and Gideon wouldn't," Jason said.

"Do you think he'd care about that?"

"About whether I become a doddery old man? Kind of?"

Roux shook her head. "Gideon loves you for who you are, not for what you look like. The fact that you're a cutie pie is a definite bonus, but I don't believe he ever saw that as the most important part of your relationship. I think he'd love you no matter what."

"Then why did he just break up with me?" Jason said, the words sharp and painful on his tongue.

Roux didn't answer.

"Anyway, it's not just about looks. If I stayed human, Gideon would have to watch me die. Is *that* fair?" Jason said.

Renie rolled over and leaned on both elbows so she could look Jason in the eye.

"That would be the same if you were both human, though. You can be married for your whole life, but one of you still has to die first," she said.

Jason picked at a loose thread on his sleeve. "It doesn't matter, though, does it? He dumped me."

Roux put her arm around him.

Someone knocked on the door.

"Who is it?" Jason called.

"Edmond."

Renie looked at Jason, silently questioning, and Jason nodded. He couldn't become a hermit over this.

Renie climbed off the bed and answered the door. Edmond walked in, his inky hair spilling around his shoulders, a smile on his lips.

"I have some news," he said.

"Please let it be good news." Jason groaned, resting his head on the board.

"It is. The prime minister contacted Ysanne today to inform her that the language of the Human Rights Act will be officially amended to include vampires. No one will be able to argue that it no longer applies to us," Edmond said.

Renie let out a little squeak. "Which means no one can argue that we should be turned out of our houses."

Edmond smiled down at her, his whole face softening. Jason's heart constricted. Gideon used to look at him like that.

"Correct," Edmond said. "McGellan and Ysanne have also reached an agreement about officially reinstating the donor system. There are still various technicalities to work through first, and changes to implement, but it is going to happen."

Renie squeaked again and flung her arms around Edmond. He hugged her, lifting her off her feet. Roux shimmied on the bed, pumping both hands in the air.

Jason felt . . . he didn't know. The relief at Edmond's news was immeasurable, along with the happiness that all the vampires he cared about were safe now, at least from that potential threat. But everything inside him still felt bleak and broken and gray, because he no longer had Gideon to celebrate with.

"So Ivar can't threaten any of this anymore?" Renie checked.

"Maybe he's not a threat anymore," Jason said, recalling the look in the Viking's eyes before he'd walked away. "Maybe he just wants to live now, same as the rest of us."

Edmond's smile slipped. "Let's hope you're right."

Jason lowered his eyes. As Gideon had so painfully proved yesterday, no one could predict the future.

Two slow, painful days passed, and Jason barely saw Gideon. He seemed to be hiding out in the north wing; maybe he was hoping that Jason would leave soon, and he could go back to normal.

Jason hadn't brought it up with anyone, but he didn't know what to do with himself now. Originally, he'd stayed because he felt he could help his vampire friends, and he had, but what happened if they had no more battles to fight? Jason could no longer stay for Gideon, so was it finally time to go home?

He had no idea how to feel about that.

He missed his family, and he still loved the house he'd grown up in, but he wasn't the same person he'd been when he first came to Belle Morte, and he didn't see how he could go back to his old life as if nothing had happened.

Even his old dream of running his own hair salon didn't reach him the way it once had.

He hadn't told his family what had happened, but he'd kept in contact with them the whole time, so when Laura's number flashed up on his phone one morning, Jason didn't think anything of it.

Until he answered the phone.

"Jason Grant?" said an unfamiliar male voice, and Jason froze.

"Who is this?" he said.

The voice was quiet for a moment, and Jason's skin prickled with fear.

Then the voice said, "We have your sister."

CHAPTER TWENTY-EIGHT

Jason

Four words.

That was all it took to shake his world to the core.

"Who is this?" he said again, clenching his fist around his phone.

"That's not important," the voice said.

"I want to talk to Laura," Jason said. There was still a chance that they were lying—

There was a scuffle on the other end of the phone, then Laura's voice, choked with tears.

"Jason?"

He closed his eyes.

It was real then.

"Are you okay? Have they hurt you?" he said, fighting to stay calm.

"I—I'm okay," Laura stuttered.

"Do you know where you are?"

More scuffling noises, and then the male voice came back on the phone.

"Do you know the empty flats just off Winnall Manor Road?"

"The crack house," said Jason flatly. "Yeah, I know it."

The flats, occupying an old Victorian building, had hit the news a couple of years ago after a police raid on the place. Jason had no idea how the flats had become a drug den, only that they had. They were empty now, but the building itself still stood, and though Jason had never been there, he knew where it was.

It wasn't hard to get to.

"Your sister's there. If you want to see her in one piece, come alone. Leave your little friends behind. The vampire boyfriend too. If you don't, we'll kill her. If you call the police, we'll kill her. If you do *anything* we don't like, we will kill her. Do you understand?"

"Yes," Jason breathed.

"You have twenty minutes. Any longer and we kill her."

"What do you *want*?" Jason said.

The phone went dead.

He stared down at it. There was no point calling back. They wouldn't answer.

"You can't go," Gideon said at once.

"I have to." Jason tried not to meet his ex's eyes. It was hard enough just being in the same room as him, knowing that he could no longer touch him, hold him, *rely* on him.

"This does sound like a job for the police," Ysanne said, resting one hip against her desk.

Jason had gone straight to her after receiving the phone call. Isabeau had already been there, and when Ysanne learned what had happened, she'd gathered Edmond, Ludovic, Renie, Roux, and Gideon. Jason would have preferred it if Gideon wasn't there, but it was too late to tell Ysanne that.

"They specifically said no police. I'm not risking Laura's life," he said.

"Jason, think about this," Isabeau cautioned. "Why do you think they want you?"

"I don't care."

"And if they plan to kill you?"

"I'm not abandoning her," Jason shouted, his chest heaving. "Whoever these bastards are, they couldn't get to me at Belle Morte, so they're using Laura as bait."

"You can't go alone," Edmond said.

"I don't have a choice. If I don't, they'll kill her."

"If you do, they could kill you."

Jason glared at him. "What the fuck do you want me to do, Edmond? Sit on my ass and do nothing?"

"No—"

"I have to go."

Ysanne held up a finger. "I could call Walsh—"

"He's *police*. We can't."

"This is crazy," Renie said, chewing her lip.

"I have to go," Jason repeated.

"Then someone has to go with you," Gideon said.

"Which part of 'come alone' is everyone not understanding?" Jason snapped.

He moved toward the office door but Gideon quickly blocked him. "Listen to me," he said.

Jason struggled to focus on the face he loved so much, but panic felt like a fog over his eyes.

"We don't know who these people are. We don't know how many of them there are. We don't know what they want. You absolutely cannot walk into that situation alone. Let me come with you."

"They'll kill her, Gid," he whispered, tears burning his eyes.

Gideon grasped his face with both hands. "I won't let anyone else know I'm there, I promise. I'm faster and quieter than any human, and I can follow you to this place. You *need* someone else there. What if you go there and they still don't release her?"

That hadn't occurred to Jason, but it was exactly the sort of thing these fucking cowards would do. He couldn't trust them.

"If I'm there, I can make sure she gets out. Then I can come back for you," Gideon said. "If they don't let either of you go then they'll have me to deal with." His voice was hard and cold, his eyes glinting red.

Jason was torn. He believed these people would kill Laura if he didn't follow their instructions, but once he was there, there wasn't anything stopping them from killing her anyway. Or killing them both.

Slowly he nodded. "Okay."

The people who'd come for the kids hadn't properly understood vampires. They'd thought crucifixes and holy water would hurt them. Maybe Laura's kidnappers were just as ill informed. Most people *didn't* know how quick and quiet a vampire could be, because they'd never seen one in action.

If Gideon said he could get there without anyone knowing, then Jason trusted him.

"Let's go," he said.

Seamus gave Jason the keys to one of the Belle Morte cars. Jason thought Gideon might ride in the back, hidden from view by the tinted windows, but Gideon insisted it was safer for him to make his way on foot.

The journey didn't take long, but Jason's heart was in this throat the whole way—a hard, solid lump that made it hard to breathe. His hands were tight around the steering wheel.

He was so fucking *scared*.

When the building came into view, his whole chest clenched into a painful ball. Laura was in there somewhere, and he'd do whatever it took to get her out.

He parked the car a short distance away and climbed out, staring up at the crack house. It was a miserable-looking place, the facade half red brick and half beige plaster, the roof sprouting thick tufts of moss. Twigs and other debris poked out of the gutter, and one of the windows was broken, leaving dull shards clinging to the frame. Metal security fencing ran around the building, but no one had bothered to board up the door or the remaining windows.

As he approached, he resisted the urge to look around for Gideon—that could give everything away. He had no idea where Gideon was, but Jason trusted that he was there, silent as a ghost.

Gideon had let him down in so many ways, but Gideon wouldn't let him down on this.

His heart hitching higher in his throat, Jason slipped between a gap in the fencing. The front door hung slightly open, and he used his foot to push it the rest of the way, hanging back in case an unpleasant surprise waited in the dank hallway.

Nothing.

Cautiously, he ventured inside. The carpet and walls were stained and scarred, and the reek of urine—animal or human, he couldn't tell—was strong in the air.

Something crunched underfoot but he didn't look down.

"Okay, I'm here," he called, hoping his voice didn't waver. He'd gladly faced down Ivar Haldorsen, but this was different. This time it was his sister at risk, and that was a whole new kind of fear.

"Keep going down the corridor," a male voice replied.

Cautiously, Jason moved farther into the building until he reached a wide area that must once have been individual flats, but now two walls had been knocked down, creating one ugly open space, with rubble still scattered here and there. There was no furniture, nothing to suggest anyone had ever lived here.

And standing in the middle of that space, spread out in a loose semicircle in front of him, were six figures. Their builds clearly showed they were male, but their faces were covered with masks—each a different animal.

There was no sign of Laura.

Jason stopped dead, keeping distance between himself and them, and held up both hands to show he was unarmed. "Where's my sister?" he said.

They ignored him.

Footsteps sounded behind him, and he whirled around, his heart slamming against his ribs. Another masked man had appeared. He deliberately knocked Jason with his shoulder as he passed, and the pettiness of it made Jason grit his teeth.

Stay calm, he told himself.

"Well?" a man in a gorilla mask asked the newcomer. "He come alone?"

The newcomer—wearing a bear mask—nodded, eyes fixed on Jason. Even through the mask's small eyeholes, Jason could see the loathing that burned there, and it made him shiver.

"The car's empty," the bear reported.

Jason fought to keep the abject relief from showing on his face. If Gideon hadn't followed on foot, if he'd come with Jason, this would have been over before it began.

"Good boy," said the gorilla.

He seemed to be the leader.

Jason sized him up.

He was taller than Jason, but wiry rather than muscular. That didn't necessarily mean Jason could take him, but he'd certainly try, if it came down to that.

"So who are you?" Jason said.

"You can call us People Before Vampires," Gorilla said.

"What do you want from me?"

"People look up to you. They see you having a relationship with a *vampire*, and they think that's okay. They think it's normal." His eyes darkened, and every instinct Jason possessed screamed *danger*.

None of the men appeared to have weapons, but there was an unmistakable edge of violence in the air.

Gorilla cracked his knuckles. "We want you to publicly denounce vampires, and that thing you call a boyfriend."

Jason didn't bother correcting him.

"Everyone will know I was forced into it," he said.

Gorilla shook his head, his eyes still malevolently gleaming.

"You're going to explain to all your fans how you've come to realize that vampires can't be trusted, and that they really are the violent monsters they pretend not to be."

"Why would anyone believe that?" Jason said.

A pause, and though nobody moved, the hairs on Jason's arms stood up.

"Because you're going to show them what your boyfriend did to you when he got angry," Gorilla said.

For a moment, Jason didn't understand. Something was going on here, but his frazzled brain couldn't quite keep up.

Then Gorilla cracked his knuckles again, and grim understanding dawned.

"You're going to beat me up then make me tell everyone that Gideon did it," Jason said, his stomach plunging.

"Give the kid a fucking cookie," said one of the other men, hiding behind a tiger mask.

Jason swallowed hard.

"As soon as you get out of here, you're going to show the world your injuries, and explain how violent and dangerous vampires really are. You're going to explain that you wanted to trust them, that you really thought you could, but at the end of the day they're not like people. They're too dangerous to be allowed to live. You're going to show everyone what happens when you trust a vampire," Gorilla said.

Jason's eyes flicked around the room, looking for a clock, but there was nothing. How long had he been here? How long before Gideon came to the rescue?

"Where's my sister?" he said, clenching his fists. "I'm not talking about anything else until I see her."

Gorilla leaned in to talk to Tiger, too quietly for Jason to hear, then Tiger nodded and broke away from the others. He headed to the back of the room, to a door that had probably once led to a bedroom or bathroom. Jason craned his neck to see inside but Tiger shut the door before he could.

"We could have hurt her," Gorilla said. "Remember that. We could have hurt your whole fucking family, and we didn't, but if you don't do what I tell you, that's going to change, fast. Play ball, then no one else gets hurt and you'll never hear from us again."

Tiger reemerged, dragging Laura with him. Her hands were tied, and they'd obviously gagged her at some point; a dirty rag was knotted loosely around her neck. Jason didn't know if People Before Vampires had removed the gag or if Laura had managed to get it off herself.

His heart jumped as he checked her over, looking for injuries.

Her face was grubby and streaked with tears, and there were marks that looked like fingerprints on her arms, but nothing worse than that. She stared back at him, her chest heaving, her eyes blazing with rage and terror.

"It'll be okay," Jason told her.

She clenched her jaw. Tears spilled down her cheeks.

"You fucking prick," she said to the man who held her.

He cuffed her around the back of the head, and she stumbled.

Everything inside Jason went deadly calm. "Touch her again and I'll kill you," he told Tiger.

The man made a sneering noise; it came out muffled behind his mask. He marched Laura closer.

"How can I trust you to keep your word?" Jason said to Gorilla.

Through the eyeholes, Gorilla's eyes crinkled at the corners. He was smiling, and though Jason couldn't see his face, he could tell it wasn't a nice smile.

"You're wasting my time, kid," he said. "So here's the new deal. You agree to do exactly what I tell you, and your sister gets to walk out in one piece. You keep screwing me around, and my lads will work the little bitch over." He gestured to the man who held Laura, and he dragged her forward. Gorilla pinched Laura's chin between his thumb and forefinger. "She's pretty, isn't she? We're already going to mess up your face, it'd be shame to mess up hers too."

Jason lunged.

They weren't expecting it, which gave him the edge of surprise he needed. He punched Gorilla in the jaw, sending him spinning away. Tiger was so startled that he dropped Laura's arm.

"Run," Jason roared.

She did.

Recovering quickly, Tiger charged after her, but Jason threw himself at the other man, and they hit the floor together. Jason got in two punches before he was dragged off.

"Get after the bitch," Gorilla yelled, his hands balled into twitching fists.

Two men tore after Laura, but she was already fleeing the building. As soon as she was outside, Gideon would be there to take care of her.

Jason almost smiled at the thought of those thugs going after his sister and finding a very pissed-off vampire instead.

Then the other four men dragged him into the middle of the room, standing between him and the exit, and he didn't feel like smiling anymore.

"You really shouldn't have done that," Gorilla said.

He punched Jason, and the blow landed on his jaw, right on the remains of his bruise. Jason reeled sideways, his face blazing with pain. He tried to straighten up, and Gorilla hit him again. Someone else kicked him in the small of the back, and he sprawled forward on the floor.

A booted foot came down on his hand, pressing until the bones ground together.

Jason clenched his teeth, fighting the cry of pain rising in his throat.

The pressure eased off his hand, and someone grabbed his hair, hauling him onto his knees.

Tiger slapped him, and somehow that was worse than the punch. It hurt less, but the contemptuousness of it made Jason's skin burn.

"You stupid kid," Gorilla said. "You think that makes a difference? We're still going to beat the shit out of you, and if you don't tell the world your boyfriend did it, we'll go after the rest of your family. Do not fuck with us."

He delivered a sudden punch to Jason's stomach that made him double over, groaning.

His attackers snickered, and he thought he heard a high five.

"Feeling cooperative yet?" Gorilla asked.

"Fuck you," Jason gasped.

Gorilla hit him again, and he felt blood spill down his chin. He spat at Gorilla.

Tiger nudged one of the other men. "Kid's got more guts than I thought."

"Maybe we did this wrong. We should have gone after his boyfriend rather than his sister," the other man replied.

The urge to laugh bubbled up in Jason's throat. "He'd snap you in half without even trying."

"Ain't that sweet," said the man in the bear mask, bending over Jason.

And then Jason did laugh, because he'd seen something behind his attackers—a beautifully familiar blond head.

"What the fuck are you laughing at?" Gorilla challenged.

"That boyfriend of mine?" Jason said, spitting more blood at the man's feet. "He's standing right behind you."

Gorilla laughed. It was a hard, scornful sound that echoed around the room. "You think I'm stupid enough to fall for that?"

Jason shrugged.

Gorilla stopped laughing. He drew back his fist for another punch—

—and Gideon grabbed his wrist, twisting the man's arm behind his back until he screamed.

Bear, bolder than the rest, ran at Gideon, trying to grab him from behind. Gideon promptly slammed his head back into the man's face. Bone crunched and the bear mask cracked. He slumped to the floor, moaning.

Gideon shoved Gorilla away, and he curled in a ball, clutching his arm.

"Who's next?" Gideon asked, spreading his arms wide.

The two remaining men exchanged looks. They'd been happy enough to mock Gideon when he wasn't there, but now they were faced with the full force of an angry vampire, and suddenly they'd lost their sense of humor.

"No volunteers?" Gideon's lips peeled back from his fangs. "That's all right, I'll pick."

He feinted toward Tiger, just enough to make him jump and squeal with fright, then changed course, and seized the man on the right by the back of the neck. He lifted his knee and slammed the man's head onto it, knocking him senseless.

Jason picked himself up, feeling a surge of savage satisfaction.

Footsteps scraped behind him, and warning bells blared in his brain. He started to turn, but a dark bag was flung over his head, and suddenly he couldn't see. He couldn't even hear properly. He tried to shout Gideon's name but got a mouthful of rough burlap instead.

Strong arms pulled him back, and he dug in his heels, but it was no good; there were too many hands pulling him. He couldn't see what was happening to Gideon, but he heard a snarl of pain that almost made his heart stop.

Debris crunched underfoot as Jason's attackers dragged him farther back, and he felt fresh air on his hands, his neck—he was outside. He heard the faint murmur of an engine, then the sound of metal doors being flung wide. Hands roughly hauled him off his feet and shoved him into the back of what he guessed was a van. He tried to shout for Gideon again but a foot slammed into his stomach, and the breath rushed out of his lungs. The pain blasted through him, red hot, and Jason curled into himself, trying to breathe through it.

The doors slammed shut.

He thought he heard Gideon's faint roar of rage, but the van was already moving, jolting him as it drove over uneven ground, and he felt it picking up speed, faster than a vampire could keep up with.

Gideon couldn't save him now.

Jason was on his own.

CHAPTER TWENTY-NINE

Jason

He quickly lost track of how long the van drove for, but it stopped jolting once it reached a proper road, and then eventually started jolting again. Jason had no idea what to make of that.

Where were they taking him and why?

What did this have to do with them framing Gideon for assault?

Finally, the van stopped.

Jason had pulled the bag off his head as soon as he could, but it hadn't helped much. The back of the van was in total darkness, no windows to let in any light, and the doors were locked.

Doors slammed—presumably his captors getting out—and he tensed, ready to fight tooth and nail when they opened those doors.

Male voices murmured, then someone screamed, making Jason jump. Something slammed into the side of the van, rocking the whole vehicle, and Jason scrambled to the other side, his heart banging against his ribs.

What the hell was going on out there?

More screams, and a crunch that sounded like breaking bones, followed by a wet, meaty noise that he didn't want to think about.

Then there was silence.

Jason's heart felt like it was on his tongue, thrashing like a trapped bird, and he tried to swallow the panic, bracing himself for whatever was on the other side of those doors.

Whatever it was, he'd fight it.

He'd never go down without a fight.

The doors opened.

Jason blinked in the sudden light, his eyes struggling to adjust. A shape formed in the bright space of the open door, and as Jason blinked a couple more times, that shape solidified into a familiar face.

"Ivar?"

The Viking vampire stared back at him, his face impassive. He still wore his blue tunic and rough trousers, but the ancient aura, that sense of danger that had seemed to surround him, was diminished now, like the last flickering flame of a dying candle.

"What are you doing here?" Jason said, his head reeling.

"I brought you here," Ivar said.

"But those men . . ."

"Were working on my orders."

A cold fist gripped Jason's heart. Red droplets were splattered across Ivar's face, and his hands were coated with them.

"I don't understand," he said.

Ivar held out one bloody hand. "Come on."

Jason didn't see that he had much choice. He climbed out of the van, though he did so without touching the vampire.

"Fuck," he breathed as soon as his feet were on solid ground.

Four men had kidnapped him. Four men lay dead on the ground. Jason registered brief flashes of blood and broken bone, gaping wide mouths and staring eyes, limbs dangling by threads of sinew, then he closed his eyes.

"You killed them," he said.

"I did." There was no emotion in Ivar's voice.

"I don't understand."

"Follow me," Ivar said.

Jason did, carefully sidestepping the pools of blood on the grass. They were out in the countryside, he realized, though he wasn't sure where. Probably the South Downs somewhere—it didn't feel like they'd driven too far.

Ivar led him up a steep grassy slope to a stretch of hill adorned with a single bare tree, and then he sat down, looking over the green swathes of field and woodland around them.

After a moment's hesitation, Jason sat down too.

"I sent those men to capture you and bring you to me," Ivar said.

Anger burned in Jason's blood. "You let them kidnap my sister for that?"

"No, I had nothing to do with that. I instructed them to capture you, but explained that the method was entirely down to them." Ivar leaned back on his hands, looking more relaxed than Jason had ever seen him. It was strangely unnerving.

"So all that stuff about them wanting to frame Gideon? Did you have anything to do with that?"

"No."

Jason believed him. "You didn't think they might have had their own agenda?"

"If they did, it wasn't my concern, as long as they did as I'd asked," Ivar said.

His indifference sparked Jason's temper even more. "Why did you even need them? You could have snatched me yourself."

"I could have," Ivar agreed. "But you would have fought me, and

I didn't want to hurt you." He gave Jason a speculative look. "I've grown strangely fond of you, boy."

Jason pointed to his own face. "You didn't mind your henchmen roughing me up?"

"I didn't ask them to do it, and I'm not responsible for the actions of others."

"Then why did you kill them?"

Ivar shrugged. "They'd served their purpose. If they hadn't hated vampires so much, I might have let them live. But they did. So I didn't." He offered Jason a thin smile. "Don't pretend you'll grieve their deaths."

"I won't. But I still don't think you should have killed them," Jason said.

Another shrug. "It's done now."

Jason rubbed his palms along his thighs. "Why am I here?" he asked.

Ivar was silent for a while, gazing at the countryside. "You remind me of me, when I was human."

"Really?" Jason hadn't expected that.

"You probably find that hard to believe."

It was Jason's turn to shrug.

"I suppose I can't blame you for your cynicism," Ivar said.

Jason pulled up a few tufts of grass. "I still don't get why I'm here."

Ivar closed his eyes, tilting his head back. Wind stirred his reddish-gold hair, blowing it around his face. "You're here because I don't want to die alone," he said.

Jason stared at him. "What are you talking about?"

"You have no idea how heavy a millennium is, do you?"

"I'm nineteen, so, no," Jason said.

Ivar's lips twitched. "Then you cannot possibly understand how tired I am. I don't belong to this world, not anymore."

"You could," Jason said.

Ivar snorted. "Go live in a Vampire House with the rest of them?"

"Why not?"

"That's not the life for me."

"Things are changing. We're building a better system for everyone," Jason said.

"Not for me," Ivar said firmly.

"Is that why we're out here?" Jason looked up at the sky. "You're going to sit here until the sun gets to be too much for you?"

"Yes."

An unexpected lump rose in Jason's throat. "I thought maybe a vampire as old as you could be out in the sun all day."

"In winter I can," Ivar said. "But I stayed outside all day yesterday, and I haven't touched a drop of blood. I won't survive another day out here."

"Couldn't you . . ." Jason trailed off because he had no idea what he was trying to say. "Tell me about your life," he said instead.

Ivar gave him a startled look. "Why?"

"Because I want to know."

He thought Ivar would refuse. Instead, the Viking leaned farther back on his elbows and started to talk. He told Jason of his childhood, how he was one of six children, three of whom had died young from various diseases and illnesses. His sister had grown up and married one of Ivar's friends, and between them they'd had eight children, five of whom had survived childhood. Ivar and his brother had eventually left Scandinavia for Britain, and settled in Lincolnshire, in what was now known as Grimsby. Ivar had been gravely wounded in battle, and was turned by another Norse vampire, though that vampire had later been killed in another battle with the Anglo-Saxons..

He told Jason of his first marriage as a human, and how she'd died in childbirth, taking their son with her, and his second marriage as a vampire. That marriage had lasted longer, though eventually illness had taken her too. He hadn't married again.

He talked about the wars he'd seen, the ones he'd fought in and the ones he'd avoided, the friends he'd loved and lost, and the many, many ways the world had changed over his long lifetime.

In turn, Jason told Ivar about his family, about his brother and sisters, and their childhood, and how his parents had met, and how Jason had come to Belle Morte and fallen in love with Gideon. He decided not to mention the part that Ivar had played in their breakup. As the hours passed, sitting under the sun together, they'd reached a strange camaraderie, and if these really were Ivar's last hours, Jason didn't want to spoil them.

Jason's phone rang on and off throughout the day but he ignored it. His friends would be going out of their minds with worry, and he felt sick for letting them suffer like this, but it might be the last thing Ivar ever asked from anyone. Not everyone would have given him this, Jason knew, but he wanted Ivar to remember that there was still good in this world, that even the person he'd threatened and intimidated could be here for him, on his last day.

As late afternoon stretched the shadows into long, dark shapes, Ivar gave a little shudder and hunched his shoulders.

"Are you okay?" Jason asked.

"I can feel it," Ivar said. He rubbed at his wrist, then his neck. "The sun. It's been so long since I felt it like this."

"Does it hurt?" Jason asked.

"Not yet, but it itches."

Jason almost said again that Ivar didn't need to do this, but something told him that Ivar wasn't backing down.

They talked quietly a little longer, until Jason could hear the strain creeping into Ivar's voice. Pinkish patches were blooming on his skin.

All day Jason had known that Ivar had come here to die, but he hadn't really grasped the *reality* of that. Ivar would burn alive in front of him, and Jason would have to watch. He didn't want to, but he couldn't let this man die alone.

"Will it hurt?" he asked, then immediately regretted the question.

Ivar gave him an amused look. "I've never experienced it before, but, yes, I should imagine so."

"Sorry," Jason muttered.

Ivar's smile faded. "I doubt it will be long now. Then *I'll* be nothing but dust and memories."

"Memories can be very powerful things. I'll remember you," Jason said quietly.

"You'll remember me as a threat, a villain," Ivar said.

Jason carefully considered his words. "I won't forget the bad things you did, and the things you *wanted* to do, but I'll choose to remember the good things, too, everything you've told me today, and this decision you've made."

Another shudder ran through Ivar. Those pink patches were darkening, turning red, and Jason's stomach twisted. "Isn't there another way? A *quicker* way?" he said.

"For so long as a younger vampire I could barely spend more than a few minutes in the sun without risking my life. When I was old enough to withstand it more, I swore I'd never take it for granted, but I've still spent so much of my life in the dark. I want to be in the light this one last time," Ivar said.

Hesitantly, Jason reached out and took Ivar's hand. Ivar stiffened, and shot him a surprised look, but didn't pull away.

"Thank you for being here with me, Jason," he said, so quietly Jason almost didn't hear it. It was the first time he'd called Jason by his name.

The sun dipped lower in the sky, spilling pink and orange and yellow across the horizon. Jason felt the warmth of it on his face, and he closed his eyes for a brief span. Ivar made a soft noise, and Jason squeezed his hand tighter, forcing himself to open his eyes. He didn't want to see the moment it happened, but he had to.

Ivar's death happened slowly, then suddenly all at once, flames licking over his body, and Jason held his hand until he couldn't anymore. Ivar didn't make another sound as he died.

When it was over, and the ancient Viking was nothing but ash, Jason let out a long, shuddery sigh.

For a long moment he stared down at Ivar's remains, the vaguely humanoid heap of ashes lying behind him, then he scooped them up, one handful after another, and gently blew them into the air, watching the wind whisk them away, across the hills and woods and fields.

Then he pulled out his phone and called the mansion.

CHAPTER THIRTY

Gideon

When Jason finally called and told the mansion what had happened, Gideon felt like he'd been trapped underwater all day and now he could breathe again. Ever since Jason had been kidnapped, he'd been in hell. He'd chased after that van until it had disappeared from view and then he'd desperately scoured the streets for any sign of it, before admitting defeat and running back to Belle Morte for help. His friends had jumped into action immediately, and Ysanne had contacted Walsh, but no one had found a trace of Jason.

All day Gideon had tormented himself with visions of what might be happening to Jason, imagining worst-case scenarios and horror stories, and when he heard that Jason had called in, that he was safe and sound, he almost collapsed with relief.

Apparently, Jason was out in the countryside somewhere, and he didn't know where, but he'd already started walking and he could see the city a few miles away. He'd call again as soon as he was somewhere he recognized and then someone could come pick him up.

Gideon wanted to rush out now, even though Jason had insisted he wasn't hurt, but he couldn't run around the South Downs looking for him. He had to wait.

It was dark when Jason finally called again, relaying the name of a street that he'd reached. Seamus was out of the door immediately, heading for a car, Roux and Renie hot on his heels, and Gideon automatically followed them.

Renie didn't say anything, but she gave him a funny look. Gideon could guess why. He was desperately worried about Jason, and he wouldn't be happy until he saw for himself that he wasn't hurt, but at the same time he was the one who'd broken Jason's heart.

Did he even have the right to worry about him now?

"Are you coming?" Renie asked, and Gideon realized the others were already in the car. Renie was holding the door open for him.

He climbed inside.

It probably only took a few minutes to reach Jason, but each second felt like a lifetime. Gideon kept picturing the moment that he'd been taken—those men throwing the sack over his head, the blades they'd wielded against Gideon when he'd tried to stop them. The slashes they'd inflicted had since healed.

Renie put her hand over his, and Gideon realized he'd been knotting his hands together. "He's okay," she said.

Gideon just nodded. He didn't know what to say.

They found Jason standing on a street corner, bathed in the artificial light from a streetlamp, his hands shoved deep in his pockets. His face was bruised and tired, his eyes hollow, and it made Gideon's heart twist.

Renie and Roux were out of the car before Seamus had even parked. They ran to their friend and flung their arms around him. Gideon climbed out of the car, too, but then he stopped, clinging to the door and wondering what he was supposed to do. He wanted to run to Jason. He wanted to hug him, to kiss him, to reassure him that he would never let anything happen to him again.

But even if they'd been together, that wasn't a promise Gideon could make, and he felt that realization like a bucket of icy water. He'd failed to protect Jason today. He could fail him again.

He watched Renie and Roux envelop Jason in their arms, watched as he murmured softly to them, watched as Seamus jogged over and clapped him on the back, beaming at him, and Gideon felt like he'd been left out in the cold. But that was his fault. He'd closed the door on their relationship, and he didn't know how to open it again.

He *couldn't* open it again.

Surely this day had proved that he'd made the right decision by ending this.

Hadn't it?

Jason

Seeing Gideon get out of that black car sent a jolt of electricity to Jason's heart. Of course, vampires were too bloody perfect to get puffy eyes or anything like that, but Gideon still looked exhausted, like someone had sucked the life right out of him, leaving a hollow shell behind.

He didn't join the girls and Seamus as they embraced Jason, and even as Jason approached the car, Gideon just stared at him, his expression indecipherable.

A thousand words sprang to Jason's lips, and they all died there, turning to dust on his tongue.

This had been quite possibly the strangest day of his life, and all he wanted was to kiss Gideon. He needed it like a drowning man needed air, and the pain of not being allowed to made everything inside him clench into a hard little ball.

He should have been angry with Gideon for giving up on them, but when he looked at the man he loved, he felt only sadness.

He remembered the shape and feel and taste of Gideon's lips, the way he slept with his face squashed into the pillow, every line of muscle in his perfect body. He remembered being in bed with Gideon—both sleeping and all the fun stuff they'd done—and the knife in his heart twisted even more, cutting him to pieces.

Could he ever look at this man and not feel destroyed?

Gideon opened his mouth, and Jason felt a terrible surge of hope in his heart, wondering what he was going to say.

He didn't get a chance to say anything.

"Let's go home," Renie said, taking Jason's hand.

The moment was over before it had begun.

Gideon climbed into the car without saying a word, and as they drove back to Belle Morte in silence, Jason wondered if Seamus and the girls could feel the suffocating tension between him and Gideon.

After they parked, they trooped into the mansion and found Isabeau waiting in the vestibule, a smile on her lips. "Come to the dining hall," she said.

They followed her in, and Jason stopped dead in the entryway. Every vampire in Belle Morte was gathered there, along with Godric and Caoimhe, several remaining security guards, and even Walsh.

A loud cheer rose up when they saw Jason.

"What's this?" he asked, looking around.

"We're celebrating," Isabeau told him. "Vampires have their legal rights now, the donor system is coming back, and Ivar is gone. We've all been through hell recently, but it's finally over."

"Hell yeah, party time," Renie cried, doing a little jig on the spot. She knocked over a chair, and Walsh yelped as it landed on his foot. Renie tried to apologize, but Edmond had already lifted her off her feet and kissed her.

Isabeau approached Gideon and held out her hand. "Dance with me?"

He placed his palm in hers, but his face was still somber, and when he glanced at Jason, Jason wondered if he was thinking the same thing—the time they'd danced in the garden, before Ivar had smashed through the wall and invaded the house.

He'd give anything to go back to that moment.

After a few minutes, Fadime wheeled in the piano from the ballroom and started playing a lively tune. Walsh produced a bottle of champagne, beaming from ear to ear, even though hardly anyone in the room could drink the stuff.

Everyone was laughing and talking and hugging and kissing. Even Ysanne had abandoned her usual composure and was kissing Isabeau like she was a horny teenager.

The cork popped, and champagne frothed over the floor. Ysanne didn't bat an eyelid, not even when it splashed onto her silk dress. Walsh took a long swig from the bottle and then passed it to Seamus, who took an even larger swig. Apparently no one was bothering with glasses.

Seamus handed the champagne to Jason, and Jason climbed onto the table. The hubbub quieted as everyone looked at him. He raised the bottle. "Here's to Belle Morte," he said, and Renie cheered. "Here's to vampires."

He glugged down champagne until the bubbles went up his nose, and then he handed the bottle back to Walsh. It wouldn't last long at this rate—he'd have to make a trip to the kitchen to get more.

Unnoticed by anyone but Jason, Gideon quietly left the room.

CHAPTER THIRTY-ONE

Jason

They celebrated long into the evening.

Seamus considered himself still on duty, so he didn't drink much more, but Walsh and Jason raided the bar and happily got as drunk as skunks, culminating in Jason trying to teach Walsh a variety of drinking games.

Ysanne was briefly called away to her office, and when she returned she told Jason that she was fighting off requests from people who were desperate to interview him about today's news from McGellan. The *Daily Topic* wanted him back on. Another show called *Today* begged to be allowed into the house the next day so they could interview him in Belle Morte, the place that had become his home.

Jason was surprised that Ysanne had agreed to that, but she reminded him that things were different now. Belle Morte would no longer be separate from the rest of the world, the way it had been these last ten years, and she thought there'd be something poignant about him being interviewed here.

He readily agreed.

As he sat precariously on a corner of the table, surrounded by empty cocktail glasses, Jason felt his heart swell with love for the people here.

Renie was dancing in the middle of the table, Edmond watching with a slightly bemused smile. Renie was not a good dancer.

Roux had burst into song several times, charming everyone with her rich, smoky voice.

Walsh had tried to chime in once or twice, but the poor guy couldn't carry a tune in a wheelbarrow. Seamus on the other hand proved he had quite a good voice.

Ysanne had regained some of her composure, and now she sat at the head of the table, her feet in Isabeau's lap, watching her house with the sort of indulgent pride a mother might give her children.

Earlier, Jason had felt drunk enough to risk giving her a hug over the back of her chair, and she'd accepted it with a small smile, patting his hand.

The dining hall had never been happier, but one vital piece was missing.

Gideon hadn't come back.

Everyone was too busy celebrating to check on him, even Godric, and Jason didn't blame them.

But he wished Gideon was here.

As he gazed around at his friends, at the way Edmond and Ludovic looked at Renie and Roux, and the way his girls looked back at them, the way Isabeau rested her head on Ysanne's shoulder, Jason felt the knife twist in his heart again.

He wanted that with Gideon.

He wanted *everything* with Gideon.

But he didn't have it anymore.

By the time the night wound to a close, Jason, Renie, and Roux were the only ones left at the table. Edmond and Ludovic had sensed Jason needed some time alone with his best friends, and everyone else was just plain exhausted.

Walsh was asleep on the table.

"I'm kind of tempted to draw a 'stache on his face," Renie said, looking at the snoring detective. "Or maybe a penis."

Jason snickered. "Not sure he'd see the funny side."

"Eh, he's lightened up a lot lately. I reckon he could cope with a dick on his cheek."

Jason made a mental note to confiscate any pens he found lying around.

"I'm sorry Gideon wasn't here," Roux said, squeezing his knee.

Suddenly, Jason didn't want the rest of his drink. He pushed the glass across the table. "Yeah, me too," he muttered. "I'd have done it, you know."

"Done what?" Renie pulled her eyes from Walsh.

"Become a vampire. That'll be one of the changes that's implemented, I'm sure of it. I'd have applied, gone through the vetting process, waited years if that was what it took. But I'd have done it. I'd have done anything for him." His eyes prickled. "But he doesn't feel the same way. He doesn't think I'm worth fighting for."

"Then he's an idiot," said Renie, and her voice hitched, either with angry passion or empathetic sadness.

Jason shook his head. "No. He's just got himself so caught up in this stupid conviction that he's doing it to keep me safe."

"Jason Grant, you are worth fighting a hundred wars for, and anyone who can't see that is an idiot," said Renie fiercely.

Jason leaned his head on her shoulder. Roux leaned her head on his shoulder.

"Will you stay with me tonight? I don't want to be alone," he whispered.

"Of course we will," said Roux.

"The guys won't mind?"

"Nah. If Edmond and Ludovic get lonely, they can have their own snuggly sleepover," said Renie.

"And a million slash fantasies just exploded into existence," said Jason.

Renie grinned.

They cuddled up in Jason's bed, Jason in the middle, his girls on either side of him. They fell asleep first, but Jason stayed awake long into the early hours. It felt good to have someone in bed with him again, and he loved having his girls here, but the person he really wanted lying next to him was Gideon.

Gideon was the one he wanted to sleep with every night and wake up with every morning.

Even with two girls in the bed, it felt empty without Gideon.

Everything felt empty.

But there was little time to mope. People from *Today* would be arriving for the interview within the next couple of hours, and though they'd probably bring their own stylists, Jason reckoned it would be better if he didn't look completely hungover when they got there.

Maybe the interview would help him forget about Gideon, at least for a little while.

Gideon

Gideon lay in bed, staring blankly at the ceiling.

He'd listened to the celebrations going on all evening, the sounds of singing and dancing and laughing. Jason's laugh stood out more than the others.

It was the first time he'd laughed since Gideon had taken a sledge-hammer to both their hearts.

Now everyone was quiet. Edmond and Ludovic had gone back to their rooms about an hour ago, but he hadn't heard Renie and Roux, so he assumed they were spending the night with Jason.

Because Jason wouldn't want to be alone.

Gideon rolled over, clenching the covers in his fists.

He wanted so badly to keep Jason safe, but was this really the right way to do it?

He was *hurting* Jason.

But if Jason was with him, then his life would always be in danger.

Wasn't it more selfish of Gideon to be with him knowing that, than to hurt him by keeping his distance?

Questions chased themselves around and around in his head. He slept now and then, short bursts of exhaustion that always ended with him waking up and feeling across the bed for Jason, then remembering that he wasn't there.

When morning came, he was as exhausted as he'd been the night before.

Before Jason, he'd been a closed book, keeping the things he felt locked inside. But Jason had unlocked him and taken the key with him when he left. Gideon couldn't close himself off any longer.

And he couldn't handle all this doubt and confusion by himself.

He sat up and kicked off the covers.

He needed help.

—

He paused outside Edmond's door, suddenly unsure if he was doing the right thing. Edmond's loyalty was to Renie, and her loyalty was to Jason. What if Edmond didn't want to see him?

Swallowing his uncertainty, Gideon knocked on the door.

When Edmond opened it, he lifted a questioning eyebrow. Clearly he hadn't expected to see Gideon standing outside his door in the early hours of the morning.

"What's going on?" he said.

Gideon searched for the words. "I . . ."

Edmond's face softened. "Why don't you come in?"

He stood to one side, and Gideon shuffled into his bedroom.

Edmond closed the door and then turned to look at Gideon, his expression expectant. There was no sign of Renie.

"I'll make an educated guess and say this has something to do with Jason," he said.

Gideon looked at the floor.

Edmond waited patiently, giving him time to gather his thoughts and find his words.

"Did I do the right thing?" he whispered.

Edmond leaned against the door and folded his arms, languid as a cat. "It depends on what you think is the right thing."

"I had to end it, or Jason would have got hurt."

Edmond lifted an eyebrow again, and Gideon realized how stupid he sounded. Jason *was* getting hurt—by Gideon.

He explained Godric's concerns and what Ivar had said to him, and Edmond quietly listened, his arms still crossed.

"To an extent I understand Ivar's perspective," Edmond said. "During some of the darker periods of my life, I no longer cared if I lived or died, and once I even came close to ending my own life. Ivar was right in saying that many other, older vampires did the same thing when it all became too much for them. But things are different now."

"How?" Gideon asked.

"Because we don't have to hide anymore. When the world didn't know we existed, the loneliness could be crippling. It seemed like there'd be no end to it. It was no wonder that some of us went mad. But now we have each other. We have the people we love, and we can rely on them when things get hard."

"I don't have the person I love," Gideon said quietly.

"But whose choice was that?"

Gideon couldn't speak.

"I understand why you've done this," Edmond said, his voice growing softer. "I know what it's like to love someone so much you would do anything to keep them from getting hurt. But don't you think Jason should have some say in this? It's his life, after all."

"Human lives are much more fragile than ours," Gideon said.

"But that doesn't give us the right to control them."

"That's not what I'm doing."

"You broke up with Jason because you thought it was for his own good, because you thought you were protecting him. But you took away his choice. It's *his* life, Gideon, and if he thinks being with you is worth the danger then shouldn't that be up to him?"

Gideon opened his mouth but still nothing came out.

"When I turned Renie, I asked her first. She was dying in my arms, bleeding to death out there in the snow. She had minutes left, if that. The only way to save her was to turn her, but I still couldn't do it without asking. The fear of losing her was more than I can put into words, but I would never have turned her against her will. The choice had to be hers, no matter how hard it was for me," Edmond continued.

"What if she hadn't said yes?" Gideon asked.

Edmond blinked, shadows filling his eyes. "Then she would have died."

"You would have let her die?"

"I would have let her make the decision about her own life. Even if it destroyed mine."

"You think I've made a mistake, don't you?" Gideon said.

"That's not my place to say. Perhaps what you need to ask yourself is how you and Jason are both handling this."

Gideon's throat constricted.

"Because from what I've seen, neither of you are handling it well at all," Edmond continued.

"I love him," Gideon whispered.

Edmond nodded, not remotely surprised. "You ended the relationship because you thought it was safer for him, but is that worth you both being this unhappy? If Jason was given the choice, he'd be with you, no matter what. It seems to me that you're sacrificing everything that makes you happy for the sake of something that might never happen."

An awful feeling crept through Gideon, sickness and regret and horror. Because Edmond was right. He *had* taken that choice away from Jason. He'd broken Jason's heart in some foolish attempt to keep him safe, but what was the point in being safe if they both spent the rest of his life in misery?

"I just walked away," he whispered, his heart twisting into knots. "I just cut him off. What the hell have I done?"

Edmond said nothing.

That awful feeling became a wave of horror, and Gideon put a hand on the nightstand for support.

"Godric said . . ." He couldn't finish that.

"Quite frankly, Gideon, who gives a damn what Godric said? This isn't about him. It's about you and Jason, and the life that *you two* want."

"The life that I've thrown away," Gideon said, digging his fingers into the tabletop.

Edmond frowned. "You think this is unsalvageable?"

"If you were Jason, would *you* give me a second chance?"

"Yes," said Edmond without hesitation. "I very much believe in second chances, and I think Jason does too. I also think he truly loves you."

"I still broke his heart." The words tasted sour in Gideon's mouth.

"Renie broke mine once," said Edmond, very quietly.

"What?"

"When she woke up after I turned her, she couldn't cope with what had happened, couldn't cope with being a vampire. Not at first. She blamed me for turning her into a monster." He winced slightly, the memory still painful. "She didn't mean any of it, of course. She was scared and hurting and she reacted badly, but Ysanne had me imprisoned before I realized any of that. I went into those cells thinking that Renie didn't love me after all, and that she'd always hate me for what I'd done to her. It wasn't until Ysanne allowed her to visit that I realized how much Renie *did* love me. She broke my heart and then she put it back together."

"You think Jason will let me do the same? Even after I've done everything I can to avoid him for days?"

"I think Jason loves you too much to close the door in your face. I'm not saying he'll fall into your arms at the first apology, though. You didn't fight for him before, so you may have to fight for him this time. You may have to prove that you're not going to hurt him again, and no one can say how long that will take," Edmond said.

It didn't matter how long it took; Gideon would do whatever was necessary to fix this. He loved Jason with everything he had, and he couldn't throw that away. He couldn't sacrifice the future they'd started to imagine together, because without Jason there *was* no future, just a bleak stretch of nothing.

Now, in the cold light of day, Gideon couldn't believe he'd actually walked away from the man he loved heart and soul.

A smile touched Edmond's lips. "Whatever it is you're thinking, go and say it to Jason."

He heard Jason's voice as he was coming out of the north wing, and his heart soared. He was going to repair the damage he'd wrought. He was going to prove that Jason meant more to him than anything, more than the whole damn world.

But by the time he reached the staircase, Jason was already disappearing into the dining hall. Gideon hurried down the stairs and stopped dead just a few steps before the bottom.

Jason wasn't alone.

A group of unfamiliar humans gathered in the vestibule, toting

cameras and lights and bags and an assortment of other equipment. One of them, a lean man in a dark suit, shook Jason's hand, introducing himself as William Grey.

Gideon had no idea who that was, or what he was doing here.

"They're from *Today*," Renie said, coming to stand beside him.

Gideon braced himself as he met her eyes, expecting to see disdain or censure. But her expression was neutral.

"*Today*?" he said.

"It's another talk show. They're here to interview Jason."

Grey and his team moved into the dining hall, and Gideon found himself moving down the remaining stairs. Jason had followed Grey without noticing that Gideon was there.

"What are you doing?" Renie asked, catching up with him.

Her question brought him up short. There was so much he wanted to say to Jason, so much he wanted to beg forgiveness for, but that was private to them. They didn't need an audience, especially not an audience of strangers.

He paused at the entryway to the dining hall, peeking inside. No one was looking his way; they were too busy setting up whatever all that equipment was.

"He said he didn't want anyone watching. It would make him nervous." Renie gave Gideon's shoulder a small squeeze. "Whatever you've got to say to him, I'm sure it can wait."

As desperate as Gideon was to see Jason, he couldn't prove his love by interrupting something this important to him.

So he waited.

—

Renie had respected Jason's wish to not be watched, but Gideon couldn't seem to tear himself away. He hovered by the entryway, out of Jason's eye line, as still and silent as only a vampire could be.

Three times, Grey checked that Jason didn't want his friends here, and three times Jason politely declined. The man's persistence was starting to annoy Gideon. If Grey had wanted the vampire inhabitants of Belle Morte to be present, he should have asked Ysanne earlier.

He watched them set up.

It seemed like a lot of equipment for one interview, but what did he know about it? Lights were positioned under the windows, cameras arranged at strategic points around the room, and boxes of makeup and styling equipment were scattered across the table.

Jason wouldn't let the makeup artist cover the bruises from yesterday's attack, saying that covering them was pretending that it hadn't happened.

He must have been nervous, but he didn't show it. He appeared calm and collected enough to make even Ysanne proud, fielding Grey's questions like he'd been doing it his whole life.

Gideon had to fight the urge not to burst into the dining hall and tell him how proud he was.

That would come later.

Assuming Jason was willing to hear it.

Grey pulled a briefcase into his lap and opened it, angling it so no one could see inside. It wasn't unusual for a man in his position to have a briefcase, but . . .

Gideon's instincts flared.

Something felt wrong.

He couldn't put his finger on it, but it was like the atmosphere had abruptly shifted, becoming something colder, more menacing. Jason didn't seem to have noticed.

Gideon's eyes flicked around the room, at the rest of Grey's team. They were all positioned out of camera shot, on the other side of the trestle table, beneath the shuttered windows, but the way they held themselves was too tense. Gideon could hear their hammering hearts. It was almost as if . . .

He narrowed his eyes.

Almost as if they were waiting for something.

"Tell me, Jason," Grey said, his voice suddenly cold as a winter wind. "Do you have anything to say to all the people who feel betrayed by the prime minister's decision?"

"I—what?" Jason blinked, thrown.

"You know how many people have suffered and died at the hands of vampires, and you still championed them. You still fought to *reward* them," Grey spat. "This is for the humans you have betrayed. People Before Vampires!"

The world narrowed to a single pinpoint.

Gideon was running before Jason could even move. He tore into the dining room and tackled Jason to the floor, using his own body as a shield.

Behind him there was an explosion.

CHAPTER THIRTY-TWO

Gideon

The world spun around him.

His ears rang with the force of the explosion; his back and shoulders were a mass of stabbing pain. Blood soaked his clothes.

Jason.

Gideon pushed himself onto his hands and knees with a soft groan, still trying to shield Jason. The smell of blood was heavy in the air, not all of it his.

Jason sat up, his face white. His lips were shaping questions but Gideon couldn't hear what he was saying over the ringing in his ears.

He cupped Jason's face with shaking hands. "Are you all right? Are you hurt?" he said, enunciating his words so that Jason could read his lips.

Jason's eyes widened. "Oh god, *Gideon*," he cried.

He touched Gideon's shoulder, and his hand came away dripping red.

Gideon had no idea how badly injured he was—the only thing that had mattered was protecting Jason.

Movement flickered in his periphery; Grey's team leaping to their feet. When the bomb went off, they'd sheltered behind the table.

Every single one of them had known this was going to happen.

Every single one was prepared for it.

Gideon tried to climb to his feet to protect Jason from whatever was coming next, but the strength flowed out of him. His feet slipped in his own blood, and he collapsed.

Jason

He thought he was going to throw up.

Pieces of William Grey decorated the dining hall, thick wet chunks of meat and bone splattered across the walls like some macabre painting.

He'd *blown himself up*, with the intention of taking Jason with him.

But Gideon had taken the brunt of the blast instead. He sprawled in a pool of blood at Jason's feet, his back a mess of nails and glass and bits of metal.

Utter terror sliced through Jason.

It had all happened so fast, and Gideon was down, and Jason didn't know what to do.

Then one of the camerapeople lunged at him, wielding a short machete. "People Before Vampires," he snarled, swinging the blade at Gideon's unprotected head.

Jason snatched his chair and leaped over Gideon's prone form. The machete flashed down, biting into the chair, and vibrations surged up Jason's arms, rattling his teeth. But he didn't drop it.

As his attacker tried to wrench the machete free, Jason kicked him square in the kneecap. His leg buckled and Jason smashed the chair onto his head with a scream of fury.

The man slumped to the floor and didn't get back up.

The others hadn't moved. They stood under the windows with

their equipment, waiting, and it wasn't until Jason's friends swarmed into the room that he realized what Grey's team was waiting for.

"No," he screamed.

More explosions ripped through the room.

Isabeau went down, hit with a piece of shrapnel from what had been the dining room table. Blood soaked her chestnut curls.

Edmond, moving fractionally faster than the others, had shielded Renie when Jason screamed a warning, and a long shard of wood jutted out of his arm. He wrenched it away with a snarl.

There was so much dust and debris in the room that Jason couldn't see what had happened to the others. There was only screaming, shouting, the ringing aftermath of bombs going off, the flash of sunlight on sharpened blades.

Sunlight . . .

Jason's eyes went to the windows. The explosions had damaged the shutters, letting winter sunlight flood into the room. It wouldn't stop the older vampires, but Renie and Roux were another story. And if Edmond and Ludovic were trying to protect the girls, they'd be at a disadvantage.

Even as Jason watched, huddled on the floor with Gideon's blood soaking into his jeans, a makeup artist charged at Roux, wielding another machete.

Ludovic got there first.

The blade sliced down his arm, opening a deep wound, but the furious vampire didn't hesitate. He punched his attacker in the chest, and even from where he was, Jason heard the *crunch* of breaking ribs.

Another man came at Roux and she whirled around, her eyes blazing red. Taking a leaf out of Nikki's book, she landed a kick between his legs that would ensure he never had kids.

A woman went for the easiest target—Isabeau—yelling the name of their group, and a beautiful blond blur came between them.

The Lady of Belle Morte stood over her fallen girlfriend, her face like fire. With one hand, she snapped the woman's neck. Then she strode forward to meet the next bastard stupid enough to attack the people she cared about.

There was a scream, and blood sprayed over Ysanne's dress. She didn't even blink.

Jason had to help them. He had to protect Gideon.

Staggering to his feet, he picked up the chair. Something hit his arm and it went numb, the chair slipping from his grasp. Before he could grab it, an arm went around his neck and dragged him across the floor. His feet slipped in Gideon's blood. He fought and writhed and struggled, but his attacker was too strong. Above him, he caught glimpses of a bearded face twisted into a grotesque mask by sheer hatred.

"You're going to die, you little bastard," the man snarled, spit hitting Jason's face. "Right here in front of everyone."

Jason saw the flash of a knife in the man's other hand, and fought desperately to get free, but the arm around his neck was the size of a tree trunk, and as solid as iron. He couldn't even breathe.

As the knife flashed down, pure rage ignited in his heart.

It couldn't end like this.

He couldn't die on the floor of Belle Morte's dining hall, not when they finally had hope for the future.

With a snarl, Gideon plowed into the man, knocking him away from Jason. They hit the floor in a tangle, but even when injured, Gideon was fast, and he twisted to his feet.

"Stay the fuck away from my boyfriend," he roared, and delivered a kick to the man's face that crushed his nose and left him out cold.

He turned to Jason, and the rage on his face slid into pain; he swayed then stumbled.

Jason rushed to catch him as he fell.

CHAPTER THIRTY-THREE

Gideon

He was lying face down on a bed and he had no idea where he was or how he'd got there.

He had no idea why everything hurt so much.

Then it rushed back—the bombs, the attack, the people who'd tried to kill Jason—and he jerked upright with a hoarse cry.

"Easy," said Edmond, putting a firm but gentle hand on his shoulder.

"What happened? What's going on?" Gideon gasped.

He realized now that it was his bed he was lying on. But hadn't he just been in the dining hall? And where was Jason?

Then the mattress shifted as Jason sat next to him and took his hand. His knuckles were scraped and bruised. "Don't try to move yet," he said. "They're still getting out the shrapnel."

Jason's face was white and his eyes red rimmed, as if he'd been crying, but he was unhurt, and Gideon closed his eyes in relief.

The cruelest twist of fate would have been to lose Jason just when he'd realized he couldn't be without him.

Pain seared his back, followed by the *clink* of something metal being dropped into a bowl, and when he looked up and saw the awful expression on Jason's face, Gideon realized that Edmond had just pulled something out of his back.

"The bomb," he said.

"William Grey had a nail bomb in his briefcase," said Renie from somewhere on his other side. "His plan was to blow Jason up on national TV, and he didn't mind dying for that. Once the rest of us rushed to the explosion, his team were supposed to kill as many of us as they could."

That was why Grey had pressured Jason to let his friends watch the interview—it would have made it easier for PBV to kill them.

"You've taken a lot of shrapnel, but you'll be all right," Edmond said.

Another stab of pain, another nail dropped into a bowl. Someone was mopping up the blood, but he couldn't see who.

"Bet you wish you hadn't woken up just yet," said Jason, trying for lighthearted. His voice and eyes were too haunted to carry it off.

Gideon realized that he must have lost consciousness in the dining hall. Someone had carried him up here. What had Jason thought during that time? Had he thought Gideon was dying?

Gideon squeezed Jason's hand harder.

"I never thought—" Jason broke off, pressing his lips together.

"None of us thought that an attack would come from a professional TV host," said Roux.

Gideon couldn't see where she was, and moving still hurt too much.

"The people he brought weren't from *Today*. Grey had been planning this for a while, his team were all radicalized members of People Before Vampires, replacing the real team at the last minute. The show is denying any knowledge or involvement, and there's a good chance they're telling the truth, but they'll still be investigated," Renie said.

"The other bombs?" Gideon said.

"Most of their equipment was rigged to blow. They knew they couldn't take us hand to hand, not if we were at full strength, and even a vampire can't walk away from an explosion unscathed."

A jolt of fear went through Gideon, and he tried to push himself onto his elbows. Only Edmond's hand kept him in place.

"Is anyone else hurt?" he said.

What if his friends had died while he was lying unconscious?

Clothing rustled, and then Isabeau crouched beside the bed, putting her face level with his. Her hair was matted with blood, and a still-healing gash marred the side of her head.

"Nothing we can't heal from," she said, squeezing Gideon's hand.

"We didn't lose anyone?"

Isabeau smiled. "No. PBV thought that if they took us by surprise, if they injured us first, they could take us down. But this is our home, and we're all family. It'll take more than a few bombs to stop us protecting that. We won't be using the dining hall for a while, though."

"One of their cameras survived the explosions," Renie said. "It captured everything. We've already given it to Walsh, but I imagine we'll be seeing the footage on today's news."

Gideon wasn't sure he wanted to.

Edmond pulled out another nail, and Gideon gritted his teeth. Every muscle felt shredded; he was so weak he wouldn't even be able to get out of bed.

An icy feeling slid through his stomach as he realized just how badly he'd been hurt. If he was human, he would have been dead. Even as a near-two-hundred-year-old vampire, it was the closest he'd ever come to dying.

The tight grip Jason had on his hand told him Jason was thinking the same thing.

"What happened to PBV?" Gideon asked.

"Four of them are dead, and the rest will be spending a very long time in prison," Ysanne said, her voice hard.

Gideon suspected she'd have rather visited a little vampire justice on the survivors, but they didn't play by those rules anymore.

The human authorities had to handle it.

Edmond gave Gideon's shoulder a quick squeeze. "This is the last one," he said.

Gideon braced himself.

Edmond pulled out the final nail, and someone covered the wound with a towel.

There was the sound of a plastic bag ripping open and the sweet smell of human blood filled the room. Roux handed the bag to Jason, and he gently lifted Gideon's head, helping him drink. He was still too weak to sit up.

Gideon drained it in two gulps, and Roux handed him a second, and then a third.

By the time he finished the last bag, the pain in his back had faded and strength was creeping back into his body. He still felt exhausted, though, completely wrung out. Even pulling himself into a sitting position was an effort.

"We should probably get some more blood," Edmond said.

Unsure how much was left in their supply, Gideon was about to protest, when he realized that Edmond was herding everyone out of the room. Leaving just Jason. Before he left, Edmond gave Gideon a meaningful look, and then he understood. Edmond was giving him time alone with Jason, so he could tell him everything he'd wanted to earlier.

He smiled gratefully at the other man.

Then the door closed, and he was finally alone with Jason.

Neither of them spoke for a long moment.

"I can't believe you took a bomb for me," Jason said.

"I'd do it again," Gideon told him.

Jason was sitting with his back to the headboard, putting him at a higher elevation than Gideon, who reclined on the pillows, and Gideon tilted his head back to look up at the beautiful face he'd come so close to losing.

Jason's expression was guarded, and Gideon suspected that he thought this whole event was just more reason for them to be apart. He was waiting for Gideon to break him again.

Never.

"I've been such an idiot," Gideon said. "I thought that being with you would put you in danger, but being apart from you doesn't change anything. It just makes us both miserable. It was wrong of me to take your decisions away. Any relationship could have risks, but I am so in love with you, Jason, and I'll fight with everything I have to win you back."

He bowed his head, resting his forehead on Jason's hip. "I'm so sorry that I hurt you," he whispered.

Jason stroked his hair, the back of his neck. "All I've ever wanted is to be with you."

"That's all I want too. I just want us to be happy, but neither of us will be unless we're together."

Jason lifted Gideon's head. "Look at me," he said, gentle but firm.

Gideon looked.

"When you walked away from us it felt like you'd ripped my heart out of my chest," Jason said.

Gideon winced. He'd ripped out his own heart too.

"But I understand why you did it. Yes, you were wrong, and I should beat you with a pillow for being such an idiot, but I love you." Jason smiled, and it filled his eyes with warmth. "And I forgive you."

Gideon sat up straighter. "Just like that?"

He'd expected to grovel. He'd expected that he'd have to prove just how much Jason meant to him, though he didn't have a clue how he would have done that.

"Just like that," Jason said.

He leaned down and kissed Gideon, and everything that had felt wrong and crooked and broken in Gideon's life was suddenly right again.

He curled his hand in Jason's collar, deepening the kiss, and Jason pushed him against the pillows, half covering him with his body.

Fresh energy flooded him, and Gideon tugged at Jason's shirt, desperate to feel the warmth of his skin beneath his hands, but Jason stopped him.

"Wait," he said, breathing hard. "This would be a little more romantic if we weren't covered in blood."

Gideon looked down at himself. Edmond—or someone else—had cut away his shirt to tend to his wounds, but his skin was still drenched in his own blood. The sheets were red and wet. The carpet was ruined. Jason was splashed all over with Gideon's blood.

"You have a point," Gideon admitted.

Jason slid off the bed, suddenly looking a little pale. "I need to shower."

It wasn't the blood per se, Gideon knew. Jason had seen blood before; he could cope with it. But it was *Gideon's* blood he was covered with, and that made a difference.

Gideon would feel exactly the same if he was covered in Jason's blood.

"Are there towels in the bathroom?" Jason asked, heading toward it.

Gideon was about to say that they didn't need towels, then he remembered the state of the bed. And the carpet. The room looked like an abattoir—nothing was happening in *this* bed anytime soon.

Jason pulled a face, coming to the same conclusion. "My room?" he suggested.

A knock came before Gideon could answer.

Jason opened the door and immediately stepped back, his face guarded.

Godric stood in the doorway, and anger flared in Gideon's chest. He'd made the decision to walk away from Jason, but that had been sparked by Godric's words. It had been sparked by his brother's failure to support him.

Again.

"I need to talk to Gideon," Godric said, but there was something hesitant in his voice, as if he was asking Jason's permission.

Jason noticed it too. He glanced back at Gideon, gauging his reaction.

Gideon didn't know how to react.

He resented Godric for planting that seed of doubt in his head, and if he found out that Godric had intentionally tried to sabotage his relationship, he'd cut all ties with his brother. But if Godric hadn't meant to cause any damage, if there was still a chance they could patch the rift between them, then Gideon didn't want to throw away that last chance.

"I'll give you two some privacy," Jason said. He leveled a hard look at Godric and lowered his voice, though Gideon could still hear him. "If you hurt him I'll make you sure you never set foot in this house again."

Godric nodded.

Jason slipped out of the room, and Gideon was left alone with his brother.

Warily, he eyed Godric.

"You wanted to talk. So talk," he said.

Godric surveyed the blood-soaked room, and a flicker of pain passed through his eyes. "I'm not sure where to start."

"I can't help you with that."

"I suppose I should start with an apology. I have a feeling that your breakup with Jason might have had something to do with what I said."

At least that saved Gideon from having to outright accuse him. He waited for him to continue.

Godric took a few steps forward, carefully avoiding the bloodiest bits of carpet. "When I told you that you were putting Jason in danger, it was because I honestly believed it was true. I really have only ever wanted what's best for you, though I realize now that I've done a very poor job of showing you that."

"I sort of thought you were deliberately sabotaging things," Gideon said.

A look of genuine pain touched Godric's features. "I would never do that."

"But you did want us to break up."

"Only because I thought it was better for you if you got out before you were in too deep."

"So it *was* sabotage," Gideon said. Just not the deliberately malicious type he'd feared.

Godric opened his mouth, shut it again. He looked stunned. "No, that— I wasn't . . ."

"But you were," Gideon said.

Godric fell back a few paces and slumped against the wall. Vampires were always pale, but Godric looked white, as if the life had suddenly drained out of him. "I'm sorry," he said. "I thought that a relationship between a vampire and a human couldn't work, and I was trying to save you both the heartache. I didn't realize how much you really care about each other."

"How much we love each other," Gideon corrected.

"How much you love each other. I was afraid that you'd get hurt, and I thought that by pointing out the problems in the relationship, I'd make you come to your senses and end it. But I can see now how utterly, horribly wrong I was."

"Because it wasn't your decision to make," said Gideon, recalling Edmond's words.

"Yes, and also because I refused to see what was right in front of my eyes. I was convinced that a human/vampire relationship could never work, and that meant I was blind to the possibilities. I'd already made up my mind, and I was too stupid and too stubborn to see that I was wrong. But I *was* wrong."

He ran a hand through his hair, disturbing its perfect neatness, and in that gesture Gideon saw the human he'd once been. He saw the brother he'd loved more than anything.

"I drove you away once before because I couldn't support you, and even when I came back, after all this time, to try and fix things, I made the same mistake all over again. I didn't support you, *again*. And in doing so I came close to destroying the lives of two people," Godric said, his voice trembling.

Gideon said nothing, just listened.

"I've done so much wrong by you, Gideon, whether or not I meant to." Godric seemed to gather his strength. "So I'll understand if you ask me to leave Belle Morte. I wanted to bridge the gap between us, and instead I fear I've made it worse than ever."

Gideon sighed. Godric had cast doubt on his relationship with Jason because he'd thought it was best for them, but Gideon had ended the relationship for the same reason. They'd both made the same mistake, so perhaps he couldn't judge his brother too harshly.

"I really did just want to be a part of your life, little brother," Godric said.

When Gideon still didn't say anything, Godric's shoulders slumped, and he nodded.

"I understand," he said. "I'll go."

His hand was on the doorknob when Gideon spoke. "Wait?"

Godric turned to look at him, his expression so hopeful, so pleading, that it cracked through Gideon's defenses and cut his heart.

"Do you truly understand that I love Jason?" he said. "Because he's the most important person in the world to me, and I need to know that you understand that."

"I do. I also think you're very lucky to have found someone like that." A faint, sad smile touched Godric's mouth. "That's how I loved Dorothy. Not being able to spend my life with her is one of my greatest regrets."

Perhaps that was where all Godric's fears had stemmed from, and what had shaped his entire outlook on relationships between humans and vampires.

Gideon mulled this over in his mind, and, finally, the anger and hurt he'd carried around for so long started to melt away.

All these years he'd thought Godric was dead. He'd raged at him and regretted not making amends, and now he had that chance.

Godric raised his head. His face was drawn, his eyes hollow. "I want to be part of your life, Gideon. I want to stay in England, with you. I want to support you. If there's even a chance you can forgive me, please tell me." His voice caught. "And if I've lost all chance at forgiveness, then I'll leave you in peace."

"You haven't," Gideon said.

Hope bloomed in Godric's eyes.

"I *do* forgive you," Gideon said, and it felt so good to say it.

Godric's face crumpled as if he was about to cry.

"I love you, Gideon," he said.

A great weight lifted from Gideon's heart. "I love you too," he whispered.

They were words he had never thought he'd say again to his brother, or even that he'd *want* to say them, but he did mean them.

Godric crossed the room and hugged him, and Gideon closed his eyes, leaning into his brother's embrace.

Jason

As soon as Gideon turned up at his door, freshly showered and dressed, Jason knew that he and Godric had worked things out. He seemed lighter somehow, as if he was no longer dragging around the baggage of the past, and Jason smiled to see it.

He didn't know why Gideon had bothered getting dressed, though. His clothes wouldn't be on for long.

"It's snowing," he said, smiling.

Roux had popped in to tell him just after he'd showered, but he'd declined to join her and Renie outside. Jason wasn't sure if Ysanne was allowing them outside again, or if his girls were breaking the rules, but he had more important things to think about.

"The last time it snowed was the first attack on the mansion. Aiden and Renie were killed." Memories of that terrible day, of Renie's blood spilling across the snow, made Jason shiver. "But it didn't end badly this time."

"I still don't think this is the last we've heard of People Before Vampires," Gideon cautioned.

"Neither do I. And I'm sure there'll be other groups like them in the future. We'll always have to deal with it, one way or another." Jason rested his forehead against Gideon's. "But we *will* deal with it. I love you, Gideon."

"I love you too," Gideon murmured.

"Whatever shit we have to deal with later down the line, for now I just want us both to be happy. We've earned it. We deserve it."

Curling his fingers into Gideon's collar, Jason pulled him toward the bed, then pushed him onto it.

Later, he'd be gentle and take the time to savor every moment.

But right now, he needed Gideon.

He tore at Gideon's shirt, and buttons flew across the room. Gideon's eyes sparked red, and Jason ran his hands down his bare chest, closing his eyes in sheer bliss at the shape of hard muscle beneath his palms, the golden hairs that teased his fingertips. Gideon's body was a work of art, and Jason would never get tired of exploring it.

He pulled off his own shirt and stretched out across Gideon, hard chest to hard chest.

Gideon's hands roamed over him, his back, his chest, his thighs, and everything in between. "I love you," he said, again, licking the pulse in Jason's neck.

"Bite me," Jason whispered, anticipation shuddering through him.

Gideon licked him again, then sank his fangs into Jason's throat and sucked hard.

Jason gasped, his eyes falling shut, his body writhing against Gideon's.

Gideon gripped his shoulders, holding him still as he drank, and Jason clutched the bedcovers, colors sparkling behind his tightly closed eyes.

He felt Gideon pulling at his zipper, sliding a hand into his jeans to stroke him, and the dual sensations were enough to make him cry out. It was almost too much to cope with . . . he felt like he was going to explode . . .

The world went white for a shattering instant, and he shuddered against Gideon, pressing his face into the side of his chest, as waves of pleasure rode him.

Gideon pulled away from his throat and licked the punctures closed. He gripped Jason's waistband, trying to push his jeans farther down, and Jason lifted himself onto his elbows, giving him better access.

The red in Gideon's eyes burned brighter as they traveled down his body.

Jason tugged at Gideon's trousers. "These need to go. Now."

Gideon grinned and stripped almost faster than Jason could blink.

For a moment, all he could do was stare. Nothing in the world was more spectacular than Gideon, naked and stretched out beneath him. He wanted to taste every inch of skin, explore every way he could make Gideon writhe and moan and cry his name, but not now. Now he just needed to be inside him.

"Look at me," he whispered, moving over him and resting his weight on his elbows.

Gideon gazed up at him, his eyes bright red with love and trust, his lips parting to show off the tips of his fangs as Jason pushed inside.

Nothing had ever felt more right.

Gideon reared up, nipping Jason's shoulder with his fangs, urging him to move faster, and Jason did, driving his hips against Gideon's with bruising force.

"I love you," he gasped, as that sweet pressure built deep inside.

He didn't take his eyes off Gideon's face as the world unraveled, as everything turned white and fuzzy at the edges, and he saw that same feeling reflected in Gideon's eyes, that same moment when everything broke apart, and there was only raw, exquisite sensation.

And then the strength faded from his arms and he collapsed onto Gideon's chest, breathing hard. Gideon trailed his fingers up and down Jason's spine.

"I want to share every day with you," he whispered. "I don't ever want to lose you again."

Jason lifted his head to stare into Gideon's eyes. "I'm not going anywhere. Not ever," he promised.

Gideon

When he opened his eyes again, he was alone. Jason's side of the bed was empty. Gideon pricked his ears, listening for the sounds of running water, but there was nothing, not even a heartbeat. Jason wasn't in the bathroom.

He frowned, sitting up.

Where was he?

He wasn't worried that something had gone wrong, but he'd looked forward to waking up with the man he loved.

Not alone.

But he trusted that Jason had his reasons.

He rolled over, taking advantage of the empty bed to stretch out his arms on either side of him. He had no idea how long he'd slept, or if it was even the same day, but it felt like a completely new beginning.

Godric was here, and he and Gideon could finally move forward and forge a new relationship.

He had Jason.

Someone knocked on the door, and he climbed out of bed, pulling on some clothes.

Renie and Roux stood on the other side, both wearing innocent expressions that were completely at odds with the excited sparkle in their eyes.

"What's going on?" Gideon asked.

They exchanged looks.

"Where's Jason?" Gideon asked.

Renie couldn't hold back a grin. "He's outside, in the garden."

"Why?"

Another shared look.

"He'd like you to go and see for yourself," Roux said.

Gideon narrowed his eyes. "Do you know what's going on?"

Now it was Roux's turn to smile. "Maybe."

"But we're not telling you," Renie added. "Like Roux said, you have to go outside and see for yourself."

Gideon headed for the garden.

It hadn't snowed as heavily as last time, but the garden was still blanketed in white, and frost made glittering patterns on the walls of the house and the trunks of the trees.

It was beautiful and almost entirely untouched, only Jason's footprints disturbing the crisp whiteness.

Jason stood a few feet from the back door, wrapped in a thick coat, with a woolly hat to protect his head. His nose was pink from the cold. A huge and yet oddly shy grin stretched across his face.

The snow in front of him was disturbed.

"What are you doing out here?" Gideon asked, moving closer.

Jason didn't answer, just looked at the disturbed snow at his feet.

Then Gideon drew closer and realized what Jason was looking at.

The words written into the snow.

Two words.

MARRY ME.

There was no question mark; of course not. Jason knew what Gideon would say.

Except he couldn't find words.

"Gideon Hartwright, you are the best thing that's ever happened to me, and I want to spend every day of the rest of my life with you. I want to marry you. I want to live in this house with you. And one day I'm going to ask you to turn me, and you're going to say yes, because we're going to spend our lives together. That day isn't today, because I'm not ready to be a vampire yet. I want to enjoy being human a little while longer. But today *is* the day that I'm asking you to marry me," Jason said.

"Are you sure? You're not worried about getting married too young?"

"I'm not saying we'll get married this year or next year, or even in five years. I'm more than happy with a long engagement. Hell, neither of us even have rings yet. I just want to know that it *will* happen."

Gideon gazed at him, this incredible, beautiful man who'd swept into his life, stolen his heart, and given him a future. He didn't know what he'd done to deserve someone like Jason, but nothing would keep him from being with him forever.

"So?" Jason said, a smile teasing his lips. "Will you marry me?"

"Yes," Gideon said. "*Yes.*"

He hugged Jason, almost lifting him off his feet, and then kissed him so hard that Jason gasped for breath.

He heard movement behind him, and then Renie, Roux, Edmond, and Ludovic were there, the girls bundled up against the sun.

"His answer better have been yes," Roux said.

"It was," Gideon said.

Renie let out a huge *whoop* and threw a handful of snow into the air. It showered down on them in small, glittering crystals. Roux ran forward and hugged Jason. Gideon was about to step back and give them a moment, but Roux pulled him into the hug, her short hair tickling the side of his face. And then Renie was hugging them, wrapping her arms around them all as far as she could.

Jason laughed, mashed between his best friends and his boyfriend—no, Gideon corrected himself, his *fiancé*—and Gideon laughed with him, because he'd finally found everything he'd never even realized he was looking for.

And he'd never been happier.

EPILOGUE

Jason

In the end, they waited two years to get married, and that was partly due to their work reshaping and reintroducing the donor system. It took up more time than either of them had expected, leaving less time to think about weddings.

But it had been worth it.

Donors had returned, though it was now illegal for any donors to be under twenty-one. They still weren't permitted visitors, but phones and computers were no longer banned, and longer-term donors were allowed to visit friends and family when they wanted to.

All Vampire Houses now had CCTV, which Ysanne had had to learn how to use—much to her dismay.

For now, the vampire kids were back in Belle Morte, living in the refurbished west wing, but construction was underway for them to have their own House. It hadn't yet been decided which vampires from which Houses would move in with the kids, to help them and teach them and generally keep an eye on them, but Gideon had suggested that Jason should consider it.

The vampires who'd been captured after Etienne and Jemima's coup had been removed from the Belle Morte cells and shipped across to Fiaigh, where they were now kept in a specially fortified outbuilding behind the castle. They'd be there for a very long time.

Every human involved in attacking the mansion in any way was behind bars.

People Before Vampires still caused trouble for donors sometimes, but there'd been no more attacks like the ones Jason had experienced.

Jason regularly visited his family, and Ysanne had allowed them to visit the mansion too. He wasn't a donor anymore and was considered as much a part of Belle Morte as any vampire.

And now, at long last, he was getting ready for the most special day of his life.

He was getting married in the ballroom of Belle Morte.

Getting married at home wouldn't have been his first choice, but it was the safest. Although there had been no more attacks on the house, and no more serious attacks on ex-donors, Jason's wedding to Gideon was the first human/vampire wedding in recorded history, truly symbolic of the new future that humans and vampires shared, and the whole world was watching.

If anyone wanted to make a point against vampires, what better way to do it than by attacking such an important event?

Despite the two years that had passed, memories of the explosions still haunted his nightmares, causing him to wake up sometimes in a cold sweat and check the other side of the bed to make sure Gideon was still there.

It was safer to have the wedding in Belle Morte rather than in a less fortified building.

Despite the countless offers from newspapers and magazines, Jason also wasn't allowing photographers or camera crews inside today, for the same reasons, although he and Gideon had agreed that they'd release a selection of photos to certain publications. The money raised from it would help fund the construction of the kids' new home.

Maybe his wedding wouldn't be quite as he'd imagined, but the man he was marrying was better than he could possibly have dreamed.

"How do I look?" he said, getting up from the dressing table Roux had moved into the bedroom she shared with Ludovic.

Roux put her head on one side, studying her handiwork. She'd applied the faintest touches of makeup to Jason's face, enough to highlight his features so subtlty that it didn't look like he was wearing any.

He thought he looked pretty damn good, if he did say so himself.

"Good enough to eat," Renie declared, flashing her fangs.

Jason hadn't bothered with stylists or makeup artists. Roux had been in charge of makeup, and he was in charge of his own hair. His girls had initially refused to let him style theirs, insisting that it was his day and he shouldn't be doing things for anyone else, but he preferred to keep his hands busy while waiting for the wedding to start.

His three bridesmaids stood in a loose semicircle around him, all clad in long dresses of emerald-green silk. Ysanne had provided the clothes, her taste impeccable as always.

Renie's hair had been curled and loosely pinned up so it looked like a great tumble of autumn leaves, studded here and there with tiny flowers. Roux's had been styled in a tousled quiff, with a single larger flower pinned to one side. Nikki's curls had been left loose, accented with a small floral hairband.

All three held small bouquets of daffodils.

All three were beaming.

When Jason had first asked Nikki to be a bridesmaid seven months ago, he'd been afraid her aunt wouldn't let her come, but somehow Nikki had persuaded her. Diane Flynn still didn't like vampires, but perhaps this was her way of compromising. And perhaps she realized that Nikki was fifteen now, well on her way to becoming an adult. If Diane wanted any kind of relationship with her niece, she had to allow Nikki to make some decisions for herself.

Jason checked his own reflection one more time, excitement churning in his stomach. The suit he'd chosen was ivory brocade with the subtlest hint of gold thread. Beneath the jacket he wore a matching waistcoat, with alternating buttons of gold and pearl. The pristine ivory color made his own bouquet look big and bright, as if he was carrying the sun in his hands.

Maybe daffodils weren't the flowers most people pictured at weddings, but they were the only ones Jason could possibly have had today.

In his breast pocket he had another daffodil, one from that messy little bunch of flowers Gideon had given him two years ago. Roux had dried and pressed it for him.

He had no idea what Gideon was wearing. His fiancé had been surprisingly good at keeping that hidden.

"Are you ready?" Roux asked.

"I think so."

"I'll go and get Isabeau."

They might not have an official photographer, but someone still had to take pictures. The humans all had their phones, as did Ludovic (although he rarely used it), but in the past two years, Isabeau, after learning what modern cameras were capable of, had developed an interest in photography.

Ysanne pretended she wasn't that interested in it, but last year Isabeau had taken a particularly gorgeous photo of the mansion in midsummer. A photo that was now enlarged, framed, and hanging in Ysanne's office.

Upon learning that Jason and Gideon weren't having an official photographer, Isabeau had jumped at the chance to take their pictures.

Roux came back into her room, Isabeau close behind, clutching her prized camera. Photography had existed for the better part of two hundred years, but for Isabeau, the modern way of doing it was still new and exciting. She guarded her camera jealously and never let anyone else touch it.

Jason had seen Ysanne try once, and Isabeau had actually smacked her hand, as if the Lady of the House was a naughty child.

The look of astonishment on Ysanne's face was something Jason would treasure forever.

Isabeau smiled softly when she saw Jason. "You look wonderful," she said.

Jason grinned back at her. "You're looking exceptionally hot yourself."

The vampire had chosen a navy-blue satin dress, embroidered with roses in cream and red, with a hem that dipped longer at the back. Her shoulders were bare, and her hair, worn loose, spilled about her pale skin.

Ysanne was a lucky woman.

The next moment Isabeau's smile was gone, and she had shifted into professional photographer mode. She took photo after photo— Jason on his own, Jason with the girls, the girls on their own, Jason with Renie and Roux, Jason hugging Nikki.

She was probably getting carried away, but who cared? It was a wedding.

Finally, she'd photographed them in every pose and from every angle, and she lowered the camera. "I'd like to get some of you all coming down the stairs," she said. "Give me a minute or two to get ready."

Jason checked his reflection once more, while Renie and Roux took their own pictures with Renie's phone. When they were done, she tucked the phone into her cleavage.

Jason raised both eyebrows.

"Hey, I don't have pockets," Renie said, indicating her dress.

"I bet Edmond would be a lot more willing to learn about technology if you showed him that trick," Jason said, and Renie giggled.

"Maybe I'll introduce him to it tonight. I think he'd like it."

Jason patted her shoulder. "Honey, he's probably going to come in his pants the second he sees you in that dress."

Roux snorted and Renie burst out laughing.

It was true, though. His girls might have very different figures, but the dresses fitted them both to perfection and complemented both Roux's lean build and Renie's curves.

The style suited Nikki, too, even though she was younger than them, the emerald silk flattering her athletic figure. She was still determined to work security at Belle Morte one day, and had dedicated herself to achieving that through a daily fitness regime.

"Let's get this show on the road, then," Roux said.

Two days ago, the current batch of donors had been temporarily sent home, and the kids had been sent to other houses, where they'd remain until the end of the week. Just for the time being, Belle Morte was a home, inhabited by the people who loved it best.

Isabeau waited at the foot of the main staircase, photographing them coming down and asking them to stop every now and then so she could try a different angle. A couple of times she insisted on them going back *up*stairs so she could try something new.

"Isabeau, honey, I can't tell you how much I appreciate this, but if we don't hurry up, I'll miss my own wedding," Jason said, laughing.

"Sorry." Isabeau lowered her camera.

When Jason came into the ballroom, his breath caught in his throat. White seats had been arranged on either side of an aisle, which was marked by a scattering of rose petals. Roses, daffodils, and lights were arranged everywhere, transforming the familiar room into something out of a fairy tale.

Although white was the classic wedding theme, Jason had wanted it because it reminded him of the snow, of the day when Gideon had agreed to marry him. The day when his whole world lit up.

The people he loved sat in those seats: His family at the front and to the left, and behind them some human friends he'd reconnected with since the dust had settled two years ago. Ysanne and Seamus were in the second-to-front row to the right, with an empty seat for Isabeau. The vampires of Belle Morte spread out behind them. Caoimhe had come over from Ireland. The front row on the right was currently empty.

At the head of the room stood Edmond and Ludovic, both wearing charcoal-gray suits, and with their hair groomed and tied back.

And in front of them, his hands twisting nervously, stood Gideon.

Everyone else faded away as Jason looked at the man he was here to marry.

Even now, after more than two years together, he was still staggered by the beauty of the man. He still sometimes pinched himself to make sure this was real and not a dream.

His fiancé had chosen a suit of gray velvet so pale it was almost silver. It clung to his broad shoulders and lean hips, the silver buttons of his waistcoat gleaming in the light. Instead of a tie he wore a lace cravat.

He had never looked more breathtaking.

The wedding march sounded, bringing the rest of the room back into focus. Isabeau had taken a place near Edmond and Ludovic so she could take pictures of the whole room, as well as Jason and the girls coming down the aisle.

Nikki went in first, her head held high.

Renie and Roux followed a moment later, their dresses sweeping along the floor.

Jason had been right about one thing—Edmond's eyes bulged when he saw Renie. If he made it through the day without pulling her off somewhere for a quickie, then Jason would actually be disappointed on Renie's behalf.

Beside the dark-haired vampire, Ludovic looked equally stunned, his eyes fixed on Roux.

Maybe there'd be two couples sneaking off for quickies.

Then it was Jason's turn.

His friends and family stood up as he came in, and for a moment he felt a flash of panic at all those eyes on him, even if they were the eyes of the people he knew and loved.

Then he looked down the aisle to the man waiting for him, to the love and amazement in Gideon's eyes.

His nerves vanished.

He walked down the aisle, only tearing his eyes away from Gideon so he could smile at his guests as he passed.

Lights glittered around him like a sea of stars.

The sweet smell of flowers filled the air.

His whole world, his entire future stared back at him from the end of the aisle, and it was a better and more beautiful future than he'd ever dared hope for.

Gideon

The day passed like a dream.

He was so transfixed by the sight of Jason in that ivory suit that he almost fumbled his vows.

The best part of the night would be getting Jason *out* of that suit.

Or maybe that would be second best.

The best part was sliding that platinum ring into Jason's finger and kissing him for the first time as his husband.

After the ceremony, canapés were served to the humans in the dining hall, and the vampires drank blood from champagne glasses. Isabeau flitted about with her camera, while Renie, Roux, and various other people took pictures with their own cameras and phones. Walsh hadn't been able to make the ceremony but he turned up to the reception, clapping Jason and Gideon on the back while managing to look slightly uncomfortable in his suit.

Perhaps he didn't go to weddings often.

During the speeches, Jason's parents spoke about how proud they were of him and how happy they were to have Gideon in the family. The attention made Gideon want to blush. It had been so long since he'd had parents that he'd almost forgotten he'd only been twenty-one when he'd died. The same age Jason was now.

Then it was Godric's turn to make a speech. He kept it short, but his words were no less poignant when he told the world how proud he was of his little brother, and how he knew Jason would make him happy for the rest of his life.

Then he embraced Jason like a brother, and Gideon's eyes burned.

As afternoon turned to evening, the wedding moved back into the ballroom.

Now the chairs had been moved to the side, and the lights were dimmed, casting the room in a twilight glow. A live band had set up their equipment in the corner, where people had used to play music to accompany balls.

Ever since that awful night two years ago when William Grey had smuggled explosives into the house, each and every visitor was checked for any kind of weaponry, and any possessions they brought in were thoroughly inspected.

The band was no exception.

Gideon had to admit that he'd been nervous about the prospect of a first dance. Despite the leaps in confidence he'd made over the years, he'd never be comfortable being the center of attention, and the thought of everyone in the room watching him made him want to squirm.

But Jason wanted it, and Gideon wasn't about to deny him.

And then, when the moment came and they moved onto the dance floor, Gideon couldn't remember what he'd been so nervous about. When he was with Jason like this, so close but not yet touching, gazing into each other's eyes, no one else even existed.

Jason had been very coy about the song he'd chosen for their first dance, and since Gideon had little concept of modern music, he'd trusted Jason to pick something appropriate. Still, he'd been expecting something slow, something romantic.

Wasn't that the tradition?

So he was taken by surprise when the music segued into a fast salsa number, and mischief sparked in Jason's eyes.

"Weren't expecting that, huh?" he said.

"Can't say that I was."

"So, husband, you feel like showing off your moves?" Jason lowered his voice so it was for Gideon's ears only. "And then later I can show off my moves in the bedroom."

Gideon smiled, showing off a hint of fang. "Absolutely, husband," he said.

He and Isabeau had started dancing again, and between practicing with her and Jason, Gideon had polished his technique until he no longer missed a single step.

"Was today everything you wanted?" Gideon asked, nuzzling his cheek.

Jason smiled and kissed him. "I've got everything I've ever wanted right here."

Halfway through the evening, Jason threw his bouquet. It was promptly caught by Nikki, though Gideon suspected that Roux, who was taller than the others, had let her win.

She told Nikki that she'd dry and press the flowers for her, like she had done with Jason's single daffodil.

After that, the wedding party continued into the early hours of the morning, until most of the exhausted guests finally went home.

On the chairs lined up on either side of the ballroom, Nikki—still clutching Jason's bouquet like a prize—had fallen asleep in Renie's lap. Renie, in turn, had fallen asleep in Edmond's lap.

Roux was taking sneaky pictures of them.

Ysanne and Isabeau had long since left.

Jason came up behind Gideon and wrapped his arms around his husband's chest. "I think it's time we got out of here, don't you?" he whispered.

Gideon's blood heated. He nodded, and Jason pulled his hand, leading him out of the ballroom. They didn't say anything to the others; that would lead to hugs and goodbyes, and suddenly Gideon couldn't wait for any of that.

He wanted to be upstairs, now.

They hadn't even got the bedroom door closed before they were kissing, hungry and urgent. Gideon wanted to rip Jason's clothes off but he forced himself to be patient, undoing each button with trembling hands. These were the clothes they had worn on their wedding day, and it would be nice to keep them in one piece. Still, despite his best efforts, at least one pearl button flew across the room.

Jason didn't seem to care.

The second he was naked, he pushed Gideon toward the bed, his eyes burning.

"God, you're so beautiful," he whispered, his voice hoarse as his eyes raked over every inch of Gideon's body.

Gideon reached for him, but Jason grabbed his hands and pinned them over his head. He could break free in an instant if he wanted to, but he loved watching the muscles tense and flex in Jason's arms as he held Gideon's hands in place.

Jason kissed Gideon's chest. He hadn't shaved today. That was for Gideon. He loved the feeling of Jason's stubble gently abrading his skin, especially when—

As if he knew exactly what Gideon was thinking, Jason moved south, his eyes gleaming. He kissed the inside of Gideon's thigh, rubbing his jaw against the skin there so Gideon could feel that slight roughness.

Gideon closed his eyes, waiting, waiting . . .

Jason's mouth closed around him, and Gideon gave a short gasp.

He loved this man so much.

He threaded his fingers in Jason's hair, his hips gently rocking, soft noises of pleasure spilling from his mouth, his other hand twisting in the bedcovers.

These precious moments—all their firsts as a married couple—he wanted to last forever.

But he couldn't make *this* last forever.

Jason had a clever mouth, and he knew exactly what Gideon liked.

A soft scrape of teeth, and Gideon saw stars.

"I love you," Jason whispered, crawling back up Gideon's body to kiss him.

He rolled Gideon over and smoothed his hands down his spine. Gideon trembled. Looking back to the day they'd first met, he could never have imagined they'd end up here. He'd never imagined he'd meet someone who would become more important to him than life itself.

Keeping him flat on the bed, Jason covered Gideon's body with his own, bracing his weight on his elbows as he gently pushed inside, Gideon gasping his name.

"I love you so much," Jason whispered, kissing his cheek, his throat, the back of his neck.

He'd been so desperate to get up here, and now that they *were* here, he wanted to savor every second.

Jason slid one arm around Gideon's chest, holding him close as he rocked their bodies together. His other hand slid over Gideon's, where it was clutching the sheets. Gideon immediately let go of the sheets and gripped Jason's hand, their fingers flexing together. The sight of Jason's wedding ring, shining on his finger, made Gideon's heart feel so full it was a wonder it didn't burst out of his chest.

For so long he'd thought he'd never find happiness like this. Often, he hadn't even thought he *deserved* it.

But as he held his husband's hand, listened to the soft noises Jason made, felt the flex of muscle in Jason's body above him, he knew that he did deserve this.

They both did.

As if he could sense exactly what he needed, Jason increased the rhythm until the bed was thudding against the wall and Gideon was shouting his name. He never took his eyes off Jason's wedding ring.

When the world shattered, it shattered for them both.

Jason fell asleep first, which wasn't surprising. It had been a long day, especially for someone without vampire stamina. Gideon couldn't see the sky outside, but birds were singing in the garden. The sun was coming up on a new day.

He pulled the covers up around Jason, making sure he was warm. Jason didn't stir, not even when Gideon dropped a kiss on his head.

Once, he'd been afraid to pursue his attraction to Jason because he'd had no idea what would wait for him at the end of that road.

Now, as he lay down and pulled his sleeping husband into his arms, Gideon realized there *was* no end to the road, only a long and blissful future with the man he loved.

He couldn't ask for anything better.

Closing his eyes and holding Jason tight, Gideon went to sleep.

ACKNOWLEDGMENTS

A nd so we come to the end.

When Wattpad Books first expressed an interest in acquiring the Belle Morte series, this moment seemed like it was forever away, but time flies when you're writing books.

The biggest thank-you goes to my incredible publishing team, for turning my dreams into a reality.

Fiona, my editor. Thank you for your patience as I dismantled draft after draft; thank you for your unwavering belief that I'd get it right in the end; and thank you for every video chat that descended into swapping stories about our cats!

Rebecca, my copy editor. Thank you for your diligence in weeding out every error.

Ysabel Enverga, thank you for this final, beautiful cover. I love everything you've done for this series.

I-Yana, my creator manager. Thank you for being there.

Kimberly, Irina, Rachel, and Maeve, thank you for everything you've done for this series.

Fire Investigator David Arthur Lock of the Hampshire and Isle of Wight Fire and Rescue Service Arson Task Force. Thank you for so generously driving all the way down to my neck of the woods to advise me on that fire scene.

Internal Communications Coordinator Megan Maddex. Thank you for finding a fire investigator who could help me.

Thank you to my family, for always being there for me. It's become something of a tradition for us to gain one more member with each book that I release, so welcome, baby Ozzie.

Thank you to my friends for understanding that I might turn into a hermit around deadline time.

And finally, thank you to my readers for taking this journey with me. It's been a pleasure to share this world and these characters with you. Here's to the next journey.

ABOUT THE AUTHOR

Bella Higgin fell in love with vampire fiction after reading an illustrated copy of Dracula as a kid, so it was inevitable that her debut novel would be about vampires. She currently lives in a small English town not far from the sea, where she writes full-time. Her works on Wattpad have amassed more than twelve million reads. One day she hopes to have enough money to build a TARDIS in her garden.